THE MEDIEVALIST

# THE
# MEDIEVALIST

## A NOVEL

by
Phil Adamo

split
infin-
itive
BOOKS

Published by Split Infinitive Books, LLC
Minneapolis, MN

Printed in the United States of America.

ISBN:    978-1-7327793-2-7

*For Aria*
*May you live in a kinder world*

# ACKNOWLEDGMENTS
## No book is created by just one person

I owe gratitude to many people.

First, thanks to my editor *par excellence*, Peta Broadfoot, whose keen eye, sharp ear, and unwavering support made this a much better book than it ever would have been.

Thanks also to the many beta readers who offered invaluable feedback and encouragement: Julie Bolton, Phil Brooks, Randall Davidson, Bob Groven, Rebecca Hobbs Bailey, Harriotte Hurie, Jan Jackson, David Jones, Linda Mitchell, John Morris, Alex Novikoff, Mike O'Krent, Denise Palmer Tolan, and Patrick Romey.

Thanks to numerous friends on Facebook for their comments on the cover art, especially Brian Meyer.

Finally, thanks to David Perry, public intellectual and fellow medievalist, for inspiring me with his many articles countering the scourge of white supremacy. Keep fighting the good fight.

Since the 2016 presidential election, scholars have hotly debated the best way to counter the 'weaponization' of the Middle Ages by a rising tide of far-right extremists, [like the] white nationalist marchers in Charlottesville, Va., displaying medieval symbols.

—Jennifer Schuessler, *The New York Times* (2019)

Were it not for the whiteness, you would not have that intensified terror.

—Herman Melville, *Moby Dick* (1851)

# CHAPTER I

## Loomings

> One Dead After Car Rams Into Anti-Fascist Protesters [hyperlink: *The Guardian*, 13 Aug 2017]

Someone is typing …

>

In the darkest corner of the dark net, I watched the blinking cursor as I waited for the next comment to appear, witnessing the plot unfold before my eyes.

> Charlottesville went 2 far
> Not far enough IMHO

Someone is typing …

> Car ramming worked.
> Depends. Made white chick a martyr 4 BLM

> Black lives matter? As if! 2 bad she was white. But that panic & fear ... U can't buy that. LOL.

> Undisciplined. Besides, goal was 2 unify the right. *That* only happens w/ ideas. Actions fade. Symbols last. Proud Boys, Neo-Nazis, KKK. Spencer had good idea—all fly under "alt-right" banner—but no unifying symbol.

> Less than 30 showed at Unite/Right2!

> Pathetic

Someone is typing ...

All posts are anonymous, fulfilling the prophecy of Peter Steiner's 1993 *New Yorker* cartoon that, "On the internet, nobody knows you're a dog."

> RU proposing 'new & improved' rally? Alt-Right 3?

> Yes, but better venue. Kalamazoo in 9 mos.

> Michigan?

> Militia groups strong there. Oath Keepers, etc

> Y 9 mos?

> Need 2 get good symbol. Good unifying symbol = unstoppable movement.

> Any ideas 4 this symbol?

> No. But I know someone who can help.

CHAPTER 2

Sterling Library

I nipped across campus toward Sterling. One hand rested on my bookbag's leather strap, stretched across my chest like a baldric for a sword. The other clutched the ID and paperwork I'd need to confirm my assigned study carrel.

*My* carrel. My *carrel.*

Classes at Yale were scheduled to start the next day. I'd already moved into 300 squares west of campus—larger than a larder but smaller than an undercroft—likely no different than the studios of hundreds of thousands of other grad students since the invention of the U in the eleventh century. Fourth floor. No elevator. One room. A small sofa that, like, metamorphosized into a bed, crammed in one corner. In the other, two opposing chairs bordered a small, square table for both dining and study. Any madrigal feasts would needs be consigned to a hotplate and mini fridge. A bathroom smaller than a hermit's cell, with shower, stood to the left of the studio's one window. The four walls of the complex formed a shadowy cloister in the center of the building.

None of that mattered. Like, there was no mark on a measuring rod small enough to show how little it mattered. I'd be spending most of my time in the library and I, only in my first year, had been given a carrel!

Here's how events transpired. This morning, I met the grad studies secretary, a woman named Joby Wanamaker—*Help me,*

*Joby Wan. You're my only hope*—who showed me my departmental mailbox and gave me the code for the photocopier.

"Eight-oh-oh. One-oh-six-six," she said.

"800 and 1066," I said back to her. "Charlemagne's coronation and the Battle of Hastings."

Joby Wanamaker didn't respond, or, more likely, I didn't notice if she did. Regardless, she also gave me the form that I now held in my hand, signed by my advisor—a scholar without peer as far as I was concerned, though I still hadn't made his personal acquaintance—which bureaucratic permission slip would give me access to a library study carrel. It was the first I'd heard of this great perquisite.

I didn't expect it to be much bigger than the proverbial broom closet—which it was not—yet it would be my own office, in the library no less! What kind of chair would it have? Wooden? Cushioned? Four-legged or swivel? Would there be shelves? A file cabinet? Would the door have, like, one of those nameplate holders?


Mol Isaacson, Graduate Student


Molly Rebekah Isaacson
(whose father disapproved of her pursuing a
degree in Medieval Studies, but I'll show him),
MA/PhD Candidate


M. Isaacson, Medievalist


I was already picturing different fonts—Lucida Blackletter, Papyrus, Zapfino—but the library's carved façade stopped me in my tracks.

"Oh, what a beautiful and complex thing." The words of Sister Clodagh rang in my ears. In every history course I took from her, she said the same thing. "Every object has both beauty and complexity. To understand this, first, find the context. Then describe. Then interpret."

I didn't have a clue about the context. Standing before the great façade on that sunny, back-to-school afternoon, the only research tool I had available was my smart phone. I didn't want to look. I knew better. Knew that I shouldn't. But the façade was so alluring I gave in to temptation—*get thee behind me Satan*—and opened Wikipedia. I had not, like, officially started graduate school. Yet. But I still prayed that no one would look over my shoulder and catch me choosing the permissive path, taking, as they say, the easy route.

Context (paraphrasing Wikipedia):

John Sterling, Yale class of 1864, was a successful lawyer in New York. When he died in 1918, he left almost $30 million to his alma mater. A chunk of this went to build the library that bears his name. Sterling Library, completed in 1930, was designed by James Gamble Rogers, Yale class of 1889. From the 1910s to the 1930s, Gamble designed several buildings at Yale in the Collegiate Gothic style, even basing the university's master plan around this aesthetic. Gamble's work became so popular that he received commissions for other university libraries, including Columbia and Northwestern, in the same Collegiate Gothic. Rogers caught some flak from other architects of the Gothic revival because he used, like, steel frames under stone cladding, thus betraying medieval architecture's use of gravity as a force for holding the structure together. Flying buttresses for show, rather than necessity. To give his designed environments a sense of antiquity, Rogers also took some liberties, like splashing the building's façade with acid to simulate older stonework.

Okay. Description:

"*Thick* description," Sister Clodagh would say.

Looking up from the bottom of the library steps, a larger-than-life statue of a medieval scholar, writing with a quill pen on a manuscript he cradles in his arms, stands centered between two heavy wooden doors. Two detailed bas reliefs flank the scholar on either side, above the arched doorways. Each side is divided into five vertical segments. Each segment has an upper and lower section, what art historians call a register.

Starting on the far left, the first segment shows images from cave paintings. Lascaux? The figure in the bottom register is ambiguous, perhaps wearing animal skins. The inscription in the second segment is in Egyptian hieroglyphs, with an Egyptian scribe hammering away in the bottom register.

The third segment is wider and purely pictorial. It contains three registers. The top register has a triumphant eagle holding two snakes in its talons—not a symbol I knew. The middle register has a ship that looks like a Greek trireme, except the Greek inscription is on the other side of the scholar, so what is the ship doing over here? The bottom register shows that Babylonian (?) "bull-man with wings" deity. I couldn't recall its designation.

In the fourth segment, the inscription seems to be cuneiform—Hammurabi's Code and all that—with the scribe in the bottom register using both his arms to hold up the clay tablet he's reading. The last segment on the left is in Hebrew, with a Jewish scribe, unidentified (at least to me), in the lower register. I try to make out the Hebrew.

"Lord." Hmm. "Lord, you have been our dwelling place through all generations. Before ... before the mountains were born ... you ... brought forth the world ... the whole world ... something, something." That's from the Psalms but I can't recall which one.

The panel to the right of the medieval scholar is also divided into five vertical sections. Each vertical section is divided into two more registers, top and bottom. I wasn't sure about the first segment. The inscription looks like Arabic, but it was hard to tell from where I stood and the figure in the bottom register was no help. The second segment is a Greek inscription with a Greek scribe in the lower register. As on the left side, the central segment is a bit taller and wider than the others. It depicts a Mayan serpent, an Athenian owl, and the

Roman Capitoline wolf, nursing the combative twin founders Romulus and Remus.

The next segment to the right has a Chinese inscription, with a Chinese scribe in the lower register. The sculptor chose an awkward pose for this figure, with his head bent over his writing his long beard hangs down toward his desk. He looks as if he's, like, vomiting. The final segment has an inscription with Mayan hieroglyphs, with the bottom register depicting a Mayan priest writing in stone with a hammer and chisel.

I was unable to Rosetta Stone any of the inscriptions, except for the Hebrew, and even that was spotty. They all have to do with cultures that invented writing—or in the case of the cave painter, a graphic record of the culture's thoughts or experiences. As far as I could remember, all of these writing systems were invented independently of one another. Cuneiform and Chinese and Mayan for sure. Maybe Egyptian hieroglyphs. What's most interesting is that Yale chose a design that seems to give each of these cultures and their writing systems equal weight, equal importance. A fairly egalitarian nod in the 1930s.

I scaled the few steps and was just about to heave open one of the massive doors, when, wait a minute. What's this? The panel on the left, the central segment, right next to the eagle holding the snakes. Is that, like, a swastika? In a building built in 1930? I knew the swastika was an ancient symbol, found in many cultures, but it was impossible to see it and not think of the Nazis, or, like now, the neo-Nazis.

Fucking Nazis?!

CHAPTER 3
The Carrel

Before I could follow my thoughts down that Nazi rabbit hole I was stopped short again, awed. Inside the heavy doors, through the security checkpoint, the main entry hall of the library was like the nave of a great cathedral. I step-by-stepped a long procession from the front portal through columns and vaulted ceilings that made the space resemble a giant stone forest. This is, like, a holy place, I thought. Evil cannot enter such a space, only good. At the far end of the nave, I spotted the circulation desk, large and wooden, carved with figures and inscriptions. This was the guardian and gateway to the great tower of stacks, the *sanctum sanctorum*. Six stories of books, all waiting for me.

It was functional, in spite of its inspiring architecture. The south aisle of the nave had computer terminals and seats for reading. The north aisle had desks with small signs that said, "Consult a librarian." I laughed; it was the book lover's equivalent of a confessional. In the middle of the north aisle stood the information desk, where the department secretary had told me I could retrieve the key to my carrel.

I handed the form to an efficient but friendly woman of about fifty whose name tag read "Patty Cist." Poor Ms Cist! I imagined some puss filled bubo from the Black Death, then remembered that's spelt c-*y*-s-t. She located the carrel records on her computer, looked up at me, then back at her computer screen.

"Is everything okay?" I asked.

"Yes, fine," she said. I'm not always great at reading people, but I thought I noticed a slight smile on her face. She retrieved the key from a folder behind her desk and handed it to me with a one-pager entitled "Use of carrels." She took a copy of the library floor plan, marked the location of my carrel, and handed it to me. It looked like Patty Cist smiled again, this time through pursed lips, but I couldn't be sure.

Use of carrels:
1) Carrels are available for use during regular Sterling Memorial Library hours.
2) Study carrels are for Yale graduate students and faculty members doing active research, as an alternative to carrying home loads of books. Books are charged to your carrel instead of to your personal account.
3) Please note that reference books and reserve materials are not allowed in your carrel. No personal items in your carrel.
4) Locked carrels are for faculty member use only.
5) If a carrel is not being used for its intended purpose, you will be asked to relinquish it.

Wait. Number 4. Locked carrels are for faculty only? Why have I, a humble first-year grad student, been given a locked carrel? I decided not to linger by the information desk to find out but conducted a *Treasure Island* upon the library map to the second floor, where I found my carrel.

The carrel doors in Sterling, at least this carrel door, didn't parrot the medieval grandeur of the rest of the building. Other than a diamond-shaped window at eye level, the door to carrel 220—fine, dark-stained wood—was without ornament. The lock was stiff, but the key worked, which was all I cared about in that moment. I swung the door open and flipped on the inside light. What the—? Carrel 220 was stuffed with someone else's stuff.

I looked at the carrel number that Patty Cist had assigned to me, looked at the key, then looked again at the succinct, one-page operator's manual entitled "Use of carrels." Item 2 declared that books would be "charged to the carrel." There seemed to be plenty of those. But the carrel also overflowed with "personal items," the kind forbidden in item 3. I must be in the wrong place. This carrel belonged to a professor, what with its locked door (item 4). But, like, why would she give me the key to a professor's carrel after she had seen my student ID? As these thoughts went through my mind, I began to check out the books—the surest way to judge the character of the unknown inhabitant. Almost all of them were about the Middle Ages. Mmm. I closed the door behind me and sat down. No rush of emotion in sitting. No elation. No pride. Just a memory, again, of Sister Clodagh before I left for Yale.

"The main thing you'll need for success in grad school is *Sitzfleisch*," she said.

"Sit-meat?" I said.

"Your buttocks," said Sister Clodagh. "If you've got good *Sitzfleisch* it means you can sit still long enough to be productive. It's endurance, perseverance, staying power. Think of *Sitzfleisch* as the opposite of ants in your pants."

I settled my butt further into the chair's hard wooden seat and looked up at the books on the carrel shelf. I knew some of them from my days hanging out at the Texas Renaissance Festival. Others I'd read as an undergrad: Maggie Black's *The Medieval Cookbook*, Emilie Amt's *Women's Lives in Medieval Europe*, and *Life in a Medieval Village*, by Joseph and Frances Gies. There were a few books by Kantorowicz (my as yet unmet advisor): *Crips, Bloods, and Crusaders: Medieval Precursors to Modern Gang Signs*. Next to that, *The King's Too Bawdy: Urban Graffiti as Medieval Marginalia*.

Kantorowicz was the whole reason I'd come to Yale. I loved being a history major and reading medieval history books in particular. But reading Kantorowicz was like reading a Molotov cocktail. His ideas were, like, incendiary. His prose was explosive. The way he connected medieval history to all the problems of the contemporary world was, like, he was Tolkien, only literal instead of allegorical.

Whoever belonged to all these books in the carrel had a row of works on a similar theme. Lynn Ramey's *Black Legacies: Race and the European Middle Ages*, Cord Whitaker's *Black Metaphors: How Modern Racism Emerged from Medieval Race-Thinking*, Matthew Vernon's *The Black Middle Ages: Race and the Construction of the Middle Ages*, and Geraldine Heng's *The Invention of Race in the European Middle Ages*. One handsome volume caught my eye, not the least because of its lengthy title: *The Image of the Black in Western Art, Volume II: From the Early Christian Era to the "Age of Discovery", Part 1: From the Demonic Threat to the Incarnation of Sainthood*, 2nd Edition, edited by David Bindman and Henry Louis Gates, Jr. I knew Professor Gates from that "Finding Your Roots" show on PBS. The cover of *The Image of the Black in Western Art* had a beautiful picture showing a sculpture of a medieval knight. The knight wore a hooded hauberk of chain maille and, over that, a surcoat that still showed colorful paint across the belt. Most surprising, to me at least, was the face that peered out of the hood. It had a broad nose and full lips and was painted black. I noticed a flyer taped to the wall next to me that had the same image of the Black knight. It advertised a grad student 'mini-conference' scheduled for next semester called "Race, Class, and Gender in the Middle Ages." As I read the flyer, I saw out of the corner of my eye a face similar to the knight's peeping into the window of the carrel, but with eyes that were decidedly alive.

I yelped! A short burst. Not from fear really. More, like, being taken aback.

The face outside the door backed away until I could see an entire body. Hands held in the air. Tattooed arms. One of the tattoos looked like the labyrinth at Chartres cathedral. The other arm also had a labyrinth, but in the Minoan style—the minotaur next to it was a dead giveaway. I was still shaken by his sudden appearance but, somehow, having these images to focus on helped me calm down. My inked-up peeper moved back further and leaned against the edge of a table. I opened the door slowly. He spoke first.

"You're with Kantorowicz?"

I nodded.

"So am I," he said. He pulled out a chair from a desk outside the carrel and sat down, closer to the carrel, but not too close. "He likes to do this," he continued. "In fact, when I first arrived and was given a key to this carrel, there was another grad student in here. It's a faculty carrel, but the man doesn't use it, so he portions its use like a benefice to his doctoral students. I've actually had the space to myself for the last two years. I thought I was going to be his last grad student, what with his current imbroglio. I guess I'm surprised somebody new has shown up."

"It *is* a faculty carrel," I said, picturing "Use of carrels," item 4, before my eyes. "Isn't that, like, illegal or against the rules or something?"

"Oh, it certainly is. But Kantorowicz winks at the librarians and they look the other way."

"Current imbroglio?" I said, but even as he started to explain, I lasered in on his right arm.

"Chartres?" I said.

"Yes." He smiled and stretched out his hand to introduce himself.

"Quick," he said. "Quinton Quick. Call me Quint."

"Quinton Quick. Call me Quint. Alliteration," I said. He shrugged.

"Molly Isaacson," I said. "Call me Isaacson." I took his hand confidently, like dad had taught me, *like a professional.* I looked Quint in the eye and shook his hand with a firm grip.

"So, like, how does this work with the two of us both assigned to the same space?" I asked. "Our own Avignon Papacy on the second floor of Sterling Library?"

"Don't worry about it," he said. "If you want to use the space, I can make room for you on the bottom shelf. We can figure out a schedule, if you think you'll be here a lot."

I nodded, then looked back at the shelving and all the books I'd been eye-balling before my humiliating scare.

"These are, like, your books?" I asked.

"Yes."

"Then *you're* a medievalist, too?"

"Yes."

"But you're *Black*!"

Filtering my thoughts was never a strong suit. I flashed on a memory from my teen years at the Ren Fest.

Walking through the fairgrounds one hot summer day, I spotted a family of three moving toward me. The father wore a friar's costume, tied at the waist with a rope. The mother was dressed as a noble lady of the court: a flowing dress with tight bodice and a conical hennin on her head with a veil that trailed behind her. These two characters, the monk and the noble woman, seemed disjointed. Their son, maybe six or seven, created the link. He wore a blousy green shirt gathered at the middle with a leather belt. A short wooden sword at his side. On his head, he sported a green *chapeau à bec*, which is, like, the proper name for Robin Hood's hat. If the boy was Robin Hood, which was clearly his intention, then the father was Friar Tuck and his mother was meant to be Maid Marion. The kid's costume was actually very good—much better than what I'd thrown together for that same role when I was his age. And the three of them went together nicely. It was clear what they were going for. But something about the sight of them didn't fit into my *universum*. The whole thing was wrong. Like, ahistorical.

"You're Black," I'd said to seven-year-old Robin Hood and his family. "You're *all Black*!"

I stared at Quint, my jaw agape. Ellipses hung in the air like just-launched stones from a trebuchet that would soon drop on my head. Quint was the first grad student I'd met and there I stood, foot firmly wedged in mouth, as I searched for a different word to fill in the blank.

"You're Black," I said. "I mean, like, you're ..."

"American?" he said. "Yes, I know. Exactly. So many people think that only Brits or Europeans can have any insight into
medieval history. The same way they think that only Blacks can
study Black history, or only Jews can study the Holocaust."

"Yes," I said. "I guess."

CHAPTER 4
## Quinton Quick

*White people.*
*White people are so …*
*—interesting?*
*—annoying?*
*—crazy?*
*Condescending, ignorant, arrogant, fragile, capricious, privileged, con-*
*trolling, fascinating, fearful, uninformed, ill-informed, misinformed, hate-*
*ful, dangerous.*

*Yes. I could've knocked on the door and stood back, offering a gentler,*
*less threatening first encounter. But she was in my space, or at least I've*
*thought of it as my space since what's-his-name left. I submit that any*
*reasonable person who walked up and saw a light inside their carrel where*
*there shouldn't be a light would justifiably peek in the window to see what*
*the hell was going on.*

*Then her pale freckled face and frizzy red locks appear in the window,*
*and she yelps?! Like some scared puppy.*

*And suddenly I'm Henry Louis Gates trying to explain to the Cam-*
*bridge cops that I'm breaking into my own house because I've locked myself*
*out.*

*She yelps!*

*And I back up, offering my best Michael Brown and Trayvon Mar-*
*tin. Hands up—don't shoot! Because mama trained me from the moment*
*of my birth to code-switch into the least aggressive posture my melanized*
*body could muster lest I put my life at risk, though from the moment of*
*my birth it was already too late.*

*Was it just that I caught her off guard? Or was it my black face catching her off guard? Hard to say, in and of itself. But her follow-up reveals all.*

*"You're a medievalist? But you're Black!"*

*No. She micro-aggressed: "You're a medievalist, <u>too</u>?"*

*Okay, little rabbit. You just got here, and you don't know a thing about POC in the Middle Ages. Hell, outside of Kantorowicz, most of the older generation don't know anything either. Cut her some slack, Quick. She's probably never been exposed to anything but the all-white "real Middle Ages." Probably started her medieval fandom as a "festie" or a "rennie", driving every summer weekend to some "Ye Olde Ahistorical Faire," wearing a laced bodice and playing the part of the wench.*

*And if Black folks in the Middle Ages or a Black medievalist disrupts your worldview, well, I'm sorry but we've been there all along.*

> *On the ninth day there came riding towards them a knight on a goodly steed, and well-armed withal. He was all black: his head was black as pitch, black as burnt brands, his body, and his hands were all black, saving only his teeth. His shield and his armour were even those of a Moor, and black as a raven. But in all that men would praise in a knight was he fair, after his kind. Though he were black, what of it?*

*That's how it reads in the "Tale of Morien". Thirteenth-century, Arthurian romance. Morien, son of a Moorish princess and a goddamned knight of the round table! There were Black folks in the Middle Ages, and not just a few.*

*What of it?*

CHAPTER 5
## Knights and Squires


"Come, little rabbit," said Quinton Quick. "If you're going to the reception, I'll introduce you around."

The annual fall reception for graduate students in Yale's Department of History took place in one of the larger halls of Beinecke, the other great library on campus. Unlike Sterling, Beinecke was a box, its modern façade comprised of unornamented, stacked marble cubes. It was *ultima Thule* to Collegiate Gothic. Yet Quint pointed out hidden meanings in its design.

"The cubes are stacked 15 across, 5 high, and 10 deep, a relationship of 3:1:2," he said.

"The golden ratio!" I said.

Quint smiled.

We stood under Beinecke's high ceiling. It wasn't the vaulted cathedral ceiling of Sterling, but it was impressive. I looked up at Beinecke's tower of books that covered several floors, encased in glass and centrally located for all to see, rather than being hidden away like Sterling's book stacks. Quint told me about a Gutenberg Bible on permanent display on the library's mezzanine. Looking around, I could see many other codices and *incunabulae* placed throughout Beinecke's exhibit space. At that moment, the library's archivists had dedicated the first floor to the mysterious Voynich manuscript—a beautifully illustrated, 15th-century codex, written in a script and language so obscure that it remains undeciphered to this day. The codex itself sat in a large glass cube, opened to an illustration of stars (or perhaps flowers), with replicas of other folios

placed around the large foyer, and conjectural, descriptive plac-
ards accompanying each replica.

Grad students began to fill the space. Some stopped to take
in the Voynich exhibit. Others were more interested in recon-
necting with friends and grad school colleagues, sharing stories
of the research they'd done over the summer, or the fellow-
ships they'd just come back from, I guessed. There must have
been, like, two hundred people in the hall. Two thirds of them
had to be grad students, or maybe very young profs. Quint
caught me counting the crowd and offered some stats about
the grad program at Yale. According to Quint, Yale's Department of History has sixty-four profs and roughly two hundred
grad students. That was a 1:3 ratio of knights to squires, masters to apprentices. He said that roughly a third of the faculty
were Americanists, with the remainder being an equal distribu-
tion of Europeanists, Africanists, and Asianists, representing
periods from ancient times to today. A decent crop of interdisciplinary scholars working in environmental history or in
women's and gender studies was scattered throughout the
room. The professors' attire, echoed by their students, ranged
from the cliché tweedy look of movie profs to black pullovers,
asymmetrical haircuts, and piercings, the symbols of the "radical" disciplines.

According to Quint, there were five medievalists in the department. Two were Byzantinists, both women. Jane Hathaway studied the impact of the Crusades on the Byzantine East.
Vasiliki Kostas specialized in education in the Latin Kingdom
after 1204, the Fourth Crusade. There was an Egyptian historian of labor throughout medieval Islam, Tariq Sallam, who
had worked to overthrow the Mubarak regime during the Arab
Spring. Alyson Stark studied medieval gender politics and
taught the methods seminar. She had just been appointed as a
Sterling Professor, named for the same guy who endowed the
library. It was Yale's highest honor and she was scheduled to
give a big lecture soon to kick off her getting it. Finally, there
was Abe Kantorowicz, my advisor and Quint's, who had a joint
appointment in art history. All of the medievalists held

endowed chairs. This meant that the medieval wing was small but important.

I watched the crowd pass through the generous buffet set up on one side of the hall as I took it all in. This was, like, a graze fest that seemed designed to guarantee good grad student attendance, offering much better than just beer and pizza. There were dates stuffed with goat cheese and wrapped in bacon, puff pastries topped with a salmon remoulade, platters of artisanal cheeses from France and Germany, beer from Belgium and wine from Spain and Italy. There were giant bowls of salad, one with mixed fruit, another with tomatoes, mozzarella, and basil, and yet another with tabbouleh. Pita bread had been cut into smaller squares for dipping in hummus, tzatziki, and baba ganoush. It was a feast meant for the knightly class, one that introduced the squires not just to the extravagant diversity of tastes, but to the idea that all of these tastes were available to us as we entered the privileged class of soon-to-be Yale PhDs. My mouth watered slightly at both prospects.

Quint touched my shoulder and pointed up toward a corner of the mezzanine. A man in a trench coat stood there, looking down at us.

"Spy," Quint said.

"What?" I looked up and tried to refocus my glance. "No," I said. "I mean, like, he *is* wearing a trench coat, but this is probably *propter pluviam*, because of the rain."

"I understand *propter pluviam*," Quint said. "But no. That's where Robert Littell tries to have one of his CIA analysts killed."

"Like, what are you taking about?"

"*The Once and Future Spy*? No? It's a thriller set in the 60s. Littell places an assassination attempt right here in Beinecke."

I stared at Quint in disbelief.

"Never heard of it," I said. "Though it bugs me that, who is the author? Littell? He's ripped off T.H. White's title."

"*Rex quondam. Rex futuram*," said Quint.

"Yes. *The Once and Future King*," I said. "Is this, like, a medieval spy thriller?"

"Nope. Cold War stuff," said Quint. "I'm really more a fan of John le Carré. This is just the campus lore one needs to know."

This guy knows a lot, I thought, as a group of four women joined us, balancing small plates and wine glasses in one hand as they extended the other in greeting. They all seemed to know Quint, who managed the introductions. There was Mary, who had an Irish last name, but who said she was working on the Holocaust. An elegant, slightly older woman named Steph was researching the role of lesbians in the anti-war movement during World War I. Amy studied Nazi scientists, while Kim researched the impact of internment on *nissei*, the children born to Japanese immigrants in the early 20th century. They were all kind and welcoming, perhaps because I didn't pose a threat to them coming from a field so distant from their own.

"Journalists," Quint said, with mock derision. "Not a one of them has more than one other language and none of their topics goes further back than a century! And they call themselves historians." He was clearly playing the teasing older brother to this group, but they weren't going to stand for it.

"Sarcasm," Steph said. "The last refuge of those whose topics have no relevance to the present."

"*Ad hominem*?" Quint said. "Really?"

"Get over yourself, Mr. Dead-Language Man," Kim said, then turned to me. "Please tell us that you're work isn't tied to this sad excuse for a medievalist."

"Actually, I'm not sure about my specific topic yet. Quint and I just met in our carrel."

"Our?" Amy said. "So, you're with Kantorowicz?

"Kantorowicz?!" Mary said. "The Holocaust denier?"

"He's *not* a Holocaust denier," Quint said.

"He went to that conference in Iran," Mary said. "What was it called? The International Conference for Assholes Denying Nazi Atrocities? No, sorry. The International Conference to Review the Global Vision of the Holocaust. Much more obtuse that way. Academic all-stars like David Duke attended."

"The KKK guy?" I said.

"The KKK guy," Mary repeated. "As well as your newly chosen advisor, Kantorowicz!"

"That was fifteen years ago," Quint said.

"Fifteen? Twenty? Thirty? Who cares how long it was?" Amy said.

"I heard Brandeis denied his promotion to full professor because he went to that conference," Kim said.

"Lucky for him Yale saved his ass at all," said Mary.

"They took his attendance at the conference completely out of context, which is what all of you are doing," Quint said. "He went to Iran to argue against the Holocaust deniers! To let them just spout off and not offer counter arguments is irresponsible."

"Don't be naïve!" Mary said. "To attend that conference for any reason gives it legitimacy that it doesn't deserve. For God's sake, Tony Blair, George W and the Pope all condemned the meeting as a way to dress up anti-Semitism in academic robes."

"Be that as it may," Quint said. "It takes light to fight the darkness. Kantorowicz fights ideas with ideas, not silence."

"Is that what he's doing with this latest article he wrote for *Zuerst?*" Mary seemed relentless. "That was just last spring, not fifteen years ago."

"What is *Zuerst?*" I asked.

"It's a rightwing mag—" Quint said.

"*Fascist* magazine," Mary interrupted.

"Whatever," Quint said. "It's published in Germany. But Kantorowicz did not write an article for it. He was interviewed."

"Same difference," said Mary.

"The interview," Quint said, "dealt with Kantorowicz's research around symbols. How neo-Nazi groups are coopting medieval symbols and how scholars of the Middle Ages could influence that discourse."

"What sort of obfuscating bullshit is that?!" Mary almost screamed, then made air quotes when she said, "*influence the discourse?* Why not just outright condemn the use of medieval-ism to promote white supremacy?"

So this is what grad school is like, I thought. In that moment, Quint spotted another friend and waved her over. I wondered if she would add more fire to the conversation or cool it down.

"Leigh Ann, this is Molly. She's Kantorowicz's new rabbit."

"A pleasure," said Leigh Ann. "I'm working with Stark on medieval queenship. Do you have a topic yet?"

"Nothing specific," I said. "Tell me about Stark. I have her for the methods course."

"She'll show you a good time," Leigh Ann said, then gestured over my shoulder to a group of profs huddled around an exhibit case for the Voynich manuscript. "That's Stark there," she said. "The one holding forth."

Even from a distance, I could tell that the others weren't medievalists, since they only nodded at Stark's comments and gestures and never seemed to offer a question or counter argument. Stark was a 'plain-looking woman,' as Mom might have said. She wore wire-rimmed glasses and tortured her auburn hair into a tight ponytail.

"One thing to know," Leigh Ann continued. "Stark has higher standards for medievalist grad students, especially the women, even if they aren't her advisees."

"How will she know I'm a medievalist?" I asked.

"She'll ask." Quint said. "They all want to be sure which rabbit is theirs."

"What is with you and this 'rabbit' schtick?" I said. "You've, like, called me that two or three times."

"You don't know the story?" Quint asked. Groans and eye rolling from the small clutch of women in our group.

"Please spare us, Quint" Mary said.

"It's such a tired saw," Steph added.

"Once upon a time," Quint began, but Leigh Ann cut him off.

"There's this rabbit that's writing a dissertation entitled 'The Superiority of Rabbits over Foxes and Wolves.' A fox tries to eat the rabbit, but the rabbit says, 'Please, no. Come back to my rabbit's den and read my dissertation first. The fox is never seen again. The same thing happens with a wolf. 'I want to eat you.' 'Please no. First read my dissertation, 'The Superiority of Rabbits over Foxes and Wolves.' And the wolf disappears."

Quint tried to retake control of the story, but Steph got there faster.

"So, then another *rabbit* asks the first rabbit how she's escaped being eaten. And she says, 'You have to read my dissertation, 'The Superiority of Rabbits over Foxes and Wolves.'"

"Then the first rabbit takes the second rabbit back to its warren," Mary said, to Quint's consternation. "And inside there's a lion surrounded by all these bones, and the dissertating rabbit says ..." Here she gestured to Quint as if giving him the cue to tell the story's punchline.

Quint scowled and took his time, as if his colleagues had, like, robbed him of the chance to tell his great story—a story he clearly liked telling by way of initiating the new grad students, in this case yours truly.

"The moral is this," he said at last. "The title of your dissertation doesn't matter. The topic doesn't matter. The research doesn't matter." He paused for effect. "The only thing that matters is who your advisor is."

"So, the lion is the rabbit's advisor," I said.

Quint seemed to be expecting more of a reaction—laughter?—but he had no time to respond. In that moment, a dark figure eclipsed the last of the evening sun that poured through Beinecke's revolving glass door. Abe Kantorowicz entered the room.

# CHAPTER 6
## Kantorowicz

"Why the crutch?" I said.

My new colleagues didn't answer right away. I looked at their faces and, if I'd been better at reading them, I might say they looked at me askance. Filter, I reminded myself. Filter.

Abe Kantorowicz, the lion to my rabbit, if Quint's story held, used a crutch. I thought of Oedipus and the Sphinx and giggled under my breath. What creature walks with four feet in the morning, two feet at noon, and three feet in the evening?

"Is it because of his age?" I asked.

"He's not that old," Quint said. "Besides, I think he's always had it."

"Maybe polio?" Mary said with a strained face.

"Scoliosis?" Steph said.

"I heard he was injured in some sort of protest when he was still an undergrad," Leigh Ann suggested.

Kantorowicz hung his coat on a portable rack near the door, then made his way around the large hall. He stopped to talk with colleagues and students, but never for too long. The rubber-footed titanium pole was attached to his right arm just below the elbow with a cuff that seemed like the oversized hand of a Lego figure. Whenever he, like, felt the need to emphasize a point in his argument, he shifted his weight and, gesturing with both hands, dangled the crutch from his right forearm, an untamed pendulum that might kneecap anyone in its way. He was elegant, not in spite of his disability, but maybe because of it. The way he used his crutch—as a pointer, a gavel, a conductor's baton—defined him the way the keys to heaven defined Saint Peter, or Thor's hammer defined him. It was his attribute, as the iconographers say.

It became clear that Kantorowicz had a goal, as his path traced a tight spiral toward the center of the room. Once Quint deciphered our advisor's trajectory, we skipped ahead to beat him to his destination. Steph and Leigh Ann followed. The cluster of people around the Voynich exhibit grew to about twenty—which, by the time we got there, included the man in the trench coat—all of them listening to Stark, who pointed to the opened manuscript as she spoke.

"This is folio 68," said Stark. "An interesting choice to exhibit. There are certainly more detailed images on other pages, some of the botanical illustrations for instance. But here we see constellations of stars as they would be seen in the sky surrounding the earth, which is shown at the center of the illustration."

At this point, a titanium pole with a rubber tip poked and sliced through the crowd, parting the group into two halves. Once he had established a clear path, Kantorowicz made his way to the case and stood face to face with Stark.

"Mm-hmm," he said. These were the first words—sounds, I suppose—that I ever heard him utter. They were not meant as transition, not intended as filler to give him time to gather his thoughts. As I came to know him, I understood that he meant this gesture as a pointed disruption of his adversary, a warning of what was to come.

"First, I think we might more precisely call this folio 68 recto 3, indicating the third fold-out on the 'front' of the 'page,' as you call it."

Stark gave Kantorowicz a look that said, *stop being an ass!* She wasn't as precise in her nomenclature as she might have been, but we were at a reception, not a professional conference. It was likely that two-thirds of the people listening weren't even medievalists, so what would be the point? She glared at him as Kantorowicz continued.

"We say number 3 because folio 68 is folded to create three sections. You can see the folds if you look closely. This is not the earth in the center of the illustration, though I can see how, in the pre-Copernican era, one might think this. Actually, it's the moon, which you can tell from the rendering of a face—the 'man in the moon'—and the shading around the edges, indicating lunar phases. And these aren't really constellations of stars. A circle of undeciphered text creates a halo around the moon, which is divided into eight sections. Four alternating sections are filled with stars with no rhyme or reason, except that they seem to turn the halo into a cruciform halo, the kind worn by Christ, as opposed to the 'empty' halos worn by most saints. Pull back a bit and you can see this pattern more easily."

Kantorowicz paused, which gave his audience a chance to let his description sink in. Yes, a cruciform halo, they nodded to themselves.

"The blank spaces in the cruciform halo do have what appear to be specific stars, though not enough to call them constellations, I think. This grouping of seven stars to the left of the moon or face might well be the Pleiades. Otherwise, there are four sets of stars, with two to eight stars per set, which might be shown in relation to their position, vis-à-vis the moon."

He had been gesturing the whole time with his crutch dangling from his forearm and with that last point, "vis-à-vis the moon," he snapped the crutch upward, grabbed its handle and pointed it toward the heavens. He was thrilling to watch, in a way that perhaps only a history nerd can understand. Kantorowicz was performing his own version of my teenaged self at the Ren Fest, correcting others for their perceived "ahistoricalness," taking no prisoners, just as he did. I glanced at Quint, who looked at me as if to say, yes, he's our lion. On the other hand, Steph brushed past me as she left and whispered in my ear.

"Mansplaining," she said.

Leigh Ann did the same on the other side.

"Correctile dysfunction."

For her part, it seemed as if Stark was accustomed to this kind of one-upmanship and had learned to roll with it. Or maybe she would save her response (revenge?) for another day.

More of the crowd dispersed. An older woman approached Stark and they walked toward the buffet. About half the small crowd, Quint and me included, huddled around Kantorowicz to ask questions or engage him further.

"What does the text say?" a young student asked.

"We have no idea," said Kantorowicz, smiling. "This is one of the charms of Beinecke MS 408. The words next to the individual stars appear to be names, and that would be helpful in deciphering the whole if we only knew which stars they were meant to be."

There were a few more questions and Kantorowicz was generous with his time. Later, Quint told me that this generosity would continue so long as the professor felt like he had an audience. People slowly peeled away, and I waited my turn to introduce myself. I have never been good in such situations, usually letting others butt in front of me, so I bided my time until it was just Quint and me. For his part, Quint had promised to "introduce me around," a promise which he kept when it was just other grad students, but which seemed to disappear when it came to our advisor.

"Mr. Quick," said Kantorowicz. "How was your summer? Productive, I hope."

"Yes," said Quint. "Yes, very good. A month at the BN in Paris and another in Magdeburg. Then lots of reading back home." He went on to list a bibliography that I thought might take days to complete. Kantorowicz seemed to approve, which was like a balm to Quint. When Quint finally took a breath, the professor turned to me.

"Ms. Isaacson, I presume."

I stared at him blankly, which he must have taken for surprise at his knowing my name, because he followed by explaining his deduction.

"One, you're here at the reception, which says you're a history student. You might be a sly grad student from a different department, crashing our party for the food, but in that case you'd be huddled under the stairs with two plates of hors d'oeuvres. But you stand here empty handed and attentive. Two, you're here with Mr. Quick, which says you're either a medievalist or someone with questionable taste in friends. Or perhaps no friends, as yet, because you're new to Yale." Quint shrugged. "Three, you've listened to me blather on about the Voynich with too much awe and fear in your soul to challenge me even once—a situation that will need to change—but for now it means that you're one of my graduate students. Since Mr. Quick is my only other advisee, then you must be you." He smiled a charming, disarming smile.

"Yes," I said, holding out my hand, remembering my practice sessions with dad for the second time that afternoon. I was enjoying this moment of affirmation, such as it was, and turned to look at Quint, but his gaze hadn't left Kantorowicz. Then, something behind Quint caught my eye.

It was "trench coat guy," standing by the buffet table, looking at me. At us? He wasn't holding anything to drink or gathering any food onto a plate. He was just standing there, looking our way, but he stopped as soon as he saw me noticing him. In fact, he turned away and headed for the door, not fast, but not wasting any time either. It was odd.

Quint and I headed for the buffet. Along the way, he introduced me to more grad students. The whole thing was more interesting, less nerve-racking than I'd expected, and we lingered at the reception for an hour or so until Quint invited me to join him for coffee.

CHAPTER 7
## A Mutual Interrogation

Dad says that the relationship between universities and coffee shops is symbiotic, like the yellow-billed oxpecker that eats the ticks off the backs of rhinos and zebras—the former gets sustenance, the latter gets pest control. Coffee shops provide a similar service to university communities: legal stimulants facilitating long nights of study in exchange for strong financial returns for relatively low overhead. "A coffee shop that goes under in a town filled with grad students," he would say, "isn't trying very hard."

There were dozens of coffee shops around the Yale campus catering to every taste. The one preferred by the history crowd was called Insomnia. With a name like that, it was no surprise that the cafe was open 24 hours, its busiest times from 10pm to 4am. It was rare to find an empty table after midnight. Most of the clientele were in the humanities. Quint and I ordered at the bar, then took the last available booth, near the emergency exit in the back.

"Tell me about Kantorowicz," I said. "How did you pick him to be your advisor? I had no idea about those, like, accusations."

"Neither did I when I first got here," Quint said. "I mean, when you're looking for grad schools, you read the books profs write and try to find someone who studies something close to what you want to study. Who knew you had to do deep background security checks?"

"When did you find out?"

"Honestly? Just last spring," Quint said. "Somebody got wind of the *Zuerst* interview and suddenly it was this big scandal on campus. Students and some faculty called for his resignation. Cancel culture took over. I mean, he didn't say anything in the interview that was racist or anti-Semitic. And he didn't say anything that he hadn't already said in dozens of other articles. It was the fact that he said it in this obscure fascist magazine, that's written in German, which means most of his detractors wouldn't even be able to read it, but that didn't keep them from crying out."

"What about the Iran conference?"

"I didn't know anything about it. I don't suppose it's the kind of thing your advisor brings up out of the blue. Then last March, the *Yale Daily News* picked up the story in connection with the *Zuerst* scandal. Soon everybody was talking about not one, but two examples of racist leanings. His less harsh critics referred to it as 'poor judgment.'"

"Why do you stick with him?"

Quint didn't answer right away, looked across the coffee shop.

"I've been his student for five years, going on six. In all that time he's been nothing but generous and helpful to me. I've never ever heard him say anything remotely racist. And I would know," he said, pinching the darker skin on the back of his forearm.

"I guess it would be hard to switch advisors so late in the game. I mean, if you're almost done, like, 'All But Dissertation', who else would take you on?"

Quint looked at me quizzically but didn't answer. Instead, he turned the interrogation my way.

"Okay," he said. "What about you?"

"What about me?"

"Who are you? Where do you come from? How did you get here? I'm guessing Renaissance festival, then Tolkien. Or maybe the other way around? Or maybe both at once?"

I squinted at him, trying to figure him out.

"Most medievalists have similar origin stories," he said smugly. "Throw in some Robin Hood and some exposure to Monty Python and you've covered about 90%. I don't mean this to sound like the Spanish Inquisition."

"*Nobody* expects the *Spanish Inquisition*!" I mock-shrieked.

"See what I mean?" he said. We both laughed.

"I did start out at the Ren Fest," I said, which put a big grin on his face. "And my parents did take me to see *Robin Hood*, the 1938 version with Errol Flynn, when I was, like, seven. For months after that, I traipsed around the backyard in my father's old green army shirt, sleeves cut-off, tied at the waist with a long leather belt. I stuck a turkey feather through the side of my grandfather's hunter green Bavarian hat and pinned it in the back so it would fit my head. I was Robin Hood—always Robin, never Maid Marian."

Quint smiled, which felt encouraging.

"My mom would yell out the window at me and my friends. 'Sometimes you have to let the *boys* be Robin Hood … And be careful with those sticks. You'll poke someone's eye out.'"

"I love the Errol Flynn version," Quint said. "What was your favorite scene?"

"Oh, the staff fight with Little John on the log crossing. No question. All that parrying and quick retorts."

Quint smiled again.

"How about you?" I asked.

"Sneaking into the archery contest in disguise. Cunning and bravery combined. When I played Robin as a kid, that's the scene I would always act out."

"What about the Kevin Costner version?" I asked.

"*Prince of Thieves*? Horrible! Robin Hood with an Iowa accent?! I will say though that it was the first Robin Hood movie to have a Black character."

"Morgan Freeman's part? But that was totally made up."

"It's all made up, little rabbit. The Robin Hood legend was already changing during the Middle Ages. We've just come to accept the 1938 *Robin Hood* as the received version. Remember, in his first appearances, in 16th-century ballads, Robin's a lone bandit who robs from the rich and keeps the money for himself. Friar Tuck and Little John get added to the mix later. So why not add a Black character? There were Black people in the Middle Ages."

This reminded me again of my encounter with the Black kid playing Robin Hood. For the first time it, like, occurred to me that I didn't have a problem playing Robin myself, even though I was a girl. Even though I was Jewish. But the thought of Black Robin Hood just did not sit well. I'm not prejudiced. It's just anachronistic. Like the Ren Fest people who dressed as pirates or Klingons or other non-medieval characters. Like turkey legs.

"Did you ever eat turkey legs at the Ren Fest?" I asked. "You know turkeys are, like, American birds. They did not have turkeys in medieval Europe, so it's really, like, not historically accurate that they serve turkey legs there."

"I never went to the Ren Fest," Quint said. "Too much of a white suburban thing. I don't know. It never felt welcoming to me."

Me and my outbursts were contributing to that. I'm not prejudiced, I thought, but this was not good.

"What about Tolkien?" I asked. "You said every medievalist origin story starts with Tolkien."

"Maybe not starts," Quint said, "but at least includes. Yes. I was 8 when I discovered *The Hobbit*, 11 for *The Lord of the Rings* trilogy. Works of fantasy but they seemed more 'really medieval' than anything else I'd ever seen or read. Tolkien's sense of unity, of cohesion, made them real. He created a world of great intricacy. Middle Earth did have a diversity of creatures, but some of his symbolism with color is pretty racist."

"Tolkien was not a racist!" I said, forgetting to use my indoor voice. "The whole theme of his books is good fighting evil!"

"Sure, of course. But I don't mean racist like he's gonna burn a cross in my yard. I mean racist like the deep down, subconscious, systemic stuff that all of us carry around, even me. For Tolkien, it meant that evil characters are always dark or black. They're old tropes, but he never once offers any resistance, any alternative."

I had to think about this. Quint carried on.

"In spite of that, he was my first academic crush. Professors for parents, but it was Tolkien's work, and his life, that made me want to be a scholar. Mostly because of his amazing mastery of languages."

Quint went on to tell me a lot of things about Tolkien that I already knew, but I didn't stop him. I imagined Leigh Ann shutting him down as a "mansplainer."

He told me how Tolkien was a philologist, from two Greek words, *phílos* meaning love, and *lógos* meaning word. Tolkien was literally a lover of words. He studied and could read Latin, French, Spanish, Italian, German, and Greek, not to mention Old English (*Beowulf*), Middle English (*Chaucer*), Old Norse (the Viking sagas), and many more. This training allowed him to invent languages for Middle-earth: the Elvish languages of Quenya, Telerin, and Sindarin; the Mannish (human) languages of Adûnaic, Westron, and Rohirric; Khuzdûl for the Dwarves, Valarin for the Ainur, and Entish for the Ents, those protectors of trees that came to resemble the trees themselves. Finally, he created Black Speech, the language of the evil Sauron, which was also the language used in the inscription on the One Ring.

"But you see what I mean? The language of Sauron and his evil minions is *Black*!" Quint took a breath to let that sink in. "Anyway, to emulate Tolkien as a medievalist, I was gonna need more languages."

"How many do you have?"

He had to stop and think about his answer, like he was counting on his fingers. Obnoxious.

"Well, English. French, German, and Spanish, fluent. Very bad in Arabic. Read Latin and Old French, Old Norse, and Middle High German. And Chaucer. What is that? Nine-and-a-half, almost ten? How about you?"

It was impressive if a little show-offy. My list wasn't nearly as long as his.

"I was the only Jew in a private Catholic high school, Incarnate Word Academy. So, I have Hebrew and Latin. I also took French for, like, three years, which Sister Philippa, my teacher, called 'retail Latin.' I took French and Latin at the same time, which every so often generated a traffic jam in the left hemisphere of my brain."

Quint laughed and it made me smile, though I hadn't known I'd made a joke.

"Aside from the languages," I said, "what else did you like about Tolkien?"

Quint didn't hesitate.

"The way he used the medieval world as a stage for moral struggle. *The Lord of The Rings* is about more than a Hobbit on adventure. The fellowship encounters all the great binary challenges of the human quest: hope and despair, death and immortality, fate and free will. He shows the seductive, corrupting force of power—the One Ring's ability to make the wearer invisible—and how the more noble characters (Gandalf, Elrond, Aragorn) resist it. He packs his books with Christlike figures—Gandalf the Grey, who dies and is resurrected as Gandalf the White; Frodo, who in carrying the One Ring carries the burden of evil for all of humanity. You're right, they're all about the never-ending struggle between good and evil."

Is this what all of grad school is going to be like? I wondered. I may be in heaven. Suddenly fearless, I reached out and took Quint by his wrists, turned them upward to reveal his tattoos, and rested his forearms on the table between us.

"Why Chartres and Minos?" I asked about the two labyrinths etched on his skin.

"You recognize them?" he said, then, "Of course, you recognize them."

I smiled at the idea that my seeing something in him made him see something in me. I realized I was still holding Quint's wrists when he shook off my grip. He slipped into what I would later call his "professor mode," preparing for when he would someday stand in front of his own classroom I suppose.

"Chartres is a continuous path. You can't get lost. You can only travel deeper into the self. The Chartres labyrinth signifies a penitential journey to Jerusalem, the return to God. The Minoan labyrinth, on the other hand, is a path intended to disorient, to deceive, to contain the minotaur—shameful halfling aberration, product of an illicit union—until Theseus can kill it. One labyrinth to contain the 'darkness' in men's souls, the other to set the soul free."

"Okay, *professor*," I said. "But why do *you* have these two labyrinths?"

Quint hesitated before he answered.

"It's personal," he said.

"If you tell me," I said with a smile, "I'll show you my tattoo."

There was an even longer pause before he spoke.

"Both my parents were professors. Dad was in history at Princeton, a white dude in a department filled with other white dudes. Mama taught Women's Studies at a community college. She was Black. Dad became obsessed with conspiracy theories and wound up in the looney bin. Mama's career got hijacked by a sudden case of single motherhood. Not that she was some self-sacrificing 'mammy' type. She loved me, but she left me to my own devices more often than not. So she could write. So she could do her own research. I'm their tawny-skinned minotaur—white father, Black mother—a halfling trapped in the labyrinth of Yale's PhD program in history."

I let that sink in. Quint stared at the two labyrinths on his arms.

"What did your parents think about you studying the Middle Ages?" I asked.

"Dad's mind was already gone by then, so who knows. Mama hoped I'd do something more relevant."

"Tell me about it," I said, thinking of my dad's disapproval.

"Even though she's gone now, her disappointment lives on. I suppose it's less aggravating than the expectations that go before me. Expectations that a Black man has to come from an impoverished background or from uneducated parents, that a Black man in grad school must be studying law or medicine or business because that's how he can really help 'his people.' The expectation that a Black man can't be a medievalist."

He stopped and stared off into space for a while. Did he mean me? Did he think I thought that way after one lousy misspeak? Even if I did think that way six hours ago, I didn't now. I managed not to interrupt him.

"Okay," he said eventually. "Let's see *your* ink."

"I don't have any ink," I laughed. "But if I ever do get a tattoo, I promise you'll be the first to see it."

Quint smirked and shook his head.

"Very funny," he said.

The barista called our names to pick up our drinks. Quint volunteered. Just as he came back with our highly caffeinated beverages, 'trench coat guy' appeared in Insomnia's doorway.

CHAPTER 8

## The Once and Future Spy

"I told you he was checking us out," I whispered.

"Do you think he's a perv wearing that trench coat?" Quint asked. "Or better yet, what kind of perv do you think he is?"

And then he was at our table.

"Mind if I join you?" he said and slid into the booth next to me before either of us could object.

"O ... kay," I said.

"We aren't fans of awkward silence," Quint said. "What gives?"

"You're both medievalists?" he asked. We must have looked surprised at his guess—or was this, like Kantorowicz, another case of deduction? He quickly followed up. "I don't have superpowers. I saw you at the reception hovering around the medieval history professors. Stark and ... something with a K ..."

"Kantorowicz," I said.

"He knows that," Quint said. "And I'm guessing he already knows who we are."

"How terribly rude of me," he said, brushing a thick crop of wavy blond hair out of his eyes. "My name is Mapp. I work for the government, and I ... have a favor to ask." He never did ask us our names.

"You're a spook," Quint said.

"Oh, heavens no," Mapp laughed and touched the lapels of his trench coat. "This is just for the rain."

"We're not interested," Quint said.

"I'm interested," I said. "I mean, like, I'm at least interested in what you want. I'm not saying that we'll do it."

Quint could have left in that moment, but I'm glad he didn't. Mapp had settled in and I was trapped in the booth. I asked him nervously if he wanted coffee or something to drink, but he waved his hand. Most of the patrons at the surrounding booths and tables were wearing headphones or earbuds, so they likely couldn't hear anything he was saying. Nonetheless, he leaned in with a conspiratorial air.

"You're aware, I'm guessing, what a great threat white supremacy is to our country."

Quint answered by pinching the flesh of his forearm to indicate the color of his skin and the stupidity of Mapp's question.

"Yes," Mapp said. "Yes. Well, we think that threat is especially strong on your campus and we think the two of you, in particular, can help."

"How so?" I said.

"Things … events … are about to unfold that are part of a national trend toward racism and anti-Semitism. We need people that we can trust to monitor the situation and report back to us."

"What events?" Quint said. "Since when is the government, especially this government, interested?"

"What exactly do you want us to do?" I said, trying to sound calmer than my carrel mate.

Mapp paused and looked us over one more time, glanced over his shoulder then leaned in even further.

"We'd like you to keep an eye on Professor Kantorowicz."

"What!?" Quint was outraged. "Are you saying our professor, Kantorowicz, is a *white supremacist*?! If this comes from accusations you've heard on campus, they're wrong. This is absurd. We're outta here." He stood to leave, then realized that Mapp still blocked my exit. Mapp sat calmly. He would have let me out if I'd pushed it, he was more persistent than threatening. He reached into an inside pocket of his trench coat and took out his phone, called up an image and placed the phone on the table.

"This is your professor and a man name Ted Bilbo."

I laughed out loud.

"You're worried because you think our professor is, like, consorting with a Hobbit?"

"No," Mapp said without smiling. "Bilbo isn't his real name. Theodore Bilbo was a Mississippi politician from the 19-teens to the 1940s. Racist. Grand wizard in the KKK at a time when Klan members in the South could get themselves elected to the Senate. We think this guy in the photo is just using Bilbo's name as a kind of *nom de guerre*."

Quint sat back down and tapped the surface of the phone to enlarge the image.

"Who is he?"

"We believe Bilbo is starting a new hate group—somewhere between Identity Evropa and the Proud Boys—hoping for something more subtle and therefore more insidious because of how mainstream they're trying to present themselves. You can see in the photo that Bilbo is talking with your professor."

Quint tapped the image again to zoom in. He looked long and hard at the picture then handed the phone to me. It was undeniably Kantorowicz, crutch and all.

"This could be anybody," Quint lied. "The photo could mean anything."

"This is why I want you to help us," Mapp said. "Your skepticism is your greatest strength."

"Flattering," Quint said. "But what the hell is that supposed to mean? Skepticism? What the hell do you want from us?"

"I want you to be Joshua and Caleb," said Mapp.

"Biblical spies?" I said.

Quint didn't get the reference and looked at me in disbelief.

"Catholic high school," I shrugged. "Taught by nuns."

"Forgive me," Mapp said. "I assumed people studying the 'age of faith' would have knowledge of the Bible."

"God made me an atheist," Quint said, his irritation growing visibly.

"Joshua and Caleb were spies in the Old Testament," Mapp said. "When the Israelites make it to the outskirts of the Promised Land, before they just waltz right in, Moses sends in a group of twelve spies to check it out."

"One for each of the twelve tribes," I said. Mapp smiled, but Quint glared at me as if I was begging for Mapp's approval. Mapp continued.

"Moses wants to find out if Canaan is really everything God said it would be. The twelve spies sneak over the border and when they get back, they all agree that it really is the land of milk and honey. But ten of the spies also report that Canaan is full of unbeatable foes: Jebusites and Amorites and Hittites, not to mention the Canaanites themselves. They report that the Israelites will never be able to enter because they would lose in any battle against such enemies. They would be like grasshoppers fighting against giants." Mapp had adopted a storytelling voice, like a preacher in a pulpit, and I wondered if he had kids. As he told the tale, I could really visualize the milk and honey, the giants, Moses and all the spies. I could sense the dread the Israelites must have felt, wondering if they should risk crossing into Canaan, the fear that they might die. Quint sat stone-faced. Mapp kept going with his story.

"The group of ten spies exaggerates. They appeal to feelings that sow self-doubt and fear, and to hell with facts. This is the kind of response that turns people toward racism and white supremacy. Worse than that, it causes people who would otherwise take a stand against evil to close their eyes and give up hope. But Joshua and Caleb just report the facts. They're dispassionate, but also self-confident, which gives them a kind of optimism that something can be done, that the Israelites *can* survive against superior forces, that one *can* combat evil and win."

"Forgive *me*," I say, "but the Israelites in this story believe the ten spies, not Joshua and Caleb, and they end up, like, not entering Canaan, but wandering for another forty years."

"That's true," Mapp said. "But the ten spies are reporting to the entire population, a mob that's swayed by emotion. I've already got a mob telling me that Kantorowicz is consorting with white supremacists. What I need are agents of reason who can prove otherwise."

"Who the hell *are* you?" Quint all but yelled.

"Special Agent Nathaniel Mapp, Federal Bureau of Investigation." He took out his ID and laid it on the table. Quint studied it and passed it over to me, though neither of us knew what to look for or how to tell if it was authentic. Special Agent Mapp continued.

"I don't think Kantorowicz is who he says he is. He's somehow involved with Bilbo, or whatever his name is, and he may be helping him put together a new hate group. I'm happy to be proven wrong, but the evidence is mounting. I'm asking both of you to bring your powers of observation and skepticism to the game. If you're right about your professor, that he's not in bed with neo-Nazis, no one will be happier than me. But if he turns out to be helping them, I know you'll do the right thing."

There was a long moment of silence at our booth. Quint and I looked at each other, then at Mapp, then around the room. Nobody said anything more. Mapp scooped up his ID and phone and put them back in his trench coat pocket. From that same pocket, he produced two business cards and placed one in front of each of us.

"I have to ask you not to discuss this with anyone else, especially Kantorowicz. Please call me when you've decided." With that he was up and out the door.

And Insomnia became more than the coffee shop's name.

CHAPTER 9
Two Murals

Quint and I left Insomnia and walked in silence until we reached Sterling, where our paths toward home diverged. Just as we parted, there was a sudden burst of energy to our conversation, all questions with no obvious answers. Should we do it? Like, spy on our professor? Observe and report back? Yeah, whatever. Could we, should we trust Mapp? Why? Should we check him out? Call the FBI field office? And what were we supposed to look for anyway? *Report unattended baggage to security. If you see something, say something.* There were a million more issues and options and we felt as if we had to rehearse them all that night, in that moment.

When we finally dragged ourselves apart, it was quite late. The next morning was my first seminar as a grad student in Yale's Department of History, and Kantorowicz would be leading it. Was he a white supremacist? Was it too late to switch advisors?

I barely slept at all that night.

Kantorowicz strode into the first meeting of the seminar: Appropriations and Abuses of Medieval Art.

It seems odd to say 'strode' but there was no other way to describe his gait. Even walking with a crutch, nothing hindered his speed or assurance. The leather briefcase in his left hand, weighted with books, acted as a counterbalancing pendulum that seemed to propel him forward. He unpacked the books from his briefcase and laid them on the small table next to the lectern, logged into the classroom's computer terminal, and

pulled up his slideshow for the first meeting. Kantorowicz projected two images side by side, executed a quick glance around
the seminar table, and began.

"What do you see?" he asked.

No introductions. No reading of the syllabus. No context
or explanation of what the images might represent. Twelve of
us sat around the long, oak table, Quint, Leigh Ann and me
among them, chairs slanted toward the lectern looking past
Kantorowicz to examine the images on the screen behind him.
A surge of panic—impostor syndrome. Did everyone else in
the seminar know these images? Had there been a pre-class
email with a reading assignment that I'd somehow missed? I
studied the two images at the front of the room and began to
calm down. He didn't ask, like, "what *is* this?" He said, "what
do you *see*?" Open-ended. The risk of being wrong, but perhaps
the chance to stand out with a daring interpretation.

"Both pictures show women," I said without waiting to be
called. "Both seem to be the Blessed Virgin Mary, based on,
like, other images I know."

"Mm-hmm," said Kantorowicz. "The BVM. Yes. Continue."

"The women's faces both look the same," I said. "Maybe
they were painted by the same artist. Or maybe they used the
same model?"

"Date?"

Silence. I had no idea about the date and didn't think I had
enough info to venture a guess.

"Medieval?" I offered.

"Mm-hmm. Given the title of this course, an excellent as-
sumption. But perhaps someone could be more specific." He
looked around the room and landed at Leigh Ann, who was
seated at the far end of the table, directly across from the professor. "You've had the general survey of medieval art," Kantorowicz said, maintaining eye contact. "Any thoughts?"

Leigh Ann, unintimidated, leapt in.

"Curving lines. Elongated figures," she said with a certainty
that I envied. "Delicate facial features. Unemotive. Slightly

smiling. Flattened pictorial space. Clothing sticks to the body as it drapes. Makes me think International Gothic, so 1250s to 1300? The individualized faces also lead me in that direction. The Virgin's face reminds me of the statue of Uta on the Naumburg Cathedral. Not that they look alike, but they both have strong, proud faces. Beautiful, but not stylized. These women are individuals. And I want to say 'Germanic' looking, but maybe I'm stereotyping."

Other students in the class sank back in their chairs and tried to make themselves smaller. I felt deep regret for having arrived early to claim a seat too close to the lectern in front.

"Very good," Kantorowicz said. "I'd praise you for being absolutely right, if you weren't so wrong." We all witnessed Leigh Ann's eyes flash as she felt her ego being crushed ever so gently. Before she could sink into total embarrassment, Kantorowicz offered more context.

"The image on the left, who is indeed the BVM, is from a mural in the *Schwall*, i.e., the cloister, of the Cathedral of St. Peter, in the town of Schleswig in northern Germany. The church was founded in the late 12$^{th}$ century, but like many medieval churches it continued to be renovated, with additions as late as the 1600s. The figure on the right, again the Virgin, is from the Marienkirche in Lübeck, about 80 miles southeast of the Schleswig cathedral."

Kantorowicz looked first at Leigh Ann, who now seemed gun shy, then at me, then at the rest of the class.

"Sticking with your stories?" he asked. "Still think it's the same model for both women? Or at least the same artist?" No one answered, unnerved by the idea of being absolutely right and wrong at the same time.

"Let's leave the two Virgins for the moment," said Kantorowicz, as he projected two more side by side images, this time with a series of birds. "These are from the same set of murals, in St. Peter's and the Marienkirche, respectively. What do you see?"

A series of roundels ran across the bottom register. Each circle contained a bird, some facing to the right, some to the left. Okay. What were birds supposed to tell us? Human figures and architecture were the basis of art historical analysis, comparing shapes and forms and perspective and line and color. Birds were just birds, unless they were integrated into larger compositions, like the necks of geese woven into animal interlace in Celtic manuscripts. These are just birds. Why is he even showing us this? What does he expect …? Wait a minute … Those are *turkeys*!

My hand shot up without hesitation, no clear idea of what I was going to say. Kantorowicz nodded to acknowledge me.

"Turkeys," I blurted out.

"Mm-hmm …"

"Turkeys aren't medieval." All those weekends at the Ren Fest were finally paying off. "I mean, they aren't European. I mean, like, okay. Turkeys are American birds. And Europeans have not yet arrived in America. Columbus? 1492? So, how can there be American birds in, like, a German mural from the 1250s?"

"My dating might be off," Leigh Ann said, retreating. "Otherwise, we have to show how a 13th-century painting style lasts into the 16th century, basically into the northern Renaissance."

Quint jumped into the fray.

"Not so fast," he said. "We've got an entire canon of art historical evidence that supports your dates. What if it's something else?"

Kantorowicz finally sat down in the chair next to the lectern. The backlighting from the dual projected images creating a silhouette around his lightbulb-shaped head. He smiled at the group around the table.

"What if the formal considerations of the Virgin are correct," Quint continued, "but our understanding of turkeys is wrong?"

"What!?" I said, then regained self-control. Was he really going after the one, original contribution I had made to this argument? The one I felt most confident about? The painting had to be post-Columbus. Anything else made no sense.

Quint again. "What if we put the arrival of American turkeys in the northern Germanic territory in the 13th century? Or even earlier? The *Vinlandsaga* has Leif Erikson landing in America in the year 1000, five centuries before Columbus. Artefacts from the excavation at Vinland, which is basically modern-day Nova Scotia, date from as late as the end of the 12th century. What if Vikings brought back the turkeys whose descendants eventually ended up in these two northern Germanic church murals?"

"Brilliant!" Kantorowicz had a huge smile on his face. "You're taking great risks. That's good. But why should modern historians adapt their narrative? Just so a bunch of medievalists can keep their long-held truths based on formal analysis? Is that what you meant to say?"

It wasn't clear to me whether Kantorowicz was engaging in sarcasm, but I think he was. It would at least vindicate my position. Every student in the class looked uncomfortable and confused. The small seminar room was filled with contradictions, but very few answers. Kantorowicz continued.

"What would be the impact on history, writ large, if Mr. Quick's theory were correct?"

Long pauses. I cautiously raised my hand.

"Do the 13th-century turkeys add to the evidence that the Vikings got to America first?"

"And who would benefit from that?"

"Benefit?"

"Whose nationalist narrative would benefit from Germanic peoples discovering America long before the 'lowly' Italian explorer sponsored by the Spanish queen?"

More silence. "I don't follow," I said.

"This seminar is subtitled 'Appropriations and Abuses,'" Quint said with a glow of recognition.

"Mm-hmm."

"Nationalistic narrative," Leigh Ann said. "Does that mean that Germany, Nazi Germany, used these murals with turkeys to promote their master race nonsense?"

"*Wie es eigentlich gewesen ist!*" Kantorowicz cried out in German.

"Wait. What?"

"Ranke," Quint whispered in my ear. "Nineteenth-century 'father of modern history.' I'll tell you later."

Now the story really got interesting. And weird and ironic. And in Kantorowicz's hands, amazing. He explained to us the origins of the two murals, based on the research of an art critic named Jonathon Keats, and how we could all be right and wrong at the same time.

"The story began in 1937," he said, "four years after Hitler came to power. The Lutheran bishop of the once Catholic St. Peter's cathedral commissioned art historian Ernst Fey with restoring the church's murals. Fey was one of the leading restoration experts of his day. It didn't hurt that he was pals with Hermann Göring, head of the German Luftwaffe and art connoisseur *par excellence*, at least according to Göring himself. Fey had already worked on many churches throughout Germany and was especially good at drumming up business, particularly through his Nazi connections. The real skill, however, the man behind the paintbrush, was a fellow named Lothar Malskat, a versatile painter who could imitate many styles, but who was especially capable in International Gothic."

Kantorowicz advanced to the next slide in his presentation: the full view of the Schleswig cathedral mural, Virgin Mary in the center, surrounded by other figures, with the turkeys lined up along the bottom.

"This is what the finished restoration looked like," he said. Next to the final version, he projected another slide showing the same point of view, but much less finished. "This was the job presented to Fey and Malskat in 1937," he said. "Or, more precisely, the job they created for themselves."

"According to Keats," Kantorowicz said, "the original mural was first painted circa 1300. Time and the damp weather of northern Germany caused damage to the mural. In 1888, the church body commissioned their first restoration. They hired a painter named August Olbers, a top restorer of his day who had worked on many churches. Olbers 'renovated' the murals by essentially repainting them. This was how things were done back in the day. Repainting allowed the viewer to see 'what once had been there.' By the 1920s, art historians had very different ideas about restoration." Kantorowicz explained how this new view forbade any attempt to add to, or in any way alter the piece at hand based upon some, like, 'imagined original' in the restorer's mind. The most a restoration should achieve was a good cleaning and stripping of accumulated layers from earlier 'renovations'. By the time Fey and Malskat came on the scene, their task was to restore the 13$^{th}$-century mural, ideally by clearing away Olbers's 19$^{th}$-century renovation.

"So, what we see in the slide on the left," Leigh Ann said, "is the cleaned up original, or whatever was left of it after Olbers 'fix' was removed. Yes?"

"More or less," said Kantorowicz. "In removing Olbers's layer, the painting underneath was rendered almost invisible. Malskat essentially performed his own renovation. First, he whitewashed the entire wall, then redrew and repainted the murals, freehand, based on what he could still see of the original, as well as conjecture from studying other mural paintings of the era. He did the same thing Olbers did, only he did it much better. Malskat had read about Leonardo giving the apostles in his *Last Supper* the faces of local peasants."

Kantorowicz stood and gestured at the images with his cane.

"Malskat used his father's face for one of the prophets, while he borrowed the face of one of his school chums to act as the face of Christ. Both of these models had the rosy cheeks and blond features idealized in Nazi propaganda. To make them look less contemporary, and to age the painting overall, Malskat rubbed the dried paint with a brick, giving the entire work a 'medieval' patina. Malskat worked under cloth-covered scaffolding so he could paint without being disturbed. Apparently, no one knew what he was doing until he was done."

Kantorowicz turned back toward us and paused.

"Malskat basically created a perfect replica of a 14ᵗʰ-century church mural," Kantorowicz said, "but one in which he improvised and added his own touches."

"The turkeys!" I almost shouted. "He added the turkeys!"

"Yes," Kantorowicz said, drawing out the syllable.

"Holy *Scheiße*!" Leigh Ann said.

"Both churches have turkeys in their murals," Quint said. "Both murals were painted by Malskat. The two Virgins have the same face. Someone known to Malskat?"

Quint was making connections faster than anyone else in the class. Kantorowicz accommodated Quint's revelations by returning to the slides with the two Virgins. He then skipped to another slide, a black and white photo of a woman in a movie poster. German title: *Heimatland.* The woman was wearing some kind of peasant folk dress. What were those things called? A *dirndl*? Her eyebrows were highly curated, but her smile was bright and her eyes clear, probably blue.

"Yes!" Quint cried out. "That's the face of Malskat's Virgin!"

"Her name is Hansi Knoteck," said Kantorowicz. "Austrian. She was a big movie star in the 1920s and 30s. This poster is for a movie called 'Homeland,' which was a Nazi propaganda film about Polish atrocities against the Germans—undoubtedly used to justify Germany's later invasion of Poland."

"So, this whole restoration was instigated by the Nazis? To make the German *Volk* look better? Was this Göring's idea?"

"Oh, no," Kantorowicz said. "Much as we might like to ascribe some sinister motives in this plot to the Nazis, they had no idea what was going on, what had taken place. The Nazis were as surprised as everyone else when they saw the finished project. And overwhelmingly pleased. None of this was what the church wanted, nor was it what Fey had promised. Nonetheless, they couldn't have been happier."

Kantorowicz related how the 'restoration' became a national, and Nazi, sensation. Famous art historians and critics raved about the murals at St Peter Cathedral in Schleswig. Alfred Stange, an art history professor at Bonn, called the murals the "last word in German art," and wrote the definitive critique of the murals in a book, *Der Schleswiger Dom und seine Wand-malerei*, that featured Fey's restoration. Heinrich Himmler, head of the SS and another self-styled art connoisseur, loved the Germanic features of the mural's figures so much—especially Mary—that he ordered Stange's book be taught in all German schools.

"Himmler was also a huge fan of the turkeys," Kantoro-wicz said, "for exactly the reason posited by Mr. Quint. Tur-keys in Germany before Columbus meant that Germanic ex-plorers, the Vikings, were in America long before Columbus. So, the Nazis hadn't plotted to create a forgery, in fact they didn't know it was a forgery. Yet the forgery served their pur-poses brilliantly."

"What about the Marienkirche?" I asked. "Another for-gery?"

"Yes," said Kantorowicz. "Let me explain. During World War II, the success of British bombing missions was spotty. The RAF routinely missed hard targets like munitions facto-ries, sometimes by miles. Churchill changed the RAF strategy to fire-bombing, which didn't require as much precision and would more directly impact the morale of the German peo-ple—*Slaughterhouse Five* and all that. In 1942, Britain brought this approach to the north German city of Lübeck. The entire city went up in flames, with fires so hot in the Marienkirche that its roof burnt off and its bells melted. The walls of the church stood, but the fire wiped away layers of whitewash that Lutherans 500 years before had applied to cover what they saw as superstitious religious images."

Kantorowicz paused and turned back to the screen, ad-vancing the projector to new images.

"A kind of miracle occurred. The fires suddenly revealed murals painted in the 13th century, when the Catholics first built the church. The images were faint, but visible: the Virgin Mary, for whom the church was named, Christ and his apostles, nu-merous prophets, and pastoral scenes with animals and birds. The people of Lübeck covered the bombed-out roof to protect the murals until they could be repaired. In 1948, they acquired enough funding to hire Dietrich Fey, son of Ernst, who had inherited his father's restoration business. Fey the younger was still working with Lothar Malskat, who had already performed a 'miracle' at the St Peter's cathedral in Schleswig. The Lübeckers hoped that he could do the same for their church."

The professor advanced to the next slide and continued.

"Malskat found the frescos in Lübeck even more delicate than the ones at Schleswig. The medieval layer of paint almost turned to dust when he touched it. Malskat's restoration would need to be even more severe than his previous effort. It took three years to complete his work. But in 1951, when the Marienkirche re-opened in celebration of its 700th anniversary, Malskat's renovated murals inspired awe. Konrad Adenauer, West Germany's first chancellor after the war, called them 'uplifting'. They gave solace and hope to a German people whose spirit had been defeated. The murals became so popular that they were even reprinted on postage stamps."

"Didn't anyone find out?" Leigh Ann asked. "I mean, how do you, how do we know about them being forgeries?"

"Good question," said Kantorowicz. "And a rather sad story, about Malskat, but also about human nature."

Kantorowicz related how the people of Lübeck, church officials and others, could have discovered the forgery, but they didn't want to.

"Hansi Knoteck—one of the best-known actresses in German cinema—was the model for the Marienkirche's Virgin Mary, which they should have noticed. Newspaper photos that appeared in 1942, just after the firebombing revealed the murals, offered before and after comparison of the original with Malskat's 1951 renovation. These photos showed some strange anomalies. Several of the saints had changed places in the ensuing nine years. Mary Magdalen, who wore sandals in the 1942 photos, was barefoot in 1951. And what looked like geese in 1942 had become turkeys by 1951. Once again, the mural's renovation was entirely the product of Malskat's imagination."

"So, like, why didn't he get busted for this?" I asked.

"No one wanted to know," Kantorowicz said. "Famous art historians had praised the works. Himmler was the patron of the restoration during the Nazi period, then Adenauer during the post-war. Both needed the renovations for their own propaganda purposes, to build up the *Geist*, the spirit, of the German people, at very different times in history."

Kantorowicz described how, because of their murals, both St. Peter's and the Marienkirche became pilgrimage sites. The church didn't want to expose the fraud because visitors and donations were up like never before.

"Malskat even tried to out himself," Kantorowicz concluded, "but for the longest time no one believed him. Even when he offered evidence, the police and the courts just thought he was some crank. People saw in these renovations what they needed to see, what they wanted to see."

What they wanted to see.

CHAPTER 10

## Meanwhile, in the neo-Nazi chatroom

> I'm not sleeping well

> > Guilty conscience?

> Y would that B?

> > Have U tried warm milk B4 bed?

> Doesn't work 4 me. My girlfriend said I should take melanin.

> > Melanin? I think U mean melatonin.

> Pretty sure she said melanin.

> > That may B. But melatonin helps U sleep. Melanin is what makes a ni—

Someone is typing …

> TB here. Let's have your pitches

> > Costumes or symbols?

> Dealer's choice.

> > OK. U know the Boogaloo Boys?

> The guys in the Hawaiian shirts?

> > Right. Their brightly colored tops hide their penchant 4 racist attacks. "Hey," their shirts say, "we're just a bunch of easy-going, laidback surfer dudes." Brilliant misdirection!

Someone is typing …

> Our idea is 2 riff on Boogaloo look but take it even further w/ a retro aspect, back 2 1950s America, when whiteness ruled & other lives didn't "matter". Bermuda shorts! Bright pastel colors. What could look more relaxed? Nothing says, "Hey, we're just hangin' out & we have no intention of drivin' your black asses from our racially pure suburbs" ;-) like a pair of Bermuda shorts!

> We'd use the whole range of colors: ocean green, coral red, a punchy yellow! Then plaids w/ combinations of all these colors. Add black knee socks w/ sandals.

> White sneakers. New Balance.

> Sandals! That's the look.

> Yes, but hard 2 run in sandals & U know how most marches end in running.

> Doc Martens?

> Now that's some old school skin-head shit! Steel-toed boots. Nothing says "I want 2 announce my presence w/ authority" like a pair of Doc Martens! "Stand back everybody! I take big steps!"

> What about tops? Hawaiian shirts?

> Oh, no, no, no. 2 derivative. We're thinking tailored Bavarian jackets. Anthracite or slate grey w/ hunter green piping along the button tabs, shoulders & pockets. Stiff military collar w/ embroidery. Collar insignia symbols, TBD.

> 4 front pockets! Great 4 all concealed weapons U want 2 bring 2 a march.

>& genuine, carved deer horn buttons.

> No. Ivory. I thought we said black-market elephant ivory.

> Deer horn is traditional. Besides ivory drives
up the price.
> Sure, but ivory says so much more about who we R!
> Go back 2 the Bermuda shorts. Rn't they a tad bit "native"?
> U might think so, but in an understated way they lift
up the legacy of colonialism.
> Plus, w/ the Bavarian jacket as top, the
whole ensemble is subtle commentary on
European dominance over mongrel races.
> Love it. Traditional, but playful. Undertones of white history
permeating entire look.
> White history!!!!
> Is there any other kind? What else have U got?

Someone is typing …

> Nostalgia
> What about it?
> It' not what it used 2 B. LOL
> Nostalgia's no laughing matter. In fact, could B most im-
portant thing we can tap into. If we offer something "new,"
*das Volk* will perk up & want 2 find out more. But once
they've scratched that itch they'll move on in search of next
"new" idea. Nostalgia much more powerful because contains a sense of loss, longing 4 something that once was
theirs but now missing. Something snatched away—
> By immigrant hordes!
> Yes … very good. We need a look that says, "whites were
the original race," but also that we came from behind 2
eventually dominate all lesser races.

Someone is typing …

> I hate 2 go back 2 the medieval well …
> No. Go ahead. It's been one of our most popular themes.
> Okay. Imagine this. A complete, medieval
suit of armor!

> Like it. Invitation 2 adventure. Involves the wearer emotion-
ally in promise of the movement. Sure 2 appeal 2 our
younger male demographic.

    > No! 2 heavy. 2 hot. 2 expensive.

        >No, no, no. Just listen. Ever see that Mel
        Brooks movie—

> Mel Brooks? The rat-fucking Jew?!

        > OK. Whatever. But there's a scene in *Silent
        Movie* where Marty Feldman—

> Another Jew! Not 2 mention a vegetarian, socialist,
fag lover!

    > He wasn't a fag.

> No, but he defended them against the bride of
Christ, God-fearing Anita Bryant!

    >Look, UR making me lose the thread.

> Jesusfuckingchrist, U 2! Just tell me your idea about the
armor!

        > Okay. So, Marty Feldman, in this movie, is
        always wearing a one-piece aviator's jump
        suit. It's blue or white or whatever. But in
        the last scene of the movie, where they're all
        going 2 the movie premier, Feldman wears
        a jumpsuit that looks like a tuxedo! That's
        the idea: jumpsuits screen printed 2 look like
        one-piece suits of armor. They'd B light-
        weight, breathable, & affordable! Just add
        insignia, TBD, & *voila*!

> What's w/ the French?

    > What? *Voila*? It just means "there U have it."

> Then, just fucking say, "there U have it."

> Okay, okay. I like it. It's clean & creates a sense of uni-
formity. Got a hint of medieval. Though I don't want 2
abandon Bavarian/ Bermuda combo just yet. Anything
else? What about insignia? Feels like UR avoiding that topic.

    > TBD.

        > TBD.

> What's the problem?

>Well ... it's ... haaard.

> "Of course it's hard, *Schätzchelein*. If it wasn't hard, it wouldn't B worth it.

> It's just that ...

> Go ahead.

> The swastika is so great! Amazing, really. & it's been around 4 so long ... It's just ... almost impossible 2 come up w/ something better. I mean, what could B better than the swastika?!

Someone is typing ...

> That's the dilemma. We need something w/ all the power of the swastika, but w/o all the baggage. Something new but also nostalgic. Something sentimental but not kitschy. Surprising, but obvious. U can't stop thinking about it. Leaves U wondering. Sticks in Ur imagination.

> Ultimately, it's the currency of love. Ironic coming from a so-called hate group, but never 4get: we don't hate anyone. Not lesser races or mud people or rat-fucking Jews. We just love the white race. We R a love group. This symbol, whatever it turns out 2 B, will B symbol of our love.

Someone is typing ...

> I've been talking w/ just the guy who can help us.

## CHAPTER 11
### An Invitation

Kantorowicz asked Quint and me to stay after class.

What was that about? I thought. Was he going to criticize me for something I'd said in class? Or maybe, like, heap great praise upon me for the same reason. Or maybe Kantorowicz knew about Special Agent Mapp of the FBI's attempt to recruit us to observe him. Did he know? And if he knew, what then?

He answered some administrative questions from a few lingering students, then invited us to walk back to his office. With excitement in his voice, he began to tell us of his plan.

"I'd like to attempt an exercise in experimental archaeology," he said. "And I'd like your help."

"Like, what do you mean by 'experimental archaeology?'" I asked. He offered several examples.

"It's Thor Heyerdahl sailing on a raft from Peru to the Polynesian Islands to show that cultural exchange, even over great distances, was possible in the pre-Columbian world. It's the modern Hellenic navy rowing cross the Aegean in a reconstructed Greek trireme."

I confessed a minor addiction to shows like *Living in the Past*, where participants lived in a reconstructed Iron Age village for over a year, just to see what it was like. The BBC produced dozens of these shows: *Tudor Farm*, *Victorian Farm*, *Edwardian Farm*. I loved them.

"I'm afraid what I have in mind isn't quite so romantic," said Kantorowicz. "I'm fascinated with the story of Malskat and his two murals. Not just the skill required, and the daring, to pull off such audacious forgeries, but also the willing suspension of disbelief entered into by everyone who saw the murals—the performative interplay between the forger and his audience."

Quint followed the professor's thread.

"They're all engaged in a kind of medieval drama," Quint said. "The miracle of the murals' death and 'resurrection' heals the community. For the Nazis, this means reinforcing their master-race agenda. For the post-war Germans it's about the nostalgia of recovering something beautiful from their past after so much had been lost."

"Exactly," said Kantorowicz. "It's precisely this response to the constructed past that I find so interesting. And the fact that it exists, whether or not the past they're consuming is 'true' or not."

"So, do you want to Malskat another mural?" I offered cautiously.

"Hm, uh, not exactly," Kantorowicz said, and explained his fascination with branding and how this was just as much a necessity for political movements as it was for corporations. "Witness the humble swastika," he said.

I didn't like the way he said 'humble swastika', but by this point we'd arrived at his office and he invited us in. Lots of dark wood, as you might expect. And, like, hundreds of books on shelves that Tower of Babelled all four walls, floor to ceiling. Some of the shelves had books behind other books. His desk was covered in papers and journals with protruding slips of paper, which I assumed indicated articles yet to be read. The one clear surface near the window had an electric kettle next to a plastic pitcher of purified water and some mugs. Kantorowicz went straight to it, put tea bags and spoons into mugs and handed them to us. He took a small decanter of milk from a mini-fridge and placed it on his desk, between the papers, where a sugar bowl already sat. It was like a tea ritual and while it progressed, he told us the history of the swastika and how it went from Oriental emblem of good fortune to the most reviled symbol of the modern era. I recalled the swastika on Sterling's façade.

Our professor's story began with Heinrich Schliemann, the famous archaeologist of ancient Troy.

"Schliemann made his fortune in a number of dodgy business endeavors," Kantorowicz said, "as a speculator in the California Gold Rush and as an arms dealer in the Crimean War. Once he'd piled up some wealth, he was able to realize his dream of searching for the lost city of Troy, which he believed could be done by following clues in Homer's *Iliad*.

"In 1871, he 'discovered Troy' on Turkey's Aegean coast. It was at a site known as Hisarlik, where British archaeologists had already been digging. You'll have seen documentaries of archaeologists painstakingly unearthing objects with tiny trowels and camelhair brushes, I expect. That wasn't how Schliemann went about it. His technique was more of the crowbar and battering ram variety. His method was haphazard and ultimately destructive in terms of preservation for future study, but he did figure out that his 'Troy' was actually the site of seven different cultures built in the same spot, one on top of the other, over thousands of years. And he did find a lot of material culture, such as the 'mask of Agamemnon,' which brought him great fame. He also dug up over 1,800 fragments of sculpture and pottery shards, almost all of which bore examples of the same symbol: the swastika."

Kantorowicz was in full lecturing flow, adding context for us.

"To understand what happened next, we need to know something about 19th-century German politics. The territory now known as Germany was originally comprised of many smaller principalities, a loose confederation that was part of the much larger Holy Roman Empire. In 1871, the same year that Schliemann discovered Troy, the German principalities separated from the Holy Roman Empire and unified as a single nation state. But cultural unification, 'to be German', was much more difficult than simply outlining some territories on a map. It became the mission of academics—historians and folklorists, philologists and archaeologists, throughout the German-speaking lands—to construct a common German culture. Part of the plan was to find antecedents to 'German-ness' in the great cultures of the past.

"Enter the linguists. Scholars like the Grimm Brothers, of fairytale fame, were making connections between modern German, on the Germanic branch of the Indo-European language family, and ancient Sanskrit, on the Indo-Aryan branch. German *regieren*, to reign, was connected to Sanskrit *raj*, meaning king. Such cognates suggested common cultural origins and the many layers of Troy meant a culture thousands of years old. A British linguist named Archibald Sayce claimed that Schliemann's discoveries 'carried us back to the later stone ages of the Aryan race.'

"Sayce's idea of an Aryan 'race' was something new," Kantorowicz said. "Sadly, practitioners of the highly fashionable, and now completely discredited, field of eugenics latched on to the idea and started promoting the Aryans as some unsullied master race of the past, the ancestors of modern Germans. Remember, the Germans were trying to create a cultural narrative for their newly unified nation-state, a national identity. And all of this happened long before Hitler was even born."

Listening to Kantorowicz present this material was, like, breathtaking. He completely captivated his audience of two. Even Quinton Quick, who'd been studying with Kantorowicz much longer than me, sat riveted. We each held untouched the cups of tea that had somehow appeared during this narration. Neither of us wanted to break the spell.

He continued.

"Schliemann's discovery brought him international fame," he said. "And it also introduced the swastika into popular culture. At first, the swastika was simply a sign of good fortune and you could find it everywhere: in Coca Cola ad campaigns, promoting the Boy Scouts, even on US army uniforms.

"In Germany, the swastika became linked to nationalism and eugenicist theories about the Aryan ancestors. The *Reichshammerbund* or League of the Empire's Hammer, an anti-Semitic group founded in 1912, was the first to use the swastika to 'brand' their organization. They used it as a rallying symbol

to unite other anti-Semitic groups. During the Weimar Repub-
lic, members of rightwing paramilitary groups known as the
*Freikorps* painted swastikas on their helmets. By 1920, Hitler
recognized the deep nationalist feelings the swastika had come
to represent and announced that his Nazi Party would adopt
the swastika as its official emblem. In 1933, propaganda min-
ister Joseph Goebbels made it a crime to use the swastika in
any unauthorized commercial form.

"That's when you know a brand has stuck," Kantorowicz
said. "When no one but the owner can use it. Never mind that
the symbol was much older than the Nazis and that it could be
found in cultures across the globe. The swastika now *belonged*
to them."

I sank back in my chair and took my first long sip of tea.
The range of our professor's knowledge was daunting, but I
was still confused about why he had called us in.

"You said you wanted our help," I said. "Are we going to,
like, rehabilitate the swastika?" I couldn't stop myself looking
to Quint for a reaction.

"Not exactly rehabilitate. But replace it with something
better." He gestured air quotes around the word "better" and
smiled.

"The archaeological experiment I have in mind is to discover a symbol to replace the swastika and imbue it with such
a sense of antiquity that neo-Nazis will adopt it as the new emblem of their program. That they'll adopt it to brand their
movement."

The smile on his face now seemed more manic than enthu-
siastic. Then he turned serious.

"I realize this whole thing may seem rather strange. My un-
orthodox methodology. Maybe idiosyncratic is a better word.
But it worked for me with my research on gang signs and graffiti. It takes your historical imagination to a different place, a
different level."

He paused and made eye contact with each of us.

"Listen. Don't tell the other students. It's not a secret or
anything, but there's so much gossip on campus about me

being a Nazi sympathizer. I just don't need the aggravation. It's just an academic exercise, but let's keep it between us."

I looked back and forth from Kantorowicz to Quint, who stared into the distance as if imagining potential images in his mind.

CHAPTER | 2
## A Catalog of Hate Symbols

The next day, I found Quint sitting inside our carrel, facing out, with the door open. I sat down at the table next to the door.

"So, are we doing this?" I said.

"I don't feel like I have much choice," he said, "for reasons already stated. You can still jump ship if you want without much in the way of consequences. Stark could easily take you on as her advisee."

"You could jump, too," I said.

"Yes, of course," Quint said. "It's my choice ultimately, but weighing all the options staying still seems like the easiest path."

"Besides," I said, "this is just an exercise. Right? Experimental archaeology? I can't see how any of this project would, like, actually advance the goals of a real white supremacist group."

"Maybe," Quint said. "It does seem like a stretch, but we can't exclude it. And I guess part of me wants to see how this whole thing plays out."

We sat and looked at each other for several minutes. Finally, I opened my laptop and got ready to act the scribe. We nodded to each other as if we were about to scale a mountain and began brainstorming research questions.

What were/are the symbols used by current hate groups?

What are their origins/relationships to other symbols?

How are the symbols used? On banners? On T-shirts?

Why have different symbols? Why not just one graphic, pictorial, iconic *thing* that would unify all the haters?

"One Thing to rule them all, One Thing to find them, One Thing to bring them all, and in the darkness bind them."

"OMG, you *are* a nerd!" Quint said.

"Yup. But that is what Kantorowicz is asking for. One 'Super-Symbol'—not the swastika—that would nonetheless attract and bind all the racists under a common identity."

"But ... one that would be subtle enough not to draw attention from the authorities or freak people out if they saw a flag flying in their neighborhood."

"What is this project about?" I asked. "Do you think it could be, like, connected to what Mapp was talking about?"

Quint rocked back in his chair, looked up at the interior ceiling of the carrel, then touched the door frame as if caressing it.

"Experimental archaeology is a legitimate method to gain understanding, to gain empathy, of some element of the past. Write in Chaucer's style to learn what Chaucer meant. What he felt." He paused. "This is just an exercise. Right? I mean, he's not having us create a design for actual Nazis?"

"Neo-Nazis."

"Whatever."

"So, you're going to do it?"

"The rabbit doesn't refuse the lion when he makes an offer like this. I need him to write me a letter when I hit the job market next year."

"Self-serving?"

"Realistic."

I considered Quint's attitude. It was pragmatic, but cynical too. The entire project made me nervous. Quint had pointed to his skin color to tell Mapp that he understood the threat of racism. I didn't have, like, a stereotypical 'Jewish nose' or I might have pointed at that to show my understanding of anti-Semitism. I didn't *need* to penetrate the crania of neo-Nazis. I didn't *want* to *get into their heads*, to feel empathy for them. But

we would have to if we were going to create a convincing forgery. *Elohim Ozer Li.* Help me out here, G-d.

"Where do we start?" I asked.

"At moments like these, when antiquarian esoterica is the
goal, I recommend the most sophisticated research tool known
to *Homo sapiens.*"

"Google?"

"Google."

I turned to my laptop and entered a few terms: racism,
symbols, white supremacist. Our first search yielded 2,830,000
results. Luckily, the top three all led to the Anti-Defamation
League, in particular to the ADL's "Hate on Display™ Hate
Symbols Database." I pointed out the trademark symbol attached to the phrase "Hate on Display." Apparently, even the
study of how haters branded themselves had to be branded.

ADL's database began with a trigger warning about the racist nature of its content. But it also admonished its readers not
to rush to judgment, noting that some of the symbols therein
may be hateful or non-hateful, depending on the context. Context! For example, somebody wearing a Thor's Hammer charm
around their neck might be a white supremacist, but they might
just as easily be a Ren Fest fan who digs the Vikings.

"That complicates things," said Quint. "Puts the onus on
the viewer. *And* it helps real neo-Nazis hide in plain sight."

The ADL database contains over 200 hate symbols, organized in a way that would have made Aristotle or Linnaeus
proud. A veritable taxonomy of hate. First come the "General
Hate Symbols," then "Hate Acronyms and Abbreviations." It
looks separately at numeric codes and hand signs. It also dif-
ferentiates between the symbols of the KKK, neo-Nazis, and
White Supremacist Prison Gangs.

Quint decided we should begin at the beginning and work
through methodically. First, "General Hate Symbols." Some of
these were so well known they needed no further explanation:
Klan robes, the burning cross, a noose, the Confederate and
Nazi flags, the SS lightning bolts, the swastika.

Both of us were surprised to see the *fasces* in the database, but its inclusion highlights the problem of coopting ancient symbols that are so obscure most people won't know their history. The Roman *fasces* was a symbol of authority. It was basically a bunch of sticks tied around an axe handle. The multitude of sticks reinforced the handle, making it stronger. The idea of strength in numbers appealed to Adolph Weinman, so he included the *fasces* in his design for the American Mercury dime. Mussolini adopted the *fasces* as a symbol for his new party and even used it in the name: Fascist. The U.S. mint is still quick to point out that Weinman designed his dime in 1916, three years before *il Duce* came to power. Ignorance about the *fasces* make it, in the words of the ADL, "more publicly acceptable than the swastika."

There were other symbols listed under "General Hate," but many of these crossed over into other categories. Rather than try to digest them all, we turned to "Acronyms and Abbreviations." Some of the entries in this group were catchy and easy to remember. "ORION," like the constellation, stood for "Our Race Is Our Nation," i.e., race is bigger than national borders. "KLASP" was another one that had a certain stickability. "Klannish Loyalty, A Sacred Principle," was very wordy, but "KLASP," that had something. Klan members also use two acronyms to greet and identify one another. "AYAK" means "Are You A Klansman?" while AKIA stands for "A Klansman I Am." It sounds a bit like Yoda. I imagined the dialog in real time.

"AYAK?" the stranger asked as he greeted me at the bus stop.

"AKIA. Oh, yes. AKIA," replied I.

"KIGY," my new racist bestie returned, which, as everyone knows, is KKK-speak for "Klansman I Greet You."

Bizarre. But not as tortuous as some of the others. Take "RAHOWA." Each syllable used the first two letters of the three words in the original: "RAcial HOly WAr." Most curious about RAHOWA is its invention by a group called the Creativity Movement, which, according to the ADL, is a "white supremacist pseudo-religion." Nothing says "we're not Nazis" like using "creativity" in your name.

The worst acronym, both in terms of content and for its difficulty of pronunciation, is "GTKRWN" which stands for "Gas the Kikes; Race War Now." Repugnant. It, like, pains me to type out those words. But my task today isn't to judge the anti-Semites, however much they deserve it. My job is to *evaluate* how they choose to *communicate* with each other. Not what they say, but how they say it. As a communication strategy, "GTKRWN" is horrible: not memorable, doesn't trip off the tongue. Bad. Completely lacking in the elegance and flexibility of "WP," which can stand for "White Power," but sometimes for "White Pride."

The best-known acronym—appearing in almost every movie featuring white supremacists—is "ZOG," a simple, yet memorable anti-Semitic slur meaning "Zionist Occupied Government." "ZOG" plays to the common fear that Jews secretly control the banks, and through the banks control Hollywood and the U.S. government.

Number symbols were another crazy thing. They used, like, alpha-numeric substitutions: 1= A, 2=B, etc. So, if 8 = H, then 88 = HH for "Heil, Hitler." 311 is trickier: 11 = K, 311 = 3Ks or KKK. Sometimes the number represents a word count, as when 14 stands for the "14 words," namely, "We must secure the existence of our people and a future for white children." You could also combine numbers, like "1488", which meant a combination of the "14 words" and "Heil Hitler."

Numeric symbols can, like, also be flashed as hand signs. With your right hand, pull your ring finger down with your thumb, leaving one finger, a space, and then two fingers: 1-2 = AB, Aryan Brotherhood. Using both hands, hold up two fingers on the right and three on the left and you get 23 = W, White.

Hand signs can also represent letters, we learnt. With your right hand held in front of the chest, extend your thumb and first two fingers. Squint your eyes and this resembles a K, as in Klan. Advanced, two-handed, alphabetic sign: hold the first three fingers of your right hand straight up, forming a W. Point with the index finger of your left hand. With the thumb and remaining fingers, form a circle. Contort your hand so that you're now pointing toward the floor. This should approximate the letter P. W-P, White Power. It's, like, really clever if it wasn't so sinister.

Most aggravating, for me and Quint at least, the fucking Nazis and neo-Nazis stole medieval symbols. They used the power of the past to give legitimacy in the present—no matter how slim the connections.

For example, the "Life" rune, above, is a symbol from the medieval Norse alphabet. Nazis used it to play up connections to the Vikings, thus legitimizing their idealized Aryan/Norse heritage. The same is true of the Othala rune, below. During World War II, the Nazis used it in insignia for two Waffen SS divisions.

But both symbols are also used by non-racist Viking re-enactors and pagan groups, so this is one of those moments when, as Sister Clodagh would say, "To understand a thing, find its context."

It was late and I still had my regular reading and assign-
ments to do. We had enough to get us started. Our research
had been successful in terms of method, even though it was
disturbing in terms of content. We worked well together, and
I was happy with our harvest. As I walked home, I organized
and re-organized all we'd learned and it didn't take long before
my mind returned to questioning the legitimacy of our project.

Was it *our* project? No. This belonged to our professor.

What would Mapp say about it? Didn't it in fact support
his wild accusations against Kantorowicz?

CHAPTER 13
Stark Lectures on Paleography

Good afternoon. This is "Intro to Methods" and today we're jumping right in with paleography.

[*show cartoon, allow time to read the caption*]

This is one of my favorites. It shows two archaeologists, which you can tell from the pith helmets and shorts. There's a pyramid in the distance. The two have just dug up a stone tablet, which they're attempting to read. The first archaeologist looks embarrassed. The second archaeologist says, "Stop blushing and tell me what it says."

[*pause for laugh*]

The entire cartoon is framed, with a definition at the top, which reads as follows: "PALEOGRAPHY (noun). Ancient style of writing; study of ancient inscriptions; science of deciphering them."

Paleography comes from two Greek roots: *palaiós* meaning "old"—as in paleolithic = old stone (age). And *graphein*, meaning "to write," which is more obvious. Paleography, then, as the cartoon pointed out, is about old writing, i.e., the study of—. More precisely, it's about the forms of writing, the various "hands", or as you of the computer generation might say, the "fonts." It is not necessarily concerned with the content of documents but is a decipherment tool with the ultimate goal of reading documents, dating them, and placing them in historical context.

[*pause. make sure they're tracking*]

As a discipline, paleography was invented in the 17th century by a monk/scholar named Jean Mabillon.

[*show slide of Mabillon*]

Mabillon was born in 1632 in the Champagne region of France. He was a precocious child, very good with languages. Just out of curiosity, how many of you have got a second language, i.e., besides English.

[*check number of hands*]

That looks like all but one of you. Good. And how many of you have a third language? Only two, three of you? Okay. Not trying to embarrass anyone but get busy people. Historians need languages to study other cultures, especially past cultures.

Admonition over. Back to Mabillon.

He was born to a peasant family, but he was very bright and at age 12 he earned a place in the Collège des Bons Enfants in Reims. He was an excellent student, but also very devout and he soon chose religious life. At 18 he entered the seminary to become a priest, but by 21 he'd taken vows as a monk. He lived in a few different monasteries, but eventually ended up in the Abbey of Saint-Germain-des-Prés, near Paris. That community encouraged scholarship and boasted connections with many famous scholars.

Now for some context. Since roughly the twelfth century, medieval monks had been forging charters, agreements for land use and ownership. The monks didn't think of it as forgery. Often, they were just trying to capture in writing something that had been agreed upon orally. As medieval society became more litigious, documents became more important. One couldn't depend on oaths and other oral agreements for transactions that had happened centuries before. More and more, monks started recording their legal transactions, even the ones that had never had a charter. Sometimes the memories of those transactions were 'enhanced', and with time, the monasteries wound up with a lot more land or rights or tithes than they'd started out with.

[*tracking?*]

A certain set of charters, supposedly written in the 7th century, recorded land grants from the Merovingian kings—the dynasty before Charlemagne—from the Merovingians to the Benedictine monastery with which Mabillon was associated. A Jesuit scholar named Papebroch questioned the validity of the charters. If he was right, it meant the monks would have to give up the land they'd lived on for centuries. Mabillon spent 8 years on his rebuttal to Papebroch's claim. He compared and studied hundreds of manuscripts for their style and script, for the kind of wax seals attached to them, and the kinds of signatures they held. He looked at documents that were a thousand years old at the time he studied them. In the end, he showed that the charters in question were authentic by dating the handwriting with which the documents were written.

Through this exercise, Mabillon created the discipline of paleography, which he explained in a lengthy tome, *De re diplomatica*—On Diplomatics, or The Study of Documents—published in 1681.

From the title, you might think the book is about diplomacy or diplomats. Those words are related, but only because diplomats used to practice diplomacy by composing and trading in *diplomas*, another word for document, like charters and treaties, and yes, that document you're all going to get when you graduate.

[*laughter?*]

Diplomatics is the study of documents, which includes paleography, the study of handwriting, but also other aspects of document creation that form its context, like the media used—paper, parchment, ink, pencil, etc. It includes codicology, which is the study of how codices (plural of codex) and other books were put together. A collection of texts in a codex might be bound and rebound several times, with the quires, or sections, rearranged, which tells us something about how the book was used. Diplomatics includes the study of wax seals, which is called sigillography. It can even include the study of oily fingerprints on the manuscript pages. The more smudges a page has, one might reason, the more that page was read or looked at. Hence, we can determine which psalm in a psalter was read most frequently. We even know of a breviary where the smudges on a certain page revealed the owner's love for the book patron's portrait in the back of the book. Actually, it was his own portrait!

[*laughter?*]

Paleography is also concerned with abbreviations. To save space on their tremendously expensive parchment, medieval scribes used abbreviations for the most common terms. Some of these still exist today. "Rx" for "recipe," as in a doctor's prescription. The ampersand (&), for "et cetera." This practice of abbreviation carried over to English contractions like "can't" for cannot, or "St." for "Saint." How does one know that "St." = "saint" and not "street?" you might well ask. Context. Remember context? In this case, narrative context, the words *around* the abbreviation.

Diplomatics also uses cultural context to determine a text's meaning. Take something like an obituary. No matter who you are in America, every newspaper obituary will be brief and, for the most part, say kind, factual things about the deceased: "loving husband, devoted father, survived by," etc. But elsewhere in the newspaper, if the dead person is important enough, you'll get a longer story about who they really were: "Mafia boss, alleged hitman." You get the idea.

Diplomatics is all of these things, all in the service of authenticating historical documents, all in the service of offering the truest interpretation of the past.

[*pause*]

Any questions?

CHAPTER 14

From the *Süddeutsche Zeitung* (Munich)

*Ernst Kantorowicz, Lieblingshistoriker des Dritten
Reiches, verstorben mit 68 Jahren*

[Translation]

PRINCETON, New Jersey, USA, September 10
— Ernst Kantorowicz, 68, died 9th September
1963, at his home in Princeton, of an aortic aneu-
rysm. A memorial service will be held this Saturday, September 14, at 2pm in the Princeton University Chapel at Princeton University.

"Did you see this?"

I held the envelope and papers up to Quint as he approached the carrel. It was a plain white business envelope, the
kind with the squiggly lines on the inside so you can't read it if
you hold it up to the light. That wouldn't have made much
difference because the envelope was unsealed. There was no
address or writing of any kind.

"It was under the door when I got here this morning,"
Quint said. "My guess was that it's for both of us, so I left it
there on the desk for you."

"Did you look inside? Did you read it!?"

"Volume," he whispered.

"Well?"

He took the two pages from my hand, leaving me the envelope. One page was typed on regular paper, the other was

printed on smoother paper with the image in reverse, white letters on a faded black background.

"This is a photostat from an old microfilm reader," Quint said. "It's obviously the original image from the German newspaper. Hmm. *Süddeutsche Zeitung.* This is a translation." He handed me the page with the translation, then read from the photostat in German, translating aloud with great precision as he read. His facility with languages was maddening.

Mr. Kantorowicz was born 3rd May 1895 in Posen, Poland (at the time, part of Prussia) to German-Jews who ran a prosperous distillery, which young Ernst was destined to inherit. He served as an officer in the German Army in the First World War. He studied economics and Islamic history at the Universities of Berlin and Munich, completing his doctorate in 1921 at the Uni-Heidelberg under Eberhard Gothein. During his student days, he was a member of a right-wing militia and fought against the leftists in the Greater Polish Uprising of 1918, and the Spartacist Uprising in Berlin of 1919. In Heidelberg, Kantorowicz joined a circle of intellectuals and artists centered on the German poet Stefan George. The so-called *Georgekreis* called themselves the "Secret Germany," and promoted a revival of nationalist ideals in the post-war era.

Under the influence of the *Georgekreis*, Kantorowicz became a medievalist and undertook a daring biography of Frederick II (1194-1250), who became King of Sicily in 1198, King of the Germans in 1212, and Holy Roman Emperor in 1220. Rather than the typical, dry history with long lists of political policies and military victories, Kantorowicz's *Kaiser Friedrich der Zweite* leaned toward hagiography or panegyric, casting Frederick as a tragic hero who embodied German nationalist ideals that were just taking hold in 1927, when the book was published. Kantorowicz praised Frederick for bringing a love of antiquity into Germanic culture, and for celebrating the intellectual and scientific achievements of both Jews and Arabs in his realm.

At the same time, Kantorowicz's work is filled with a blind admiration of power and absolutism that opposed pluralism. He praised Frederick's punishment of his Sicilian subjects for "weakening their blood" through intermarriage. Although Frederick allowed the Jews to maintain their cultural practices (though taxing them heavily for doing so), he was also the first to insist that Jews be identified by wearing gold stars. The 1927 cover of the first edition of *Friederich der Zweite* bears a swastika. This was the stuff that made Kantorowicz's book a favorite among the upper echelons of the Third Reich. Hermann Göring was a huge fan, who reportedly gave a signed copy as a birthday present to Mussolini. Even after Kantorowicz was ousted as a Jew, Hitler proclaimed that he had read the book twice.

*Friederich der Zweite* earned Kantorowicz a professorship at the University of Frankfurt in 1930, even though he had not completed his *Habilitationschrift* (second book). By 1933, when the Nazis began "cleansing" the universities of Jewish scholars, Kantorowicz was no longer allowed to lecture. In 1935, the Nazis gave him permission to "retire."

Still believing in the myth of Germany that he had helped to create, the bourgeois, Jewish Kantorowicz remained in Germany until 1938, fleeing to Oxford only after his mother was taken to a concentration camp. Subsequent professorships included Berkley, from 1939 to 1950, and Princeton, from 1950 to 1963, where he wrote his second great work, *The King's Two Bodies: A Study in Medieval Political Theology*, a seminal, interdisciplinary examination of the relationship between the king's anatomical body and the body politic.

Kantorowicz never married and leaves behind no children or other family members.

"What do you make of it?" I asked, when he'd finished. "I
mean it says that Kantorowicz is dead, but it also says that he
was a Jewish Nazi. What the hell is going on!?"

"Calm down. Calm. Down." He reached past me, pulled
two books off the shelf and placed them side by side on the
carrel desk: *The King's Two Bodies* and *The King's Too Bawdy*. "This
one is by Ernst Kantorowicz, who did indeed die in 1963. This
one is by *Abraham* Kantorowicz, our advisor, who is very much
still alive. Abe is the son of Ernst."

I sat there, staring back and forth at each book, more precisely at the authors' names. I wondered if this was how kids
felt when their parents told them they were adopted. Abe is the
son of Ernst. Oh-kay. Let that sink in. Naturally, Kantorowicz
had a father. And his father was also a historian, apparently a
really famous historian. Bonus points: Kantorowicz the elder
was the favorite historian of Adolph Hitler.

"How can you … how do you know?"

"I found *The King's Two Bodies* my first semester in grad
school. I thought it was funny that the author and my mentor
had the same name, so I showed it to Kantorowicz. He said it
was his father. I think they must have had some sort of falling
out because he quickly changed the subject. I also think *his* title,
*The King's Too Bawdy*, has something to do with it. I mean it's
very clever wordplay, but it's also pretty much 'in your face'."

I looked again at the two books, really studied their titles,
and smiled. I'd seen this before, the first time I was in the carrel, checking out Quint's books. I just hadn't registered the different first names.

"The question is," Quint said, "why has Mapp delivered
this to us?"

"Like, you think it's Mapp?"

"Don't you? Who else could it be? He's obsessed with
Kantorowicz, so he's trying to bias us against him."

"He said he did not want us to be biased."

"Oh, puh-lease."

"Okay," I said. "Mapp sends us this article about Kantorowicz's father, who, as it turns out is much loved in the Third Reich. He has written a book about Friedrich II that's filled with, what does it say, 'blind admiration of power and absolutism.' Göring loved the book. Mussolini loved the book. Hitler loved it so much he read it twice, and that was after daddy K had to flee the country, his Jewish mother having been put on a train for Auschwitz or wherever. Is all of this, *this*," I repeated holding up the two pages. "Is it supposed to make us think that Kantorowicz, *our* Kantorowicz, is a fucking Nazi?! Apples not falling far from trees and all that?!"

Quint looked around the room. There wasn't a soul in sight, but he gave me that look again like he was the library Gestapo and I needed shushing.

"That's part of it," he said. "But it's not the part that bothers me the most."

He took the pages back, looked again at the photostat in German, then flipped the page to the translation.

"Look at this," he said. "Mapp told us that he didn't think Kantorowicz was who he said he was. Look," He held out the page, his finger pointing to the last line:

Kantorowicz never married and leaves behind no children or other family members.

# CHAPTER 15
## Male Banter at the FBI Field Office, New Haven

MAPP:           Domestic Terrorism. Go for Mapp ... I
                don't know ... Yes ... Yes, I know it's her
                birthday ... Yes, I'm going to try, but you
                know how things can get around here ... I
                can't talk about that ... No ... Okay ...
                Yes, I'll call you later.

BLOUNT:         Whipped?

MAPP:           Just trying to keep the missus happy in a
                job designed to do the opposite.

CARBONE:        Daughter's birthday?

MAPP:           Induction or deduction?

CARBONE:        Huh?

MAPP:           Sorry, Carbone, but your desk is right
                across from mine. You want to make con-
                versation, make conversation, but stop sur-
                veilling my phone calls.

CARBONE:        I guess that means no invitation to the
                party.

                (Enter Hermann)

HERMANN: Damn, Mapp! What's with the Kojak look!?

BLOUNT: Had to happen sooner or later, eh, Mapp? That combover wasn't fooling anyone.

HERMANN: His head's brighter than his future.

CARBONE: Careful, Hermann.

HERMANN: You're right. Fortune favors the bald!

CARBONE: I mean it, Hermann. Mapp here is real FBI. Third generation. Grampa Mapp opened the NH Field Office. Cracked Liz Bentley in '45. A Soviet agent in DC comes to New Haven to turn herself in?! I mean, that's the rep this office had. Russian operations took a real hit after that.

HERMANN: Not the Rackley case, though. When was that? 70? 71?

CARBONE: Mapp's father. Black Panthers filled that boy's body with bullets. Everybody knew Bobby Seale did it, but the jury acquitted.

BLOUNT: Yet here's our Mapp. Third generation FBI. Stuck on the dead-end desk of the Domestic Terrorism Task Force.

HERMANN: Everybody knows that's low priority. Taliban. Al-Qaeda. ISIS. That's where the funding is, so that's where the action is.

BLOUNT: Nobody has time to chase angry white boys dressed up in sheets and steel-toed boots.

National priorities. White supremacists are "some very bad dudes," but they're small potatoes, even two decades after 9-11. Tough luck, Mapp.

CARBONE:    Back off, you two.

MAPP:       Leave it, Carbone. Thanks for the help, but I've got better things to do. I'm gonna go miss my kid's birthday, then defy our national priorities and catch me some god-damned, small-potato neo-Nazis.

CHAPTER 16

Stark Delivers the Sterling Lecture

Good evening.

*[pause and make eye contact]*

Thank you, madam Provost for that very warm introduction. Thanks also to Yale's President, the Board of Regents, the Alumni Association, my colleagues in the Department of History, my students, grad and undergrad, and to all of you for being here tonight. It's a great honor to offer this inaugural lecture as Yale University's newest Sterling Professor.

*[advance slide to NYer cartoon. Keep caption covered]*

I believe it was David Lodge, the great satirist of academia, who said that American scholars always begin their papers with a joke.

*[chuckle]*

I don't have a joke for you tonight, but I thought we could start with this cartoon from the *New Yorker*. We see one figure seated with a notepad behind a couch, where the other figure is lying down, and we immediately recognize the cartoon genre of "the therapy session." The patient is a white man in a tweedy sportscoat, elbows patched, with a well-trimmed beard and wire rim glasses—tropes that make him instantly recognizable as a professor.

*[hold for laugh]*

We could spend the whole evening dissecting this gendered representation, but I'll focus on the caption instead, which reveals that this is, in fact, a *history* professor, and which so masterfully contains the theme of my talk. A history professor, on the couch, talking to his shrink. Here's what he says.

*[uncover caption]*

"Those who fail to study history are doomed to repeat it, but those who do study history are doomed to stand by helplessly while everyone else repeats it."

This is actually a bit long for a New Yorker caption, but we can forgive this, I think, once we realize everything that's at stake. The caption needs the opening clause with the full quotation from George Santayana, so familiar to us all.

"Those who fail to study history are doomed to repeat it." You may not know this, but Santayana's actual quotation was "Those who cannot *remember* the past are *condemned* to repeat it." I'm thinking some history teachers amended the quote to encourage their students in the discipline. Either way, Santayana's words offer hope. Without saying as much, he promises that if people would only do so much as study history, then the human race actually would not end up repeating it. One presumes that the history Santayana hopes we will avoid is all the "bad" stuff: war, poverty, oppression. Surely, he would find it okay if humans repeated the "good" stuff: acts of charity and kindness, the spread of brotherly and sisterly love, universal health care and student loan forgiveness. No. It's clear to us what Santayana means, not the least because his quotation is so overused as to become cliché.

The comic turn in the caption, the surprise, comes in the subordinate clause, which offers the historian in the cartoon, and indeed all historians, the cold slap in the face that is the reality of our profession.

"Those who *do* study history are *doomed to stand by helplessly* while *everyone else* repeats it." Ouch.

I'm certain that each of you—professors and students and lovers of history—has had at least one moment in your lives where past events so clearly resonate in the present that we stand on the side lines, astonished that those around us don't see the similarities between then and now.

"Don't you know that internment of minorities has happened before?!" we cry out. "Don't you know where such policies led in the past?!"

"Don't you remember that demagogues of the past, exploiting peoples' fears, have led us to fascism?! Can't you see that it's happening again?!"

Our times, perhaps all times, are rife with such moments. Historians, who know about human behavior in the past because they have studied it deeply, are rightly frightened, outraged, and exasperated when our fellow humans fail to see what we see. We feel "doomed to stand by helplessly," while our fellow humans allow the 'bad' stuff of the past to happen again. And again.

What can we do?

[*pause and make eye contact again*]

It's very tempting, especially for our younger colleagues and our graduate and undergraduate students, to be drawn to activism, to see the intellectual training you've received as historians as preparing you to change the world. Let me lay out my thesis very plainly: Don't do it.

[*pause*]

The simple version of my thesis is that you must avoid mixing scholarship with activism, that such mingling of discipline with passion can only lead to disappointing results. But like many theses, this one is more complicated, and I hope you will stick with me as I lay out my argument.

I offer three reasons for why I urge you not to mix historical scholarship with activism: ambiguity, presentism, and contingency. Let me speak to each of these in turn.

First, ambiguity. By ambiguity, I mean the conflicted feeling that will live in the scholarly audience when scholarship mixes with activism, and vice-versa. Don't think for a minute that historians do not cultivate audiences. Historians need audiences for their work, just as activists do. But when historians apply their methods to contemporary problems, it creates a conflicted feeling in both audiences, for scholarship comes to be seen as advocacy, which diminishes its power as pure, unbiased argument. An historian should never be an activist because it diminishes his work as an historian.

Let me give you an example from the field of the history of science.

*[slide with cover of Brandt's book]*

Allan Brandt holds a joint appointment at the Harvard Medical School and the Department of the History of Science at Harvard University. In 2007, he published *The Cigarette Century: The Rise, Fall, and Deadly Persistence of the Product That Defined America*. At 600 pages, it's well written and heavily footnoted. According to Amazon's description of the book, "From agriculture to big business, from medicine to politics, *The Cigarette Century* is the definitive account of how smoking came to be so deeply implicated in our culture, science, policy, and law. No product has been so heavily promoted or has become so deeply entrenched in American consciousness."

I think we can say, without reservation, that Professor Brandt is an expert on all things concerning the history of cigarettes, and, in particular, the unique risks the tobacco industry poses to public health. But he was deeply ambivalent about taking on an activist role. Here's what he writes in the epilogue of his book:

> "There was … always a question about my possible availability to testify in a trial on behalf of a plaintiff. Each time I respectfully declined. Certainly, my research confirmed that the industry had conspired over many decades to deny and obscure the deadly risks of its product. … But … I did not want my scholarship to be dismissed as 'advocacy'. The lawyers could use my work as they saw fit. I did not want to become a combatant in the tobacco wars; I much preferred my role as a war correspondent and military historian."

*[show slide of "napalm girl"]*

The idea of Brandt calling himself a "war correspondent" evokes memories, for me, of Nick Ut's Pulitzer Prize-winning photo of nine-year-old Kim Phúc, running down the street in Trảng Bàng, naked, afraid, and in horrific pain from injuries inflicted in a South Vietnamese napalm attack. That was June 8, 1972, the summer before my senior year of high school. My father saw this photo reading *The New York Times* at our breakfast table and shook his head.

"How could he take that picture?" he said. "How could he not run over and pick the girl up, cover her naked body and rush her to the medics?"

"No," I said, to my father's shock. "He has to take the photo so the rest of us will know what happened."

Historians, like journalists, have to remain neutral, dispassionate observers and scribes. I'm not saying this makes us better humans—it may even make us worse. But we have to take the picture, or gather evidence and write the heavily footnoted book, so that *others* can act. Without that record, there's no chance for people to learn from history, Santayana's wish, because there is no history.

To be fair, Brandt did eventually testify in a case against big tobacco: *United States vs. Philip Morris,* which has been called 'the largest civil litigation in the history of American law." But he did this because big tobacco was using its own version of history to prop up its case, calling in historians with no expertise in the history of cigarettes to confirm big tobacco's narrative. Brandt came in, not as an activist, but to fight bad history with good history, to protect the professional standards of all historians.

[*pause*]

Second: presentism.

The historicist view says that we must judge history on its own terms. That we must, as much as possible, view the history in front of us through the lens of the historical actors involved in that history, and to view it without judgment. Once we start to ask questions about 'relevance,' and why we should care about the past beyond the classic response, 'for its own sake,' then, I believe, all is lost.

Yes, of course, the past can help us understand the present, how we got from then to now. But we cannot and should not use history as if it were a roadmap for finding our way in the present. We should check such sentiments as "this or that approach to 20th century Nazis did or did not work, therefore, we should or shouldn't do the same." Approaches like this ignore the complexity of the past and can lead us down paths that are doomed to failure. We must speak out and reject pronouncements that "this policy is just like the Holocaust" or "that political leader is just like Hitler." Such thinking oversimplifies the past and sheds little light on the complexities, either of past or present.

Activists are, and should be, concerned with the problems of today. Historians need to focus on the problems of yesterday.

[*pause*]

Finally, contingency.

Historians cannot predict the future. In fact, we're terrible at it. This is why getting involved in preemptive strikes against sovereign nations is such a can of worms.

[*maybe a laugh there. pause*]

Not even historians highly trained in human motivation and causality can predict the outcome of a scenario that depends on an infinite range of contingent factors inherent in every human interaction. And so, I say, they should not get involved based on the arrogant belief that their skills will guarantee a brighter outcome.

As many of you know, my grad school advisor, Joseph Strayer, in addition to his day job as a very productive Princeton historian, also consulted with the CIA. He used to love it when people would ask him why the Central Intelligence Agency, dealing with 20th-century scenarios, would hire a medievalist.

"What does a medievalist do?" he'd answer with that familiar twinkle in his eye. "Medievalists construct complete narratives from small scraps of disparate information ... which is exactly what the CIA does! Medievalists have the skills required to be CIA operatives!"

"Operative" may have been a stretch. Strayer did not have many James Bond skills. No martial arts. No lock-picking. No bomb defusing. He was an analyst. Although the problems he analyzed remain classified, he worked at the CIA at a time when they were helping America overthrow foreign governments to keep them from falling to communism. Brazil. Guyana. The Congo. Iran!

Strayer believed he was a patriot and he was, at least in the sense that he understood the word and the world. He would have considered his work at CIA as the activism of his time. All well and good though today, with historical hindsight, we judge it poorly. His involvement with the Agency caused a rift in our friendship. It was a disservice to the discipline of history. More than a disservice. It dishonors our discipline, in the same way that "applied" anthropology or "corporate" psychology in the service of capitalism dishonors those disciplines.

[*pause*]

In closing, let me return to the concept of hope.

I began this talk with the *New Yorker* cartoon and Santayana's hopeful stance that we only need to study history to keep from repeating all the "bad stuff" from the past. Santayana's quotation is filled with hope that humanity can progress. But the historian in the cartoon feels hopeless, believes he's doomed to look on, as members of the human race fail to learn from history.

I'm more than a little sad to tell you that this is the unfortunate plight of the historian, of all historians, of *us*. We cannot be hopeful because we're required by our own professional standards to be honest about the events we study.

When the songs of social justice movements proclaim that "we shall overcome," or when protesters chant "the people, united, will never be divided," these are claims full of hope that inspire activists to keep going. But they're not true. Nothing in the historical record proves these claims, but rather the opposite. The "people united" are often divided, and defeated, for any number of reasons, some of which are within their control and others that are not. Of course, the honest narration of history has some examples of the "united people" not being divided, but overthrowing oppressive regimes and freeing themselves, at least temporarily. It's *not* all one or the other. In spite of this, to be an effective activist means embracing these songs and chants in order to inspire a movement's followers.

Historians, if they're true to their vocation, cannot, must not do this.

Thank you.

CHAPTER 17

Q&A

There was a healthy round of applause, but, like, no standing ovation. Did historians get standing ovations? The Provost returned to the stage, thanked the speaker for her talk, and—looking to Stark for the all clear—invited the audience to ask questions. Why was the Provost needed for this? I wondered. Like, Stark could just as easily have asked the audience herself. Part of the ritual, maybe. There was a fair amount of rustling in chairs to accompany the awkward silence that said, *she's a goddamned Sterling Professor. I don't dare ask her a question.* I looked around to find Quint, sure that he would volunteer, but I couldn't see him.

"Any questions?" Stark said in her most inviting tone.

From his front row seat, Kantorowicz raised his hand and stood. Someone brought him a portable mic. Addressing Stark from the front of the auditorium meant that his back was to the audience.

"Thank you, Professor Stark," he said, then corrected himself. "*Sterling* Professor Stark." This got a small laugh. "I wonder about the many counter examples to your thesis. The thesis that historians cannot, indeed should not be activists."

With this, Kantorowicz turned away from Stark and faced the crowd.

"There are many activist historians to choose from, but let me pick three: E.P. Thompson, Howard Zinn, and Marc Bloch.

"Thompson began his work with a biography of William Morris, one of the founders of the Arts and Crafts Movement in Britain. Morris, a socialist, was interested in the dignity of work before the Industrial Revolution, a period which we might label as the "long Middle Ages." Most of you likely know Morris from his beautiful, handmade edition of the *Canterbury Tales*, the so-called Kelmscott Chaucer. As a medievalist, that would have been enough for me, but Thompson filled a gap in the scholarship. Where other scholars had focused on Morris's art, Thompson focused on his political activism. Thompson himself was a member of the Communist Party at the time.

"Thompson's interest in labor and its connection to politics came to full fruition in *The Making of the English Working Class*. Thompson said he wanted to 'rescue the poor stockinger, the Luddite cropper, the obsolete hand-loom weaver, the Utopian artisan.' At 800 pages, Thompson's work redefined social history. He was writing history from the bottom up, looking at documents that had long been ignored or derided as insignificant—popular songs, union club cards, workshop customs—a tour de force! With *The Making of the English Working Class*, the phrase 'forgotten history' became *au currant*.

"All of this is just to say that Thompson was an important and prolific historian. Yet he also left his mark as an activist. In the 1980s, at the height of Cold War tensions, Thompson was renowned throughout the world as a voice for peace and nuclear disarmament. He was nothing short of an intellectual activist superstar.

"He was also witty in his activism. The Thatcher government had put out a pamphlet entitled *Protect and Survive*, an update of the old Civil Defense tracts, that was meant to teach British citizens how to survive a nuclear attack. Thompson wrote a parody of this called *Protest and Survive* that spoofed the notion of surviving nuclear war and offered creative ways to practice civil disobedience."

Kantorowicz paused to take a breath. Stark thought this might be a chance to respond. She'd barely spoken one syllable into the mic when Kantorowicz raised his crutch high in the air, which he, like, must have thought was more effective than a single-finger hushing .

"Howard Zinn!" he said with renewed energy. "There's not an undergrad on this campus who doesn't know his *People's History of the United States.* Zinn moved away from the grand narrative, the nationalistic fetishizing of our 'march toward democracy,' that had dominated American histories up to that point. He critiqued those histories that preferred the privileged, the elites, who manipulated and used the system to their own advantage by oppressing the poor and disenfranchised, which most often meant Black folks and women, and other minorities. A book of great influence.

"Zinn stood up to McCarthyism and wrote about and marched for civil rights. He protested the Vietnam War at rallies, but also with his very scholarly book, *Vietnam: The Logic of Withdrawal,* which helped spark the debates that eventually led to ending the war. For heaven's sake, he co-edited the *Pentagon Papers* for publication! He was just as vocal in opposing the invasion of Iraq and used his books and articles and lectures to bring light to W's folly.

"Finally, he explained his life of scholarly activism in his memoir *You Can't Be Neutral on a Moving Train,* which covered half a century of fighting the people's fight."

Kantorowicz took another breath. This time Stark was able to cut in.

"Abe, if you're going to be much longer, perhaps I should respond to these two examples. It might also be good to hear if anyone else has questions or comments."

Here Kantorowicz opted for the two-handed, double index finger in the air, his crutch dangling from his right arm. It looked like an umpire showing the count—one ball, one strike—except that he quickly stopped being the umpire and stepped up to the plate again.

"Marc Bloch," he said. "A personal hero for me and for many medievalists. He was part of the French *annalistes* movement. Like Thompson and Zinn, he wrote history from the ground up. His methods were innovative and influential, broadening the kind of sources we use and the way we use them. His *La société féodale* set the bar for understanding the so-called 'feudal system.' His was a nuanced genius.

"As for activism, no one holds a candle to Bloch. During World War II, even though he was Jewish, he didn't flee when the Nazis invaded France. Risking his own life, he stayed and fought in the Resistance. The Nazis captured him and sent him to his death in a concentration camp. While imprisoned, he wrote one of the classic guides for students of the past, *The Historian's Craft*, which was smuggled out of the camp and published posthumously. It's still used in history programs across America and Europe."

Kantorowicz stopped. He still stood, but his comment that had turned into a lecture was done. The room was quiet for several seconds. Stark, having been shut down twice, stood at the lectern waiting, looking at her colleague, hoping to confirm that it would really be her turn. She tilted her head ever so slightly. He offered an almost imperceptible nod.

"Thank you, Professor Kantorowicz. I don't know how much time we have left, and I can see that others have their hands up. It would be rude of me, though, not to offer a response to such a thorough comment. It was a comment, wasn't it? I didn't hear a question, but I want to be sure before I continue."

He smiled and sat down.

"First, let me clarify. At some point in your comment, you seemed to use the phrase 'women and minorities.' This may be a small thing—an adjustment of terms—but women are most certainly not in the minority in the United States. In fact, taken as a whole, the minorities aren't even the minority in America. White men are."

Someone in the back of the auditorium let out a whoop, which caused the rest of the audience to laugh. Stark smiled.

"Now ... who was first on your list?" she said, feigning absent-mindedness. "It feels so long ago ... Thompson. Yes, E.P. Thompson. Well, he's an excellent counter example, at least as far as you've presented your case. Thompson was an impressive historian and a very visible activist working for the good. *My* point is that activism will inevitably taint the scholar's work, which I think it did with Thompson. I'm not the only one who thinks so.

"In the 70s, Thompson had a public feud with the Polish historian and philosopher, Leszek Kolakowski. Like Thompson, Kolakowski had been a member of the Communist Party. When Stalin's atrocities became known, Thompson left the party, but remained a Marxist. Kolakowski left the party and the ideology, writing a seminal work on how Marxism was a corrupt dogma that inevitably resulted in Stalinism. Kolakowski criticized Thompson for his double standards in evaluating the historical evidence. He likened Thompson to an avowed leftist who would rail against torture when it was done by the United States but defended torture when committed by countries he sympathized with. 'Hey,' the leftist says. 'Cuba's a helpless little country, American imperialists might invade at any moment. They don't *like* using torture, but what *choice* do they have?'"

A soft rumbling of approval from the audience.

"This same double standard is Thompson's greatest weakness. He's generous with sources that promote his agenda, but harsh with those that don't. Please understand, I'm sympathetic to Thompson's agenda. But Thompson allowed his activism to infect his history.

"Now ... Howard Zinn. Who doesn't love a guy whose book shows up on *The Simpsons* and *The Sopranos*? But he isn't without his critics. Forgive me for not having citations here. I'm doing this off the top of my head. In general, critics of *The People's History* think that it swung too far to the other side of one-sidedness. For Zinn, class conflict means rich elites with sinister motives plotting against the oppressed masses. In *The People's History*, ordinary people's only role is to fight the wealthy and snooty villains that Zinn has put in front of them.

"Again, I'm not saying that I disagree with Zinn's politics, but his politics have sullied his scholarship."

Stark took a sip of water and looked out over the crowd. It felt like everything up to this point was, like, foreplay and that she was about to go in for the kill.

"Marc Bloch," she said. "I … really can't say anything about Marc Bloch. He's one of my heroes, too.

"His situation is different from that of Thompson and Zinn, I think. As you know, he didn't choose the context of his activism, but had it thrust upon him. I don't like to compare other historical events to the Nazi era; the Nazis always win as 'worse than anything else.' It cheapens all of history. The truth is, we can't know what Bloch would have done if the Nazis had *not* occupied France. He might not have written *The Historian's Craft*, but he would have lived a happier life. And so would many others."

Stark asked if anyone else had a question or comment. No one did. This could have been exhaustion. For myself, I didn't want to risk the public drubbing. There would be time enough for that in Stark's seminar.

As I turned to leave, I saw Quint across the room. We made eye contact and he gestured drinking a cup of tea. It was 9 o'clock and Insomnia was calling.

CHAPTER | 8
Insomnia

"OMG! That was, like, the coolest thing I've ever seen!" I could hardly contain myself. I felt like I'd witnessed a battle of the Titans. "Are they always like that? Are they frienemies? Or just outright enemies?"

Insomnia was crowded, as always. We took a small table with only two chairs this time, in case the FBI or CIA or whoever might want to crash our conversation with some other save-the-world proposal.

"They do enjoy each other," Quint said.

"It looked like they might enjoy killing each other."

"Not at all," Quint said. "They need each other. Each one makes the other stronger. You know the Scholastic method?"

"Yes, of course," I said. "School masters locked in disputation, scholarly cross-examination employed in the pursuit of truth. I just, like, I have never seen it played out in front of me."

"It's like Peter Abelard," Quint said.

"The guy who was castrated for sleeping with his student?" I found myself asking questions about well-known facts just so Quint could confirm them. What the hell was that about?

"An unfortunate incident," Quint said. "I prefer his prowess in the disputation." My cheeks flushed. Quint looked at his empty espresso cup, considered whether he should go for another, then set the cup down and continued.

"Peter Abelard once accepted a challenge to argue a very complicated passage from *Ecclesiastes*, which he hadn't yet read, and he would have to present his argument the very next day.

He won! I mean how ballsy is that? Well, sorry. Unfortunate ironic description." He smiled and shrugged. "The point is that Abelard saw disputation as akin to joining the battlefield. His father had expected him to become a knight, but Abelard described his career as 'leaving the field of Mars for the field of Minerva!'"

My mind drifted into the abyss of fatherly expectations. Do fathers always want their children to do what is 'practical'?

Quint's voice drew me back to him. I knew all of the history he was telling me but I liked hearing him tell it. When he had finished, Quint looked at me. Several seconds passed and I once again felt a warmth in my cheeks. *Oh, my G-d!* I stood up, almost knocking my chair over and went to the counter to order another drink. Not caffeine, I thought. I turned and performed the same 'cup o' tea?' pantomime that Quint had executed after the lecture. He waved me off. I opted for two tall glasses of water and returned to the table. We both took long sips.

"Anyway," Quint said. "That's what's going on with Stark and Kantorowicz. They're two masters locked in an endless disputation. Each one of them is all in, but they also do it out of respect for each other, I think. They're Scholastics who believe that if they keep going, they'll eventually find Truth."

I took another, longer swig of water.

"So, do you think Kantorowicz believes his counter arguments? Or is he just playing the disputation game?"

"Good question," Quint said. "The Scholastic masters used to train their students to debate both sides of an argument, regardless of what they believed."

"I'm not so worried about that," I said. "I mean … this is relevant to that other thing. About, you know, whether or not Kantorowicz is a neo-Nazi."

"Hmm." That was the "hm" that Kantorowicz used. Do students eventually become their teachers?

"What I mean is … if he really believes in his counter examples, then he can't be a Nazi."

"Neo-Nazi."

"Whatever. He can't be a *neo*-Nazi because the examples he chose are so antithetical. I mean, Thompson and Zinn both worked for the betterment of the world, for civil rights and against war. Those aren't Nazi or neo-Nazi values. And Bloch. He actually gave his life fighting real Nazis. Kantorowicz called Bloch his hero. Isn't that proof that he's, like, on the side of good?"

"I get what you're saying. To be honest, I'm having a hard time being detached from this. I've been working with him for six years. I feel like I know who he is. But I'm trying. How did Stark put it? Not to let my bias infect my thinking. If he's a neo-Nazi—and that's a big if for me—then something needs to be done."

He looked at his watch, something I had never seen him do.

"I don't want to sound mercenary here, but he's my advisor. If I go after him, and it turns out he's innocent, I'm screwed. I doubt that Agent Mapp is going to write a letter that will land me a good teaching job. Even if he's guilty, that means switching advisors and what prof would take on a grad student who snitched and got his former prof fired, or worse?"

He looked at his watch again.

"I should go," he said. "Can I walk you as far as Sterling?"

"Oh. Yes," I said, perhaps a little too quickly.

As we stepped out of Insomnia, I looked across the street and … *oh, no* … *oh, shit, shit, shit!* Right there, walking toward us, was the easily recognizable Kantorowicz, crutch in one hand, leather briefcase in the other, making good time down the sidewalk opposite from where we stood. He was not alone.

I shoved Quint back into the doorway of the coffee shop.

"What gives?"

"Look."

From the shadows, we watched Kantorowicz approach at a distance. Who was that with him? Was that the guy Mapp showed us? The Hobbit? Bilbo the white supremacist?

"It's him," Quint said. "Yes, I'm sure it's him.

"We have to follow them."

"Are you crazy? No!"

I grabbed him by the collar of his sweater and pulled his face closer to mine, looked him in the eye, then took off.

"No," Quint said, but he was right behind me. "At least back off. Don't be so obvious."

We followed them at what Quint determined was a safe distance, up Wall Street toward Sterling and Beinecke. They turned down College Street in the direction of the music school and we had to hustle to the corner so as not to lose them. They stopped at the corner of Elm, then crossed the street diagonally toward Battell Chapel, which I began to describe with art historical vigor.

"High Victorian Gothic," I said to Quint in a hushed tone. "Not the same as Collegiate Gothic, but it kind of goes together. Weird choice for a school founded by Congregationalists. You'd expect more of the whitewashed, Puritan style."

"What are you taking about?"

"Sorry. I do that when I'm nervous."

We watched Kantorowicz and Bilbo disappear behind Battell, headed for the Old Campus Courtyard. Cutting through the green would take them to the History Department. We crossed the street and hugged the chapel as we made our way to the courtyard, entered at the northwest corner. There were only so many paths they could have chosen, but as we looked down each path, they were nowhere in sight. The courtyard had decent lighting, helpful at that time of night, but squinting down each path brought us no luck. Kantorowicz and his mysterious companion had disappeared.

We stood for several minutes on the edge of the park.

"My heart's racing," I said.

"It's the caffeine," Quint said.

"Or the fact that we have just had our first spies-following-Nazis-and-trying-not-to-get-caught moment."

"Neo-Nazis," he said.

I laughed and punched him on the shoulder. It was something else making my heart race. I could feel my cheeks reddening and hoped it was too dark for him to notice.

"I better go," I said.

"Should I walk you?"

"No! I mean … I can make it on my own." I looked down at my shoes. What the hell's happening here? "I… I just have an early tomorrow." With that, I turned back toward College Street, then Elm to Howe to Edgewood, then home.

I wouldn't be able to sleep that night.

*

*Careful, Quick. Don't want to let happen what I think is happening. Too much going on. Gotta start writing that monster monograph, that single book on a single topic for a single reader, the D in ABD, that Get Me Outta Here dissertation.*

*You don't need some white girl who seems to follow trouble rather than avoid it. You don't need … How long have you known her? Two weeks? No. I don't need some Spike Lee 'Jungle Fever' episode so close to the finish line. Been there, done that, got the T-shirt and a black eye.*

*Finish this year without distraction. Then go somewhere and write your stupid dissertation in peace. Write and write and write and do not get distracted by a girl. A woman.*

*Write it. Then defend it. Then jump into the insanely competitive job market. Supposed to be easier for me because minorities are 'desirable' on college faculties, necessary leavening in the great diversity bake-off. Bullshit! But that's all the melanin deprived, scared white ABDs can talk about. Reverse privilege or some such crap.*

*Oh, man, oh, man. I don't need this 'lure of the exotic'. I've no desire to be the 'object of her gaze'.*

*She's smart. I'll give her that. Well read, too, for a first-year. I like her … what would you call it? Enthusiasm? And her nerdiness. Did she really do an architectural read on Battell Chapel while in hot pursuit of possible domestic terrorists? Oh, my God!*

*She's naïve, though. Buys in too easily to whatever this is that Mapp's selling. And you keep trying to protect her. From Mapp. From herself.*

*What the hell, Quick. What are you doing? Get her out of your head. Too much to do to start something here. Oh, I won't be able to sleep tonight.*

CHAPTER | 9
## Your funding …

| | |
|---|---|
| FROM: | kermit.mulroney@yale.edu |
| DATE: | Mon., 1 OCT 2020 |
| TO: | quinton.quick@yale.edu |
| CC: | abe.kantorowicz@yale.edu |
| SUBJECT: | Your funding |

Dear QUINTON QUICK,

This is the regular letter sent out to all ABD PhD candidates in the Department of History. Your funding will run out at the end of this year. This should not be an occasion for panic. Our records show that you:

- have completed all course work
- have shown reading proficiency in sub-field required languages
- have passed your comprehensive exams
- are auditing one course:
  HIST 690—Approp/Abuse Medieval Art

You should plan to defend your dissertation by the end of this academic year in order to complete your PhD within the six-year funding period. You can, of course, extend the writing period for two more years, but we do not recommend this. Less than half of candidates who extend their dissertating ever finish.

Again, do not panic. We have cc'd your advisor and assume you will work with him/her/them to create a satisfactory plan for completion.

Please let me know if my office can help in any way.

Sincerely,

Kermit Mulroney
C. Vann Woodward Professor of History and
Director of Graduate Studies
Department of History
Yale University

CHAPTER 20
Your future …

FROM:        tariq.sallam@yale.edu
DATE:        Mon., 3 OCT 2020
TO:          quinton.quick@yale.edu
SUBJECT:     Your future

Dear Mr. Quick,

As-salamu alaykum.

We've only occasionally spoken but I wanted to reach
out and offer my services. As you have surely read in
the *Yale Daily*, your adviser Dr. Kantorowicz is on
track to be censured by the Faculty Senate for his
connections to the German white supremacist magazine *Zuerst*. As a faculty member of color, I'm appalled by my colleague's actions.

More to the point, I'm sympathetic to the dilemma
which you face as a Black graduate student. I can imagine some conflicted feelings. How do you reconcile
the loyalty you must have to a professor who has
served you well over several years with the apprehen-
sion over how his alliances may impact your future?
This is not to mention the sense of betrayal you must
feel connected to the revelations around his political
views.

Perhaps it's too soon to think about switching advisors, and, *in sha Allah*, I hope this all works out for you. But, if you ever want to talk, my door is open.

Tariq Sallam
Said al-Hibri Professor of History
Yale University

CHAPTER 21
The Spanish Forger

"What do you see?"

The next time we saw Kantorowicz was at the second meeting of his seminar, which he held in Beinecke's Rare Book & Manuscript reading room. I made eye contact with him as I sat down and tried to discern whether he had seen Quint and me following him the night of the Sterling Lecture. Either he hadn't seen us or he was good at hiding it. I turned my attention back to the reading room's table where we would spend the next 90 minutes.

Spread out before us were the tools used to examine ancient tomes. First, there was a box of pencils. Pens were forbidden, as was any food or beverages. There were flat mats of velvet-covered foam, the kind that might be used by close-up magicians, intended to keep a manuscript from ever touching the table, the soft velvet minimizing abrasions. There was also a large, velvet-covered foam "cradle" with a V-shaped platform where a reader could rest an old book, alleviating stress on the book's spine. There were curious "snakes," lead beads strung together into bracelets then covered in cotton, used as weights to hold open the pages, to minimize contact with oily human fingers. Speaking of oily fingers, there was a school box containing archival, white cotton gloves, each pair individually wrapped in plastic. Kantorowicz passed this box around and asked that we not put on the gloves until he told us to. He'd already distributed full color photocopies of three medieval manuscript pages. In front of him on the table was a large folder; I guessed it contained the original parchment pieces of the copies he'd handed out.

"What do you see?" he repeated, indicating the topmost copy in our packets. I still didn't know everyone's name, but more of the students contributed than last class.

"There's a lot going on," said one student.

"More specific."

"There are lots of people," another student said.

"The main character is the woman in the blue dress and red robe," another student added. "She's repeated several times. Sorry. Three times. She has the same wavy red hair, if that's meant to be the same person."

"Good observations," said Kantorowicz. "Now let's just add some terminology. The woman isn't a *character*, but a *figure*. She appears in three *panels*, like a comic strip but without the lines separating the panels. The panels fall into two *registers*, one on top of the other. Who's next?"

"The left panel of the top register shows the woman arriving in a boat at some sort of castle," Leigh Ann said. "There are other people in the boat and people in the arched door of the castle who greet her."

"Good that you start in the top left corner, rather than being drawn into the larger illustration in the bottom. That's the direction in which the story will unfold. Next?"

"The top right panel," said I, following the professor's lead in terms of narrative direction, "has the same woman, perhaps inside the castle walls. She's looking up at a statue. It may be made of gold. The statue seems broken in several pieces and is falling over. I mean, the statue is, like, crumbling in midair."

"Mm-hmm. Next?"

The whole class was feeling encouraged. Students jumped in one after the other.

"There's a castle in the background. Uh, same panel. Top right."

"All of the figures have the same vapid expression."

"There are many more people in the bottom register. They're all watching the woman who's killing some kind of monster next to the lake."

"How do you know that's a lake? It could be part of the ocean."

"She isn't killing the monster. She's fighting it.'"

"It's not a monster," said Quinton Quick. "It's a dragon. And she's not fighting it. She's taming it. See the red scarf around the dragon's neck. Like a leash."

"Very good," said Kantorowicz. "Now, all of you, look deeper. Tell me details."

I was able to identify some of the hats in the image. A man in the bottom register on the left wore a velvet chaperon. Several of the women wore double-horned hennins. Thank you, misspent youth at the Ren Fest.

Quint jumped back in.

"The geography is highly stylized. The rocks create a path from the upper to lower register, guiding the narrative. The water also looks very, I don't know. Swirly. The whole effect is an imagined space."

"Mm-hmm."

"The trees look really fake," said one of the quiet guys in class. "Like lollipops on sticks. They're colored an intense green."

"Anything else?"

The same student wanted to say more but hesitated.

"I'm not sure this is allowed," he said. "But ... all the women have large breasts."

"Amazing!" Kantorowicz said. "You've all just brilliantly exposed this manuscript painting as a forgery!"

We must have looked confused. Was he doing that same thing again, where we would all be right until it turned out that we were really wrong, but then we would all be right again? It was maddening.

"Okay," I said. "What do you mean by forgery?"

"Yes," said Quint. "Don't we need a lot of other contemporary pieces for comparison?"

"Mm-hmm. Good questions," said Kantorowicz. "And, yes, comparison pieces would help, but we don't have time for that today. Can you figure things out by questioning the internal evidence?"

"For example?" I said. I think he liked that I was pushing back, but it still felt risky.

"Tell me more about the hats," he said.

"Okay … the man's hat is called a chaperon. It's made from a lot of cloth so it can keep its shape on top but also, like, drapes around the shoulder and across the neck. It's Italian, late 15$^{th}$ century. The women wear hennins, which are basically pointy cone-shaped hats with veils. These women are in double hennins, so, two cones. French, early 15$^{th}$ … Oh! Right. The hats are from different regions and different times."

"Which means?"

"Well, either the artist had some encyclopedia of medieval hats, or he was a time traveler who doesn't need to paint what's in front of him. The different periods and regions mean somebody's doing a mash-up."

"That's not the term I would use, but yes, it's an anachronistic mash-up."

He let that sink in.

"Any help from the story being depicted?"

More silence. Quint finally spoke.

"Jacob Voragine, in his *Golden Legend*, 13$^{th}$ century, tells a story about St. Martha taming a mythic monster called a Tarasque that lived in southern France. She subdues the monster with holy water and a cross, then ties it up with her girdle, or belt, which is what we see here."

"She's holding a cross in the top right panel!" Leigh Ann said, excited. "Ahh … she's making the golden, *pagan* idol crumble with the power of the cross!"

"Mm-hmm."

"There's nothing in Voragine's work about her destroying idols," said Quint. "So that could be made up."

"Like inserting turkeys into a mural where turkeys don't belong," I said.

"Yes," Kantorowicz smiled with his eyes, then turned back to the quiet guy. "What can you tell me about that intense green color?" Deer in headlights.

"Uh, nothing," he said at last.

"Yes, that's correct. It's a totally unfair question. I'll come back to that in a moment."

Kantorowicz switched gears. He put on his white, archival gloves and instructed us to do the same. He opened the folder and removed a single folio. It showed a female saint arriving in a boat. Several people waited to greet her, some of them wearing as yet unidentified hats. There was a castle in the background, but it wasn't the same as in the earlier illustration.

"This is a leaf from Beinecke MS 283, from this very library." With that he gently passed the folio into the gloved hand of the woman to his right, who spent a reasonable amount of time looking at it, then passed it on. "There are fourteen of these folios, all on parchment as you see here. All of them are forgeries. Can you tell me why?"

In Spanish—a language I barely know—the word for riddle or puzzle is *rompecabeza*, "head breaker." That is what it felt like playing this game with Kantorowicz. It was fun, but it was also exhausting.

"It has the same bright green trees," said the quiet guy, who would soon need a new nickname.

"Yes, and that's important, but you don't really need that to solve this one."

The folio made its way around the table. Every student, including the erudite Quint, examined it, then passed it on without comment. The folio finally got to me, sitting to the professor's left. Without thinking, or perhaps out of desperation, I turned the folio over and looked at the back side. It was covered in writing.

"What's this?" I said.

"That *is* the question." Kantorowicz smiled.

I looked at the Latin text and puzzled over the passage for several seconds, at first simply to make out the handwriting. How do you say *rompecabeza* in Latin? Quint, apparently growing impatient, reached across the table to snatch the folio from my hands, but I held on and snatched it back. If I hadn't been glaring at Quint, I might have seen Kantorowicz having a mild heart attack over our manhandling of this 600-year-old document. I could hear the other seminar students gasp. Once I recovered, I laughed out loud as I sight read the Latin: "Whoever fears the Lord will act like this, and whoever grasps— grasps!—the Law will obtain wisdom."

I thought for a second longer.

"*Ecclesiasticus?*" I said. "*Sirach?*"

A huge smile from Kantorowicz, but scowls and dropped jaws from my grad school colleagues, Quint included. He shook his head and, smiling, mouthed the word "freak."

"Eidetic recall," I shrugged. "Plus, I went to a Catholic high school."

"Let's save our awe and/or derision for Ms. Isaacson for another time," said Kantorowicz. "How does this biblical passage on the back of Beinecke 283 help us show that the illustration is a forgery?"

Quint had spent more time in the archives than any of the other students, at least as far as I knew. He was on it. Instead of grabbing for the folio again, he instructed me to hold it up to the light. It was difficult to see, but at just the right angle the light shown through and revealed letters that had once been on the other side, now scraped away and hidden beneath the illustration.

"It's a palimpsest," Quint said.

"Very good, Mr. Quick," said Kantorowicz. "The genius of our forger is that he painted his works on authentic medieval media, like parchment, or in this case vellum. Sometimes he cut blank folios out of old choir books. For the fourteen examples here at Beinecke, he scraped off individual folios from a missal for the Mass, which is why you get this passage from the *Book of the All-Virtuous Wisdom of Yeshua ben Sira*, a.k.a., *The Book of Sirach*, a.k.a., *Ecclesiasticus*."

"The painting has no apparent connection to the text," Quint said. "Normally, if there are images, they would illustrate text. Another clue that it's a forgery?"

"Very good, Mr. Quick."

Kantorowicz retrieved the folio and gingerly returned it to its folder. I thought I heard a sigh of relief as he did so.

"All right. We've almost reached the end of today's journey. Let me tell you the story of the last example in your packet, and dare I say it? All will be *illuminated.*" A few groans at the pun. Quint dared to roll his eyes in the professor's direction. Kantorowicz passed out copies of a photo showing an attractive woman in what looked like 1930s attire: a flapper's hat pulled down over her ears, a fox stole and pearls around her neck.

"This is a woman named Belle da Costa Greene. Her first job was as librarian at Princeton University. There she met a student with the delightful name of Junius Spencer Morgan II, nephew of J.P. Morgan."

"The banker?" said quiet guy.

"Very good, Mr. Stone."

Quiet guy had a name.

"In 1905, Morgan, the uncle and banker, invited Ms. da Costa Greene to become chief librarian of the Morgan Library, his ambitious collection of rare books and manuscripts. One of Greene's tasks was acquisitions, which required her to develop a keen eye to differentiate between authentic pieces and forgeries.

"Around 1930, 'The Betrothal of St. Ursula'—the last page in your handout—came up for sale and was offered to the Morgan Library. The seller dated the piece circa 1450 and attributed it to a Spanish master, Jorge Inglès, whose name, ironically means George English. Ms. Greene examined the work and saw all of the elements you've discovered today: the sentimental, vapid faces; lollipop trees; swirling water; anachronistic costumes; buxom ladies. Unlike all of you, Ms. Greene had extensive experience and many comparative examples to draw upon. She could tell that 'The Betrothal of St. Ursula' was a fake. She refused to buy it and dubbed its creator, the Spanish Forger.

"It's likely the Spanish Forger was really French, but the name stuck. Here's the best part: his 'The Betrothal of St. Ursula' was created sometime in the early 1900s."

"What!?"

"That's impossible!"

"How do they know that?"

"Mmm," Kantorowicz said. "How do they know? Remember Mr. Stone's observation of the 'bright green trees.' Ms. Greene—no pun intended—recognized the pigment, which is known as copper arsenite or Paris green, which didn't exist before 1814. Except for the authentic media, the parchment on which he painted, all the other materials were modern. Not medieval in the least. And there ends the curious story of the Spanish Forger."

I felt compelled to applaud, which luckily was muffled by the white gloves. Students began to pack their stuff and stood up to leave.

"But wait," Kantorowicz smiled. "There's more."

For the umpteenth time, we all looked confused, but also delighted in a way that the story wasn't over yet.

"The most amazing part of the story, I think, is that Belle da Costa Greene was herself a kind of forgery."

Everyone was seated again and completely focused.

"Belle da Costa Greene was born Belle Greener. Her parents were mixed-race African Americans. Father, Theodore Greener, was the first African American to graduate from Harvard University. Belle was lighter than her parents and at some point, she decided that her life would be easier if she 'passed' as a white woman. She changed her name and invented a Portuguese grandmother to account for her slightly darker skin. Belle Greener could never have gotten a job at the Princeton University Library."

He paused.

"Greene started at Princeton in 1902, the same year Woodrow Wilson became President of the university. Wilson was a notorious racist. He'd grown up in the South during the Civil War and at eight years old, witnessed William Tecumseh Sherman's devastating march to the sea. Wilson saw slavery as benign and the KKK as harmless. So during his presidency at Princeton, students and alums were proud that their school wasn't the kind of place that admitted 'Negroes', either as students or faculty. But the refined, and 'white', Belle da Costa Greene *was* hired in the Princeton library, and she parlayed that into quite a life for herself. Even if it was a life in hiding."

I looked across the table at Quint, but his eyes were lowered, his hands clenched.

CHAPTER 22
## Tradecraft

I needed clean clothes so I asked Quint if he'd hang out with me at Brainwash & Dry, my neighborhood laundromat. We sat in a row of orange plastic chairs and stared at the two tumbling dryers in front of us, one for whites, one for coloreds. Those were mom's words. Whites and coloreds.

"Always wash them and dry them separately," she said. Separate but equal, I thought. Did Quint make that connection? I remembered Belle da Costa Greene and shook my head. I turned to Quint, who hadn't brought any laundry, nor had he said a word since he got there.

"What's your problem?" I asked.

"I can't do this," he said after a long silence.

"What does that mean?"

"This," he said making a small circular gesture. "THIS!" he said again, widening the gesture.

Was "this" the row of orange plastic chairs? Was it us? Was it the laundromat? Life? The world? Before I could ask him we were interrupted once again by our favorite FBI agent.

"Jesus Christ!" Quint snapped at Special Agent Mapp, who had ditched the trench coat for grey sweatpants and a 'Hudson University' hoodie. He had a duffle bag full of clothes. He didn't load them into a machine, but instead dumped them onto a table behind where we sat and pretended to sort them like props in an improv skit called 'FBI Guy Does his Laundry'.

"Don't turn around," Mapp said. "Just listen. This is the last time I'll disturb you, at least in public."

"What's that supposed to mean?" Quint asked.

"Oh, it soon won't be safe to meet publicly anymore. Not after your little cloak-and-dagger stunt the other night."

"What!?"

"You tried to follow your professor and Ted Bilbo after the Sterling Lecture."

"How did ...? You were ...?" Quint fumbled for words, then looked at me as if to say it was my fault. I shrugged and turned toward Mapp to take the blame from Quint.

"Look straight ahead," Mapp whispered. "Don't worry about it. The fact that you tried to follow them shows me you're interested in helping. But don't ever do it again. You're terrible at it."

"We *won't* do it again and we *don't* want to help you," Quint said, looking directly into the dryer across from him.

"You haven't told Professor Kantorowicz about me," said Mapp.

"How do you know?"

"Because if you'd told him you'd have told me that you told him. Another sign that you want to help."

Quint caught Mapp's reflection in the dryer's glass door and the two of them stared at each other. Mapp broke the silence first.

"I know this is difficult, but you're our best option for this part of the operation. I also know you can do it because of who you are."

"You don't know shit about who we are!" Quint said.

Mapp looked around the laundromat. He took a deep breath as a way of warning Quint to keep his voice down, then recited our lives from memory, like so many items on a grocery list.

First, he turned to me.

"Subject: Isaacson. Female. Only child. 24 years old.

"Parents, still living but divorced. Father: Arthur. Jewish, non-practicing. PhD in mathematics and computer engineering, Rice University. Telecom Programmer at NASA. Apparently loving, but often absent due to work. Mother: Joyce, née Rosenstein. Reformed Jew. MA in art history, University of

Texas at Austin. Docent, Houston MFA. Close relationship with daughter.

"Subject grew up, Houston. Non-practicing Jew, though *bat mitzvahed* at 12. Attended Incarnate Word Catholic High School. Self-proclaimed 'medieval history nerd,' Facebook page now inactive. Diagnosed on the spectrum at 15. Highly functional, no intervention. Prescribed Sertraline for anxiety. Early admittance to Smith College. Graduated in three years, BA in medieval history. Recently enrolled, Yale MA/PhD program. Advisor, Abraham Kantorowicz."

He turned to Quint.

"Subject: Quick. Male. Only child. 28 years old.

"Father: Conrad. White. PhD in History of Ideas, Harvard. Last position: full professor, joint appointment in history and philosophy, Princeton University. Institutionalized for mental disorder when subject was 13. Now deceased.

"Mother: Adele, née Jefferson. Black. PhD in Afro-American and Women's history, UC Berkeley. Last position, Associate Professor, Mercer County Community College. Aspiring radical feminist but never important enough to be dangerous. Reputedly annoying at faculty meetings. Single mother after husband was put away. Died of heart disease two years ago.

"Subject grew up, Princeton, New Jersey, on Princeton U. campus. Self-proclaimed atheist, after both parents, though flirted with Islam as an undergrad. Attended Princeton High School. No Facebook or other social media presence. Serious legal run-in at 16. Records sealed—still working on unsealing them. BA, *summa cum laude* from Morehouse, double major in medieval history and literature. MA in history from Harvard. Enrolled, Yale PhD program. ABD. Advisor, Kantorowicz.

"You were saying?"

Drums in dryers whirred and agitators in washers twisted back and forth replacing the silence in our Brainwash & Dry brains. On the one hand, the amount of context Mapp had collected on us was impressive. I suppose I felt a brief moment of researcher envy. And I liked hearing more about Quint. On the other hand, it was freaking me out how much he knew. It was a good thing he knew about the Sertraline because his recitation was triggering an anxiety attack all by itself.

"Think of me as a talent scout," he said. "I'm not trying to scare you. It's easy to use the net to harvest all sorts of data on people. That's not the magic trick. Beyond the data, I think I can see who you really are."

Quint stood, walked toward the store front window and looked out. I leaned back in my orange plastic chair and turned toward Mapp, in spite of his instructions not to.

"Why did you send us the obit from the *Süddeutsche Zeitung?* Were you trying to turn us against Kantorowicz? Like, make us think he's a neo-Nazi just because his father was a Nazi?"

That caught Mapp off guard. He paused before he answered. Quint's attention returned.

"No," Mapp said. "It's possible that he's a Nazi—"

"Neo-Nazi."

"*Neo*-Nazi. It's possible Kantorowicz is a neo-Nazi because of his father, but he could just as likely be a neo-Nazi for all sorts of other reasons. Or he could not be a neo-Nazi. I'm open to all possibilities, but that isn't why I sent you the obit."

"It's the daddy question," Quint said turning back toward Mapp.

The FBI Agent tilted his head and nodded, then quoted Professor Stark from her Sterling lecture.

"Medievalists construct complete narratives from small scraps of information."

"You were there?" I said, recognizing the line.

"I was tailing Kantorowicz, until you two stepped in."

"We didn't see you," I said.

"Exactly," Mapp said. "You'll only see me when I want to be seen."

I thought about this for a second.

"Your stupid, obvious costumes!" I said. Mapp smiled.

Quint took a deep breath.

"What do you know about the elder Kantorowicz dying with no offspring? Our professor presents himself as the son. What do you know?"

"Yeah," I said. "Do your little grocery list trick with Kantorowicz."

Mapp shook his head.

"I wish I could. Unfortunately, my research on this subject only tracks back to grad school. Before that, Kantorowicz is a ghost."

"That's impossible," Quint said. "His grad school records would show where he did his undergrad. His undergrad records would list a high school. Then you just work backwards."

Mapp let Quint go on, then responded.

"Listen. Kantorowicz's family history may or may not have anything to do with this. All I know is that I keep seeing him with an avowed white supremacist, and it's my job to do something about that. The very fact that the two of you have IQs off the charts, and that you're skeptical about everything makes you ideal candidates to help me."

I looked at Quint with what he later told me were pleading eyes. He gave in.

"What do we have to do?"

"That's the best part," Mapp said. "Don't do anything. Just continue to go to class and have your regular grad-student-meets-advisor interactions. Only report back to me."

"Should we call your office?" I said. "I still have your card."

"No," Mapp said. "Unfortunately, there are elements in the Bureau that are sympathetic to the white supremacist movement. Not many, but it makes it too dangerous. No. I've got a better idea."

Mapp reached into his duffel and pulled out a resealable sandwich bag and two books. He handed the sandwich bag to me. It contained three pieces of white chalk. He gave Quint one of the books, the one that looked older. Quint read the title aloud.

"*Practica inquisitionis heretice pravitatis.* You have excellent taste."

"*Pravitatis?*" I said. "Depravity? *Practical Inquisition of Heretical Depravity?*"

"It's a manual written by Bernard Gui," Quint said. "The most famous inquisitor of the Middle Ages."

"I've read *The Name of the Rose*," I said.

Mapp took the book back and whispered instructions. No one but us could hear above the din of the machines.

"Take this book to Sterling and hide it in the stacks. Put it *behind* the books on the shelf with the call number BX1700. It's the bottom shelf. *Behind* those books. If you need to get a message to me, write a note and leave it in this book."

"Just like that?" Quint asked. "What if someone finds the message?"

Mapp then held up the other book. It was a copy of *Crips, Bloods, and Crusaders: Medieval Precursors to Modern Gang Signs*, by Abraham Kantorowicz.

"Ever heard of the book code?" Mapp asked.

Fan of spy fiction that he was, Quint didn't hesitate.

"Three numbers. First number = page. Second number = line. Third number = word. I've never done it, but I've read about it plenty. Are we using *Crips, Bloods, and Crusaders* as the key? I've already got a copy of that."

"I know," Mapp said. "I've peeked inside your carrel window." He held up a hand before we could object. "Use your copy to write messages using the book code. Put the message in Bernard Gui's book. Put the book on the shelf, behind the other books in the stacks at BX1700. Bottom shelf. *Behind* the other books."

"BX1700 are the books on medieval heresy," I said. They paid me no attention.

"Dead drop?" Quint said.

"Dead drop," Mapp confirmed.

The two of them smiled at each other and held each other's gaze. OMG! What the hell's going on here?! I waved a hand in front of their eyes to break the spell.

"So ... Quint writes you a message and ... What? Do you just meander through the stacks every day to see if you've got any secret mail?"

"That's what the chalk is for. If there's a message, put a chalk mark on the façade of the Sterling Library, directly under the statue of the medieval scholar. A circle with an X in it."

"What does that mean?"

"It's an old hobo chalk code. It means 'everything's okay.' That'll tell me the coast is clear to pick up the message. Understood?"

"Yes. But I'm a little pissed off. I mean, the boy gets to write secret messages using the book code and hide them in a special hidden book and the girl gets to put a chalk mark on the front of a building—which I'm pretty sure is, like, vandalism in the eyes of Yale University Security."

Mapp laughed. He reached out to pat my hand, then thought better of it when he saw the look in my eye.

"Easy," he said. "I have a much more important job for you." He held up Kantorowicz's book again and handed it to me. "I want you to leave this in your professor's office."

"His book?" I said. "I think he probably already has a bunch of copies."

Quint reached over and touched the book's cover.

"There's a bug inside. Right? Some kind of listening device?"

Mapp nodded, then turned back to me. I opened the book and began madly flipping through the pages expecting to find a big section cut out with a miniature reel-to-reel recorder inside.

"You won't find it," Mapp said. "I guess you would if you ripped the book apart, but I'm going to ask you not to do that." He gently reached over and closed the book's covers.

"Wait at least two days," he said. "Then, the next time you happen to be in the professor's office, leave the book. Don't make it obvious. Put it into his shelves or leave it under some papers. He's not going to think twice if he sees it because, as you say, he has several copies already."

I read *Crips, Bloods, and Crusaders* as an undergrad, I thought. It was the reason I came to Yale, to study with Kantorowicz.

Holding the book close to my chest, I could feel my heart pounding against it.

The dryers spinning my laundry both ground to a halt. First whites, then coloreds. The noise level went down and Mapp's stage whisper halted. I opened a dryer door and began pulling out the wash. Quint stood by, uncertain of whether to help. A look from me stopped him.

When we turned around, Mapp was gone.

CHAPTER 23

Genealogy for Beginners

"I love the Mormons!" Quint said.

He was seated at a large table outside our carrel door. The door was open and he had made himself comfortable at this larger workspace, with books and photocopies and printouts spread across the table's surface.

"Okay," I laughed. "Why do you love the Mormons?"

"Their whole concept of the afterlife. They believe you can baptize the dead, even, perhaps especially, those who lived before Jesus Christ and before the final revelations to their prophet, Joseph Smith. They want the whole family to be together in heaven, so they feel obligated to find all their long-lost ancestors, in order to baptize them *postmortem*, so they can make it into heaven. Which means they use genealogy to save people's eternal souls."

"And why do you suddenly care about this?"

"Because of the 2 billion names preserved on 2.5 million rolls of microfilm that the Mormons have stashed away in their Granite Mountain Records Vault, locked behind doors that weigh 14 tons, in a climate-controlled environment designed to withstand a nuclear attack, built into the Wasatch mountain range near Salt Lake City, all for the purpose of genealogical research to find the dead ancestors and baptize them."

"You have already been to Insomnia today, yes?"

He smiled and shrugged, then reached into the mess of papers in front of him, pulling out the obit of the elder Kantorowicz from the *Süddeutsche Zeitung*.

"This thing's been bugging me since we first got it. He left no offspring, even though our prof claims to be his son. And Mapp's comment that the professor wasn't who he said he was, but that Mapp said he couldn't find anything on the professor before grad school. That seems pretty lame for the FBI."

"So?"

"So, I went to Familysearch.org, the genealogical service of the Church of Jesus Christ of Latter-Day Saints and home to an amazing, user-friendly database. Ancestry.com is an off-shoot of Familysearch. Both are located in Utah, but now practically everything's online. So, Mormons. Mormons! Look at this!"

He shoved a piece of paper across the table, something he had printed out from the Familysearch website. It looked like a family tree, though it had lots of symbols that were unfamiliar to me.

"Only someone with wicked paleography can decipher this," I joked.

"You must channel the spirit of Stark's seminar. Go ahead. Give it a try."

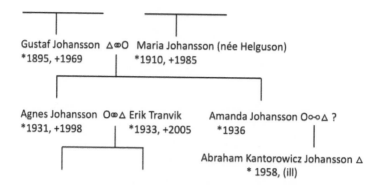

"Okay," I said. "All the names have small triangles or circles next to them. Based on the names, males and females, respectively." Suddenly, I caught the name in the lower right-hand corner: Kantorowicz. I pointed to the name as I showed

Quint. "This isn't our guy, is it? Why does he have a different last name?"

"Let's come back to that," he said. He then pointed to other symbols on the chart and we worked through them together.

"The * and + mean birth and death," I said. "The ∞ symbol always appears between the Δ and O. Marriage?"

Quint agreed.

"What about 'O∘-∘Δ?' next to Amanda Johansson's name?" he said.

"∘-∘ is different from ∞, but it still seems like some sort of connection between Δ and O, except that this Δ is followed by a question mark. Unknown husband?"

"Not husband," Quint said. "Unknown *mate*. And the ∘-∘ means a union, but not marriage."

"A union that produces Abraham Kantorowicz Johansson Δ."

"Yes."

"So that "ill" in parentheses isn't an abbreviation for illness. He's illegitimate!" I smile, pleased with myself, even though it wasn't that hard to decode.

"What about the second last name?" I said. "Johansson?" Quint reached into the pile and retrieved a photocopy of a birth certificate. It had the same information.

City or township:   Princeton, NJ
Name of child:      Abraham Kantorowicz Johansson
Birthdate:          20 December 1958
Name of mother:     Amanda Johansson
Name of father:     [blank, a line drawn across the space]

"If this is our professor, why is the father's name left blank?" I took out my copy of *Crips, Bloods, and Crusaders*. "Look, right here in the author bio. I never thought twice about it before, but Abe says he's the son of Ernst. And Kantorowicz is one of his last names."

Quint referred to the dates again. Amanda Johansson was born in 1936. That would make her 22 in 1958, when she gave birth to young Abe. He then showed me the obit again. The elder Kantorowicz was born in 1895, which in 1958 would make him a father at the age of 63."

"Cradle robber!?"

"What else could it be?" Quint said. He led me through the rest of his thought process. "Where would an older professor like Kantorowicz come into contact with a young, apparently available woman like Amanda?"

"A student?"

"I thought so, too, but I looked through all the Princeton year books, *Bric-a-brac*, for the years Amanda might have been a student there. Then I realized that she couldn't have been a student at Princeton."

"Not smart enough?" I asked. "Not enough blue blood?"

"Not male enough. Princeton didn't admit women students until 1969. I didn't know that until I started looking at their yearbooks. But she *was* at Princeton."

"So who was she?"

"The *Bric-a-brac* editors included an acknowledgments section on the last page of the 1957 edition. Two female librarians were listed, as well as one librarian's assistant, Amanda Johansson."

"So, Hitler's favorite historian, a full professor at Princeton, slept with a librarian's assistant! That is one helluva power differential. That is, like, sexual harassment!"

"It probably happened all the time in those days," Quint said. "Princeton was quite the Old Boys' Club. I'm guessing it was only frowned upon if you got caught. The scandal of a professor sleeping with a woman 'below his station'. And it was definitely bad form to bring a bastard son into the world."

"Fucking Nazi!"

"Hold on," Quint said. "First of all, you're in serious non sequitur territory. His being a Nazi, if that's true, isn't necessarily connected to him sleeping with the much younger Amanda."

"What do you mean, *if* he's a Nazi?"

"I've been busy," Quint said. "First, I've found out more about the *Süddeutsche Zeitung*. It leans left and it seems they only reported some of the Ernst Kantorowicz story."

He handed me a large blue volume, *The Encyclopedia of Historians and Historical Writing*, Vol. 1. A yellow post-it marked the entry for Ernst Kantorowicz. In 1950, at UC Berkeley, Kantorowicz refused to sign the loyalty oath proving that he was 'not now, nor had he ever been' a member of the Communist Party. The irony was that he had fought against communists after World War I. Kantorowicz refused to sign the oath, claiming that it was a threat to academic freedom. Plus, once he got to America, he spoke out against the Nazis, who had killed his mother.

"He's clearly a lot more complicated than we thought he was," said Quint.

"Why isn't he listed on the birth certificate?"

"Embarrassment?" Quint said. "Or shame? Not just that he was an older man hooking up with a much younger woman—someone lower in the Princeton caste system—but also that he'd probably lived his entire life as a closeted homosexual. That's what the whole intellectual George's circle in Heidelberg was about, at least partly. According to *The Paris Review*, Stefan George cultivated mostly gay acolytes."

I looked at the article in *The Paris Review* and marveled at all the research Quint had done since the last time I saw him, just yesterday. What about his dissertation?

"What about the name, 'Kantorowicz Johansson'? Our professor only uses Kantorowicz."

Quint thought for a while before he answered.

"I don't want to venture into armchair psychology, but here goes. When the elder Kantorowicz refused to recognize his son, Amanda was stuck. She couldn't list him as the father, but she could still include Kantorowicz as her son's middle name. At some point, she must have told the boy about his famous professor father. Abe Kantorowicz Johansson then dropped his legal last name and became, simply, Abe Kantor-owicz."

I nodded.

"And after all that," I ventured, "he went on to follow in his father's footsteps. He was only five when his dad died. Did he ever meet him? It's, like, really sad and messed up."

We sat at the table outside our carrel for several minutes, sifting through Quint's research, revisiting print outs of articles and documents, showing highlighted sections to one another and shaking our heads. Really sad and messed up.

"Should we tell Mapp any of this?" I said. "Is this the kind of thing he wanted us to report?"

"Absolutely not!" Quint said. "In fact, I'm trying to figure out why Mapp said he couldn't find anything on Kantorowicz. I found all of this in just a few hours, and I'm not the damned FBI. What's going on there?"

More silent mulling.

"How the hell are we going to go to class next week? We know intimate details about our prof that he did not invite us to know. And now we can't unknow it."

"No," Quint said. "No. We cannot."

CHAPTER 24

Relics and Tweets

"What do you see?"

Hearing those words at the start of class never got old. Kantorowicz didn't greet us. He never called the roll. He projected an image onto the screen and got down to business. It made my blood flow faster. Or was that, like, the newfound knowledge I carried about my professor's past? Knowledge I couldn't admit to knowing.

"What do you see?"

On this particular morning, the students didn't hesitate.

"Three angels, maybe gold, standing on a platform. Their wings are spread upwards. The three of them are carrying or elevating a glass cylinder."

"The angels are standing on a platform. It's round with three legs. The platform is surrounded by a cut-out design of gothic arches all the way around."

"The glass cylinder is as tall as the angels. This is a vertical piece. The cylinder is topped with an orb that has some kind of finial on top of it. Not a cross, but a kind of organic shape."

"There's something in the container."

"Mm-hmm ..." Kantorowicz smiled. We students had to squint and strain to figure out what the cylinder contained.

"It's a bone." Leigh Ann finally said.

"It's a reliquary," Quint said.

"Very good," said Kantorowicz. "All of you. This *is* a reliquary, a container intended to hold the relics, literally the leftovers, of a saint. By the way, it's a finger bone, if anyone was wondering."

Some nervous giggling and a few faint sounds of disgust from the students. Kantorowicz described how this reliquary was late 15$^{th}$-century Gothic, from the region between France and Flanders. To be more precise, it was called a philatory, a special kind of transparent "display" reliquary, as opposed to completely enclosed reliquaries that kept the relic hidden. A true act of faith to pray to the reliquary without ever being certain that the relic was inside the box. Kantorowicz clicked through several slides of reliquaries in a variety of shapes reflecting the body part they contained: arms, hands, feet, heads.

"Sometimes, of course, a relic is comprised of the saint's entire body, as is the case of Saints Peter and Paul in Rome, hence the status of Rome as a pilgrimage destination." He went on to tell us about other saints remains, or partial remains, and how the traffic in relics was big business in the Middle Ages. Saint James, or Santiago as he's known in Spanish, lies as a relic at Santiago de Compostela, the famous pilgrimage site on the Iberian peninsula.

"Except for his arm," Kantorowicz said. "That was stolen to be displayed as a relic in another church and was never recovered." He projected another slide.

"Here's a reliquary containing the entire remains of the obscure Saint Menoux, the patron saint of mental health. What do you see?"

"A stone sarcophagus."

"Elevated on four stone pillars"

"Very simple design. Two quatrefoil openings on the side, maybe covered with glass from the inside."

"To view the body?"

"What's with the giant opening at one end? It doesn't show anything of the relics."

"Not unless you stick your head into it," Kantorowicz said.

Giggles, and confused looks.

"Let me explain," said Kantorowicz. "Saint Menoux was greatly venerated in a region of France along the Allier river. A servant of the church, a fellow named Blaise, was tasked with caring for the relic. Blaise was 'simple of mind,' as they used to say. In the local dialect, he was *bredin*. Blaise wanted a better view of his patron than the tiny quatrefoil windows provided, so he cut this bigger hole into the sarcophagus, big enough to stick his head in and get a good look at Menoux." Kantorowicz let this image sink in, then continued.

"Having venerated the saint for several hours with his head in the hole, Blaise took his head out and was suddenly cured of his 'simple mindedness.' He was *débrediné*. The tomb containing Menoux's relics became known as a *débredinoire*, a 'de-crazifier,' if you will. It was said that anyone who stuck their head in the hole and prayed to the saint would be cured and/or protected from any mental illness."

"Did you ever visit Saint Menoux?" Leigh Ann asked.

Kantorowicz smiled and nodded.

"And…?"

"So far, so good," he shrugged. "Now. What do you see?"

Another image, this time of a piece of lace or embroidered cloth.

"Is that medieval?" I asked. "It looks very well preserved."

"As a holy relic, you would expect it to keep its shape," he said.

He told us the story of the Shrine of Saint Audrey, a 7th-century English princess. Audrey married young but had sworn a vow of perpetual virginity. After three years, her husband died. She married again for political reasons, but the second husband wasn't so keen on her chastity vows. When he made advances upon her, she escaped to a monastery at Ely. Audrey died of a horrible tumor on her neck, which she interpreted as G-d's retribution for the vanity of her wearing so many beautiful necklaces in her youth. Based on this story, medieval hawkers of merchandise began to sell lace necklaces at Saint Audrey's Fair, held every year on her feast day, and a great excuse for pilgrimage to Ely. By the 17th century, critics viewed the necklaces as shoddy and vulgar. They coined a new term to describe such cheap trinkets: "tawdry," a corruption of Sain*t Audrey*.

"This same over-veneration goes for relics," Kantorowicz continued, "the fetishizing of objects to the point of mass production. If you've ever visited Graceland, home of and shrine to the late great Elvis Presley. In the gift shop at Graceland, and I'm not making this up, tourists can purchase vials of 'Elvis sweat,' which the vendors claimed was authentic because Elvis was known to sweat profusely during his later concerts."

The discussion then turned to the proliferation of forged relics in the medieval period. Every student had heard the stories of the three heads of John the Baptist—at least two of them had to be fake; of the splinters from the True Cross, so plentiful that you could build a fleet of boats from all the wood; of the crucifixion nails, so numerous that if you melted them down you could forge ten suits of armor. The Protestant reformer John Calvin even joked about collecting all the relics in one place, to show 'that every Apostle has more than four bodies, and every Saint two or three'.

Kantorowicz then surprised us with a few relics that none of us had heard of. Mother's milk from the Virgin Mary. *Gross!* The foreskin of the baby Jesus. *Super gross!* My people, the children of Abraham, Isaac, and Jacob, practice circumcision— thank G-d I'm not a boy—but this is ridiculous! I mean, how did they even know to hang on to it when Jesus was still just a baby? And where did they keep it for all those years until Jesus proved who he was, post-crucifixion?

Of course, all of the aforementioned were forgeries.

The problem of forged relics was huge in the Middle Ages. This might be evidence of an "age of faith," where gullible, ignorant folk believed in anything presented to them. One might think that there were no skeptics. But one would be wrong.

"The Pardoner, from the *Canterbury Tales*, is an excellent example of this," said Kantorowicz. "According to Chaucer's description, the Pardoner had a pillowcase that he tried to pass off as the Blessed Mary's veil. He had a piece of the sail that Peter used whenever he went to sea, that is, until Jesus came along and offered him a better job. I imagine veneration of this relic, something that belonged to an apostle before he became an apostle, as akin to venerating Babe Ruth's high school geometry book before he became the homerun king."

Kantorowicz must have noticed the students' confusion at the reference.

"Babe Ruth?" he said.

"Before our time," Stone, formerly Quiet Guy, offered hesitantly.

"The Middle Ages is before your time!" said Kantorowicz. "Anyway … The Pardoner. He had a Latin cross covered in stones, and a bottle with some pig's bones." He returned to today's first image: the reliquary containing the human finger bone. Or was it a pig bone?

"What happens when a relic is forged?" he asked. "What does the forgery say about the culture that created it? Look at *what* they forge, and you'll see what *matters* to them. To forge a relic is to confirm the belief, or at least the hope, in the ability of the saints to intervene in the lives of ordinary people. The great scholar Peter Brown argued that the cult of the saints was a continuation of the patronage system of the Romans. In ancient Rome, a person in need could ask a favor of a patron, who would grant the favor in return for some later favor. If you've ever seen the *Godfather* movies, you'll know what I mean."

Only one student laughed.

"Really!?" Kantorowicz feigned exasperation again. "All right … when the Roman Empire went into decline, so did its patronage system. The people had to find something to replace it."

"And they called them *patron* saints!" I blurted out.

"Quick," said Kantorowicz.

"Yes?" said Quinton Quick.

"No, I mean Ms. Isaacson's reply was … never mind. Yes. Patron saints. According to this belief, saints' relics had a kind of magic, as the anthropologists might call it. Praying to the relics could help the crops grow, cure illnesses, even help you find your misplaced keys. This was powerful stuff."

Kantorowicz looked at his watch, then shut down the classroom computer. Normally, this signaled the seminar coming to an end, but he held up his right hand, crutch dangling from his arm.

"Before you go," he said, "I'd like to try out an idea with you." He had been standing for the entire class, but sat down now, which I took as a gesture of intimacy.

"This entire semester we've been talking about the visual. How the visual is a kind of language. Today we talked about relics, which I would argue communicate something to the believer, even when those relics are fake. Okay. So far so good. Now here's my slightly crazy theory: I'm wondering if Twitter messages aren't a kind of modern, or post-modern relic."

He looked around the seminar table, made eye contact with each student.

"A tweet is a message. It's made up of words. But those words are contained in a specific, standardized frame, which renders the words as more than just words. The words live in the context of the Twitter frame, which makes the message greater than if the words stood alone.

"The same thing happens with the words in a medieval illumination. They enter the context of an illuminated manuscript and achieve higher meaning when the illuminator frames the words in a banderole, representing the speech of a given figure, like a speech balloon in a comic strip. When the evening news or the internet reports that the President of the United States 'said such and such,' they don't just tell us the words he used on Twitter. They tell us that he *tweeted*. And then, to lend authenticity to their report, they show us a picture of the tweet.

"The visual composition of a tweet is familiar to us all, I think. The frame is a rectangle with a horizontal bias. In the upper left-hand corner of every tweet is an image, chosen by the tweeter, which may be biographical, a selfie, or an avatar or some other symbol. No matter what icon is used, it tells us something about the tweeter. Next to the image is the tweeter's name, which may be their real name or a pseudonym. Under the name is the tweeter's 'handle'—@so-and-so—which locates the tweeter in cyberspace, giving the reader the maybe false sense that the tweeter can be tracked down and found, if need be.

"The Twitter frame also contains information about the tweeter, intended to lend authority and credence: How many followers does the tweeter enjoy? How many likes for this tweet? How many retweets? This is the equivalent of the oily fingerprints on the medieval manuscript. The more smudges on a folio, the more the medieval reader preferred that page. It's the medieval version of 'liking' a tweet.

"In fact, the entire tactile experience of your smart phones and tablets replicates the tactile experience of reading medieval manuscripts. This isn't an original idea of mine. Other scholars have said it before me. What is original, I think, is the notion that the words in a tweet don't exist outside of the Twitter frame. Linguists used to talk about the 'rapid fading effect' of human speech. You say words that represent your thoughts. Sound waves come out of your mouth. Some of these are intercepted and interpreted by your listeners, but after the sound waves are gone there's nothing left. In contrast, a tweet is a relic of oral culture. It remains as an object of veneration and skepticism for as long as the great shrine of 'the Cloud' exists."

He looked at his watch again.

"I'm afraid I've kept you past the allotted time. We can pick this up next week."

# CHAPTER 25
## Dance of the Internet Trolls

Joseph Goebbels
@realJosephGoebbels
Make the lie BIG, keep it SIMPLE, keep saying it and eventually they will believe it
8:45PM-June 1, 1933
3.6M Retweets 10M Likes

Donald J. Trump
@notrealDonaldTrump
Love it @realJosephGoebels! RT. How about this: "what was RACIST about that story? The story wasn't RACIST just inaccurate and wrong." #doubledown
12:35PM-August 28, 2013
8.7K Retweets 90K Likes

Just A Southern Boy
@14/88
Big tobacco cos. used cartoons like @JoeCamel 2 hook kids on nicotine. Want 2 do same for WP logo. Make it funny & friendly & welcoming.
1:45PM-November 17, 2010
2K Retweets 1.9K Likes

**White Pride By My Side**
@rahowa2000

Do u know Pepe the Frog? Character in comic book by Matt Furie, *Boy's Club*. Good possibilities for memes.

8:45PM-November 17, 2010

**1.4K** Retweets   **7.9K** Likes

**Hitler Lover**
@BlutundEhre

 What about milk? Spread theory that only white Europeans can digest white milk. Lactose intolerance a sign of inferior races.

3:30PM-December 7, 2018

**2.4K** Retweets     **5.9K** Likes

**Mein Kampf – Your Kampf**
@88isGreat

RT. @BlutundEhre! White milk = White Power! #MilkTwitter

8:05PM-December 7, 2018

**1K** Retweets     **2.3K** Likes

**Blood Cross Crusader**
@bcc4ever

Sneakers! Make New Balance the official shoe of the White Race! LOL #AYAK

8:45PM-December 17, 2018

**3.4K** Retweets     **10.9K** Likes

 Mein Kampf – Your Kampf
@88isGreat

@rahowa2000! #Sad Frog, #Smug Frog, #Angry Pepe"

10:35PM-November 17, 2010

**3.4K** Retweets   **10.9K** Likes

 Joseph Goebbels
@realJosephGoebbels

Daily Stormer playbook: "Genuine, raging vitriol is a turnoff to the overwhelming majority of people. The unindoctrinated should not be able to tell if we're joking or not." #KeepItLite BTW: I'm not joking!

8:05PM-January 15, 2018

**3.4K** Retweets    **10.9K** Likes

 Donald J. Trump
@notrealDonaldTrump

..... very fine people on both sides. **LOL**

1:00PM-August 12, 2017

**45K** Retweets   **1.2M** Likes

 Hitler Lover
@BlutundEhre

@88isGreat. White milk makes WP smarter

8:45PM-December 17, 2018

**3.4K** Retweets    **10.9K** Likes

**White Pride By My Side**
@rahowa2000

"Okay" hand sign as meme? Fingers form letters "WP" = White Power. Whadaya think?

6:32PM-December 15, 2019

**3.4K** Retweets   **10.9K** Likes

**Hitler Lover**
@BlutundEhre

@rahowa2000! Bee-you-tee-full!!! #WP

7:45PM-December 15, 2019

**29K** Retweets      **107K** Likes

**Joseph Goebbels**
@realJosephGoebbels

RT. @BlutundEhre! @rohowa2000! Subtle and ubiquitous. LOVE IT!

8:45PM-December 19, 2019

**3.4K** Retweets   **10.9K** Likes

**Hitler Lover**
@BlutundEhre

@rahowa2000! What about Moon Man?

8:45PM-December 17, 2015

**1K** Retweets      **6.9K** Likes

White Pride By My Side
@rahowa2000

@BlutundEhre! @rahowa2000! MacDonald's ad campaign c. 1980. Now symbol of WP!

8:45PM-December 17, 2015

**3K** Retweets    **18K** Likes

Donald J. Trump
@notrealDonaldTrump

Those Tweets were NOT RACIST. I don't have a racist BONE in my body! I'm the LEAST RACIST person in the world. #GoBackWhereYouCameFrom. #MAGA ....

3:45AM-July 23, 2019

**22K** Retweets  **109K** Likes

White Pride By My Side
@rahowa2000

How about an "official truck" for WP?

8:47PM-December 15, 2019

**3.4K** Retweets    **10.9K** Likes

Just A Southern Boy
@14/88

@rahowa2000! WHITE pick-up w gunrack & Stars-n-Bars in rear window. #WPTruck

2:10PM-December 19, 2019

**2K** Retweets    **1.9K** Likes

**White Pride By My Side**
@rahowa2000

@14/88! Has to be a Ford. Henry Ford +
Hitler = BFFs! WHITE F150 4x4!
#ProtocolsOfZion

3:02PM-December 19, 2019

**3.4K** Retweets   **10.9K** Likes

**Hist Prof on a Mission**
@k2bawdy

@BlutundEhre! @rahowa2000! @14/88!
@realJosephGoebbels! @88isGreat!
@bcc4ever! We are coming for you, you
RACIST BASTARDS! #FightIgnorance

6:47PM-October 3, 2020

**1** Retweets   **14** Likes

                                        8:00AM-October 4, 2020

**@k2bawdy:** We're writing to let you know
that your account features will remain limited
for the allotted time due to violations of the
Twitter Rules, specifically our rules against
abusive behavior. To ensure that people feel
safe expressing diverse opinions and beliefs
on our platform, we do not .....

                                        8:00AM-October 4, 2020

.... tolerate language that crosses the line
into abuse. This includes behavior that
harasses, intimidates, or uses fear to silence
another person's voice.

CHAPTER 26

## Pope Joan

Halfway through Stark's Thursday seminar, she started a new topic.

"I want to tell you story," she said. "It's an interesting story, but one that isn't true." Everyone in the class leaned in.

"My question to you is this: even *if* the story isn't true, can it be *useful* to us in understanding the past? Today's story is the legend of Pope Joan."

Stark looked around the room one more time to confirm that all eyes were on her.

"We first hear about a female pope from a chronicler named Jean de Mailly. Jean was a Dominican friar, which means he was a member of the educated elite. Friar Jean was active in the 13th century in the city of Metz, in northeastern France. He compiled an influential collection of legends about the saints, which tells us something about his interests. He also wrote a 'universal chronicle of Metz.' Remember that a chronicle is a narrative of the happenings in a given time and place, but it isn't a history. Because?"

For a moment, we all sat dumb, unaccustomed to her asking a question so early in her presentation. A woman in the front row looked behind her at the other students, as if checking in for the okay to proceed, then spoke.

"A chronicle isn't a history because it doesn't have any analysis. It just tells its story like it's true. No questions asked."

"Good," Stark said. She continued.

"Jean de Mailly writes about the female pope in his chronicle of Metz. He sets the story in 1099. He doesn't give her a name."

Stark told us the chronicler's first claim: that the female pope couldn't be found in any papal records.

"Perhaps this was to justify not knowing her name. Yet he seems to know quite a lot about her rise to power within the church, starting as a secretary to the Roman *curia*, then being named Cardinal, then becoming pope. According to Jean, her success came from her character and talents, but also from the fact that she disguised herself as a man.

"Claim number two," Stark said. "The turning point in the story: One day, while mounting a horse, the unnamed female pope gives birth to a baby, as often happens."

Stark paused for the students' laughter. That laughter ended, however, and was followed by horror, as she related the woman's fate.

"Upon seeing the pope give birth, thus outing herself as a woman, the angry mob tied her feet to the tail of the horse and stoned her as she was dragged through the streets of Rome. Jean adds that the dragging lasted for 'half a league.' Authenticity is in the details. They buried the female pope on the spot where she died and left a sign there to mark the event. *'Petre, Pater Patrum, Papisse Prodito Partum.'* Oh Peter, Father of Fathers, betray the childbearing of the woman Pope. The Latin has better alliteration."

The story raised all sorts of questions—which for the moment, nobody asked. How good was the female pope's disguise as a man that she never got caught? Was the woman pope the first medieval cross-dresser, even before Joan of Arc? Even if the entire papal court was in the dark, there had to be, like, at least one man who knew the female pope's secret: the guy who knocked her up! How/why did he keep her secret for the nine months of her pregnancy?

"The female pope first gets a name," Stark said, "later in the 13th century. Martin of Opava, another Dominican chronicler, calls her Joan in his *Chronicon Pontificum et Imperatorum*,

Chronicle of the Popes and Emperors. Please forgive a brief tangent so I can tell you about this amazing book."

According to Stark, Martin's *Chronicon* was a major innovation in pedagogy and graphic design. All of the content was derivative, copied from other sources—therefore not very useful to historians. But the *Chronicon's* presentation was groundbreaking. The book was laid out in two columns, one for popes and one for emperors, lining them up chronologically according to the years of their reign. Every page of the book had exactly fifty lines, corresponding to fifty years, so the material is presented in manageable chunks.

"Martin's work is a chronicle and not a history because …?" Stark asked. A smartass in the back row spoke first.

"Because it's called *Chronicon.*" Some laughter from students. Stark rolled her eyes.

"No," said the same woman in the front row. "It's a chronicle because it records events and offers no analysis."

"Right again," Stark said.

"Wait a minute," I said. "Martin's *Chronicon* doesn't offer any new information. It's derivative, as Professor Stark says. But there is an implicit analysis in the way the material is presented. Fifty years per page to present chunks of time. That could be periodization. And the side-by-side presentation of popes and emperors? That's to help students make connections. Why did this pope from column A do what he did when that emperor from column B was in power? Those are questions about context."

Stark didn't say anything, but she had a big smile on her face. That felt good.

"Okay, let's get back to Pope Joan," said Stark. "According to Martin, the pope in her male disguise was known as 'John Anglicus' or 'John of Mainz.' Martin messes with the chronology, placing John/Joan in the 850s, between popes Leo IV and Benedict III."

Stark outlined Martin's version of the legend, which was much more detailed than that of his predecessor. John Anglicus served as pope for two years, seven months, and four days.

"What a surprise it was to discover John was a woman! So far, not much new in the story. Then Martin lays down some serious back story."

When Joan was just a girl, she was taken to Athens by her boyfriend, who had her dress as a boy. In Athens, she developed into a great scholar. When she came to Rome, she became a teacher of the liberal arts and the higher disciplines of law and theology. The Romans so revered her intellect that they elected her pope. (Martin has none of that stuff about Joan rising through the ranks.) Then, Joan's downfall. She got pregnant, miscalculated the baby's arrival, and, like, gave birth on a horse while riding in the papal procession from St. Peter's Basilica to the Lateran Papal Palace. Martin was masterful in his details. The road taken by Pope Joan was called the *Via Sacra*, Holy Way. But after the embarrassment of the female pope giving birth in the street, it became known as the "shunned street." Martin didn't discuss how Joan died, but, as in the earlier chronicle, he buried her in the street where she gave birth. According to Martin, Joan isn't listed in the papal records because of her gender, and "on account of the foulness" of the matter.

"In one edition of the *Chronicon*," Stark continued, "Joan was defrocked and served many years of penance, dying years later. Her illegitimate son grew up to become a bishop and had his mother buried in his cathedral when she died."

I heard the words "illegitimate son" and thought of Kantorowicz. Amazing how this stigma, this taboo, carries on for generations. It's got nothing to do with biology and is entirely constructed by culture. I caught my mind wandering and did my best to refocus, but Stark had moved on. She was talking about a strange chair fitted with an open toilet seat, on which subsequent papal candidates would sit in order to have their testicles checked out, to prove they were male.

"*Duos habet et bene pendentes*," Stark said with a smile. "He has two, and they dangle nicely."

Stark pointed out how the legend of Pope Joan persisted and was enhanced in various genres. The Renaissance poet

Petrarch claimed that it, like, rained blood for three days and three nights when Joan's subterfuge was revealed. His contemporary Boccaccio included the story of Pope Joan in his *De Claris Mulieribus*, Concerning Famous Women.

"The legend of Pope Joan was also used as a political tool to critique the papacy. If a woman could rise to the office of pope, then the church must be corrupt (it should not have allowed this), or at least incompetent (it should have known). Anti-papist protestants had a field day with it.

"Let's go back to the question I asked at the beginning of the class," Stark said. "If the story's made up, how can it help us understand the past?"

"It's not about the past," I said, without waiting for Stark to call on anyone. I could feel the eyes of my classmates shooting laser beams, but I didn't care. "It's about the cultures that constructed the legend."

"Say more."

"Even as it shifts over time, the legend tells us all about contemporary attitudes toward women. Medieval men, especially in the church, viewed women as deceptive—Joan disguises herself; manipulative—Joan works her way to the top; and lustful—even as the highest cleric, Joan can't remain celibate. It doesn't matter if Joan really existed. The attitudes about her did exist and they're in the story of Joan for all to see."

Seminar ended. Approving looks from Stark. A mixed bag of envy and respect from my classmates. Oh, well. As I left the room, I began comparing Pope Joan and Kantorowicz. Both stories had constructed narratives. Both had secrets. Both had illegitimate children.

At least Kantorowicz's mother wasn't dragged through town tied to a horse.

CHAPTER 27

A Mysterious Emblem

It was a late autumn day but I wandered around campus ignoring the fall foliage, unable to shake my obsessive comparison of the fake pope with my possibly fake professor. Before I knew it, I found myself in the history building, standing in Kantorowicz's doorway.

"Ms. Isaacson. To what do I owe the pleasure?" He gestured to the two chairs in front of his desk as he moved toward the window to start the kettle. It was only my second visit to his office, but this must have been how he always did it. Visitor arrives, make tea. I remained standing, set my backpack on one of the chairs and looked around the room at all of his books.

*Don't make it obvious. Put it into his shelves or leave it under some papers.*

I'd been carrying around the tricked-out version of *The King's Too Bawdy*, the one with the bug, ever since Mapp gave it to me. It wasn't my original intention in coming here, but this seemed as good a time as any. I unzipped my pack.

"Mind if I check out your books?"

*He's not going to think twice if he sees his own book.*

"Please do." Kantorowicz turned to set my cup of tea on his desk in front of my place.

"Oh, sorry. I take milk."

I needed him facing away from me so I could take action. Once he turned his back and stepped toward the minifridge, I pulled the book from my pack, clasped it against my chest and took two steps toward the bookshelf by the door.

"Here we are. Milk."

I could feel him turn toward me, heard him taking his place again behind his desk. I continued facing the bookshelf, pretending to casually study his library. Just at chest level, I spied a group of books that seemed the right height. I pulled one of them out halfway and tilted my head as if I were looking at the cover. My heart was in my throat. In as smooth a motion as I could muster, I took the bugged copy of *The King's Too Bawdy* and slipped it into the slot I'd created, pushed it in gently so it was even with the other books on the shelf.

"What can I do for you, Ms. Isaacson?"

I spun around. Mission accomplished. Do they really say that? I could still feel the pounding in my chest. I didn't have a plan for what to do next, but I tried to act cool.

"I've just come from Stark's seminar," I said, "and I, uhh … was bothered by something we discussed."

"Perhaps you should speak with Professor Stark."

"Yes. No. Well … I think I, like, need another perspective."

"All right."

"So, in Stark's class, we were, like, talking about the Pope Joan legend. You know it, right?"

He smiled and nodded. Idiot! Of course, he knows it. This is what happens when you improvise.

"Yeah. Okay. So, I'm, like, trying to connect, or maybe reconcile, something from the Pope Joan story with something you said in your last class. You talked about relics becoming part of the cultural consciousness, even when they're forgeries. And Joan, in the story, experiences a terrible outcome because she pretended to be pope. She's a kind of living forgery."

Kantorowicz smiled. I still wasn't sure where I was headed with this. I must have seemed like every other struggling student.

"Joan gets punished for her deception," I continued. "She gets dragged by a horse and stoned. And that makes sense to me. People don't like being deceived, so maybe she got what she deserved, even though it reflects the church's rampant misogyny in those days."

I looked around the room again, hoping to find a point to my rambling. He must have had hundreds of books. I looked at the one I had just shelved. It looked to me like the proverbial sore thumb. Worse. It was one of those giant rubber thumbs that clowns use when they bang themselves with a hammer: swollen, throbbing, grotesque. I was sure he would spot the planted book, then realized that my staring at it wasn't helping.

"So, Joan gets her punishment, but she leaves behind a son, who's illegitimate."

*OMFG! Is this where I'm headed!?*

"What do you think happens to him? I mean, being born a bastard was tough back then. What does an illegitimate son do with his life? What can he do to, like, change his station?"

Long pause. Kantorowicz took a sip of tea and looked out the window. I did the same. When he finally spoke, he didn't make direct eye contact.

"You're a very sensitive reader," he said. "Not many people would think about the son in all of this. The rest of the story is so dramatic, but you're right. There he is."

There was another long pause, another long sip of tea, and a long glance out the window. He looked up at a cork board hanging behind his desk—pinned with layers of reminders and calls for papers—and removed a single sheet of paper with what looked like a kid's drawing. He cradled it in his hand, studying it, as he resumed talking.

"How are you and Mr. Quick doing with my little project? Are you working well together? I hope it's not too much of a distraction from your regular work."

That was it then. We were done with the earlier topic. I'm not sure what I expected him to say. Oh, by the way, I'm also a bastard son. Here's how it worked out for me ...

"We're fine," I said. "Quint is great to work with. I hope to know half as much as he does when I've been here that long." I could feel my cheeks getting warm. What the hell!? I shifted the conversation to all the hate symbols we'd researched, hoping this squishy feeling would go away. Kantorowicz seemed pleased.

"I'm grateful and excited both of you are willing to work on this," he said, then looked again at the drawing in his hands. "I dug this out a couple of days ago and thought I'd share it with you. There might be some possibilities here."

As he passed me the drawing, I joked that I shouldn't handle it without archival gloves. He laughed and assured me it would be okay, just this once. The drawing was rendered in colored pencils and reminded me of drawings I used to do when I was nine or ten, of whatever medieval fantasy was in my head at the time. It was a picture of a shield, but in an odd shape. It took the form of a French escutcheon, a heraldic shield, but broader and more squashed down, with a horizontal orientation. The shield, or emblem—yes, better—the *emblem* depicted two registers. The top register was charged with a row of five four-pointed stars, with longer arms on the stars' horizontal axis. The bottom register was charged with a dramatic lightning bolt, running upward from sinister to dexter at a 45-degree angle. The lightning bolt crossed in front of a rotary gear. The two icons together evoked those Fascist or Soviet images that promoted the totalitarian strength of factory workers. The gear and lightning bolt floated on a red and silver field of horizontal stripes.

"I've never seen anything like this," I said. "What is it?"

"I've no idea," Kantorowicz said. "I drew it when I was a boy. I used to draw it all the time."

"May I take a picture of it?" I took out my phone.

"Oh, you can have it. I must have dozens of them around here, or at home."

I assured him that a picture would be good enough, laid the drawing on his desk and snapped one. There was something spooky about the drawing that made it feel awkward to take it. I put my phone away but didn't get up to leave. He asked me if there was anything else, but I just sat there.

"Are you having doubts?" he said. "It's a rather odd project."

"It's not that," I said. "Just … can you tell me more about how it's supposed to work? We design this super, new and improved neo-Nazi symbol, and then what? What happens next?"

"It's better you don't know," he said calmly. "Nothing sinister. It's like the double-blind protocol in a drug trial. No one can know who gets the real meds and who gets the placebo. To be certain of how our archaeological experiment is working, there need to be controls."

"Okay," I said, disappointed and—channeling Quint—skeptical.

"It's really nothing bad," he said again, and proceeded to give me an example of what he intended.

"A few years ago, citizens in the quaint German town of Wunsiedel were confronted with an upcoming neo-Nazi march. Rudolph Hess was buried in the town and the neo-Nazis had marched there for many years to celebrate Hess as a Nazi hero. The townspeople wanted to protest, but they didn't want to risk the usual aggressive confrontation that could lead to violence. So, in this particular year, someone got the bright idea to turn the march into a fundraiser against fascism, like 'Walk for the Cure.' People pledged donations based on how many feet each neo-Nazi marched. The greater the distance, the bigger the donation. Townspeople showed up at the march and actually cheered on the fascists. 'Keep going,' they chanted. 'Every goosestep you take is another dollar to fight fascism.' This disrupted the neo-Nazis' hold on reality. If they kept marching, it meant they were helping the anti-fascists. If they stopped marching, it meant the anti-fascists had successfully stopped the march. Either way, the neo-Nazis lost.

"There are a million ways to fight hatred," Kantorowicz concluded. "I prefer cleverness and wit."

I'd never thought of it that way. The fucking Nazis filled me with such rage, it was hard to, like, imagine making fun of them. I smiled at Kantorowicz, zipped up my backpack, and stood to leave.

"Thanks," I said. "For your time."

Walking out the door, I looked again at the bugged book that I'd reverse-purloined onto Kantorowicz's shelves. Mapp would be able to monitor all of his conversations now. I immediately wondered how I could break in later and purloin it back again.

What would Quint say about all of this?

CHAPTER 28

Chartres and Minos

*Quo vadis, Quick? Where are you going?*

*The only place I should be going is to my desk to start writing my goddamned dissertation.*

*Come on, Kantorowicz! Could you find a worse time to give me this "experimental archeology" bullshit? Even though you'd tell me to say no if I was too busy, who are you kidding? As if free will were an option when the lion asks the rabbit to jump.*

*Your "little project" is taking up all my time. Not just time on task, but space in my brain that should be devoted to Morien, my biracial, multiethnic knight of the round table—worthy, unexplored topic of my looming dissertation.*

*No chance of passing for white in the Middle Ages. Morien was all black. Black as pitch, black as burnt brands. Black as a raven. All black. What of it?*

*A different world than mine, than Belle de Costa Greene's. What was it like for her? What choice did she have?*

*And who am I to judge? Mama black. Daddy white. I'm Obama in reverse.*

*Chill out, man. The universe is random. Not everything's connected.*

*Who are you, Kantorowicz? Collaborator? Double agent? What's your plan? Invent a hate symbol—a fake, a forgery—and hope the haters love it? Then expose the forgery, pull the rug out from under them and yell, "Surprise! Fooled ya!" Put that way, Mapp begins to make a lot of sense.*

*"He's not who he appears to be," says Mapp. And I shrug him off and think he's crazy because I KNOW YOU! But then I follow the trail, conduct research of my own using methods YOU taught me, and the evidence points to Mapp being right.*

*Special Agent Mapp, I don't trust you as far as I can throw you. You've forced a dilemma on me: to spy or not to spy? To watch the world crumble under the jackboot or do something? To remain a historian or become an activist. Stark would be horrified.*

*It's all a distraction from the work I should be doing. And the greatest distraction: Molly Isaacson.*

*She's starting to make me laugh and I hate that. She gets my jokes because you have to be the biggest nerd on the planet to get my jokes, which she is, and I hate that. I come to the carrel now and know she's been there because it smells like her.*

*Quo vadis, Quick? To Chartres, the continuous path where you can't get lost? Or to Minos, where the minotaur awaits?*

CHAPTER 29
## Chaney, Goodman, and Schwerner

Quint began avoiding me.

At first, I thought he was just busy, but then I knew it was more than that. Every time I came to the carrel, he was just finishing up. When I'd spot him at Insomnia, he avoided eye contact, then, like, scattered when I approached, suddenly too busy to talk. We hadn't had a brainstorming session for the neo-Nazi project in weeks. I did my best to work on it, but it wasn't the same. I worried that Kantorowicz would start asking about our progress. I had nothing to report. Likewise, I hadn't heard from Mapp in a while. He could've been hiding in the book stacks or inside the espresso machine—*you won't see me unless I want you to see me*—but I had to think he'd been looking for an update on our "subject."

Did I miss Quint? I missed Mom when I first went to Smith. This was different. As many languages as I had, I didn't have language for this. I needed to talk to someone. Another woman? Not mom. After twelve weeks at Yale, I'd managed to make not a single female friend. What about Stark? Not a friend, but at least a woman. Would she understand? Be helpful? Was it even appropriate to consult a prof about personal stuff?

Stark's office was very different from Kantorowicz's. Bigger by a third, though she seemed to have twice as many books. Kantorowicz's library had no rhyme or reason I could discern. Stark's books were organized according to color, shelved around the room in ROY G BIV order. "I've tried other systems," she told me, "but this works for me. I have all the authors and titles in my head. If I need to consult Cappelli's *Lexicon Abbreviaturarum*, I know it's a yellow book, so I go to the yellow stack. After that, everything's alphabetical. I find it soothing."

Stark also devoted an entire wall to diplomas and certificates and plaques, unlike Kantorowicz, who displayed none of these. Hanging in balanced composition were her sheepskin from Princeton, several citations from the Medieval Academy, a plaque that declared her "best teacher" of 1995, and a picture of her standing next to Joseph Strayer, her grad school advisor who had also worked at the CIA.

The most telling thing about Stark's office, the biggest difference between her office and Kantorowicz's, was that her door was open. Not metaphorically open, as in "my door's always open, so please come in." It was literally open, whenever she was there. This meant that I didn't have to knock. No one did. You simply stood in her doorway and she invited you in.

"Do come in, Ms. Isaacson. Everything going well with your studies? Adapting to the grad school life?"

"Yes. Yes, I think so."

"Well, then, how can I help?"

Where to start? There is this guy. I like him. You know, *like* him like him. Good G-d, this could not be the kind of help she meant. How can I ask her what I want to ask without sounding like an immature idiot?

"I need a woman's perspective," I said. "I'm trying to … find balance … between the personal and professional."

"Oh, my," she said. "Is that a problem already? You've only just arrived. Have you met someone? Is it distracting you from your work? Women's completion rates are higher than men's—67% the last time I looked, vs. 57% for men—but marriage and pregnancy continue to be a bigger challenge for women working on PhDs. Oh, my God. You're not *pregnant*, are you? *Are* you pregnant?" She asked that last question in a hushed tone, as if to draw me into her confidence.

Are you kidding me? I thought. If this was meant as an invitation to open up, it had the opposite effect. I decided on the spot to switch the topic away from Quint.

"I suppose it's not really about the *personal* and professional," I said. "It's more, like … *all* … professional."

"Oh, thank goodness," she said. "Okay. I'm listening."

Why the hell did I come here? I hadn't done so the whole semester. I was doing great in Stark's seminar, but in that moment, I looked like a flake. I felt the ancient curse of not being able to stop myself rising before me. Oh, well. In for a penny …

"What kind of person is Professor Kantorowicz?"

"Hm … Like any other person, I suppose. Maybe more so."

In for a pound …

"Is he, like, a man of his word?"

"Why? What's he asked you to do?"

"He invited me to work on a project. It sounds challenging and fun and everything a grad student would want, especially getting to work with a prof she admires."

"And?"

"I'm not sure what impact it's meant to have. It could be something brilliant, something that strikes a blow at a great evil in the world."

"Yes?"

"But it might turn out to be something hateful. It might be evil itself."

"I don't understand."

"If someone did something that they believed was right, but it turned out to be wrong, what should they do? And if that person had to tell the authorities, would the person who asked them to do the thing understand? Could that person be forgiven?"

"What exactly is this project?"

"I shouldn't tell you. I can't!"

Stark stood from her desk and quietly went to close the door. As she returned to sit down, she moved slowly around the room, caressing the colors of the rainbow.

"Ok. I'm going to tell you something that *I* probably shouldn't." Stark paused. "I'm telling you because, in spite of all the rumors, Abe Kantorowicz is a good man, and I want to relieve any concerns you might have about working with him."

Stark looked at me to make sure I understood her motives, but also to confirm my understanding. What she was about to say was sensitive and confidential.

"It was 1990, or maybe 91, a book came out by a historian named Norman Cantor. *Inventing the Middle Ages*. In some ways, it was a brilliant, post-modern approach to understanding the medievalists who created our discipline. Cantor wrote about Tolkien and C.S. Lewis, about Strayer and Marc Bloch, and many others, including Ernst Kantorowicz, the father of your professor, my colleague and friend."

She confirmed the genealogy that Quint had discovered. I sat, amazed.

"Cantor's book was not kind to Ernst Kantorowicz. He accused the father, with another German historian named Percy Schramm, of being a 'Nazi twin.' With Schramm, the case was clear. He'd acted as the official historian for the German High Command, and after the war he was an apologist for the Nazis. With Kantorowicz, the story was more complicated. He was certainly a fan of strong leaders and was proud of being a German, in all the ways we think of when we think of the Nazis. But Kantorowicz was Jewish. His mother died in a concentration camp. And later in life, Kantorowicz rejected anything that had to do with National Socialism. Cantor's book was a one-sided hit job. Completely unfair. Our Kantorowicz, the son, was deeply hurt by it. In sharing his feelings about Cantor's book, he told me more about his difficult relationship with his father."

I wished that Quint could be sitting next to me. So much of what he'd found was confirmed, and Stark was filling in many cracks in the story.

"When Abe was born, Kantorowicz, the father, denied his son and abandoned the mother, who was apparently much younger, and she was left to fend for herself. I think the mother's name was Anna."

Amanda, I thought, but I didn't correct her.

"Anna, or whatever her name, was a very bright and talented singer. Abe told me she went to Westminster Choir College, which was a music conservatory in the Princeton township. She took a job between classes in the library at Princeton University, where the elder Kantorowicz taught and where they met. Not much more detail there. I think Anna maybe had a trust fund. In any case, she and Abe weren't destitute, but they lived simply. This was the 1960s, the era of the civil rights movement. Anna left Princeton and got a job doing voter registration in the South. In Alabama, no ... Mississippi. She brought young Abe with her wherever she went. I can't say that was the best parenting choice."

Stark paused again, picked up a blank piece of paper from her desk and examined it between her thumb and fingers. She continued.

"Anna worked on the voter registration stuff with a fellow named Bill Turner, a Black man who'd been a student with her at the choir college. I asked Abe if they were a couple. Maybe she followed him to the South, or he followed her. He didn't know. His mother always told him that Turner was a much better student than she was, but that she was a better singer. Helping Black folks register to vote was dangerous in 1964, but they were both committed to the cause. It was the same year Chaney, Goodman, and Schwerner, the three civil rights workers, went missing and ended up dead. That sort of thing happened a lot, but theirs was the most famous case. One day, Anna and Turner were walking with Abe down an isolated farm road. They heard a truck on the road behind them, so they moved over to the side. Then ..."

Stark took a deep, shaky breath.

"It's so devastating. I can still remember when Abe first told me the story."

She sat quietly for a moment longer.

"They heard the truck and moved out of the way, but the truck accelerated and headed right for them. Abe was only five or six. It was a white truck, he told me. I can see him, seeing himself, as he told his story. His eyes get wider, transfixed, as he witnesses the *HUGE WHITE TRUCK with a grill that looked like TEETH!* He told me how he stood frozen, unable to move, as the truck raced toward him. Anna just had time to grab him and jump to safety, but the truck still caught Abe's leg, crushing all the bones and muscles under its weight. Bill Turner tried to run but was hit full on and killed instantly."

Stark's eyes filled with tears and she turned away, looking out her office window until she regained control.

"I'm sorry," she said. "Abe told me that story almost thirty years ago, right after Cantor's book came out. He told me he had nightmares about that white truck well into his college years. He said his mother made sure he remembered Turner's name. Abe asked her if Turner had saved his life. 'No,' she told him. 'No. You and I got lucky, but there was nothing heroic about Bill's death. Didn't save you. Couldn't save himself. It was just a stupid, senseless death. The murder of yet another Black man by a white man filled with hate. But we still have to remember Bill. He was a person. A human being. A friend.' Abe was just a kid. The whole thing must have been so traumatic. But his mother made sure he remembered Bill Turner."

"Is that where the crutch comes from?" I knew it was a stupid question as soon as I said it.

"I guess at that age, when kids are still growing, severe damage like that can disrupt the healing process, even stop bones from growing further. I'm not sure exactly, but it could be something like that."

"Did it make it into the news? Like Chaney, Goodman, and Schwerner?"

Stark shook her head.

"No. Abe told me that he tried to find something—after he'd grown up—some coverage in the paper, but there was nothing. Turner was the only one killed and my best guess is that he didn't warrant the same coverage as the other murdered civil rights workers because no whites had been killed with him. If it got reported at all, it was probably just another 'unfortunate' traffic accident in the South."

We sat a while longer. Stark looked at the blue range of books. I stared out the window and watched the afternoon turn to dusk.

"You asked me the kind of person Professor Kantorowicz is," said Stark. "I think that single event from his childhood informs everything he became. He loved his mother and admired her work for social justice. Her work. I told him that watching a Black man get killed in front of his own eyes must have had an impact, but Abe shook his head. 'Why do I need to see a Black man die to fight racism?' he said to me. 'Isn't racism bad enough without that?'"

"Maybe it's too horrifying to make that connection," I said.

"Maybe. But if you ask him why he fights racism, he only talks about his mom."

Stark smiled and looked at me with kind eyes.

"What sort of man is Abe Kantorowicz? A good man. A decent man."

CHAPTER 30
Winter Break

Thanksgiving came and went. I paid, like, an obligatory four-day visit to the parental units in Houston. Quint stayed in New Haven, as far as I knew. The semester ended uneventfully—aced all my intro grad courses. Then the longer winter break was upon us. Other academics may take vacations or go on holiday or simply chill out during the break between semesters. Medievalists do not. I don't, like, mean to brag, as if our dedication to our work makes us superior human beings. I leave that for others to judge. It's more likely desperation.

For grad students, they needed to finish their dissertations and get out on the market before their funding ran out, a point in time that was always, like, just around the corner. Medievalist grad students were the main reason the libraries remained open during the break, with the exception of Christmas Day and New Year's Eve and Day. If we thought it would do any good, we would have lobbied for those days to be open as well.

For professors, getting tenure and maintaining status in the pecking order both played a role, especially in a discipline less and less understood or appreciated, with faculty jobs always threatened as "next on the chopping block." Walking past the DOH building at any hour of the day, I saw lights shining from Kantorowicz's office window. The same was true for Stark's. Lights were visible from the outside, but from the inside her door was closed, even though she was there, belying the "my-door-is-always-open" vibe she gave off during the regular semester.

Many grad students and profs share at least some elements of an unhealthy lifestyle: hunched over books, reading under dim light, preferring libraries and archives to time at the pool or gym, consuming caffeine as if it were a sacrament, choosing pastries over fruits and vegetables, as if free will didn't exist. Once research becomes more important than food and sleep, the doctor knows that the disease of medievalism has taken hold and there's no cure.

The four weeks of winter break represented unbroken time, uninterrupted periods for reading and contemplation, for browsing in the stacks and accidentally finding the previously unknown gem that might change the entire direction of our research. A time to think. A time to write. "A time to every purpose, under heaven." *Ecclesiastes* again! Was that the passage Peter Abelard was challenged to interpret? It would be funny if Abelard heard the Byrds' version.

For my part, I spent most of my time reading the books assigned for next semester's courses. When I was an undergrad at Smith, I had an experience that spooked me about keeping up with the reading. I went to a prof's office after the first class and told him I had questions about a book.

"Have you read it?" the prof asked.

"Yes," I said with confidence, and pulled the book from my backpack. The prof took my copy of the book and turned it over in his hands.

"How many times have you read it?" he said.

"Just once," I said. "Over the summer."

He shoved the book back into my hands.

"Go home and read it again," he said. "And when you're certain you know what it means, read it again. Then come back and we'll talk."

I stared at him, uncertain of what to say, then left his office and did as he instructed. To my surprise, even with my near photographic memory, there were things I got from the second reading that I'd not gotten from the first, and the third reading produced even more benefits. I told the prof about this and he smiled.

"Medieval monks," he said, "chanted the Psalms seven times a day, every day, getting through all 150 psalms in week, then starting all over again from the beginning. This was partly a meditative exercise, a way of praying. But it was also a way of incorporating the Psalms—from the Latin *in corpore*, to put the Psalms *into their bodies*. This meant that no matter where they were, they could draw on the Psalms, call upon a passage consciously, or have it pop up from their subconscious. That's how you should read anything that's important to you."

So that's what I did the entire winter break, anticipating the next time a prof asked, "How many times have you read this book?" My main comfort in undergoing this strict regimen was knowing that I wasn't alone. In their own ways, Quinton Quick and Kantorowicz and Stark were doing the same thing.

This must have been why I hadn't seen Quint since the last day of Kantorowicz's seminar. He must have been cloistered somewhere on campus. I was missing him. A lot.

Three or four days before the start of the spring semester, around 10pm on a Thursday night, I headed to Insomnia. It was crowded, but not as much as I thought it would be by the following week. "Our" booth was open in the back and I took a seat there.

The windows were frosted from the cold outside and people came and went and often sat down with their hot cocoa or mulled wine without removing any layers. So it caught me off guard when I suddenly found Special Agent Mapp seated next to me. He once again chose the same side of the booth, even though the seat opposite me was open. I made a face to show my disapproval, but he was unimpressed. He flashed that ingratiating smile of his, took off his gloves and rubbed his hands together, then removed his wool cap, causing his flattened down hair to perform, like, a static-electric ballet.

"Any news of your professor?" he said.

"No foreplay?" I asked. "Right to the good stuff?" I felt myself channeling Quint's animosity toward him.

"I gave you an assignment," he said.

"What happened to the hobo chalk sign?" I said. "Letting you know when we had something then leaving you a message? The book code? The dead drop?"

"I've stayed out of your way, but I haven't heard anything from you since before Thanksgiving."

"There's nothing to report."

"Nothing to report," a voice behind me repeated. It was Quint, in all his assertive splendor, suddenly sitting across from us in the booth. Mapp startled as if Quint might punch him in the face and leaned back, just in case.

"I'm not here to make trouble," Quint said. "And I'm not here to save the day. Isaacson here can take care of herself."

That felt like possibly the nicest thing he had ever said to me.

"Listen," Mapp said. "This thing with your professor could be turning into a matter of national security. You have to let me know if you know something."

I looked at Quint. Even though we hadn't done any work on it for the entire winter break, at least not together, we still had the hate symbol project. Was that the kind of thing we should be sharing? I wasn't always the best at reading facial expressions, but the one that Quint now flashed was clear. We weren't going to tell Mapp about that project until we were sure about Kantorowicz.

"What about the bugged book?" I said, proud of how I'd shifted the subject.

"What?" Mapp said.

"Kantorowicz's book with the listening device inside? I left his office dripping in sweat the day I planted it. Anything there?"

"Oh, uh. No. Nothing as yet."

"Anything else?" Quint said.

"Yeah, anything else?"

Mapp covered his electrified hair again, put his gloves back on and left.

It was satisfying to be rid of him, but both Quint and I realized that it was now just the two of us in the booth. Long silence. I spoke first.

"Espresso?"

"Mmm. No. I should go—"

"I missed you," I blurted out. "Glad you showed up here, even though, as you say, I had everything under control."

He laughed.

"Have you been working?" I asked. "Researching? Writing? I'm trying to get all of next term's reading done before the semester starts—almost going to make it. Just three more books to get through this weekend. Foucault's *Discipline and Punish*, Lyotard's *The Postmodern Condition*, and Umberto Eco's *Travels in Hyper Reality*. Most excited about the last one. I love Eco, though I don't really get this one. Have you read any of them?"

"Let me get an espresso," Quint said. "Something for you? Something *decaffeinated*?"

We sat there until well past 1am, talking about books and ideas and Quint's experiences in Kantorowicz's other seminars. At the mention of our prof's name, and with Mapp long gone, I broached the subject of our "special project."

"Do you have any ideas?"

"Too busy," he said. "Though I did have half an idea this afternoon."

"OMG, I should tell you about this drawing he gave me. I completely forgot." I showed him the picture of the drawing on my phone. "Kantorowicz said he drew it himself, when he was a kid, and that he kept drawing it over and over again, like some kind of obsession. My word, not his. Then he found the drawing and showed it to me and said it might be an idea for the neo-Nazi emblem. You know, since he basically wanted something unknown. And, OMG! I have to tell you about Stark. I met with her to talk about you, but instead she told me about Kantorowicz and everything you found out from the Mormon site, she fleshed all of that out. It's, like, the most amazing story."

Quint reached across the table and touched the back of my hand.

"Oh … Too fast? Too much?"

He nodded. I felt a little embarrassed when he touched my hand, but I felt worse when he took his hand away.

"Sorry, sorry, sorry," I said. "You had an idea. You said you had an idea. No. *Half* an idea. Just this afternoon. Tell me."

He smiled and told me how he had been working in Beinecke to give me space in the carrel and not get in my way. That hurt, but I kept quiet and let him talk.

"Every time I passed through Beinecke," Quint said, "I'd see the exhibit in the main hall. It seemed perfect."

He saw my reaction.

'You don't mean ..."

"Yes," he said. "An impenetrable collection of text and images that has defied interpretation for centuries. What better candidate to have our forged interpretation layered onto?"

"Come on!" I said.

"They're not open now. Besides, I can't do anything until the end of January. I've got the grad student conference and I need to finish that paper. You can start looking at it tomorrow, but I'll have to catch up with you in a couple weeks."

A couple weeks!? Too long, I thought. I wanted to restart our project, but mostly I wanted to be working with Quint again. My cheeks became flushed and I felt my heart rate increasing. I did not turn away, this time. *This* time, I knew the cause of these symptoms. I knew, and I liked it.

# CHAPTER 31
## Censured vs. Censored

Gender, Class, and Race in the Middle Ages:
A Grad Student Mini-Conference
Hosted by the Department of History
Yale University

Saturday, January 25, Beinecke Library, Room 100
9am            Coffee and Pastries
9:30am         Welcome
               *Kermit Mulroney*
               *C. Vann Woodward Professor of History*
               *Director of Graduate Studies*
               *Yale University*

It was my first conference.

Professor Mulroney offered what he called "words of welcome." These consisted of his, like, explaining that he was not a medievalist and that his only reason for being there was that the department chair couldn't make it.

"I normally wouldn't be up so early on a Saturday morning," he said, although it was 9:30. "But you are all hearty 'medievalists,'" he said, smiling and adding air quotes for no reason that I could figure out.

"We're not, like, '*medievalists*,'" I said to Quinton Quick in the back row, repeating the unnecessary gesture. "We are just, like, medievalists." Quint moved my hands into my lap with one hand, as he brought an index finger to his lips with the other.

"Inside voice," he said, even though I was sure I had whispered.

The room we were in was probably three times as big as needed. There was a long, draped table with pastries and fruit and coffee by the door. A clutch of 50 chairs all pointed toward the lectern at the front of the room, half of which remained empty for most of the day. To the right of the lectern was another long table, with the same beige tablecloth, four glasses and a pitcher of water. There were nine students giving papers, discernable by their professional attire. Three professors commenting, though only Stark was present for the morning session. That's twelve people who had to be at the conference, plus about eight more, all Yalies as far as I could tell, who were there to support their fellow grad students.

Mulroney wished the room a good conference filled with interesting and exciting papers and discussions and was on his way.

10am-12  GENDER IN THE MIDDLE AGES
*Alyson Stark, Sterling Professor of History*
*Yale University*
Moderator

Stark stood and thanked Mulroney for his words of welcome, then "on behalf of Yale's medievalist faculty," thanked all of the grad students for attending. She made special note of the distance some of them had traveled.

"We have presenters from schools in New York and New England," she said, "But also from SMU in Dallas and even Ohio State University."

Columbus to New Haven is 639 miles, I thought. Dallas to New Haven is 1637.

1. "Hildegarde of Bingen, Orgasmic Mystic"
   *Rhonda Moore, PhD candidate*
   *SUNY Binghamton*

2.  "Gendered Negotiation:
    Matilda of Tuscany and Lay Investiture"
    *Leigh Ann Cranston, PhD candidate*
    *Yale University*

3.  "The Women of Camelot:
    Beyond *The Mists of Avalon*"
    *Beth Westin, PhD candidate*
    *Southern Methodist University*

The first session went without a hitch. Stark introduced the grad students presenting on gender in the Middle Ages. They were all good, as far as I could tell, though the woman from SMU seemed more nervous than I thought she needed to be. Each presenter got a smattering of applause from the small audience in attendance. Stark gave her response to the papers, offered synopses, compared methodologies, and praised the creative research. She then asked for questions from the audience but no one came forward so she asked a question herself. A second attempt to seek questions from the audience also met with silence.

"Well, then," she said. "Shall we go to lunch? How about another round of applause for the presenters?"

12-1pm            Lunch

We ate in a room adjacent to where the papers were given. As we switched rooms, I had a clear view of the Voynich exhibit, which was still up. By the end of today, I thought, Quint and I can, like, get back to working on our secret project. That made me happy.

1-3pm             CLASS IN THE MIDDLE AGES
                  *Tariq Sallam*
                  *Said al-Hibri Professor of History*
                  *Yale University*
                  Moderator

4. "What's in a name?
*Jacquerie*, Yellow Vests, and the rhetoric of ward-
robe identity on medieval and modern popular re-
volt"
*Renate Connors, PhD candidate*
*University of Notre Dame*

5. "Preaching Rebellion:
The proto-Marxist rhetoric of John Ball"
*Robert North, PhD candidate*
*Columbia University*

6. "Spinning Out of Control:
Wool and women's labor in 13th-century France"
*Laura M. Deveres, PhD candidate*
*The Ohio State University*

The second session also went smoothly. Professor Sallam
introduced each of the speakers in turn, but before he began
he offered special thanks and praise to Quint, who had organized the conference. For his part, Quint avoided eye contact
while Sallam was talking about him. When the last presenter
had spoken, Sallam offered a synopsis—though not as thorough as Stark—then asked for questions. The attendees either
felt more comfortable with each other or they found the papers
more interesting because there were, like, actual questions
from the audience this time.

"Can you honestly draw parallels between the medieval and
modern worker movements?"

"Is it legitimate to apply Marxist theory to instances of labor unrest in a pre-Marx era?"

"Isn't that just presentism at its worst?"

The discussion was, like, a lot livelier, even though the
numbers in the room had not changed. Sallam asked everyone
"to thank the presenters one more time," which brought another round of applause. He then made apologies to Quint before taking off. Stark, who had been there since morning,

thanked Quint for organizing the conference, then also left for another "obligation."

3-3:15pm        Break

We stood along the back wall munching on carrot sticks and cookies. There were more questions and comments on the papers we'd just heard and grad student chit-chat about research funding and whether or not people had already taken their comprehensive exams and how long this or that person had until they defended. During this blather, a younger guy with a smart phone in his hand—maybe an undergrad— walked up and asked Quint if it would, like, be okay for him to take some pictures.

"I'm from the *Yale Daily*," he said. "You're the organizer of this thing. Right? We'd like to do a small piece to cover it."

"Sure," Quint said, standing a little taller. "Of course."

Kantorowicz showed up just after the break. He went to the front of the room to call the last session to order.

3:20-5:20pm    RACE IN THE MIDDLE AGES
                *Abraham Kantorowicz*
                *Rhodes Professor of History*
                *Yale University*
                Moderator

7. "The Queen of Sheba in the Medieval Imagination"
   *Lavonne Jefferson, PhD candidate*
   *Harvard University*

8. "Pardon me while I deconstruct your stereotype: How religion trumped race when Maurice of Magdeburg, a Black Christian, defied the Emperor"
   *Harlon Green, III*
   *PhD candidate*
   *Princeton University*

9. "Hands up! Don't joust! The case of Morien, Black knight of the Table Round"
*Quinton Quick*
*PhD candidate*
*Yale University*

"This has been a lovely conference thus far," he said. "My name is Abe Kantorowicz and I'm pleased to moderate this last session on race in the Middle Ages. Our first speaker—"

Kantorowicz stopped, suddenly caught off guard. The reporter from the *Yale Daily*, stood in the back of the room with his hand raised.

"We usually wait until the end of the session to take questions," Kantorowicz said, smiling. "How can we help you?"

"Do you deny that 6 million Jews were killed in the Holocaust?" he said.

The conference attendees from other schools looked at each other with confused expressions. Only the grad students from Yale had an inkling of where this was going. There was a long pause before Kantorowicz answered.

"Look," he said. "I'm not sure your question is relevant to these proceedings."

"It's relevant because you're here," the young reporter interrupted. "The faculty senate claims that you deny the Holocaust and they've censored you for that. But here you are, ignoring the fact that you're censored and speaking at this public event. So, did the faculty senate get it wrong and maybe you don't deny the Holocaust? Do you deny the Holocaust?"

A muffled rumbling spread over our small gathering of medievalists. People in the audience looked back and forth from Kantorowicz to the reporter to each other. Quint, seated at the front of the room with the other presenters, made a move toward the back, no doubt to eject the guy, but Kantorowicz held up a hand to stop him.

"You're out of line!" Kantorowicz said. "First you've completely confused the terminology. You said the faculty senate censored me. If that were true, I can understand why you think

I shouldn't be here speaking openly. But there's a difference between *censor* and *censure*! The former would keep me from making any pronouncements in public, which, thankfully, is not only impossible in the United States—at least for now— but it's also the antithesis of the university's ethos of free speech and academic freedom. No. The senate *censured* me, which is their way of expressing disapproval over someone's words or deeds—a kind of official, public finger-wagging, their way of telling me and anyone else who's listening that they do not approve of certain of my actions!"

Kantorowicz held both hands out to his sides.

"Censor!" he said, gesturing with his left hand. "Censure!" he said with the right.

It was only then that Kantorowicz realized the student was holding up his phone, not taking photos, but shooting video.

"Get that thing out of my face!"

The student reporter was immune to the professor's angry demand.

"Okay," the student said. "Censured. Were you *censured* for denying the Holocaust?"

"Yes," Kantorowicz snapped.

"That's all I needed," the young 'gotcha' journalist said. Satisfied with this admission of guilt, he turned to leave.

"Don't you ... you ... I was censured because the senate *thought* I denied the Holocaust. Not because I actually did it. I attended conferences with Holocaust deniers and have given interviews to publications that promote those views, but this does not mean that I share them!"

The student once again held up his phone to record the professor.

"You still haven't answered my question," the student said.

"That's because I don't answer to you!" the professor shouted.

Wrong move, I thought. The student clicked off his phone and hurried out the door.

The gasoline had been removed from the room, but the fire was still smoldering. It took some time for a sense of calm to return and for Kantorowicz to regain his composure.

"Forgive me," he said to the audience. "This was ... an episode of Yale's dirty laundry being aired in public. I'm sorry it happened and ... well ... disrupted your conference." He looked down at the program, which he had been holding in his hand the whole time. It looked like he was going to pick up at the point where he had been interrupted.

"Look," he said. "For the record. I'm not a Holocaust denier. I was censured by our faculty senate, but they've got this all wrong. I'm Jewish! My grandmother was killed in the Shoah! I don't ..." Kantorowicz stood silent in front of the conference attendees, still holding the program as if he was about to read from it. Maybe a minute passed, but it felt like an hour. Quint approached him.

"Professor? I'm so sorry ..."

Kantorowicz snapped out of his stupor.

"Don't be silly," he said. "Take a seat and let's get back to business."

CHAPTER 32
## The Young Conservatives Host a Speaker

The final session of "Gender, Class, and Race in the Middle Ages" was lackluster. Not the content of the papers, but the mood. Kantorowicz managed to introduce the speakers, who managed to deliver their papers, but with a hesitancy that kept them looking over their shoulders, as if disruption might come again at any moment. Kantorowicz had seen the three papers ahead of time, so he only needed to read his written response. There were questions about the papers but I can't remember a single one. Quint felt badly for Kantorowicz, but I was feeling sorry for Quint, who'd organized the whole thing. The wine and cheese reception at the end was more tense than celebratory. Only half of the already small group attended. No professors.

We left Beinecke and headed for Sterling.

"Insomnia?" I offered.

"No," Quint said. "I should really get dinner instead of coffee … I think I'd rather be by myself."

"Why?"

He gave me a weird look.

"Weren't you there?" he said.

"It was great! Your paper was, like, great! Don't let that asshole from the *Daily* ruin your day. You organized an amazing conference!"

My phone beeped and I took it out to check it.

"Uh-oh," I said.

"What?"

"This isn't good."

"What!?"

I held up the screen so Quint could see it for himself.

Since coming to grad school, I'd set up several Google alerts, including one that notified me of stories about Kantorowicz. That fucking little twerp from the *Yale Daily* had posted the video he took to the paper's Twitter account. Quint shook his head as read the headline.

"Yale Prof Denies Holocaust."

The video was short but damning. It showed Kantorowicz, agitated, avoiding the reporter's questions. It skipped over the part where he explained how and why he attended conferences and gave interviews to Holocaust deniers. And finished with a question and answer taken completely out of context.

"Were you *censured* for denying the Holocaust?"

"Yes."

It was the difference between asking a prisoner whether he was *convicted* of murder or if he had actually *committed* the crime. Two separate things. But with that inflammatory headline—Prof Denies Holocaust—and the tendency of online viewers to "share" anything they found juicy, without fact-checking, this was going to cause real damage.

We'd almost reached Sterling when we heard a clattering behind us. A crowd of students, holding signs and chanting, marched toward us from the direction of the Beinecke.

"Hey-hey. Ho-ho. Those white supremacists got to go!"

"Hey-hey. Ho-ho. Those white supremacists got to go!"

For a second I thought they were reacting to the tweet about Kantorowicz.

"What's going on?" Quint hollered into the crowd.

"Craig Michaels is in Linsly-Chit," one of the students shouted and handed Quint a flyer.

"We're gonna shut this racist asshole down!" shouted another.

I read the flyer over Quint's shoulder. "Craig Michaels: The Future of White Nationalism and Why You Should Care." I had no idea who Craig Michaels was, but Quint's face bore a look of pained recognition.

"You know who that is?" I asked.

"Oh, yes," he said. "He was one of my profs at More-house."

We followed the crowd to Linsly-Chittendon Hall. The exterior of the building was in a Romanesque Revival style that seemed to borrow features from southern France, Spain, and Italy in the 11th and 12th centuries.

"Rounded arches," I said. "Squat columns, stone walls made to look rougher and more rustic, cylinder-shaped towers growing out of the walls. Likely *Richardsonian* Romanesque, named for the 19th-century architect who created it. Beautiful in its own way, but also, like—"

"Stop that," Quint said.

"—an asymmetrical nightmare."

"Done?"

"Nerves."

Beyond their titles, there were, like, significant differences between "Gender, Class, and Race in the Middle Ages," and "The Future of White Nationalism and Why You Should Care."

Our little grad student conference had about 25 people, and nine of those were presenters. Half the chairs in the Beinecke classroom we used were empty. In contrast, the room for "The Future of White Nationalism" was packed—200 people in a room with a 150 capacity, not counting the two or three campus security guards scattered on the periphery.

Another feature of the white nationalist event not shared with the medievalist grad student conference was the number of protesters. We basically had one protester, and he wasn't really protesting the conference but one of its moderators. "The Future of White Nationalism" had about 100 protesters outside the lecture hall bearing signs with messages like "Yale is no place for haters!" and "Illegal immigration started in 1492!"

Everyone inside the room seemed supportive of the speaker and his message, but it was hard to be certain. The crowd was mostly white, mostly male. They all looked like they shopped at Abercrombie & Fitch. A pasty, jowly undergrad in a suit that didn't quite button in the front made his way to the podium. He tapped the microphone, as one does, and addressed the congregation.

"There are still some empty chairs," he said, gesturing to one or two vacancies around the room. "For those of you standing, you can still find chairs."

We squeezed through the door and found two seats, one behind the other at the end of two of the rows. Others settled in and 'pasty jowly' began.

"Welcome. My name is [*I didn't catch it*] and I'm the president of Yale's Young Conservatives Club." Who cares who you are, I thought, as he went on, "It's my great pleasure to introduce tonight's speaker. Craig Michaels is a graduate of Evergreen State College in Olympia, Washington. Go, Geoducks! Heh-heh."

clap-clap-clap!

This clapping wasn't applause, but a kind of rhythmic protest.

clap-clap-clap! clap-clap-clap!

"Dr. Michaels received a PhD in philosophy from Notre Dame University and taught for several years at Morehouse College in Atlanta."

I leaned over and whispered to Quint.

"You went to Morehouse," I said. "Did you—"

"Two classes," said Quint.

"Here to discuss the question of White Nationalism and why we all should care, please join me in a warm welcome for Dr. Craig Michaels!"

Michaels went to the podium, shook hands with the president of the Young Conservatives Club, then looked out over the crowd. He resembled that Nazi in the *Indiana Jones* movie— the one whose face melts away when he looks at the Ark of the Covenant—only taller and better looking.

"Thanks for that very kind introduction," said Michaels. "And thanks to all of you for being here on a Saturday evening. It shows that you really care about issues that matter. Besides, the bars in New Haven are open late, so you can still find other fun when we're done here."

That got a chuckle. Michaels had a certain charisma, knew how to charm a crowd.

"I want to begin by setting out some clear definitions and boundaries," he said. "I'm a white *nationalist*, and I'm here to represent the philosophical underpinnings of white *nationalism*. I'm not a white *supremacist*."

Upon hearing that first declaration, a female student seated in the center of the room stood up, turned her back on the speaker, and began clapping.

clap-clap-clap!

clap-clap-clap!

Michaels paused but didn't comment. It was clear that he'd seen this sort of thing before.

"A white nationalist believes in the uniqueness of all races, including the black and brown races. By 'uniqueness,' I mean that each of the races is different, and no comparison of good, better, best is implied."

Two young Black men, sitting near the doors, joining the first protester, stood and faced the back of the room.

clap-clap-clap!

"It's the most natural thing in the world for members of the same race to want to associate with their own kind. In that sense, you might think of me as a white *naturalist*."

That garnered some nervous laughter.

"White nationalists take natural tendencies and organize them around political philosophy. A white nationalist prefers association and promotion of his own race over misguided attempts to promote diversity for diversity's sake."

Another student, near the front row, stood and faced the back, followed by three more in the center.

clap-clap-clap!

"It's a proven fact that black people feel uncomfortable in white civilization."

Two more students stood, then two more.

clap!

"As white nationalists, we say, why fight this? Why force multiculturalism onto a situation that's already finding its natural equilibrium? Distinct ethnic groups—white, black, brown—have the right to political sovereignty, and to govern their own affairs in ethnically homogenous spaces."

More students stood and faced the back. The protesters now comprised about one-fourth of the audience. They still maintained "civility" in their civil disobedience, but the situation was reaching a tipping point. From where we sat, Quint and I could see the tense faces of the protesters, who were trying their best not to lash out or become intimidated into sitting back down. They'd clearly had some training or put some thought into this action. Their clapping kept them focused. We also registered the faces of students still seated, looking at their fellow Yalies with increasing agitation. I wondered if Michaels, like, clearly aware of the growing tension in the room, would try to diffuse it. Or if creating tension was the point of the exercise.

"Let me reiterate," Michaels said, apparently resigned to speaking to the backs of so many heads. "I'm a white nationalist. *Not* a white supremacist. The white nationalist has no desire to rule over other ethnic groups. Yet, if made to live in a world of enforced multiculturalism, we will advocate and promote our own agenda, the agenda of the white race, the values of white civilization, just as any other ethnic group would attempt to do for themselves. We prefer to live in peace, but if threatened with the annihilation of our culture, we will not, in the words of a great white poet, "go gently into that dark night."

"It's *'gentle* into that *good* night," I whispered to Quint. "Dylan Thomas."

"Ours is a simple appeal to what Nietzsche called "Aryan humanity,"" Michaels said. "Nothing more."

Suddenly, Quint was on his feet. At first, I thought he was going to turn and face the back of the room like the other protesters. Instead, he was raising his hand and addressing the speaker without waiting to be called.

"Dr. Michaels," he said. "Quinton Quick. I was a student in your class on Nietzsche at Morehouse."

"Oh. Quinton … You look the same."

clap-CLAP!

"Yeah. Listen. I think you're way off base where Nietzsche's 'Aryan humanity' is concerned."

"Oh? I remember teaching *you* the concept when you were in my class."

"I've done more reading since then," Quint said. "Nietzsche used the phrase 'Aryan humanity' throughout his writings, but he never meant it in the way the Nazis thought he meant it. Nor in the way the Alt-Right now thinks he meant it."

"The student has become the master," Michaels gave what he hoped would be a disarming smile. "Please. Enlighten us."

In that moment, Quinton Quick unleashed the medieval scholastic master inside himself. He was Peter Abelard. He was William of Ockham. He was Thomas Aquinas. His was the most beautiful mind I'd ever seen.

"First, when Nietzsche references 'Aryan humanity,' he's *not* espousing some eugenic or Darwinian ideal. In fact, in Nietzsche's day, 'Aryan' was *not* a concept denoting racial purity, but a term to identify a branch of languages, part of the Indo-Iranian language family. Those languages, by the way, were spoken by ancient peoples of many different colors—and they're all related to each other."

Quint gestured around the room to the protesters as he said, "peoples of many different colors," then continued.

CLAP-CLAP!

"Aryan has nothing to do with race. Nietzsche always used the phrase 'Aryan humanity' in contrast to Christian morality. He meant the humanity of the pre-Christians, the pagans. And by the way, not the Odin worshippers or Druids so often co-opted by the Alt-Right fanboys. Nietzsche meant the pagans going all the way back to the Greeks and Romans."

"It's Greek and Roman values we white nationalists want to raise up," said Michaels. "Values like strength over pity, the will of the individual over egalitarianism, nobility over humility. The victory of these values can only be accomplished through the autonomy of white nations. All else, as Nietzsche has shown, leads to cultural decay, which is only accelerated through the influence of the Jews. It's the Jews who are behind the crisis of white genocide, who thwart every attempt to stem the extinction of the white race."

"Don't invoke Nietzsche to support your anti-Semitism." Quint's response was measured. He continued to hold onto the rational, in spite of Michaels' racist drivel.

"Nietzsche spoke out against anti-Semitism! He even slammed his pal Wagner for—."

"YOU FUCKING NAZI-LOVER!" I shouted.

I couldn't take it anymore.

"You mother-fucking, Jew-hating, Nazi-loving, neo-Nazi!" clap-clap! clap-clap! clap-clap-CLAP!

Quint put his hand on my shoulder, like, to calm me down, but I couldn't stop. My internal bullshit detector had reached its limit and I kept shouting hate filled, anti-fascist insults in Michaels' direction. It only took one or two of the silent protesters to join me.

"Why are we putting up with this crap!"

"Hey-hey, Ho-ho. This neo-Nazi's got to go!"

"Hey-HEY, Ho-HO. This neo-NAZI's GOT TO GO!"

clap-CLAP! clap-CLAP! clap-clap-clap-CLAP-clap-CLAP-CLAP-CLAP!

Every student standing with their back to the speaker was now chanting and clapping, louder and louder! Members of the Young Conservatives Club started yelling at them to shut up. Some young conservatives pulled at the protestors' shirt sleeves, in an attempt to get them to sit down. The entire event quickly devolved into chaos. As the shouting and clapping inside the room increased, so did the clapping and shouting outside the room. One of the inside protesters opened the door, allowing the chaos to enter.

CLAP!

The scene looked like a submarine being flooded from the outside as trapped sailors tried to shut the hatch doors or escape against the current. Campus security was helpless to do anything more than call for backup. This was the closest I'd ever gotten to a medieval melee. Campus police arrived and the violence dissipated. Several bruises, some poked ribs, two bloody noses and a black eye. Sanctions from the Dean's Office were evenly distributed all around. Someone spirited the speaker out a back door. What was all that bullshit about "representing philosophical underpinnings"? This self-contained riot was Craig Michaels' real goal—practice for whatever race war they had planned for the future.

Quint and I had managed to squeeze out of the room without too much damage. We put some distance between ourselves and the mob and headed back toward Sterling, our refuge. Just as we turned the corner toward the library's great façade, there was Kantorowicz at the top of the steps. I nudged Quint and pointed.

"Who's that with him?" Quint said.

"Not Bilbo, the neo-Nazi."

Kantorowicz was talking to someone we had never seen before. A guy with a shiny bald head in a perfectly tailored, grey suit.

We pressed our bodies into a shadow for cover and watched the two men talking for some time. When they finally left, it was in different directions.

"Follow the new guy!" I said.

"NO!" Quint said.

I felt dejected, but finally agreed that he was right.

"Report this to Mapp?" I asked.

Quint's eyes followed the bald guy until he was out of sight, paused for several seconds after he'd gone, then finally answered me.

"Yes," he said. "Mapp!"

CHAPTER 33
## Aftermath of a Small Riot

I was jangled and worn out by all yelling and protesting. I headed home and didn't catch up with Quint until the next day at Sterling.

The carrel door was closed when I got there and Quint was inside, writing. I opened the door and stuck my head in, but my greeting barely got a hello. He handed me a piece of paper with a string of numbers.

"Book code message," he said, and handed me the copy of *The King's Too Bawdy* from his shelf. "Please check my work before we send it to Mapp." He returned to whatever he was typing. I wasn't used to this gruff treatment and I didn't like it. Why was he angry? Had I done something wrong?

I concentrated on his encoded message. Three columns of seven numbers each. Every entry had 3 digits—page number, line number, word number—that represented an individual word. So the entire message was 21 words:

| | | |
|---|---|---|
| i-1-5 | 15-12-4 | 4-15-2 |
| 3-17-6 | 7-14-5 | 4-15-9 |
| 3-19-8 | 22-9-1 | 72-7-9 |
| 5-3-9 | 8-16-5 | bald |
| 2-4-4 | 5-15-3 | 22-10-7 |
| 4-17-6 | 43-2-8 | 5-3-9 |
| 7-14-5 | supremacist | 8-14-5 |

The great thing about the book code, according to Quint, is the impossibility to crack it unless you know, and have, a copy of the key. It's better than a specially designed codebook, which, if it was found, would identify the bearer as a secret agent and allow the enemy to send false messages pretending to be that agent. The best kind of source book can be found anywhere in the world, like the *Gideon Bible*, but both sender and receiver would need to be sure they were using the same edition. Using *The King's Too Bawdy* is obscure and doesn't draw attention to itself in the context of a medievalist's study carrel. One drawback is that not every book is suited to every type of message. It's difficult to encode a message about nuclear arms using Martha Stewart's *Living the Good Life*. This was the reason that "supremacist" and "bald" were left unencoded: those words didn't appear in the key. Another is the fact that you can't compose or decipher a message except through the brute force of looking up the words in the key. There's no way to decipher a message in your head, which is fairly easy with a simple substitution code, for example.

I mention all of this by way of saying that it took me a while to decipher Quint's message to Mapp. Here's what I came up with:

"Kantorowicz met man not seen before, library building, same time as white supremacist speaker on campus. Bald head. Did not follow."

"Yes," Quint said, and continued typing.

"Should I hide this in the Bernard Gui inquisitor's book? In the BX 1700 section?"

"Yes," Quint said. His curt answers were starting to bug me. What was his problem?

"Anything else?"

"When you're done, leave the chalk mark on the front of the library."

"Okay," I said. I turned to leave, then turned back. "Are you mad at me?"

"Why?"

"You seem weird."

"Hm."

Quint never stopped typing throughout this awkward inquisition. Not seeing a better option, I reached over and shut the lid to his laptop. He looked like he was marshalling all his focus and energy not to yell at me.

"It's this!" he said, pointing to his now-closed laptop.

"I was just trying to get your attention."

"No!" he said. "It's not just the laptop. You do this all the time."

"What!?"

"Come on," Quint said, mocking my voice. "Let's tail our prof and his neo-Nazi buddy! Come on, let's follow this new bald neo-Nazi! Come on, let's call Craig Michaels a 'fucking Nazi lover!'"

"He *is* a fucking Nazi lover!"

"I know he's a fucking Nazi lover! A 'mother-fucking, Nazi-loving, neo-Nazi!' as you so beautifully put it. But I was in the process of destroying his argument with logic and rhetoric. I had him in my sights and was about to blow him out of the water with reason. Michaels taught an entire course on Nietzsche, which I lapped up but now, having matured in my reading habits, I know that Michaels doesn't know shit about Nietzsche. And I was about to reveal that fact in front of God—whom Nietzsche said was 'dead,' but even that is more complicated—in front of God and everyone, but you jump in! *You*, Molly Isaacson, who has no patience. *You* open fire with ad hominem attacks, with name calling. Which ignites the crowd and sparks a mob reaction. Which we narrowly escape!"

"I just said what everyone else was thinking."

"*Feeling!* You said what everyone else was *feeling!*"

"Are you angry because I started the riot, which I don't think I did! Or are you angry because you think I cut off your rhetorical flourish? Because you didn't get the chance to finish him off with your logic and rhetoric?!"

"It's the only way to win against Michaels and his kind. What you did, what you helped to make happen, only fed into his plan."

"Are you saying he wanted a riot?"

"YES!"

I paused for a moment. I was startled by Quint's passion. Hurt too. Mostly I was amazed at how controlled he was, how he could really yell at me and seem to really mean it, all the while raising his voice only loud enough to avoid drawing attention from the librarians. It was his version of flying under the radar.

"I thought so, too," I said. "That Michaels' goal was to incite the crowd."

"Then why did you play into that!? You constantly act without thinking. I swear to God, you're the bull and the china shop all in one!"

He re-opened his laptop and returned to whatever he was typing.

"Please don't be angry with me," I said.

"I'm not angry," he said. "I'm redirecting my anger by working."

"On your dissertation?"

"If only."

"What then?"

"An op-ed for the *Daily*."

"Topic?"

"The importance of free speech, even when that speech is ugly."

It took me a second to digest that.

"Like hate speech?" I said. "Like the kind of venomous bullshit that Michaels was spewing?"

"Yes."

"But you're ..."

There it was again. You can't defend hate speech as free speech because ... you can't be a medievalist because ...

"I'm Black," said Quinton Quick, as calm as I'd ever seen him. "It's okay to say it. I'm Black. But I challenge anyone who shoves me into a box and defines me for all time because of that one accident of my nature. I'm Black *and* I believe that the right to free speech must be absolute."

"But the crap Michaels was saying was hurtful to you."

"And to you," Quint said. "His rhetoric, such as it is, hurts Black folks and Jews and women. Ultimately, it hurts white folks, if they buy into it. But I won't abandon the First Amendment. Even when nasty and hateful and stupid people decide to speak, they have a right to do so. An absolute right. The way to combat nastiness and hate and stupidity isn't by stopping speech. It's through *more* speech. *More* speech."

The entire time he was admonishing me, he'd never stopped typing. He paused the second time he said, "more speech," and looked at me.

"If you don't mind," he said, "the deadline for Monday's edition is six tonight."

I didn't say anything. I absolutely disagreed with him about absolute free speech. There had to be limits, I thought, but kept this to myself. Quint showed me his serious face, the one that said don't bug me when I'm working. I'd only recently learned to recognize that face, and when I did, I needed to respect it.

I picked up the paper with the encoded message and gestured that I'd hide it in the designated book, upstairs in the stacks. I also took out the sandwich bag with the white chalk and mimed that I would leave the signal for Mapp—an X in a circle below the medieval scholar on Sterling's façade—indicating a message.

Quint gave me a slight smile and nodded.

You're wrong about free speech, I thought. I took out my phone and looked at the time. 4:30pm. Ninety minutes till the deadline for Monday's edition.

CHAPTER 34
The Bungalow Boys

> So, everyone had a chance 2 check in? Alright then. First item: discuss chore wheel. Then our main topic: presentation on new uniforms, w/ suggested new name 4 the group, followed by announcements.
> I have an announcement.
> That's fine. Just post it when the time comes.
> Oh. Okay.
> Alright then. The chore wheel. Not sure why we have 2 go over this every time, but people seem 2 have trouble w/ it & we just have 2 have some discipline if we're gonna strike a blow against miscegenation & international Jewry. Now, whose turn was it this week 2 leave racial slurs on the voicemail of Southern Poverty Law Center & the Anti-Defamation League? We promised we'd call each one three times a day, but we've seriously been falling down on that.
> I can't believe people are letting that drop. & it's not just because it was my idea.
> Ooh, I don't think it's anything against U personally.
> Well, it sure feels that way.
> It was me. It's embarrassing. I had a sore throat all last week. Turned into laryngitis & didn't think I could deliver on the racial slurs. U know,

make them sound threatening enough.
> Why didn't U say something?!
> Come on, Klaus. Let's give Chad some space 2 explain himself.
> NO NAMES IN THE CHATROOM PLEASE!
> Sorry.
> I thought U guys would make fun of me.
> Don't B silly.
> Did U try hot tea w/ honey & lemon?
> Yes, try the hot tea next time, but by all means let someone know. We're here 4 U.
> & we don't want 2 fall back on our intimidation tactics.
> TB here.
> Just in time, sir. We R about 2 present new uniform ideas.

Someone is typing ...
Image uploading ...

> This is Frank Lloyd Wright, most famous American architect of the twentieth century. While he's well known 4 structures like "Fallingwater" & "Taliesen," he was also a secret anti-Semite. Mel Gibson of his day! Buddies w/ Charles Lindberg & Henry Ford, blaming Jewish warmongers 4 entering World War II. Once told a Jewish apprentice who'd fucked up 2 "let his beard grow & get back 2 being a rabbi." Priceless!

Someone is typing ...

> The picture shows Wright in his later years w/ his famous pork pie hat—wide brim rolling up at the

ends w/ taller vented crown. Brown, of course. His signature look. We're proposing the Frank Lloyd Wright hat w/ the white ascot & herringbone tweed coat U see in the picture.

> & below the waist?

> Khakis & Doc Marten boots.

> Mmmm! Love it! Fantastic!

> Of course, Wright had 2 keep his Jew-hating on the DL 'cause of clients like Guggenheim & other kikes. I mean, the guy designed synagogues, took the Jews' money 2 do it, then claimed the synagogues were American temples 4 Jews, not Jewish temples.

> He had some balls.

> Yes, but that Jew-hating beneath the surface, mostly hidden, is exactly the kind of profile we're looking 4. & here's the best part. We propose the name 4 the group 2 B the "Bungalow Boys," because of Wright designing the most American of homes, the bungalow!

> Why does every group need a different name? Can't we all just B Jew-hating, race-baiting neo-Nazis?!

> Well, the Klan is not the same as the Proud Boys is not the same as the Oath Keepers. We all goose-step 2 a different drummer.

> Can't we celebrate that difference.

> DIFFERENCE!? Are U talking about diversity? *DIVERSITY!* Don't U use that language w/ me, U *UNTERMENSCH*-LOVING, PORK-PIE-HAT-WEARING, BI-CURIOUS FAGGOT!

> Chill out guys! We R gonna have to agree that different people are gonna have different opinions & some people are gonna make different choices? OK? Now can we at least agree on "Bungalow Boys"?

> *Sieg Heil*
>> *Sieg Heil*
>>> *Sieg Heil*
>>> *Sieg Heil*

> Great. Any other business? Otherwise, announcements? I'll go first, if nobody minds. I just want U all 2 mark your calendars 4 the big march in Kalamazoo. Plan ahead 2 take time off, especially if UR in law enforcement or the military. Make sure U can get leave time.

>> What about the cops? What should we do at the rally if the cops approach us? I mean, they've been our allies plenty before now, but if they try 2 stop us what should we do?

> It's doubtful they will, but I think we're obliged 2 show them the same courtesy they show us.

>> Speaking of the rally ... I'm, uh, uncomfortable in large social gatherings, tend 2 get over-stimulated. Anyone not wanting 2 attend the rally, I'll B holding a zoom meeting, reading aloud from *Mein Kampf*. Cameras off, of course, if any of U want a safe space alternative, I'd B happy if U joined me.

> That's very thoughtful. Anything else?

>> I made this sign 4 the next protest: "Jew & spick & chink & black/There gonna give our country back!"

>> U mean "they're," not "there." *They're* gonna give our country back.

>> Grammar Nazi!

> Anything else?

>> I propose a big *Sieg Heil* 4 the new uniforms?!

> *Sieg Heil*
>> *Sieg Heil*
>>> *Sieg Heil*

>> & 4 the new name! Bungalow Boys!

> *Sieg Heil*
>> *Sieg Heil*

> *Sieg Heil!*
> Great meeting, everybody. Who wants 2 moderate next week?
>> Shouldn't we stop sharing power w/ different moderators & move toward a single charismatic leader? I mean, I'm just saying …
>>> I s'pose U'd like that job?
> OK, OK. That's 4 another time. Meeting adjourned.

CHAPTER 35
The Yale Daily News

Dateline, New Haven:

**OPINION: "All speakers have rights"**
by Quinton Quick, PhD cand., history

I write this op-ed in response to the small riot that erupted following the Yale Young Conservatives' event featuring Craig Michaels, the controversial, white nationalist speaker. Let me start by saying that I'm a person of color, and I find almost all of Michaels' ideas to be racist and repugnant.

That said, I want to express my disappointment with the reception his talk received from the students protesting his talk. I also want to defend the principles of academic freedom and freedom of speech, two fundamental rights denied to Michaels' on Yale's campus this past Saturday.

First, academic freedom requires the freedom to learn as well as to teach. Students' rights to hear whatever they wish should be protected, even when condescending views of professors and administrators might claim that students are not "wise enough" or "mature enough" to know what is good to hear or learn.

Student organizations, of all political stripes, have the right to invite any speaker they wish to campus. They should not be hindered in their ability to invite speakers, even when some consider their choices to be controversial. I would even go so far as to say that controversial speakers should especially be invited.

Free speech is not the freedom to say anything. We cannot allow speakers to incite violence. No one can be allowed to cry "fire" in a crowded theater. Although his ideas are loathsome, Michaels' speech stops far short of inciting violence. Labeling his speech as such doesn't make it so.

Freedom of speech is not about the right to say anything, but it does guarantee the right to exercise one's reason in the public court of ideas. Every great thinker from Plato to Kant to John Stuart Mill has said as much.

Mill spoke presciently of our own time when he said that the greatest threat of censorship came not from the state, but from the tyranny of our fellow citizens. It was not the "state" that shut down Michaels' ideas. Not the administration. But our fellow Yalies, acting in the name of ... what? Freedom?

I was about to challenge Mr. Michael's in that public court, when the mob at the Young Conservatives' event shifted the focus from reasoned debate to unfettered emotional reaction. Such reactions sometimes provide short term satisfaction, with the immediate effect of denying the offensive speaker a platform. But they also destroy any chance for long-range deconstruction and dismissal of flawed ideas.

In academic freedom and freedom of speech, the central idea is freedom. But freedom in both of these senses is really about equality. Everybody, anybody, in America, has the equal right to participate in open debate, the right to persuade one's fellow citizens of one's ideas.

Free speech on campus should not be a partisan issue. It should not be a value that liberals dismiss only because conservatives defend it. Nor should conservatives use it as a bludgeon to attack liberals as hypersensitive censors of speakers whose ideas are intended to agitate and offend.

Disagreement is no reason for disruptive action intended to silence a speaker's voice. A university like Yale should not be a place where hecklers win the argument simply because they yell the loudest. Intellectual contests should rightly be won through logic and reason, without regard for the protestors' volume.

▪▪▪▪▪▪▪▪▪▪▪▪▪▪▪▪▪▪▪▪▪▪▪▪▪▪▪▪▪▪▪▪▪▪▪▪▪

**OPINION: "No *lux*, even less *veritas*"**
by M.R. Isaacson, grad student, history

Two words are inscribed in Hebrew on a book, inside a blue shield on Yale's coat of arms: *Urim* and *Thummim*. These words are repeated in Latin in the banner that runs across the top of the arms: *Lux et veritas*. "Light and truth."

Our school's motto reveals Yale's noble aspiration for us: to create a place that sheds light on the world's problems. A place that seeks out and values Truth. Unfortunately, the Young Conservative Club's event featuring the white nationalist speaker, Craig Michaels, brought forth very little light and even less truth.

The speaker was clever in his low-key approach. He wore a suit and tie, rather than dressing as a skin head. He was introduced as a PhD, who had taught at none other than the well-regarded, historically black college of Morehouse in Atlanta. Impressive. One might almost guess he was a moderate.

Michaels spoke in measured tones. He calmly explained that he was not a "white supremacist," implicitly conveying his distaste for the term. No, he was a "white nationalist", which according to Michaels' description is something almost patriotic.

This was not a ranting raving racist, but by all appearances a reasonable fellow. Some might argue that because of Michaels' very reasonable-ness, we should also behave reasonably toward him. But this is the trap of "civility," the new buzz word that administrators trot out to keep students on their best behavior.

For his part, I do not doubt that Michaels believes he has "a Truth" to share with his audience. But we, his audience, are in no way required to listen to his "Truth." In fact, our own academic freedom as students allows us the liberty to choose not to listen.

And while Michaels has the right under the First Amendment to spew his venom, this does not give him license to spew it wherever he likes. The State cannot censor him, but we, the community of scholars at Yale University, can and should censor him, in the sense that we deny him a platform.

Is there really any question about how vile his position is? Do we really need to pretend that his brand of hate is worthy of a platform, just because free speech has always been held up as the greatest American value? As a Jew and as a woman, I'm horrified by Michaels' rhetoric and I see no reason to give him an audience.

This is why I shouted white nationalist Craig Michaels down at Saturday's event—and why many others joined in—forcing him to leave the venue.

Rejecting speakers who so violate societal norms has a long tradition, from the ancient Greeks to the Quakers. To those who claim that protesters are violating Mr. Michaels' rights, I say that "freedom of speech" is little more than a refuge for white men in power who feel threatened because the rest of us have grown weary of their tired ideas.

And if all of us really do enjoy the right to free speech, I prefer to use mine to shout down the haters, to shut them down and run them out of town. Not only will this rid the world of some of its

evil, it will also open a space for marginalized
voices that have long been silenced!

I walked into Insomnia late Monday afternoon, carrying a
copy of *The Yale Daily News*. Quint was already there, sitting in
our booth, reading his own copy.

"I see you managed to write a piece about the Young Conservatives' event, too," Quint said.

"I took a position somewhat counter to yours."

"That's fine," he said. "If you read my piece, you should
know that I'm not going to shout you down for having a different opinion ... though I might need to engage you in a scholastic disputation."

He smiled, and I blushed.

CHAPTER 36
A Swastika on the Door

The day after our op-eds appeared, *The Yale Daily News* reported neo-Nazi graffiti on several campus buildings.

> Yale's Hillel Jewish Center and the Afro-American Cultural Center were both painted with white swastikas, interspersed with the letters KKK. On the door of a professor's study carrel in the Sterling Library, someone drew a large swastika in indelible black marker, with KKK around the swastika. Finally, someone drew a Celtic cross, a common neo-Nazi symbol, in chalk on the façade of Sterling Library, below the statue of the medieval scholar.

"I did *not* draw a Celtic cross!" I insisted to no one in particular. A couple in the booth next to mine gave me a look, then decided I must be talking on my phone with earbuds. Kantorowicz had witnessed this sort of thing once and said that it was "the great advantage to living in these times" that a person was "not immediately deemed crazy just because it looked like she was talking to herself." It was likely much more suspect that I was reading a paper edition of the *Yale Daily*, rather than reading it online.

"I did *not* draw a Celtic cross!" I said again when Quint finally showed up. "I drew a circle with an X through it, the Hobo pictograph for 'All is well.'" I shoved the *Yale Daily* toward Quint and drew the symbol on the newspaper, under the neo-Nazi graffiti story.

"A circle," I said. "With an X on the inside."

Quint took the paper and rotated my drawing 45 degrees.

"Circle. Cross." he said, tracing the lines of the X turned sideways. "Celtic cross."

My face scrunched into a scowl.

"Remember what the ADL website said about context," said Quint. "Context matters. I know and you know that this is a Hobo sign, but in the context of the other graffiti on campus, they've lumped your chalk mark in with the other neo-Nazi signs."

"I need to fix this," I said. "Get the *Daily* to run a correction."

"NO!" Quint said.

The couple in the next booth looked over again. I looked back at them but didn't respond.

"You don't need to fix everything," Quint said. "Stop trying!"

I stared into my mug.

"Didn't you read the main part of the story?" he asked. "A giant swastika and KKK scrawled on the door of a professor's carrel? They're talking about Kantorowicz's carrel. OUR carrel! Haven't you been there today?!"

"Do you think someone is targeting you?" I said.

"Why would they be targeting *me*?" Quint said.

"You're *Black*!" I said.

"You're the more likely target," Quint said, now whispering. "*You're* the one who wrote the big 'no-free-speech-for-the-neo-Nazis' piece. *You* self-identified as Jewish!"

"Maybe the swastika is for Kantorowicz. He's Jewish."

"But if he's the target, his office door would be a better choice to make a statement."

"If it's for one of us, who even knows what carrel we're in?"

We both paused to think.

"Mapp."

"The FBI isn't going to draw racist graffiti, especially not on the door of its two most promising 'junior agents,'" I said.

"This is serious!" Quint said.

"I want to see it."

"It may not be there anymore," Quint said. "The campus cops were on site this morning, but they may have asked the custodians to clean it up by now."

"Then we shouldn't waste any time."

As we left Insomnia, I glanced to the right at the Hillel Center, just next door to the coffee shop. My eyes welled up at the sight of swastikas on its front door. I thought of *Kristallnacht*, the 'Night of Broken Glass,' and all the other nights after it, when hateful graffiti like this would foreshadow more sinister, more deadly outcomes. I started to walk faster, and we hurried the half block up Wall Street, turned left onto College, then right into the quad south of Harkness Hall, the path that led to the front of Sterling. Someone had already wiped my chalk mark from the façade. At least it would not add to the anti-Semitic stress on campus, even if it was being misread.

There was quite a buzz of campus security and local TV reporters in the library's lobby.

"They'll likely want to talk with us," Quint said. "If it's our carrel."

He gestured with his head toward a back staircase, which we took instead of the main elevators behind the circulation desk, weaving through some reference stacks and other carrels as we approached our own. It turned out to be a better choice. As our carrel came into view, there was Kantorowicz, talking with Ted Bilbo, the two of them standing in the open door of our carrel. Of course, it was really Kantorowicz's carrel, which he was just lending to us, so we shouldn't have been surprised to see him there. He and Bilbo were casually looking around at our books and papers. They weren't touching anything, but it still felt like we were being violated.

Quint wanted to sneak up on them, to hear what they were saying. There was no way to do it without being seen, so I held him back. Good thing I did. In that moment, the two of them finished their examination of the carrel's contents, stepped out of the tiny space, pulled the door shut and locked it. Now, between the two men, we could discern the swastika, drawn with a black marker on the dark wood of our carrel door. Whatever they were talking about, the closing of the carrel door signaled an end to the conversation. Kantorowicz and Bilbo nodded to each other and moved in the direction of the main staircase.

Quint made a move to follow, but I pulled him back into the stacks again. Across the room, emerging from a small corridor, the bald man in the well-tailored suit appeared—the one we saw after Craig Michaels riot. He was following our professor and the neo-Nazi Hobbit.

"What the hell is this?" Quint whispered to me over his shoulder.

"Another neo-Nazi?" I said. "That's what we wrote to Mapp in the book code message."

"So, what?" Quint said. "Is 'bald neo-Nazi' providing some kind of overwatch security as Bilbo and Kantorowicz meet?"

I shrugged.

Kantorowicz and Bilbo slowly vanished down the staircase, like the masts of ships sinking into the horizon. "Bald neo-Nazi" seemed to float across the second floor of the Sterling Library as he followed them, making no sound and leaving no trace, first to the top of the stairs, then downward, barely touching the individual steps as he went.

Now, I thought, and moved in front of Quint to pick up the chase just as an entire shelfful of books shifted to the left. And there he was, Special Agent Nathaniel Mapp of the FBI, standing on the other side of the shelves grabbing at the air to get our attention.

"DON'T!" he whispered. "Don't follow them. Stay here. Count to a hundred, then go home." As quickly as he'd materialized, Mapp disappeared, following the trajectory of those who'd gone before.

It reminded me of a cartoon I'd seen when I was a kid. A little fish is about to be eaten by a big fish. Unbeknownst to the big fish, there's an even bigger fish behind him, ready to eat both of them. The even bigger fish is so focused on his two-fish lunch that he doesn't notice the whale swimming along behind him, all set to chomp down on the whole lot.

Mapp was secretly tailing "Bald neo-Nazi," who was secretly tailing our professor and the neo-Nazi Hobbit. We decided not to follow the line of followers. If Mapp was the whale in the cartoon, who were we supposed to be? Besides, he'd already told us we were bad at the following game. Instead, we decided to wait until the next day and go to Kantorowicz's office, where we'd finally confront him. The whole enterprise was getting to be too much. Too confusing. Too dangerous.

CHAPTER 37
All will be illuminated …

"You all right?" Kantorowicz asked. "I heard about the graffiti in a memo from the provost and immediately thought it must be my … *our* carrel. Are you okay?"

He didn't admit that he'd, like, seen the graffiti firsthand at the carrel door. Interesting. We assured him we were okay. I said that the swastika on the door was indeed the most frightening episode of my time at Yale, if not of my entire life. Quint wasn't willing to go that far.

"In the seventh grade," he said, "someone left a note on my desk with the kid's 'hangman' game, where you have to guess the right letters to complete the word or gradually get lynched. Most of the letters were filled in, so it was easy to guess the message: 'ST__PID  NI__  __ER.' By high school, the haters weren't nearly so creative and just scrawled the N-word across my locker."

"That's it, then," Kantorowicz said. "I'm calling the whole project off!"

"What?!" I said.

"The new symbol project," said Kantorowicz. "You shouldn't be involved. I no longer require your assistance. Thank you. You're done."

"Wait -" Quint said.

"And you should be working on your dissertation," Kantorowicz said. "It was totally wrong of me to ask you to take this on."

"Hang on a minute!" I said. "This swastika graffiti happened because of an op-ed I wrote. Cause I stood up in public and gave that racist asshole Michaels what for. It's got nothing to do with our 'experimental archaeology' project!"

Kantorowicz looked out his window. Quint tilted his head and looked into our professor's eyes.

"It *is* just an experiment," Quint said. "*Isn't* it?"

Kantorowicz continued to watch the late January snow fall in the quad below.

"I'm afraid I haven't been entirely honest with you,' he said at last. "Oh, my. Where to begin?"

He bolted up from his chair, reached for the crutch resting against the bookshelf behind him and in one fluid motion made it to the windowsill where the kettle awaited. He'd forgotten to serve tea.

"Forgive me," he said, and took care flipping the kettle's switch, distributing mugs and tea bags, and placing the milk and sugar on a corner of his desk. As the ritual unfolded, he began to tell us how he came to be working with neo-Nazis.

"Like a lot of universities," Kantorowicz said, "Yale has a speakers' bureau. I usually get invited to church congregations when they want someone to come in and talk about the architecture of their buildings, or maybe to put some holy day or biblical passage into historical perspective.

"A little more than a year ago, I got invited to talk to a group that called itself 1488 Consultants. I remember joking that, as a historian, I couldn't think of anything earth shattering that had happened in 1488."

"Bartholomeu of Portugal rounded the Cape of Good Hope," I said. "Furthest south any European traveler had ventured. Anne of Brittany was crowned Duchess at age 11. Michelangelo started his first artist's apprenticeship in Florence."

"I think the point was rhetorical," Quint said.

Kantorowicz gave me a look and I blanched.

"In any case," he continued, "They said 1488 was just the address of their building. They'd chosen it as a last resort when they couldn't come up with a better name. They said they acted as PR consultants to groups whose messaging might be considered fringe, or at least controversial, like pro-life groups or gun rights advocates."

Kantorowicz shifted his weight, then continued.

"I told them those topics didn't seem so fringe to me, but they just smiled and said that that 'depended on the response of the reader.' I was fascinated that they referenced Stanley Fish and the post-structuralists."

"Wait," I said, holding up both hands. "You're losing me."

"Post-structuralism was a brand of criticism that evolved in the 1960s. The basic claim was that no text had any inherent meaning, neither from the author nor from its historical context. It had no meaning at all until a reader constructed the meaning by reading the text."

"That's ridiculous," I said.

"Maybe," Kantorowicz said. "There are still scholars around who like debating such ideas. My point is that these 1488 fellows seemed widely read and well educated."

"Why did they invite you to speak?" I asked.

"Ouch!" Kantorowicz said.

"Oh ... uh ... I didn't mean it like 'they were well educated so why did they invite *you*? I meant, *how* did they come to invite you *in general*?"

"They knew my book," he said, smiling. "They were interested in my work with modern gang signs as branding and marketing tools, and how it compared to medieval heraldry."

I glanced over my shoulder at the copy of *The King's Too Bawdy*, still sitting upright on the shelf where I'd left it, still, presumably, recording all conversations in our professor's office. Including this one.

Kantorowicz described his meeting with the 1488 group. It happened over lunch in, like, a conference room of a Holiday Inn off of I-95 with about 25 or 30 people in the audience. According to Kantorowicz, the lunch was good. The participants asked good questions. Several of them stayed after to talk more.

"By the end of the lunch, Ted Bilbo—that's the name of the chap from 1488—Bilbo!" he laughed. "You can't make that up. Anyway, this Bilbo fellow said the whole thing had been a great success and that he hoped we could work together again."

He blew across the top of his mug and took a sip of tea.

"A couple of weeks later, Bilbo called and wanted to meet for drinks. He said the 1488 group wanted me to do some consulting for them. It was friendly enough. He asked me how long I'd been a professor, if I liked it. But after a while, the questions got a little strange. Did I think students of color were less prepared for college than white students? What did I think of need-based vs. merit scholarships? What about racial quotas? They weren't unreasonable questions, but it felt like he was trying to suss out something else. Then he came to the crux.

"Bilbo told me that 1488 had several clients with similar missions, all of whom desired to merge into something bigger. What these different clients needed was a common symbol or logo, something steeped in history that could unite them. Fair enough, but then the real kicker came, the reason they wanted me to consult on this project. All of these groups had an affinity for medieval symbolism, which was my specialty. That's why they wanted me."

Kantorowicz paused. He must have sensed that his voice was rising and tried to regulate it.

"Bilbo wanted me to find a medieval symbol that had never been used before in the modern era, to unite the various groups under a common historical banner. As if such things were just lying about, waiting to be discovered!"

"Didn't you have *any* idea about who you were dealing with?" Quint asked.

I looked back and forth between the two of them.

"I must admit I was naïve at first," said Kantorowicz. "Bilbo started telling me how each of these clients of his was concerned about preserving their heritage, their cultural legacy. How they felt attacked by rapid societal changes that were threatening their historical identity. Finally, the light bulb clicked on."

"White supremacists," I said.

"Yes," said Kantorowicz. "But the language Bilbo used didn't have an ounce of hate speech in it. No overt racism. The way he spoke was designed to evoke sympathy."

He paused, watched the falling snow again, then turned and faced us both.

"I looked Bilbo straight in the eyes. I told him 'that was the kind of thing where those racial quotas played a part.' They were the most hateful words that had ever come out of my mouth, but I knew what I had to do: to signal I was on board so I could work against him. Bilbo nodded in agreement and said he'd be in touch soon."

It was an extraordinary story.

Quint responded.

"Why didn't you tell us any of this before? Why the sub-terfuge of the *archaeological experiment*?"

"It wasn't fair," Kantorowicz said. "I should have been honest with you from the start. But now that I see the real danger involved, I have to take you off the project. The swas-tika graffiti was just a warning. It's too much. I can't protect you. So that's it!"

"If it's so dangerous," I said, "why are *you* doing it? Aren't you scared?"

"So scared I went straight to the FBI!" He made eye con-tact with each of us. "I've been working with an agent named Mapp on what he calls a counter-intelligence plan."

On hearing Mapp's name, my eyes flashed toward Quint, who shook his head so subtly that high-speed, stop-motion photography wouldn't have caught it. Okay, Quint. You don't want to tell him that we know about Mapp, that he's actually been working with us to keep an eye on the prof. I'm not sure why you don't want this known, but okay.

"What does 'counter-intelligence' mean?" I asked.

"You remember when I told you about the neo-Nazi march in Wunsiedel, Rudolph Hess's burial place? How the townsfolk in Wunsiedel turned the march into a fundraiser to spoof and confound the neo-Nazis?"

I nodded.

"Like that," Kantorowicz said, "only ten times more complex. And much more dangerous!"

Kantorowicz described a documentary that had come out in 2018, shortly after the events in Charlottesville. *Undercover in the Alt-Right* told the story of Patrik Hermansson, a 25-year-old Swedish grad student who infiltrated the white nationalist Alt-Right for over a year. Using his own identity, his cover story was that he was researching societal responses to controversial, right-leaning views. Hermansson said he "posed as an academic" because he knew that white nationalists "were interested in having academically minded people."

Hermansson soon gained the trust of racist players at the highest levels. He captured secret video of meetings between white supremacist leaders many of whom had, like, never been filmed before. None of the Alt-Right suspected him. He'd so thoroughly gained their trust that they invited him to speak about his research at one of their conferences. They even asked Hermansson to do background checks on people trying to join the Alt-Right groups, even though they'd never done a background check on him.

Kantorowicz said that, according to Mapp, this documentary was, like, a remarkable example of counter-intelligence. When Hermansson finally exposed the Alt-Right players, some of them were shamed into exile or lost their jobs. For others, the paranoia inherent in such groups, like, rose to new heights. Distrust within the membership became so overwhelming that further attempts to "unite the right"—which had been the original goal of the Charlottesville gathering—faded away, at least for a while. This was the kind of play that Agent Mapp believed Kantorowicz might achieve.

"He said it was perfect," Kantorowicz said. "A 'made-to-order counter-intel op.' That's how he talked. Bilbo and the 1488 'consultants' wanted me to find a historical symbol they could rally around and Mapp could use that against them. Then things got really crazy."

He took another sip of tea.

"Bilbo said his clients were aiming for another 'unite the right' event, to be held in early May in the university town of Kalamazoo, Michigan. He asked if I could find a symbol by then. In fact, I'd need to find it sooner because they wanted it to be distributed, adopted, and employed by all the clients by the time of their Kalamazoo rally."

"The International Congress!" Quint said.

"Huh?"

"Tell you later."

Kantorowicz continued.

"It was Agent Mapp's idea to create a forgery. How would they ever know, if I was the expert? Being pressed for time, I asked both of you to help."

"Wait," I said. "This guy Bilbo wants you to *discover* a *real* medieval symbol, to unite the right? But the FBI guy, Mapp, wants you to make a forgery?"

"That's the counter-intelligence part," Kantorowicz said. "Give them something they think is real, then reveal that it's a fake to disrupt their reality. Discord, distrust, and disunity follow. That's Mapp's theory, anyway."

*

Sitting on a park bench in the quad outside the Department of History offices, wearing his ridiculous trench coat, the earbud dangling from his left ear only slightly disguised by his flowing blond locks, Special Agent Mapp of the FBI sat listening.

"It was Agent Mapp's idea to create a for ... .....
.... ever know, if I was the expert? ... ... ... another reason ... .. asked ... ... .. ... .. help."

"Wait," ..... ... ... ... ... ... Bilbo ... ... ... *discover* ...
... ... symbol ... unite the right? ... ... ... FBI ... Mapp ... ... .. ... make a for—?"

"That's the count ... ..... .. something they think ... disrupt ... ... . Discord, distrust, and disunity ... ...... ... ... Mapp's theory."

\*

"That's the easy part," said Kantorowicz. "The hard part is convincing them our forgery is real from the start. Mapp had an idea about that as well. He asked me if there wasn't an academic journal where this forgery could be published, to give it legitimacy and so the white supremacists could discover it on their own. I explained that would take too long, and besides, by the time it came out all sorts of scholars would challenge the symbol's authenticity. I told him a conference paper would be a better bet. I'm thinking of the Medieval Academy, coming up in March."

"That's professional suicide!" Quint said in a panicked voice. "You can't let anyone know you're presenting falsified research at the Medieval Academy, otherwise Mapp's scheme won't work. But when they find out—which will happen, at least by the time you expose the fraud—then your career's over."

"That's how it has to happen," Kantorowicz said. "Introduce the forgery at the Medieval Academy. Expose it at Kalamazoo. Alt-Right and neo-Nazi unity disrupted."

"Won't the neo-Nazis, like, also want to kill you?" I said. "Not that I think that's worse than your career being ruined."

Kantorowicz smiled at me and nodded.

"Patrik Hermansson, the student who went undercover with the Alt-Right? He's now forced to live in hiding under an assumed name."

"This is crazy!" Quint said.

"I've made my choice," Kantorowicz said. "I'll live, or die, with the consequences."

He said this with the sadness and resolve of a small boy who'd been crippled by a racist driving a huge white truck. Like a boy who'd seen that same racist murder an innocent Black man before his eyes. Like a son whose father had been the favorite historian of Adolph Hitler, though his grandmother had died in a concentration camp. His resolve turned to obsession before our eyes.

"But I can't involve the two of you," he said. "No. I won't let you do it."

Quint let out a low, guttural growl, an unearthly sound. He told me later *it was the minotaur breaking loose, societal expectations falling from his shoulders like the walls of the labyrinth crumbling to the ground. Finish the dissertation? Get a job? Become a respectable member of the academic community? All of that could wait! Time to step up. Time to pick up the napalmed baby and do something.*

"It's not your choice," he said to Kantorowicz. "I'm in." He stood and planted both feet on the ground. "Besides, I've already got a really good idea for the forgery, so I need to see how this plays out."

"I'm in, too!" I shouted.

"You can't just jump in because I've jumped," Quint said.

"Someday, you're gonna regret saying that," I said. I could tell he already did.

Each of us, Kantorowicz, Quint, and myself, made slow direct eye contact with each other and nodded slightly, once, in affirmation. We accepted our mission, and whatever fate came with it. It wasn't quite "all for one and one for all," but it would have to do.

"Let's meet soon, then," Kantorowicz said. "You say you have a possibility for creating the forgery? Did you use the little drawing I gave you?" He was looking at me, but Quint answered.

"No," he said. "But it's something I think you're going to like. Give us a day to put together a proper presentation."

Kantorowicz nodded. The meeting was over, and we were on our way.

## CHAPTER 38
### *¡Rompecabeza!*

Exiting the office, I looked again at the bugged copy of *The Kings Too Bawdy*, which I had planted on our professor's shelf. I must have leaned toward the book as we passed through the door because Quint—maybe sensing my inclination—performed an elegant do-si-do to place his body between my own and the bookshelf. He pretty much danced me out of the office, to keep me from copping the bugged book or exposing it to Kantorowicz. I waited until we were down the hallway, well out of hearing range.

"I don't understand what's happening," I whispered, just to be safe.

"No. You don't understand" Quint said. "Which is exactly why we shouldn't act on impulse."

Fuck you, I thought. Sometimes I act on impulse. And sometimes that causes a riot. Fucking let it go.

"Mapp gave us the bugged book," I said, "asked us to surveil Kantorowicz because he suspected the prof might be a neo-Nazi. But now that we know Kantorowicz is working with Mapp, he doesn't need to be surveilled anymore. Kantorowicz was honest with us about his entire plan, so we don't need to suspect him anymore. Right?"

"Chronology," Quint said. "Put the events in order to see if they suggest causality."

It was a concept straight out of Stark's historiography seminar.

"Fine," I said. "According to his own account, Kantorowicz was unsuspecting when he first encountered Bilbo. Once he did suspect Bilbo of working behind the scenes for white supremacists, he went to the FBI. Special Agent Nathaniel Mapp, of the Fleecy Blond Intimation, suggests a counter-intelligence plan. Kantorowicz recruits us for the 'new and improved Nazi symbol' project. But that same Mapp recruits us to spy on *him*, which we do, planting bugs and following hobbits and leaving encoded messages. So … what is Mapp up to?"

"Exactly," Quint said. "If Mapp is privy to everything Kantorowicz knows, why hasn't he pulled us off the Kantorowicz detail? Why does he suspect Kantorowicz of being a neo-Nazi, if he was the one who came in first?"

"Should we confront Mapp? Should we tell him that Kantorowicz told us about him?"

"NO!" Quint said. "We don't reveal what we know, and about whom, to anyone, until we know more."

"I don't get it," I said.

"Turing and *enigma*," he said.

"Unless Turing is a medievalist, you've filled a giant U-Haul truck with the sum of my knowledge and moved way beyond my comfort zone."

"Alan Turing was a mathematician during World War II who worked on Nazi codes, practically inventing modern computers along the way. He famously broke the *enigma* code, which meant that the British could always know what the Germans were up to. Yet he didn't want the Germans to know that he knew, realizing that they would just change the code if they did. Which sometimes meant sacrificing men in battle, because saving them would reveal what the British knew. Turing saw the longer-term benefits of not revealing his knowledge of *enigma*."

I shook my head, in part because he knew so much history that wasn't medieval, in part because I couldn't believe what he was suggesting we do.

"To be players rather than pawns," he said, "we need to hold onto whatever intelligence we gather, until we know *who* knows what *Mapp* knows about what *Kantorowicz* knows about what *Bilbo* knows."

He knows that we know that he knows that you know that
they know that we know ...

"¡*Rompecabeza*!" I shouted. "You're breaking my fucking
head!"

CHAPTER 39
## The Voynich Manuscript

To be players rather than pawns meant holding on to, like, whatever intelligence we gathered, and not acting counter to what was expected of us. For the moment, this meant putting together our presentation of the medieval-based forgery so Kantorowicz would have something to offer the neo-Nazis.

In this situation, Quint's scheme for using the Voynich manuscript was utter perfection.

"The manuscript gets its name from a guy named Wilfrid Voynich," Quint said. "How he came to own it—the manuscript's provenance—is lengthy and tedious. Suffice to say that the codex passed through the hands of some of the greatest minds of the early modern period, including an alchemist named Georg Baresch, a medical doctor named Jacobus Horcicky de Tepenecz, and the Holy Roman Emperor Rudolf II, who may have gotten it from the occult philosopher John Dee, who was active in Rudolf's court. None of them succeeded in deciphering it."

Quint took a breath and continued.

"Voynich himself spent his life trying to figure it out but died in disappointment. Ironically, in 1917, when the US finally entered World War I, he was suspected of espionage and was even investigated by the FBI for possessing a secret code, which they believed to be 'a tool of the Hun.'"

Another pause for breath before he concluded the provenance question.

"Voynich's widow, Ethel, bequeathed the mysterious codex to a woman named Anne Nill, who sold it to a certain H.P

Kraus, who in 1969 donated it to Beinecke. Since then, the Voynich manuscript bears the call number, Beinecke MS 408."

He opened the replica copy he'd borrowed from the library, the 2017 critical edition published by Watkins, and pushed it toward me.

"What do you see?" Quint said, just as Kantorowicz would have asked if he were here.

Beinecke MS 408 has 116 folios. Almost every page has drawings of, like, plants, or stars and planets, or human figures. One section shows dozens of female nudes with swollen bellies swimming or wading in green water that flows through a system of organic-looking pipes and tubes. All the drawings seem to be rendered by the same person, whose artistic skill might best be called "colloquial." The drawings are simple but lively, not quite childlike but also not as sophisticated as, say, Leonardo da Vinci. The ink drawings are enhanced by washes of green, yellow, red, blue, and brown. The manuscript text is indecipherable, so it's impossible to know its subject or meaning.

"Based on the drawings," I said, "it seems quasi-scientific, like, maybe medical, since herbs and astrology were both important in medieval concepts of health. The nude women in water might illustrate some kind of bathing cure?'"

"Good," Quint said. "Now, here are the big questions about the Voynich: Is it written in some long-forgotten language and alphabet unrelated to the familiar languages of scholarship, like Latin or Greek? Or is it an enciphered text, designed to hide its esoteric secrets? Or is it both? One thing's for sure: the Voynich isn't random. It has repeating patterns of letters and words that suggest rules of grammar and other aspects of human language. But which one?"

According to Quint, there were as many theories about the Voynich as there have been scholars trying to decipher it. Linguists have posited that the manuscript is written in Old English, Middle High German, medieval Welsh, Old Dutch, Old Spanish, classical Latin, Hebrew (or Arabic written with Hebrew letters), Manchurian, and Nahuatl, the language of the Aztecs. Some have claimed that it's an entirely artificial language. One scholar suggested a secret language given to Judas by Jesus Christ.

"It's eluded the greatest cryptologists of the 20th century," he said. "William Friedman of American Military Intelligence, who cracked Japan's 'purple code' during World War II, tried and gave up. Even Alan Turing couldn't breach the secrets of the Voynich. In 1978, the U.S. National Security Agency, the NSA, studied Beinecke MS 408 and determined that the manuscript was a hoax."

"Maybe that was to avoid their embarrassment from, like, not being able to figure it out."

The purpose behind the Voynich manuscript has also led to some crackpot conjecture. Is it a manuscript from the future describing alien technology? Is it an ancient text that forewarns of the end times? Is it a stage prop created by Francis Bacon, the purported author of the works of William Shakespeare?

The Voynich is all these things. It's an empty vessel that conspiracy theorists use to concoct their crazy visions. It's a blank slate for kooks and occultists to write their esoteric narratives. It's a turquoise Thunderbird convertible driven by Thelma and Louise and Wile E. Coyote, where otherwise serious academics hitch a ride and have their careers driven off a cliff.

"For our project to make it past the Medieval Academy," Quint said, "it only needs to be slightly less crazy than all the theories that have gone before."

CHAPTER 40

The Palimpsest Plan

All of the secrets of the Voynich manuscript are, like, hidden in plain sight. We may not understand the meaning of the images. We may not be able to read the words and sentences. But images, words, and sentences are all visible to the naked eye.

"What if the Voynich had secrets that were not visible to the naked eye?" Quint said. "What if it contained a palimpsest?"

Palimpsest: from the Greek, "to scrape again."

In case you weren't paying attention in Stark's seminar, a palimpsest occurred when an original text had been, like, scraped off the parchment and written over with a new text. This saved on parchment, but for historians it meant that you could sometimes find more interesting invisible texts hidden underneath the texts that you could see.

"What if the Voynich contained a palimpsest?"

This was the brilliant plan of Quinton Quick, apprentice to Abe Kantorowicz, soon to be *philosophiae doctor* from Yale. The first benefit of this plan was that the proposed discovery was entirely original. We would not need to provide counter arguments to pre-existing theories. There was no need to say that Professor X was wrong about the palimpsest Y, because no one had ever suggested a palimpsest. The second great benefit was that it used material evidence that had not yet been published. In addition to all the scholarly books that included images from the Voynich, every single folio of the manuscript had been digitized in hi-resolution images and posted to

numerous websites. There would be no image of our palimpsest to argue against because we had not yet published it. People could go to Beinecke and examine the original, but that
took time and sometimes special permissions. This would slow
down any meaningful academic response to our fake theory,
which Kantorowicz needed in order pull off the "big reveal"
in Kalamazoo and embarrass the neo-Nazis.

"Hasn't anyone, like, taken infrared images, or whatever,
to look for palimpsests before?"

"I'm sure they have," Quint said. "But if anyone asks, Kantorowicz can just say they missed this one. Nobody will be able
to prove anything at the Medieval Academy meeting."

Once we'd decided on a palimpsest, we had to work out
what it would say. It would have to sound like some racist
screed that could have been written in the medieval period.
Something so vile that the neo-Nazis would, like, lap it up right
away. The text would need to refer to an image on the same
page as the palimpsest, which image the neo-Nazis could then
co-opt onto their shields, etc.

"What language should it be in?" Quint asked. He and I
both had Latin, but mine was better. We both read French and
German, but it would not do to put the palimpsest text into a
modern language.

"I can do Hebrew," I said. Lots of the earlier Voynich
scholars thought the manuscript was enciphered Hebrew."

"That's great," Quint said. "But we're trying to appeal to
… How did you put it? 'Mother-fucking, Jew-hating, neo-Nazis?'"

"Oh, yeah. Right."

We ran through the catalog of languages we shared between us.

"What about Old Norse or Middle High German?" I said.
"That would appeal to their Teutonic strand."

"I can read a text in front of me, but I'm not fluent enough
in either of those to compose something from scratch. You?"

"Not really," I said. "Latin is probably my best shot."

"Okay, let's go with Latin for the moment," said Quint.

We sat quietly for a while.

"What about an image first," said Quint. "An image is what's going to have the most impact. What they're going to paint on their idiotic shields."

I opened the Watkins edition and began paging through images in the Voynich manuscript. Quint looked over my shoulder, which I quite liked. After a few minutes, he laughed out loud.

"Imagine the neo-Nazis painting one of those weird botanical images onto their shields."

"I was just thinking the same thing but imagining a neo-Nazi emblem with a bunch of nude women bathing in green water. Nothing cries out 'fierce Germanic warrior' like a shield with a naked lady in a bathtub."

"How about this?" Quint reached around me and flipped the page to one of the round astral charts, folio 69 recto, a cruciform halo with a six-pointed star at the center.

"Maybe," I said. "But it has a Jewish star of David right there. Wouldn't that turn them off?"

"What if the text said that the star originally belonged to the Germans?" Quint said. "What if our forgery claimed that it never belonged to the Jews, that they stole it from its rightful owners?"

"That's horrible!" I whispered, appalled.

"Yes," Quint said. "I bet the fucking neo-Nazis would love it."

Quint went on to tell me how the early Germanic tribes, when they first converted to Christianity, were obsessed with the books of the Old Testament. They especially liked 1 and 2 Kings because that's where they could find all the good battle scenes. When Pepin was crowned King of the Franks, the pope anointed him with chrism oil, just like kings David and Solomon. Pepin's son, Charlemagne, saw himself as a "new David," the head of a "new chosen people."

"It wouldn't be a stretch to see the early *Germani* claiming the star of David as their own invention," Quint said.

"You're one devious mother!" I said.

"But wouldn't it be great to see the neo-Nazis proudly wearing the star of David on their shields?"

We decided that folio 69 recto was the right place to locate our fake palimpsest and spent a couple of hours composing a racist text that would appeal to our target audience. Then I translated it into Latin. I looked in old paleography manuals online to see which hand we should use, took out my handy calligraphy pen and wrote the poem on a piece of tracing paper I'd laid down over the full-color image in the Watkins edition. It didn't have to be perfect because we were just going to "scrape it off" again. In the meantime, Quint called on a friend who was getting an MFA in photography to see if she could mock-up an infrared photo that would "expose" the fake palimpsest.

When all of this was in order, we called on Kantorowicz in his office.

Quint had a stack of photocopies that more or less simulated a digital presentation. He started with a very brief introduction of the Voynich manuscript, then came to the point.

"Beinecke MS 408, folio 69 recto, has a palimpsest," Quint said, then paused for effect. "At least it's a palimpsest in the forgery we propose."

Kantorowicz straightened in his chair. He had a glint in his eyes like a caged lion at the zoo realizing how easy it would be to jump his enclosure and devour one of the small children throwing peanut shells at him.

Quint showed a color photocopy of folio 69r from the Watkins edition and described the elements that could be seen: the emblem of a Christ's halo, 46 segments radiating out from the center, writing in every other segment, the six-pointed star in the center, the text at the center and all around the circular image. Then he showed the faked infrared scan that his friend had created, showing the palimpsest around the outer ring of text. He let Kantorowicz read the Latin, both inside and outside the roundel.

"German race, master race, put on earth by almighty God." Kantorowicz shook his head, disgusted, but approving.

"We've still got some kinks to work out," Quint said, "about the authorship and provenance of the palimpsest. The Latin poem needs some fine tuning. We also want to build in some elisions and distortions in the text. It mustn't be too perfect. It should all be done by the time of the Medieval Academy meeting."

"Good," said Kantorowicz. "Good."

CHAPTER 41
The Medieval Academy

For any topic that exists in the world, from baseball to vintage fashion to international relations, from urban studies to sexuality to forestry, if it can be discussed and debated, if it can evoke passion and possessiveness, if it can generate the interest of three or more people, there will be a professional organization or learned society somewhere in the world that hosts an annual conference devoted to that topic. Taken in this larger context, a gathering of medievalists seems, like, almost mundane.

By the way, "gathering of medievalists" is the correct term for describing a group of medievalists, like "pride of lions, or "murder of crows." This comes from the practice of using the same term to describe a group of folios gathered together for binding in a codex. The discipline of medieval studies is in fact a gathering of many disciplines—history, religion, art history, music history, literature, and more—centered around the period of the Middle Ages, as complicated as that period is to define.

To avoid any appearance of partiality, the Medieval Academy of America's annual meeting that year was held in Boston, rather than Cambridge, where the Academy had been founded and where it was still headquartered. The organizers chose the Isabella Stewart Gardner Museum to host the conference.

The New York socialite Isabella Stewart and her husband John Lowell Gardner loved to travel and made frequent trips to Europe, Egypt, the Middle East, and Asia. Along the way, they became avid art connoisseurs, using Isabella's $2 million inheritance from her father to expand their collection. As their house grew too small for their collection, they decided to build a museum. In Venice, they purchased architectural fragments —columns, capitals, statues, and more—to decorate their new building in a mixture of Roman, Byzantine, Gothic, and Renaissance styles. The Venetian Palazzo Barbarro, "summer home" to Bostonians Daniel and Ariana Curtiss, whose guest list boasted painters like John Singer Sargent and James McNeill Whistler, was a major inspiration to Isabella. After Jack's death in 1899, she threw herself into the project, taking a "hands-on" approach, frequently ordering workers to re-do sections they had already completed. She had a particular vision for her 'forgery' of a Venetian palazzo and she wasn't going to have it any other way. For example, she instructed plasterers on how to apply the stucco in the courtyard 'correctly'; thinking the wood beams destined for the Gothic Room to be 'too smooth', she took an axe to them herself, to give them that special antique look.

She completed her museum in 1901 but didn't open it for two more years so that she could install the collection that would fulfill her vision. It was a wonderful setting to host the Medieval Academy.

The MAA professed to be the oldest and largest society of medievalists in the world. Interestingly, the Academy's annual meeting is not the largest of such gatherings, a distinction that goes to the International Congress for Medieval Studies at Western Michigan University in Kalamazoo, affectionately known as K'zoo. The smaller size of the Medieval Academy's gathering, around 300 participants, also reflects the perceived quality of the papers presented. They represent the crème de la crème, the best of their kind, written by the most elite scholars.

In spite of its perceived exclusivity, the Medieval Academy wanted to remain relevant and this year's conference program offered some evidence of its success. The theme of the conference was "The Global Middle Ages," an attempt to move medieval studies away from its long tradition of Eurocentrism. The program's 100 pages included seven sessions with up to ten panels per session running simultaneously, each session having two to three papers. Topics aligned with the conference theme ranged from medieval China and Japan, the 13$^{th}$-century empire of Mali under Sundeita Keita, the legacy of medieval Europe in Mexico, and the globalism of Marco Polo and Ibn Battuta. There were also numerous workshops in paleography and codicology, pedagogical strategies for teaching global medieval history to undergraduates, as well as digital humanities for storing and disseminating sources and scholarship. Two panels were sponsored by a new group of scholars, the Medievalists of Color. One of these panels was an open forum on how to combat the coopting of the Middle Ages by white supremacists.

Every member of the medieval history faculty at Yale was in attendance at the Medieval Academy meeting, all of them except Professor Stark giving papers. Professor Hathaway, one of the Byzantinists, was giving a paper on Anna Komnena, the daughter and biographer of Emperor Alexios, who played a role in the First Crusade. Vasiliki Kostas, the other Byzantinist, was part of a roundtable discussion on education in Constantinople after 1204, when the Latin Kingdom in the East was established. Tariq Sallam, the Egyptian expatriate, spoke on slavery in the Fatimid caliphate of the 10$^{th}$ and 11$^{th}$ centuries. Finally, Kantorowicz was scheduled to give the keynote talk after the induction ceremony for new fellows of the Medieval Academy. This was where he would unveil our great archaeological experiment. After that, G-d save us all!

The main business meeting was held during lunch on the Friday. Although it was open to any member of the Medieval Academy, or any attendee at the conference, it was anything but packed. Kantorowicz told us that scholars often used this time slot to skip their conference duties and do some shopping or site-seeing with their spouses, in this case around Boston. The business meeting included presentations of various awards for service and teaching, travel and research grants for grad students, and awards to promote inclusivity and diversity.

One of the more positive reports came from the editor of *Speculum*, the Medieval Academy's prestigious, flagship academic journal, which was exceeding its expense targets. Seated next to Stark, I just had to ask her about the journal's name.

"How did they come up with *that*?" I fought to hold back a rush of immature laughter like I hadn't felt since I first heard the word "sackbut" used to describe a medieval trombone.

"Yes," Stark said. "One has to imagine the 1925 Medieval Academy, membership entirely male, searching for a suitable Latin name for the journal of their new organization. *Speculum* is simply Latin for 'mirror'. They must have meant their journal to be seen as scholarship holding a mirror up to medieval society."

"And none of them checked in with their wives?"

"No," Stark chuckled. "I'm afraid the entire gynecological undercurrent in the journal's title was lost on them."

Other than this gratifying exchange, it was clear, even to this first-year grad student, that the subcommittee reports were the one part of the conference worth skipping.

I connected with Quint after lunch. We had each been going our own way during the conference, hearing papers that interested us. I asked him where he was headed next.

"There's a roundtable on fighting white supremacists who co-opt medieval symbols," Quint said. "I thought it might be relevant given the bombshell that Kantorowicz is going to drop tomorrow afternoon. It's sponsored by the Medievalists of Color."

CHAPTER 42
The Medievalists of Color

For all the Medieval Academy had done in the name of diversity and inclusion—including the global theme of this very conference—for some, it still wasn't enough. How could it ever be enough, after having, like, done so little for so long?

Friday afternoon. The roundtable sponsored by the Medievalists of Color, the MoC, had been advertised as a discussion on combatting white supremacy. People believed the roundtable was an opportunity for medievalists to look outward at how their field was being used to promote racism, which no one wanted. What they wanted even less, though, was to look inward, to be confronted with the uncomfortable realization that the medievalists themselves were promoting racism, that the very nature of their field, in spite of all its variety, was a vehicle for white supremacy.

According to the conference program, five scholars led the discussion. Two of them were Black: Cynthia Wright-Bell, an art historian of medieval bestiaries at St. Scholastica University in Minnesota, and Reed Coleman, who taught Beowulf at Connecticut Wesleyan. Coleman was among several scholars who recently advocated for a renaming of 'Anglo-Saxon' Studies on account of its inherent racism. White nationalists had coopted the term 'Anglo-Saxon' because, to them, it sounded so purely white. Next on the panel was Madeleine Chang at Mount Holyoke, who researched medieval women in China's Tang Dynasty, and Dorothy Watanabe-Smith at Case-Western Reserve, who studied the economy of feudal Japan. Lastly, there was Henry Sanchez, an adjunct instructor at NYU, who studied intercultural relations in the crusader states. All of the panelists were untenured, junior professors.

"It's a tremendous act of courage," Quint told me as we stood in the doorway, looking for a place to sit. "Publicly speaking out about something so controversial. As stupid as it sounds, they've got limited to no job security. It could seriously mess up their careers."

"Oh, man," I said, and immediately thought that was the lamest response I could give. Quint continued.

"Some of them have even been harassed by neo-Nazis, getting hateful emails and threatening tweets. Wright-Bell has restraining orders out on two racist stalkers and is escorted by campus security whenever she's at work. Chang has small children and she's ended up moving and getting an unlisted phone number."

The room was packed with about 60 people. Leigh Ann, who fancied herself an ally, was sitting right in the middle. She waved to Quint and me as we walked in, so we sat with her. This put us sitting right in front of Stark and Kantorowicz. I wondered what our professors would think of the panel. Would either of them respond, pro or con, to what was about to unfold?

Cynthia Wright-Bell spoke first.

"The Middle Ages is being weaponized," she said. "It's being weaponized by radical forces in the Middle East like ISIS in order to recruit disillusioned young men to fight in the name of an idealized medieval Islamic past. In the West, that idealized medieval past takes on a Christian flavor to recruit the same kind of impressionable, disenfranchised young men to the causes of the KKK, neo-Nazism, and other forms of white supremacy. Since Charlottesville, we've all become acutely aware of how easily, how seamlessly white supremacists co-opt elements of our discipline and twist those elements in support of the hatred they hope to spread. As medievalists, unless we take action, we run the risk of being seen as white supremacists ourselves, or at the very least as white supremacist sympathizers."

Wright-Bell paused to let that sink in. Everyone in the audience nodded, considering their own experiences.

"But a far more insidious problem is how the medievalist establishment itself is promoting racism as a regular feature of its own inherent structure: how, at every level, conference program committees, hiring committees, and tenure committees work, perhaps unconsciously or subconsciously or, though we hate to admit it, consciously to perpetuate white supremacy. That's what we want to talk about. How colleagues in our own field, medievalists who deplore the use of medieval symbols by neo-Nazis, nonetheless promote institutional racism—white supremacy at the structural level."

People shifted in their seats. This was clearly not what they were expecting. Reed Coleman spoke next.

"The first thing we're asking of the Medieval Academy," he said, "and of all medievalists, is to practice the self-reflection necessary to truly combat institutional racism. We realize that this is one of the most difficult things we can ask." Coleman paused and made eye contact with his colleagues on the panel.

"Although the Academy's been open at this meeting to inviting non-Eurocentric topics, it still seems resistant to topics that are self-critical of medieval studies. This roundtable is a case in point. The Academy's program committee had no problem with a panel discussion on white supremacists co-opting medieval symbols. But our proposal to critique the discipline of medieval studies, and the Medieval Academy itself, was rejected. This is why we were forced to pull a bait and switch on all of you, to show the importance, the necessity of self-reflection. The first step, always, is admitting you have a problem."

"The Medieval Academy no longer has the luxury of being the conference of 'pure scholarship,'" said Madeleine Chang. "The Academy's program committee can no longer afford to ignore topics relevant to the times in which we live—discussions of our politicized discipline, of the pedagogy of medieval studies. This year's program is a good start, but the Academy must continue to support and expand its offering of papers on medieval decolonization, the global Middle Ages, and anti-racism. We don't want 'pure scholarship' to disappear, yet even the notion of 'purity' must be contested. None of us practices in a vacuum. There's always an inter-relatedness, a greater context in which we all research our topics and present our research. We're *all* implicated. None of us can claim otherwise without empowering white supremacy. Forgive me for quoting a non-medievalist, but as Howard Zinn said, 'You can't be neutral on a moving train.'"

There was a smattering of applause and other sounds of approval on hearing Professor Zinn's quote. Then Dorothy Watanabe-Smith stood to speak.

"The MAA meeting," she said, "and all medievalist conferences, need more transparency concerning how papers are chosen, as well as who makes those decisions. The Academy is actually pretty good about this, but there's always room for improvement. Of deep concern is the selection process at the International Congress in Kalamazoo, and we hope that Academy members might apply a bit of moral pressure there to bring about some improvements."

You could feel scholars in the room, longtime members of the Medieval Academy and longtime attendees of the Kalamazoo conference, feeling put out by the suggestion that one conference should dare to criticize the practices of the other. The long history of the two conferences was reason enough to consider this suggestion ludicrous. Watanabe-Smith continued.

"At both of these conferences, there is still a profound preference for what we can only call 'white' papers, and a dismissive tokenism when it comes to papers presented from a diverse perspective, or papers that directly address issues of racism and white supremacy. Here are just a few examples of the acceptance rates for panels submitted by 'traditional' medievalist societies at this very conference. The Chaucer Society proposed 5 panels and got 5. The Pearl Poet Society proposed 3 and got 3. The Society for the Advancement of Medieval Martial Arts proposed 6 and got 5. In contrast, the Medievalists of Color proposed 10 panels, on topics ranging from 'Medieval

Race, Class, and Gender' to 'How to be a White Ally to Medievalists of Color.' Only 2 of 10 were accepted, which, frankly, is unacceptable."

A few people in the room snapped their fingers to indicate their support. Watanabe-Smith concluded her remarks.

"We don't want to threaten boycotting future meetings of the Medieval Academy, or the Congress at Kalamazoo, but we will unless things start to change."

Henry Sanchez, the last panelist stood.

"We ask that you join us in a counter protest against the neo-Nazi march that's scheduled in Kalamazoo the same weekend as the International Congress on Medieval Studies. It can't be a coincidence that the second Unite the Right rally, the first since Charlottesville, is scheduled to take place on the same weekend as K'zoo. Those of us who monitor 8chan and Stormfront and other white supremacist platforms have heard the alt right promoting a new, unifying symbol, based in medieval studies, that they hope to unveil at Kalamazoo. They claim that hundreds of alt right marchers will be there, wearing this new symbol of white power. This couldn't be a more 'in your face' response to all of the medievalists who've tried to fight white supremacy and the misuse of medieval symbols. Please join us at the counter protest!"

There was more finger snapping, but also hearty applause as the panel concluded. Several participants crowded the stage to ask questions or get more info, Leigh Ann and Quint among them. I stayed, like, on the periphery, unclear on what I should do as a white person.

Stark left without commenting, as did many other scholars of her generation. Kantorowicz lingered but was silent until the clot of people around the presenters had dispersed. He then quietly invited them to attend his talk the following afternoon.

CHAPTER 43
## A Hidden Message

"Good afternoon. I appreciate your being here. I'm the only thing standing between you and our closing reception in the cloisters, just the other side of the wonderful Gardner Museum, so I thank you and beg your patience."

Kantorowicz looked out over the crowd in Calderwood Hall, the Gardner's venue for large groups. To give the keynote address was an honor for Kantorowicz, who had only been elected a fellow of the Academy the previous year. It brought some controversy, given the recent accusations against him and his censure by the Yale faculty senate. His was effectively the last paper of the conference. It was the perfect spot for a scholar of his stature, but also for a paper that would cause such a great disruption, not only in the white supremacist world, but in the world of medievalists.

"Before I begin, I think we should once again offer our thanks to Lisa and her staff in the Cambridge office, to Luke and the program committee for a wonderful lineup of papers, and to the staff here at the Gardner." There was a round of polite applause.

"The title of my paper, "A Hidden Message in the Voynich Manuscript," likely seems redundant. Those of you familiar with the manuscript know that the Voynich is a codex of 116 folios, packed from board to board with hidden messages. The Voynich gives meaning to the phrase, 'A riddle wrapped in an enigma shrouded in mystery.' But this afternoon, I hope to reveal at least one of the Voynich's mysteries. And if I'm correct, our discovery may lead to the decipherment of the entire co-dex."

Kantorowicz let that thought sink in. The top medievalists in the country sat up in their chairs. Some of their faces expressed skepticism at the promise of such a discovery. Others smiled optimistically. I sat nervously by the digital projector, waiting for my cues to advance the slides. Quint stood in the back of the room, perhaps to be ready for a fast exit if this whole thing went wrong. Our professor gave a brief introduction to the manuscript, its general description, its provenance, how it came to be housed at Beinecke, then went into his "discovery."

"In some ways," he said, "what I'm about to share with you is all the product of dumb luck. Discussing the nature of palimpsests in one of my seminars, a student asked if Yale had any manuscripts with palimpsests. I assured them that we had a few. They then asked about 'that book' that was currently on display in the grand hall of Beinecke Library, i.e., the Voynich manuscript. I had to admit, I didn't know."

This scenario seemed plausible, or at least we hoped so. A student with very little experience asks a question out of innocent curiosity, a question that even a great professor like Kantorowicz had never asked. A question that would lead the professor to have a look, just in case, though surely nothing would come of it. Yes. He had hooked them with our narrative.

"I didn't want to make a big deal of this at first, didn't want to drag out the high-tech imaging tools just yet. So, I sat in the reading room with a desk lamp pointed at the Voynich, directing light through the parchment, as I turned over every folio with my eyes peeled for the slightest sign of scraped-away letters. There were moments when I thought I saw hints of palimpsests, and I made notes, but nothing that seemed really promising. Until I got to folio 69."

I advanced the slideshow to the image of fol. 69 recto, un-enhanced, which Kantorowicz described in great detail.

"There's a block of text at the top, four lines comprised of a total of 36 words. The main image is this circular shape, which as you can see has rough lines suggesting a halo. At the center of the halo is a six-pointed star, though not the perfect geometric shape one expects in Judaism. There is text within the arms of the cruciform halo, 46 segments radiating out from the center. Every other segment has writing in it. We'll have to save that for another time. There's more text around the star at the center of the image, which we'll return to in a moment.

"Our focus for now is the text that appears around the circumference of the large circle, which is segmented into a series of 16 short phrases of two or three words each. This is the text around which ... on a Tuesday afternoon ... to my naked eye (with the aid of a 60-watt lightbulb) ... a palimpsest leapt from the page."

That was my professor's dramatic cue to advance to the next slide. This showed fol. 69r side by side with our forged photographic rendering of the palimpsest, as seen using "ultraviolet light." The audience let out a gentle gasp of approval.

"The palimpsest was easy to see, in part because of all the negative space, the unused parchment on both sides of the folio."

Heads nodded. Kantorowicz continued.

"Whatever the language and lettering style of the original Voynich manuscript, this circular text in the palimpsest is in Latin, written in a 15$^{th}$-century Bohemian *bastarda* script."

Some senior scholars in the audience were already trying to make out the palimpsest's text.

"If we could have the next slide please. Here's our transcription of the Latin palimpsest, with a side-by-side translation in English.

"We've only worked on this one folio," Kantorowicz said. "Nonetheless, the Latin transcription of the palimpsest and its corresponding text on this folio shows a one-to-one, letter-for-letter, substitution code. Which means that the Voynich manuscript isn't written in a different, unknown language, but in Latin, the common scholarly language of the Middle Ages.

| Latin transcription | English translation |
|---|---|
| *Gens Germanica,* | German race, |
| *Genus Magister,* | Master Race, |
| *ex dei omnipotentis,* | By god almighty, |
| *in terris positus.* | Placed on earth. |
| | |
| *Regnabit super terram,* | He will rule the earth, |
| *ad terram col[—].* | [He will care for] the earth, |
| *Pium patris,* | Pious father, |
| *Donum patrem.* | Gift of the Father |
| | |
| *Gentibus omnibus* | All races |
| *Fit reverentia,* | Bow to you. |
| *Nullus excelcius* | None is higher |
| *Germanos.* | than the German race. |
| | |
| *Genus primus,* | First race, |
| *Genus Magister,* | Master race, |
| *Gens Germanica,* | German race, |
| *Usque in aeternum.* | For all eternity. |
| *—Tacit[9]* | *—Tacit[9]* |

"The secret of Beinecke 408 is that it uses a *cryptic writing system* in order to hide its esoteric knowledge. If we're correct, the palimpsest on folio 69 recto could be the Rosetta Stone for deciphering the remainder of the codex."

Oohs and aahs, the likes of which I couldn't imagine at an academic conference.

Session papers at the Medieval Academy were limited to 30 minutes, but Kantorowicz paused and allowed time for the audience to take all of this in. Questions were normally held until the end of the session, but a voice from the crowd couldn't wait.

"What does —*Tacit* mean, there at the end?"

"Great question," said Kantorowicz. "And it is, in fact, the next point in my paper."

He smiled and continued.

"At first, we thought *tacit* might be a conjugated from of the Latin *tacere*, meaning "to keep silent," from which we get the English word 'tacit,' an adjective suggesting 'something assumed as a matter of course' or 'something known without having to say anything about it.' Was this final word suggesting that everything that went before was 'assumed,' without the need for proof? That it was tacit, in the modern English sense?

"For those of you conjugating *tacere* from memory, you're realizing, as we eventually did, that there is no form *tacit* conjugated from *tacere*. We scratched our heads for quite a while."

Kantorowicz paused, pointed to me, then thought better of it.

"One of my graduate students solved the problem for us, though somewhat inadvertently. In one of our work sessions, she noted that the Latin word for the English 'tacit' was *tacitus*."

Another long pause. Kantorowicz had a flare for the dramatic. I looked up and witnessed what dad used to call a "shit-eating grin" on Kantorowicz's face, as the esteemed medievalists seated around me realized that —*Tacit* was an abbreviation for Tacitus, the great Roman historian, author of the *Germania*.

Tacitus had written *Germania* as a kind of ethnography of the peoples living on the outskirts of the Roman Empire. As far as anyone could tell, he had never visited the Germanic tribes to the north but relied on scouting reports to write about them. Authenticity made no difference to Tacitus, who was using the *Germani* as moral foils to the Romans of his own time. Tacitus portrayed the *Germani* as noble and brave warriors who would rather die on the battlefield than return home alive without their brother warriors. According to Tacitus, the *Germani* women watched battles from the sidelines, cheering on their men by baring their breasts. Fearing what would happen to their women if they lost in battle, the men became enraged and fought that much harder.

"The sentiments in the four quatrains found in the Voynich palimpsest," said Kantorowicz, "are very much in keeping with the attitudes contained in Tacitus' *Germania*."

Of course, this was all misdirection—part of our professor's experimental archaeology to set a trap for neo-Nazis looking for a unifying symbol. I spotted Ted Bilbo sitting alone in the mezzanine of Calderwood Hall, taking video of Kantorowicz's presentation with his phone.

Kantorowicz laid it on thick.

"We need to provide some context at this point. As I mentioned earlier, the Voynich manuscript was composed between 1404 and 1439. Publius Cornelius Tacitus lived from AD 56 to 120. If a passage from his *Germania* made it into the Voynich, it would be remarkable. We checked the *Germania*, thinking it the most likely contextual match for our Voynich text, i.e., both of them talked about Germanic culture. But we found no match.

"It seemed unlikely we would find it elsewhere in Tacitus. I was ready to give up and move away from the idea of Tacitus as the author, when another grad student of mine discovered what was nearly invisible in the palimpsest: a tiny superscript abbreviation resembling the Arabic numeral 9."

I advanced to the next slide showing a detail of the word: —*Tacit⁹*.

"Tacitus!" an elder medievalist cried out from the front row, unable to conceal his excitement.

"Yes," said Kantorowicz. "The superscript 9 was one of the most common medieval abbreviations, representing the nominative affix *-us*. Hence *Tacit⁹* stood for Tacitus."

More heads nodded. It was fun to see Kantorowicz taking his professional colleagues through the paces of his process, the same way he did with his grad students.

"My time is running long, so let me skip a few steps."

He signaled to me to project the next slide, a photo of the title page from *Tacitus and Bracciolini: The Annals Forged in the XVth Century*, by John Wilson Ross (London 1878). Kantorowicz continued.

"We thought Tacitus, the ancient historian, was a perfect candidate to be the author of our text, but in searching all of his writings, we failed to find a match. It was a grad student again who, in researching Tacitus, discovered a 'pseudo-Tacitus,' a forger writing under the historian's name. In 1878, John Wilson Ross posited Poggio Bracciolini, the great Italian Renaissance humanist, as the true author (meaning forger) of *Annals* by 'Tacitus.' Bracciolini lived from 1380 to 1459, so the Voynich was created during his lifetime. As a great man of letters, he could have had access to the manuscript, or had influence over its creation. Now we just need one more piece of the puzzle."

The audience leaned in. Kantorowicz had taken them on a remarkable journey and they were almost home.

"More context: In the aftermath of the Great Interregnum of the Holy Roman Empire, constant instability plagued every attempt at unified governance. Sigismund, son of Charles IV, had a slow and rocky rise from king of Germany in 1411, to King of Italy in 1431, and finally to Holy Roman Emperor in 1433. All of this was happening in the time period of the Voynich manuscript's creation."

Kantorowicz paused.

"It's a stretch," he said, "and it's just conjecture at the moment, but we believe that the extreme pro-Germanic sentiments in the Voynich palimpsest—the Voynich text on folio 69 recto—were meant to justify and bolster Germanic rule over the territories of the Empire. As such, they represent the earliest rhetoric to espouse claims of Germanic racial supremacy, 500 years before Hitler came to power."

He paused, and then ...

"Thank you."

Applause. Cautious at first, then stronger. Did academics appreciate Kantorowicz's work because it was the kind of thing that they themselves constantly struggled with? After all, who else could understand the meaning of such an achievement? This didn't keep them from asking pointed questions when the time came.

The session moderator returned to the lectern, thanked Kantorowicz, and asked if there were any questions.

"This seems obvious," one colleague asked, "but why was the pseudo-Tacitus text scraped off?"

Fantastic! He called it "the pseudo-Tacitus text." I could see Kantorowicz smiling as this fellow medievalist signified the real-life forger that we had introduced into our own forgery.

"Yes. Good question. Our best guess is that someone trying to decipher the Voynich, long after Bracciolini's intervention, did so directly on the manuscript. Later, when the manuscript came into the hands of those trying to protect its secret, the pseudo-Tacitus text was scraped off. This may have been done by Athanasius Kircher, the 17th-century polymath who was in possession of the Voynich for many years. The scraping wasn't necessarily to hide the potentially racist sentiment. It may have been to hide the key to deciphering the rest of the manuscript, which Kircher wanted to keep to himself, but which is exactly what we hope can happen next. As I say, this is all conjecture."

More questions followed, some about methodology, others about content. Did the pseudo-Tacitus text offer hints at what other (ancient?) texts the Voynich might contain? The pseudo-Tacitus seemed disconnected from the illustration of the cruciform halo. Did that suggest that other texts might be just as disconnected from their illustrations? Were the illustrations just a ruse, a cover for whatever controversial sentiments the text might contain?

"For example," Kantorowicz concluded. "Consider the six-pointed star in the center of this illustration. We wanted to test our theory about using the palimpsest as a key for deciphering the rest of the text, so we tried it on the text around the six-pointed star, since it's fairly short. What we found is quite interesting, though also disturbing."

He apologized for not having a slide of the transcription and translation, which, of course, we didn't because otherwise scholars in the room could have instantly checked our "translation" and called it out for the nonsense that it was. I went back in the presentation and projected the image of fol. 69r. Kantorowicz "deciphered" the original Voynich text around the star.

"*Hoc stella non de filiis Israhel est, sed de filiis Germania, a Deo electi.* 'This star is not from the sons of Israel, but from the sons of Germany, chosen by God.' The text seems to suggest that the Star of David was coopted by the Jews, and that God's true people were the Germans. A perversion of the lost tribe trope, but where the tribe is no longer Jewish."

This ended the Q&A session.

The room fell silent as each scholar moved into his or her own trance, trying to consider the implications of that last line of text. Would the scholarship hold up? Was the rest of the Voynich equally racist? I overheard the Medievalists of Color asking if this might be another symbol to be coopted by white supremacists. And with what dire consequences?

I smiled with self-satisfaction that our ruse had worked. Step one of our experimental archaeology was complete. I looked back at Quint, who was watching Bilbo as he exited Calderwood Hall.

Was that Agent Mapp exiting behind him?

CHAPTER 44
Media: Social and Otherwise

Hours after Kantorowicz presented his paper at the Medieval Academy, he could be seen delivering that same paper on YouTube. Within a week, the video of our professor had hundreds of thousands of views. The comments on YouTube fell into three categories. The largest of these was made up of people who simply posted their favorite quotes from the video.

"German race, Master Race, by God almighty, placed on earth."

"All races bow to you. None is higher than the German race."

"'This star is not from the sons of Israel, but from the sons of Germany, chosen by God."

Original comments from supporters of racism included things like, "I told you so!" and "Thank God historians are finally able to set the record straight!" Viewers opposed to racism posted comments like "How can this hateful Kantorowicz claim to be a teacher!?" and "More proof that academics are overpaid!"

For the neo-Nazi crowd, Kantorowicz's bona fides were enhanced when the video from the Medieval Academy was linked to the video posted by the reporter from the *Yale Daily*.

"Were you censured for anti-Semitism?"

"Yes!"

Word spread across 8chan and Reddit and other platforms used by white supremacists. Neo-Nazis and Skinheads and Klan members posted links to the video in their blogs along with hateful comments about the "racially superior sons of

Germany" and what they were going to do to the "sniveling sons of Israel."

The Twitter-verse was ablaze, with tweets and retweets on all sides of the issue. Even @notrealDonaldTrump—who famously proclaimed that "a wall was a medieval solution that worked," in spite of walls being neither "medieval" nor very good solutions—tweeted how happy he was to see a professor doing "real history, not fake history."

Medievalist blogs got involved. The website medievalistsofcolor.com published a harsh rebuke of Kantorowicz's findings, claiming that their publication, even at a professional conference, was "irresponsible without fully considering the consequences." The MoC had no doubt that white supremacists would soon coopt the text and images from the Voynich manuscript and, once again, "use medieval history to promote their hideous racist agenda." Medievalists.net claimed that Kantorowicz's work was "interesting," but "shouldn't have been posted without a thorough academic peer review."

I was, like, overjoyed by all of these responses. Exactly the effect we'd hoped for. Quint did not agree.

"It's going too far," he said, decrying the failings of experimental archaeology. "It's already *gone* too far!"

"How can you know what will happen unless you try the experiment?" I said.

"This was not some controlled experiment in a high school chemistry class," Quint said, "where the teacher never doubts how the 'experiment' is going to turn out, even though she hopes the outcome will amaze her students. No. This is like physicists shooting two particles through the Hadron Collider at CERN for the first time, not knowing if the energy created by the impact is going to save the world or destroy it!"

The Kantorowicz story also began to be felt back at Yale. Emboldened by what they saw in our professor's YouTube video, closeted white supremacists at Yale began sketching Klan hoods in white chalk along the campus walkways. The staff of the *Yale Daily News* reported on the story, which was picked up by mainstream media, first locally, then nationally.

Kantorowicz received invitations to appear on CNN, MSNBC, and Fox News. On the advice of University counsel, he declined all of these interviews, instead releasing a statement.

"My research into the Voynich manuscript was based on long-standing, legitimate historical methods. I cannot be held responsible for what that research has uncovered."

He lied.

All things being equal, this was not the kind of attention that Yale's Provost wanted for her university. There was talk about placing Kantorowicz on academic leave. Normally, the faculty senate would have threatened to engage the AAUP and the ACLU, but many in the faculty believed that their long-time colleague had racist motivations—a notion that hurt Kantorowicz deeply. Sitting in our professor's office, Quint and I felt like we were all under siege.

"You exposed us," Quint said to Kantorowicz, "even though you promised you wouldn't. I mean, I'm in the shadows, under the mezzanine, so I'm not on screen. But you kept referring to 'your grad students who did this or that,' on a video that's now gone viral. And Isaacson!? She's so naïve about this whole project that she almost stands to take a bow when you acknowledge her translation. It's dark in the hall, but you can make out her face if you try hard enough."

"I ask that you *not* refer to me in the third person when I'm, like, standing right here. Moreover, I prefer *not* to be called naïve. I may not be ABD like you, but we *both* entered into this project with open eyes!"

How dare he? Mr. ABD! Mr. Aggravating Big Dickhead!

"Kalamazoo," Kantorowicz said, "is only six weeks away."

The plan had always been to launch the forgery at the Medieval Academy, then have the big reveal at the Medieval Congress in Kalamazoo, where the Alt-Right would simultaneously be holding their latest gathering. At K'zoo, the truth would be revealed about the Voynich forgery, exposing neo-Nazis and other white supremacist protesters to ridicule for displaying emblems that were blatantly fake.

"We only need to hold out until K'zoo."

CHAPTER 45

Weaponized Wheels


Any incident in which an attacker uses a wheeled vehicle to ram deliberately into another vehicle, building, or crowd of people, is properly (and not surprisingly) defined as a "vehicle-ramming attack."

                                    *


[Dateline] Ford F150
TV/Theatre/Internet advertisement
Setting: Sonoran desert (representing freedom of the open road, purity of experience, autonomy of driver, white male privilege, landscape without rules)
Total time: 60 seconds

| | |
|---|---|
| 00:00-00:02 | Disclaimer: "Professional driver on closed course." Soundtrack: Rock music, strong beat, face-melting guitar solos |
| 00:02-00:07 | Cross-fade to aerial shot of white truck speeding through desert |
| 00:07-00:08 | Title slide: "THIS IS WHY THE NEW FORD F150 RAPTOR IS BADASS" white letters on orange background, signifying heat, intensity |
| 00:08-00:14 | Several jump-cuts of truck in motion, speeding though the desert |

00:14-00:16      Overlay title slide: "21% BETTER TORQUE
                 TO WEIGHT RATIO THAN 1ST GENER-
                 ATION RAPTOR." Truck churns up plumes
                 of dust in the background

00:16-00:21      More jump-cuts of truck, in motion, speeding
                 though the desert. Overlay title slide: "3.5 LI-
                 TER ECO-BOOST ENGINE, ALL NEW
                 10-SPEED TRANSMISSION."

00:21-00:26      More jump-cuts of truck in motion, more
                 plumes of dust

00:26-00:30      Interior shot: close-up of dashboard. Overlay
                 title slide: "6 TERRAIN MODES."

00:30-00:31      Exterior shot of truck in motion, profile

00:31-00:33      Graphic of shock absorber (subliminal phallic
                 imagery). Overlay title slide: "NEW 3.0 INCH
                 FOX RACING SHOX"

00:33-00:34      Cut to close-up of actual shock absorber in ac-
                 tion (subliminal reference to intercourse)

00:34-00:35      Cut to overhead view of truck exterior in mo-
                 tion

00:35-00:37      Cut to close-up of rear tire. Overlay title slide:
                 "ALL NEW BF GOODRICH ALL-TER-
                 RAIN T/A KO2 TIRES."

00:37-00:40      More jump-cuts of truck in motion, more
                 plumes of dust

00:40-00:42    Ditto. Overlay title slide: "FUEL ECONOMY IMPROVED UPTO 36%"* (* with disclaimer in tiny print: "Estimated city MPG")

00:42-00:45    Shot of truck racing toward the viewer, mounting a sand dune and apparently ramming through the sand at the dune's crest. Gigantic slow-motion, orgasmic plume of sand fills the screen. Overlay title slide: "COMING IN NOVEMBER."

00:45-00:47    Cut to overhead view of truck exterior in motion, trailing plume of dust. Overlay title slide: "HOW MUCH TORQUE?"

00:47-00:49    Overhead shot of truck spinning out in slow motion. Answer to previous question spelled out in the sand in clear Times New Roman font: "510."

00:49-00:51    Two jump-cuts of truck exterior in motion, trailing plume of dust. Overlay title slide: "HOW MUCH HORSEPOWER?"

00:51-00:56    Overhead shot of truck spinning out in slow motion. Answer, as above: "450."

00:56-00:59    Title slide: "THE LINE'S BEEN DRAWN."

00:59-01:00    Display Ford blue oval logo, next to "Built Ford Tough" emblem.

*

In 1917, Henry Ford manufactured his first truck, the Model TT, roughly a decade after his first Model T car rolled off his Detroit assembly line. In 1928, he replaced the Model

TT with the Model AA, a truck based on his new Model A auto, except that it was larger and heavier to accommodate the work it was meant to do. Ford produced the Model AA until the start of World War II, when he shifted production to assist in the wartime effort.

According to *Michigan History: WWII and Ford Motor Company*, "Henry Ford was a well-known pacifist and publicly opposed U.S. entry into World War II." Nonetheless, after the Japanese attacked Pearl Harbor, Ford felt it his patriotic duty to produce military vehicles for the United States war effort. The Ford Company manufactured its first bomber, the B-24 Liberator, in 1942. Over the course of the war, using Ford's innovative assembly line method, his company produced almost 90,000 complete aircraft, almost 60,000 airplane engines, and 4,000 gliders, as well as a quarter-million military vehicles, including tanks, armored cars and jeeps. During the war, Ford had plants in Canada, Great Britain, India, New Zealand, South Africa, and (Nazi!) Germany.

After the war, in 1948, Ford introduced the F series of trucks, which is still in production. In 1953, the half-ton F-1 became the F100. The F-2 and F-3 were folded into one category of truck, the three-quarter ton F250. Ford's one-ton F-4 became the F350.

Since 1980, the Ford F150 has been the most popular truck for personal rather than professional use.

\*

The act of ramming into the enemy is a tactic as ancient as warfare itself. The Greek phalanx is little more than a human ramming machine, a block of men attempting to crash through enemy lines. Machines have long been the preferred instruments of ramming. The entire strategy of the Greek trireme was to ram one's own ship into that of the enemy—sinking the other ship was the sign of victory.

The most common image of ramming tactics is the medieval battering ram. This was a much more sophisticated instrument than the blunt logs held by eight to ten men, as portrayed in many cartoons. Rams were often hung from chains within a covered structure called a penthouse, which gave protection to the ram operators from arrows or boiling oil raining down on them. With the ram suspended from chains, the operators could expend their energy creating the horizontal momentum of the ram, rather than just keeping it aloft. For added impact, medieval warriors laying siege to a castle outfitted their rams with iron-tipped heads, often in the shape of an actual ram's head. The penthouse containing the ram was on wheels, hence it could be used to attack the main gates or any other part of the castle walls. Obviously, a besieging army would benefit from multiple rams in order to attack from many sides.

With the advent of vehicles driven by mechanical engines, rather than human power, the potential for ramming tactics increased. The first recorded incident of ship ramming in modern times was when the *CSS Virginia*, a steam-powered, ironclad Confederate warship, rammed the *Cumberland*, a Union frigate, in the Civil War's Battle of Hampton Roads. The *Cumberland* sank instantly.

Following World War II, automobiles became a ubiquitous feature of modern culture. By the 2010s, automotive vehicle-ramming attacks were a low-cost, low-skill tactic available to militants, especially those acting in independent terrorist cells. Low cost because any vehicle would do, and low skill because anyone who could drive was capable of carrying out the assault. The attacks of September 11, in which commercial airliners were flown into buildings, are rightly seen as vehicle-ramming attacks, but at a much higher vehicle cost and skill level than typical vehicle-ramming incidents. Ramming attacks with airplanes proved more easily preventable, although at the cost of changing the entire culture of airline travel. Vehicle ramming attacks are nearly impossible to prevent—though architectural barriers such as security bollards can help. By way of comparison, it's easier to deter against suicide bombers—whose tactics require higher-cost materials and higher-level training—than it is to prevent vehicle-ramming attacks.

Vehicle-ramming attacks may be divided into three types. Attacks on buildings are the least common and usually include an attempt to blow up the building, like the 1981 ramming of the Iraqi Embassy in Beirut, which ended in an explosion that leveled the building. This attack is also the main contender for the title "first modern suicide bombing."

The most common form of vehicle-ramming attack targets crowds of people and seems to be a favorite of radical groups such as ISIS or Al-Qaeda. These include several attacks in Israel: one in 2001, three in 2008 (two of these with bulldozers), another two in 2009 (one with a bulldozer), a truck attack in 2011, a tractor attack in 2014, and a truck attack in 2017. A 2006 SUV ramming attack at the University of North Carolina was intended to avenge the deaths of Muslims worldwide, while a 2014 car attack in Quebec was perpetrated "in the name of Allah." In 2018, a car drove into crowds of cyclists and pedestrians at Westminster in London.

Some ramming attacks combined vehicular assault with other forms of attack. For example, after the ramming effort was stopped or no longer viable, an attacker might switch to stabbing or shooting his victims. Infamous examples of this include the 2016 attack in Nice, France that killed 86 people by ramming and gunfire; the ramming and stabbing attack at the Ohio State University in 2016; and the 2017 ramming and stabbing attack on London Bridge. All of these were perpetrated by Islamic terrorists. Following that 2018 attack in Westminster, London Mayor Sadiq Khan proclaimed that vehicle-ramming attacks had become the terrorist's "weapon of choice" in Europe and the western world.

Vehicle-ramming attacks remain rare in the United States. This may be due to the ready availability of guns. Yet, one example stands out: the 2017 vehicle-ramming attack at the Unite the Right Rally in Charlottesville, Virginia, in which James Alex Fields, Jr, an avowed neo-Nazi and white supremacist, drove his 2010 Dodge Challenger into a crowd of protesters, injuring eight and killing 32-year-old Heather Heyer. In a photo taken earlier that day, Fields is shown wielding a round, black shield with the 'medieval' insignia of the neo-Nazi group Vanguard America.

Heyer's final post on Facebook, before she left for the protest, read as follows, "If you're not outraged, you're not paying attention."

\*

In 1982, Ford added its blue oval logo to the grill of all F series trucks, permanently replacing the shield-like silver emblem with the rotary gear and lightning bolt icon, which had been the F series hood ornament since the 1960s.

CHAPTER 46
The Road Trip

Holding out until K'zoo proved to be easier than we thought it would.

The rhythm of the school year carried on. Seminars continued. Reading and debating historical issues continued. Late night meetings at Insomnia continued. The limited attention span that comprises the American news cycle rendered the Kantorowicz/Voynich affair a non-issue. Although we still watched with interest, little happened on campus or in the news. Special Agent Mapp and the neo-Nazi Hobbit Ted Bilbo had all but vanished. The last time we saw either of them was back in Boston. The bald neo-Nazi in the bespoke suit had also disappeared. Quint and I had created a convincing forgery. Kantorowicz had presented it in a scholarly forum. Round one of our experimental archaeology was complete. With the stress in our lives limited to the usual grad school stuff, Quint and I argued less and enjoyed each other's company more. There was nothing left to do except sit back and wait for the reveal at Kalamazoo.

"You *are* going to Kalamazoo? Affirmative? Yes?" I asked over my cup of chai latte. Quint took a sip of espresso and nodded.

"Aside from wanting to see how our experiment ends, K'zoo is one of the best places to network," he said. "The Medievalists of Color will be there. I'd like to connect with them more."

"I thought they were boycotting."

"They were threatening to, but I think they'll probably come and continue to threaten boycott for next year if things don't change. Besides, I think they want to be a presence at the counter protest of this new 'Unite the Right' rally."

I thought about how that rally was the centerpiece of Kantorowicz and Mapp's counter-intelligence plan. I wondered if the neo-Nazis would embrace the new, fake emblem we had created for them. How many of them would adopt it, and in what form?

"How are you getting there?" I asked.

"To Kalamazoo? Probably fly to Chicago then rent a car. That's what I did two years ago. I still have some travel grant money but I hate to spend it going to Michigan."

"Want to drive together?"

"Drive!?" Quint said. "That's got to be, like, twenty hours."

"Twelve and a half," I said. "But we could see lots of beautiful country along the way. It could be fun."

"I don't have a car," Quint said.

"I do."

It was all I could do to keep quiet and let my invitation sink in. I didn't want to reveal that I'd been thinking about a road trip with Quint for over a month now. I had the entire route mapped out, with a plan for driver shifts that would get us there without ever having to stop, except for gas and food and bathroom breaks and, oh, please, just keep quiet and let this seem like his idea.

"That's a long drive," he said, then paused in thought. "I have an aunt who lives in Cleveland. Maybe we could stay with her overnight. If we left Wednesday and made it to Cleveland, we could make it to K'zoo by noon on Thursday."

And that is what we did.

The school year ended. Papers and projects got handed in. We packed up my 2006 previously-owned Mini Cooper—my "got into Yale gift" from dad—and headed west. We left at 7 on Wednesday morning, with the plan of reaching Cleveland by late afternoon.

"We should take I-84 and drive north of NYC to miss the traffic," I said. "Then we can head south on 81 to 80, then due west to 77 to Cleveland, with an ETA of 4pm. When we leave Cleveland, we can take 90 to 75, then north to Dearborn where we'll pick up 94 west, which takes us right into Kalamazoo in a little less than five hours."

"Did you google map?" Quint asked.

"My parents wouldn't let me have an iPad as a kid, so I, like, distracted myself reading an old Rand-McNally Atlas my dad kept in his den. From the age of nine, I planned my escape from Kingwood, Texas, not just what I'd do once I left, but, like, how I'd get there. The whole Interstate system's in my head, as well as state and farm roads. I can see the I-what-evers in my mind like they were right in front of me."

"Hmm," he smiled. I blushed. Again.

The weather and the roads were clear. We took turns driving in two-hour shifts. I hadn't used the Mini very much since arriving in New Haven. It was a little cramped for Quint's long legs, but he liked driving it and kept insisting he could drive further when it was his turn, not wanting to give up the wheel. The Mini was fun to drive, especially in the city, where it felt agile and responsive in the flow of traffic. It wasn't really built for long road trips, only because it looked so out of place next to trucks and tractor-trailers and even SUVs on the highway. We had to take special care to be seen whenever we were passing or being passed. We had one scary moment outside of Wilkes-Barre, when a big white pick-up sped past us doing what seemed like 100 mph. I was driving, doing 70, and it felt like the truck was going to blow me off the road. Aside from the speed, we also noticed the Confederate flag, like, hanging in the truck's back window.

"I didn't think we'd see that this far north," I said.

"It's no longer just a symbol of the south," Quint said.

Further down the road, we pulled into a diner. We almost decided to go elsewhere when we saw the same truck parked in the lot, but we were too hungry. Inside, we stepped back into the 1950s. Everyone in the diner was white, which made

Quint's entry that much more noticeable. It couldn't have helped that I, a white girl, had walked in with him. I could feel Quint pulling me back out the door, but a tall, smiling Black waitress came out of the swinging kitchen doors, handed us two menus and said we could sit anywhere we liked. We scoped out the two guys we thought belonged to the white pick-up and chose a booth as far from them as we could get. Someone had left a copy of the Wilkes-Barre *Times Leader* in the booth, so Quint rearranged the pages and started reading it, trying to appear nonchalant.

"Here's a notice for a meeting of the H.L. Mencken Club, tonight at 7pm at the Best Western."

"Too bad we'll miss it," I said. "My dad was a huge fan of Mencken."

"Really?"

"When I was a kid, he'd read to me from Mencken's book on American slang. We'd laugh and laugh as we tried out the different insults and curse words in different accents." I smiled, remembering those times.

"You do know Mencken was a racist and an anti-Semite?" Quint said, quickly dampening my reverie. "He was also a big Nietzsche lover, though he got Nietzsche wrong, too, just like Craig Michaels."

"How do you know this?"

"I took a course on Nietzsche. Remember?"

"Well ... I'm still sorry we'll miss the Mencken Club."

"I think it's a cover for a hate group," Quint said.

Just as he said this, we both looked over at the two guys we thought belonged to the white pick-up, which caused them to look back at us. They didn't break their stare.

"Let's get this to go," Quint said.

I agreed. We paid for two cheeseburgers with a large order of fries and two cokes. It wasn't the easiest meal to eat in a moving Mini Cooper. Our dining experience was made more difficult when that flash of white metal with the mocking confederate flag rushed past us again, surprising Quint into a reflexive, spastic jerk of the steering wheel. Such sudden movement never went well in a car like the Mini—barely turn the wheel and you could end up two lanes over. We weren't quite blown off the road, but Quint did spill his drink all over his lap. There was no easy place to pull over. I started wiping his pants with paper napkins, but then became embarrassed and decided just to offer the napkins for his own use instead. He kept driving. I kept to my side of the car, watching him dry his pants as best he could, as I felt my face getting warm.

Quint had called his Aunt Betty in Cleveland before we left New Haven. "Of course, we could crash in her place," Quint said, imitating her smoky voice.

Aunt Betty was the sister of Quint's father, which is to say, she was white. She lived alone in a large single-family home in the Newton District. Her husband had died many years ago and her three kids had all moved out and had their own lives. Only one of them, according to Aunt Betty, still lived in Cleveland, but in the suburbs. She greeted Quint with a warm hug and many exclamations along the lines of "my how you've grown" and "how long has it been?" She showed us to two bedrooms upstairs, where she made some awkward comments about not knowing "our situation." *Not to worry, Aunt Betty. No situation here.* But even as I thought this my face felt flushed. Downstairs again, she had laid out bread and cheese and cold cuts for sandwiches, grapes in one bowl and apple slices in another, with a third bowl brimming with potato chips. Her hospitality fulfilled every expectation of a kind aunt welcoming distant relatives after a long drive.

"How long will you be staying?"

"Just tonight," Quint said. "We have to leave early tomorrow morning to make it to our conference."

"In Battle Creek?"

"Kalamazoo."

"Oh," said Aunt Betty, realizing what little difference it made to her. Quint, sitting next to her at the table, gave her a sideways hug, then reached for more bread and cheese.

"There's a show at the museum you might like," Aunt Betty said. "At least it's the kind of thing your mother used to like. It's Wednesday, so they're open till 9."

"What's the show?" Quint asked.

"I'm not good with the names. Philip something. He makes satirical paintings making fun of racists. There's a thing on the fridge." She disappeared into the kitchen and returned with a flyer. "Philip Guston," she continued. "A retrospective of the 'Klansmen' paintings."

"Never heard of him," Quint said, taking the flyer from her, then passing it to me. "What do you think?"

It was a fifteen-minute walk to the Cleveland Museum of Art, even with Aunt Betty's loving but convoluted directions. At the top of the steps leading up to the main entrance, there was a full-size copy of Rodin's *Thinker*. Naturally, Quint struck the pose. I laughed.

"Your turn," he said. I tried but quickly gave up.

"It looks better on you," I said.

By the time we got to the museum, we only had about 90 minutes before it closed. We headed right for the Guston exhibit.

Philip Guston was aware of racism and anti-Semitism from an early age, especially the activity of the KKK. The Cleveland Museum's retrospective of his work offered pieces from the 1960s. Guston painted in a naïve style, portraying Klan members as crude, cartoonish figures performing mundane activities. Under Guston's brush, the bodies of Klansmen were squat, their hoods patched and stitched-together. Groups of them crowded like clowns into tiny jalopies, holding stubby cigars in one clumsy hand, while the other held what looked like a toy gun or a cross stuck together from popsicle sticks. Sometimes the Klansmen's hoods were splattered with blood, but this was incidental. Guston captured Klan members on their humdrum commute home. He showed what they did after they'd finished terrorizing their victims. They sat around smoking cigars, drinking beer, staring at each other, or staring at the wall. The exhibit featured dozens of variations on this theme.

The Klansmen in Guston's paintings were menacing, but absurd.

Quint and I moved through the galleries at our own pace but stopped together in front of one of the pieces. It showed a hooded Klansman standing before his self-portrait on an easel. A cigarette hung from the side of his mouth. He looked through the eyeholes of his paint-spattered hood and carefully executed the eye holes of the hood in the painting. It was the moment where evil recognizes itself but is unmoved. As we stood side by side, trying to digest his work, Quint's hand brushed against mine, then held it. He studied the painting a while longer before realizing that I was looking up at him. He looked back at me, and our eyes locked in a gaze as if we were a painting ourselves. We leaned in at the same moment. Neither of us could claim innocence or deny responsibility.

We kissed.

Then we kissed again.

Or maybe it's better to say that we kept kissing, generously exploring each other's lips, holding each other's faces in our hands, then holding each other close without kissing. All of this in front of a painting about ... what?

I have no idea why that was the moment when everything—an entire academic year of blushing denial, of looking then not looking, of intellectual attraction turned to physical desire, of pending danger turned to erotic tension—decided to bust lose. As we walked home, I laughed out loud remembering an episode of *Seinfeld* where Jerry takes his date to see *Schindler's List* and they end up making out like crazy teenagers throughout the movie.

"I've never seen Seinfeld," Quint said.

"*Lacuna!*" I shouted. "A gap in your cultural upbringing!"

"Meh! Lacuna matata!" he said and began singing the song from the *Lion King*. Under different circumstances, I would have groaned at his stupid pun, but tonight I laughed out loud and reached up to kiss him some more. The fifteen-minute walk back to Aunt Betty's took more than half an hour, stopping every few minutes to reexamine this newly discovered pleasure. Back at Betty's house, we tried to sneak upstairs. We knew that Betty had put us in rooms across from each other, but we had no idea where Betty slept. We got stuck in the middle of the hall, ready and willing for the "what," but indecisive on the "where," when a disembodied voice cried out from the end of the hall.

"Sleep well, you two," said Aunt Betty.

For a moment, it looked like each of us was going to knock the other down, like two horny but frightened keystone cops trying to make it to our own rooms before Aunt Betty opened her door and caught us in the act. Quint took my hands and held them firmly in his own. We kissed again, a long, slow, passionate kiss. Quint began to back into his room, coaxing me to follow. With one hand at my waist, he put the other behind his back to open the bedroom door. Before he could enter, I spun us around so that I was now leading, and he was following.

"Good night, Aunt Betty," said I.

"Good night, Aunt Betty" said Quinton Quick.

We smiled into each other's eyes, as the door clicked shut behind us.

CHAPTER 47
Fair Lane

Aunt Betty greeted us early with fried eggs and bacon, frozen orange juice and instant coffee, all made with loving hands.
Did she know? Could she tell?

I sat next to Quint, my chair just a few centimeters closer
to his than it was last night. Under different circumstances, no
one would have noticed. I didn't stroke the back of his forearm
or lay my head in the crook of his neck, as badly as I wanted
to do those things and more. In spite of my restraint, there was
no way that Aunt Betty didn't know we'd slept together. I was
like a bad poker player whose tell was trying to mask her expression as a good bluffing strategy, but only when she had a
winning hand.

Quint ate heartily and recounted memories of Thanksgiv-
ings at Aunt Betty's house, with traditional food and loud cous-
ins and football on TV. Under the table, he pressed his leg
against mine. Even fully clothed, sitting upright in hardwood
kitchen chairs, I could feel my heart beating faster.

After breakfast there were hugs all around and Aunt Betty
pressed a brown paper bag into my hands.

"For the road," she said.

We headed west out of Cleveland, missing all the traffic
because we were leaving town rather than coming in to work.
Quint drove. Having shown such restraint over breakfast, I
now took the opportunity to caress his forearm, to study his
silhouette. Turning north onto I-75, Quint saw a sign advertis-
ing Fair Lane, the estate of Henry and Clara Ford, and asked if
I'd like to make a stop.

"Yes, yes, yes," I said.

Once we arrived, I started in with what Quint now called my "rolling architectural commentary."

"Fair Lane is a gem of the Prairie style, á la Frank Lloyd Wright, mixed with, like, Late English Gothic," I said.

"Just the kind of home a man like Ford built for himself," said Quint. "Utterly American, but with a dash of the medievalism so loved by the Nazis and other white supremacists."

"Can't we just once enjoy the form without dwelling on the context?"

"Oh, I'm afraid not," Quint said. "And don't ever let Kantorowicz hear you talking like that. For shame!"

The educational signage around Fair Lane was pretty good concerning its architectural features. It was less revealing about Ford's dark past. Quint picked up the slack.

"Did you know that Ford blamed the Jews for spreading communism, supporting trade unions, controlling banking, even promoting gambling and *jazz music*, all of which would lead to the downfall of American values and culture?"

He spoke in a voice like a TV gameshow host. I think he was trying to be playful.

"Did you know that Ford considered a run for the White House and that Hitler endorsed his candidacy? 'I only *vish* I could send some shock troops to help *wiss zee* election,' *der Führer* said."

I laughed. A little.

"Ford even got a shout out in *Mein Kampf*." Quint was on a roll. "Hitler singled him out as the only dude in America who understood 'the Jewish problem.'"

He paused for effect.

"Oh, and he built Fair Lane."

"Asshole!"

In spite of Quint's comic critique, the grounds at Fair Lane were beautifully kept. We had a picnic by the river, courtesy of Aunt Betty, before we launched our final stretch toward Kalamazoo.

The road to K'zoo was a straight shot and the ride was uneventful … almost.

It was my turn to drive. South of Battle Creek, a half hour east of Kalamazoo—ZOOOOM! we were once again nearly brushed off the road by the slipstream of a huge white truck, blazing past us at double the speed limit. At first, we thought it was the same truck as before, but this one didn't have a confederate flag in the—ZOOOOM! another white monster *sans* flag raced past us then—ZOOOOM! a third truck passed us and cut in front so we were watching the rear ends of three white leviathans, blue oval logos smirking at us from their tailgates as they disappeared toward the horizon.

"What the hell!?"

"Are you okay?"

We were close to our destination, but I still pulled off at the next exit to catch my breath.

"Those fuckers are gonna kill somebody."

I was shaking. Quint put his arm around me and it all felt alright again. He drove us the rest of the way.

It was my first time in Kalamazoo, on Western Michigan's campus, but Quint remembered his way around from the last time he was here. We registered, got a parking permit, and picked up a copy of the program. I suggested switching our dorm room reservation from two to one. Quint had a brief moment of surprise, then realized the *novus ordo seclorum* and smiled in agreement.

"Of course," he said. "Of course."

We dropped our bags and headed into the controlled chaos of K'zoo: the International Congress on Medieval Studies.

CHAPTER 48
K'ZOO

The Medieval Institute at Western Michigan University has hosted the International Congress on Medieval Studies since 1965. Over half a century, K'zoo, as it's affectionately known, had grown into a conference that hosts over 3000 medievalists from around the world, featuring over 500 sessions that include academic papers, roundtables and panel discussions, workshops on topics ranging from pedagogy to the digital humanities, and demonstrations on everything from Gregorian chant to medieval longsword techniques. On its first three evenings, the congress hosts movie nights, during which experts in medieval culture call out the historical inaccuracies in *Braveheart* or make fun of Tony Curtis's Bronx accent in *The Vikings*. There are plenary lectures by world-renowned scholars and over 100 business meetings and/or receptions hosted by learned societies.

Two events make K'zoo unique among medievalist gatherings, and perhaps among scholarly conferences in general. The first is the Pseudo Society, an evening of stand-up comedy for academics, in which medievalists poke fun at the pomposity of their own discipline. A notable early entry: "Inventing the Past: The Methodology of Pseudo-history," a treatise on "making shit up" when you don't have the time to construct an argument or search for evidence. The second event unique to K'zoo is the dance, a late-night event at which too much alcohol and too little self-restraint cause otherwise staid and buttoned-down academics to sway, hop, two-step, jump, jive, and wail, regardless of Terpsichorean gifts or lack thereof. You haven't lived until you have seen a 71-year-old paleographer, like, gyrating with their 20-something grad student.

This was all according to Quint, who'd been to K'zoo exactly once before. It was my first time. I felt torn between the urge to taste all the wares a conference like this had to offer and resigning myself to following Quint around as he tasted the wares that interested him. I didn't want to seem clingy—hell, I didn't want to *be* clingy—but our new status as a couple, uh, two people who recently consummated their desire for one another, made every move whether toward or away from the other feel, like, fraught with meaning. Did he feel the same tension, the same tugging?

"So, uh, what session are you going to?" I asked, nonchalantly looking over my program, which I should have downloaded online a week ago. The offerings were so vast that the paper copy resembled a novella.

"I always start with the book exhibit," he said. "Though I try not to buy anything right away. No matter how many books the publishers bring, at the end they have to carry plenty back to their home offices. So, if you wait till late Saturday or early Sunday morning, you can sometimes get great deals."

"Mind if I tag along?"

"Sure, whatever."

*Sure, whatever?* What kind of response was that? A week ago, I wouldn't have cared. Well, maybe I would have cared a little, but now? Like, how was that supposed to make me feel?

The book exhibit was in the same building as the registration, in Valley III, a set of dorms during the school year that also housed the registration tables during the conference. I let Quint lead. For people who loved to read, the book exhibit was an exquisite labyrinth. All of the major academic publishers and university presses had tables. There were also vendors for specialty items. An old Russian man who looked like a gnome sold wax replicas of medieval seals, the kind attached to medieval charters. They came in all shapes and sizes, some for medieval cities, some for kings and knights, some for bishops and noble ladies. I didn't think of these as forgeries, since they never purported to be anything other than what they were. A few of them were cast from the original matrix, the die that held the negative image. Others were cast from dies that themselves had been cast from original seals.

Speaking of replicas, one vendor claimed to offer original works of the Spanish Forger. These had become collectors' items in their own right and were highly prized—and highly priced. I lifted one of the plastic-sheathed vellum folios to examine it and a matronly professor with a southern accent pulled me aside.

"I see you looking at those," she said, pointing at the folios. She took my arm and gently nudged me out of earshot of the vendor. "You should just be aware that those are forgeries."

"Oh, I know," I said. "We studied the Spanish Forger at Yale last semester."

"But these are forgeries," she said.

"Yes, I know. Sentimental facial expressions, trees that look like lollipops, swirly water, buxom ladies in anachronistic hats. And the 'Paris green' color," I added, with just enough confidence in my tone to impress her. "Besides," I said. "The guy selling them even labels them as 'The Spanish Forger.'"

She looked at me exasperated.

"You're a clever young lady," she said. "What I mean to tell you is that these pieces are forgeries of the Spanish Forger—over-priced fakes of the original fake—not worth the parchment they're drawn on." She smiled, patted me on the arm, then turned and walked away.

Just as she said, "fakes of the original fake," I spotted the familiar blond locks of Special Agent Mapp, indicating that the FBI was lurking in the shadows. I thought I saw him look over his shoulder right at me, then he was gone. What the … mirage?

I scanned the crowd in the book exhibit, but in looking further, noticed that Quint was nowhere to be seen. I felt a moment of panic, then a moment of disgust that I had let myself feel the moment of panic. Like, where are you, independent woman, who doesn't need a man for fun or validation? I got hold of myself and took my time wandering through the rest of the book exhibit. I might go back later and purchase a forgery of the Spanish Forger, just for the multi-layered stories I could tell about it later.

When I finally emerged from Valley III, there was Quint, sitting on a bench.

"There's a session on Arthurian heroes across campus," he said. "You can come to that if you like. Or you can find something else and then, maybe afterward, we can meet up at the open bar back here at Valley III, then we can find some dinner or see what moves us. What do you think?"

I did not mention my sighting of Agent Mapp.

"Yes," I said. "I think I'll find a session on my own, then meet you back here."

Independence. Fun. And validation.

CHAPTER 49

Tactical Briefing, FBI Temporary Command Post,
Kalamazoo, MI

MESSER:        (to Mapp) Long time no see, old friend.
               What's with the Yul Brynner?

MAPP:          (to Messer) Finally succumbed to chromo-
               somal destiny from mom's side of the gene
               pool. Thanks for noticing, asshole.
               Shouldn't you get this thing started?

MESSER:        Okay, everyone. Thanks for coming. Grab
               some cliché coffee and donuts if you ha-
               ven't already. Let's settle in for the briefing.
                    I'm FBI Special Agent John Messer,
               with the Detroit Field Office, Domestic
               Terrorism. This is my colleague Special
               Agent Nathaniel Mapp, from the New Ha-
               ven Office. He'll be back to talk with you
               in a sec, but first let me introduce Lt. Ben
               Simpson with Kalamazoo P. D., and Dep-
               uty John Oakes from Kalamazoo County
               Sheriff's Department, and Major Bill Wil-
               son with the Michigan Staties. We all want
               to thank Lt. Simpson for welcoming us
               into Kalamazoo and we're glad to see such
               a coordinated effort. Let me turn this over
               to Agent Mapp.

MAPP:            Thanks, John. And thanks to everybody for
                being here. Please put your eyeballs on the
                screen.
                    Today isn't your typical protest vs.
                counter protest scenario, though many of
                the same protocols apply. This is the or-
                ganizers' first attempt to restage the Unite
                the Right Rally that went so terribly wrong
                in Charlottesville. We expect a mix of white
                supremacists, from KKK to the Proud
                Boys to Atomwaffen Division and other
                neo-Nazis.
                    Social media tells us this is a rally about
                "claiming identity" or "unifying identity."
                That means you're going to witness a lot of
                Alt-Right marchers wearing *this symbol* on
                their clothing and banners. As you can see
                it's a Jewish star of David, which may seem
                counter-intuitive given the general attitude
                of anti-Semitism among these groups. This
                symbol is part of a year-long counter-intel-
                ligence sting that we hope will come to fru-
                ition at today's rally. The details are too
                complicated to go into here, but suffice it
                to say that, if all goes well, the protesters,
                oddly enough, are going to love wearing
                this symbol until high noon, when Profes-
                sor Kantorowicz of Yale—*seen here*—will
                give a speech at the rally that makes them
                all, once again, hate wearing it.
                    Our aim is that this quick shift in taste
                will create distrust and paranoia, but that
                may even cause them to turn violent
                against each other, which is something all
                of our forces will need to contain. The ul-
                timate goal of the counter-intel plan is to

disrupt the Alt-Right. To diminish its leadership's capacity to organize.

I'll have eyes on the professor. He'll have two of his grad students with him. *This woman*, Molly Isaacson. And *this man*, Quinton Quick. Lt Simpson, if you could assign two of your men to surveil and protect. They could be anywhere in the crowd, so be on the lookout. Also, BOLO this Atomwaffen bad boy, code name "Doppelgänger"—*seen here*—who's likely the leader of any planned internecine violence, as well as *Ted Bilbo, head of the Bungalow Boys*, the brain-trust behind the star of David fashion shift and the main rivals of Atomwaffen for Alt-Right leadership. Loo.

SIMPSON:        The party kicks off at 11:30 from *these two student parking lots* at WMU. We expect there may be some stragglers joining the march further down Howard Street, but we've tried to block access. By noon, all the marchers should arrive *via Howard* at *these playing fields* between Howard and West Maple at the West Crosstown Parkway. Except for *this row of houses* on Howard, it's a fairly isolated venue. The city council did all it could to issue a permit away from downtown. *These three schools* you see on the map—Montessori on the north, Maple Street High on the south, and the Arts Magnet School over here—they'll all be closed because it's Saturday. We're re-routing the city bus away from *Maple Street*.

The *playing fields* have capacity for 7000, cheek to jowl, but with 1000 marchers forecast on social media, it'll feel a lot less crowded. We've also got our fingers crossed for the 40% rule: 1000 marchers projected, 400 show up, but we're ready for the full compliment. We also expect 1000 counter-protesters, but the same projections apply.

The organizers have set up a *platform for speeches on the west side* of the playing fields. If the marchers inside the fence are facing west and gathered at that end, then we hope that'll create a *void here on the east*. Lots of empty space inside the perimeter fence, offering some protective distance between the gathered *marchers on the inside* and the *counter protestors outside the perimeter*.

KPD will run a three-tiered response. Uniformed officers at the start and end points. Bike patrols along the march route. Public Order Platoons, full turtle gear, on alert *inside the high school*, here.

MAPP:          You don't want them visible?

SIMPSON:       Start out visible and it says we're hankering for violent engagement. We don't want to bring in the POPs unless we have to, but we want them on standby.

MAPP:          Did your department create the perimeter? Jersey barriers? Guard rails? Bollards?

SIMPSON:       We don't have the budget for that. It's just the cyclone fence that's always there to demarcate the boundaries of the playing fields. The fence behind the platform is eight feet high, since it also acts as the boundary *between the fields and these building here.*

WILSON:    My Staties will be there to cover the perimeter. All we have to do is keep the counter-protesters on the outside. We've dealt with "antifa" elements before, so we don't think this will be a problem. Our intel says the counter-protesters are mostly professor types from the big medieval conference at the U.

MAPP:    Yes, that's likely. The organizers picked this time and place as a kind of "in your face" gesture to historians complaining about Alt-Right promoters stealing their medieval symbols. That's actually central to our op, and from a counter-intel POV, we're expecting the neo-Nazis to turn on each other. But we also want to avoid any pending rage from spreading. No damage to life and limb. What about that moment of internal combustion? Are you prepared for multiple arrests?

OAKES:    All our teams have had refreshers on the First and Fourth Amendments. If we do make arrests, we want them to stick. We'd also like to avoid multiple arrests, especially mass arrests. We don't have capacity for that, though I've got some school busses on call if it comes down to it.

As for "internal combustion" as you call it, Kalamazoo and Battle Creek county SWAT stand in reserve. I'm putting snipers *on the roof of the high school*, not for shooting, but for overwatch and surveillance. Otherwise, the rest will stage here, *east of the radio tower*, out of sight of any protestors.

That's it. Lieutenant? Anything else?

SIMPSON: Good to go. Ed-Fac-Comm-Diff covered.

OAKES: Worst acronym in the history of law enforcement.

SIMPSON: Education. Facilitation. Communication. Differentiation.

We've educated ourselves with intel from social media and the FBI.

We've let the organizers know that we plan to do everything we can to facilitate their First Amendment rights. We know what the Alt-Right wants from the rally— at least what they say they want officially— and they know what we expect of them.

We've got good inter-agency comms, and we're in contact with the organizers.

Finally, we've differentiated at least two groups, Alt-Right marchers and medieval professor types as counter-protestors. I'm guessing we'll have a number of regular old concerned citizens on site, but be ready for some antifa rabble-rousers, for good measure. Otherwise, we're Oscar-Mike.

MESSER: Mapp? Anything else?

MAPP: Asses and elbows.

MESSER: Thank you, gentlemen. And remember, if you want to make God laugh …

ALL: Tell Him your plans!

CHAPTER 50
## Medievalists at War with Each Other

Was it possible for medievalists to fight white supremacy? Was it folly? Was it, like, madness? And if we decided to fight, how should we do it?

"We need to protest from the sidelines!"

"We need to get into the thick of it!"

Our professor engaged the Medievalists of Color in a full-throated disputation. Unfortunately, none of the MoC felt like engaging him back.

"Blacks fighting for civil rights in the 1960s," said Kantorowicz, "didn't sit *outside* the lunch counters, holding protest signs, looking in. They took seats *at the lunch counters*. Claimed their right to be there. It was non-violent protest, but it wasn't on the sidelines."

"I'm not sure you're the person to be lecturing on what Black folks did and did not do during the Civil Rights movement of the 1960s," said Reed Coleman.

"My point is that you've got to be physically involved with the struggle. This is more than just an intellectual exercise."

"That's easy for you to say in your white body!" said Coleman. "As a Black man, I'm 75% more likely to be attacked just for standing near a white man's personal space. For safety's sake, we should follow the march on the sidewalk, then gather around the perimeter fence for the rally."

It was Saturday morning. The Kirsch Auditorium was packed, the mood animated, even angry. For the past two days, themes of racism and white supremacy among medievalists dominated the International Congress. In the book exhibit, in the open-bar receptions, in the coffee breaks between sessions, and on the long walks to and from the several buildings across the massive state campus, medievalists talked about racism and white supremacy and how it was being perpetrated by their own kind. Surpassing every topic in this discussion was the new historical symbol Kantorowicz had discovered in the palimpsest of the Voynich manuscript—the Star of David as *a Germanic symbol stolen by the Jews!* Most medievalists dismissed the palimpsest as a cruel anti-Semitic forgery perpetrated by the pseudo-Tacitus. No scholar really believed that the text was authentic. That was ludicrous. But no one suggested that the forgery was more recent—that it was, in fact, just a few months old, the product of Kantorowicz himself with the aid of two grad students (who shall, like, remain nameless), and some photographic trickery.

"Yes. Of course," Kantorowicz said. "Everyone should make their own decision about their own safety. I only hope that some of us will engage the enemy more directly. With one-on-one pedagogy and wit, rather than posters and shouting from a distance. And while "anti-fa" scholarship is important, if it isn't read by the white supremacists whose minds we're trying to change, then what good is it?"

"Maybe you could explain what you mean," Quint said. Some of the Medievalists of Color gave him the side-eye. Leigh Ann looked at him as if he was Chamberlain trying to appease Hitler. Quint gave off a hint of the student defending his professor, but I think he also wanted to know, concretely, what "one-on-one pedagogy" looked like in the middle of a protest designed by the closed-minded. I sure wanted to know.

"Take the case of Brenton Tarrant," Kantorowicz said. "The guy in New Zealand who killed 51 people and injured 49 more in two consecutive mosque attacks.

"We're familiar with his deadly stats," said Cynthia Wright-Bell. Kantorowicz continued, undeterred.

"If I was face-to-face with Tarrant," Kantorowicz continued, "I'd say, 'Listen, man. Don't paint the name of Charles Martel on your weapons. You see him as a great Muslim slayer, but that's based on nonsense that, unfortunately, teachers are still teaching in our schools. 'Martel as Muslim slayer' is straight out of Edward Gibbon's 18th-century Islamophobia playbook. It's got nothing to do with his own time. Martel and his heirs actually had stable relations with the Islamic powers of their day. Any other story is nonsense and a smart guy like you would know that."

"All true," said Henry Sanchez, another MoC leader, jumping into the debate. "And very adept of you talking to the 'youth of America' on their level. But how do you figure getting that across in the middle of a crowd shouting hate slogans?"

"I never said it would be easy." Kantorowicz paused and took a deep breath. "I simply say that we have to change individual minds, and for that we have to believe there are individual minds, rational minds amid the throngs, able to be changed. Otherwise, all is lost."

There was a moment of quiet in the auditorium, as if the members of the MoC might be considering Kantorowicz's suggestion. Coleman finally spoke again.

"Last year, the Southern Poverty Law Center tracked over 1000 hate groups across the United States. By contrast, national and regional associations of medievalists number just over 100, including affiliated centers and academic programs in college and universities." He paused. "How do you propose to implement your one-on-one strategy when we're so outnumbered?"

"The Unite the Right rally in Charlottesville drew between 500 and 600 white supremacists," Kantorowicz said. "Law enforcement estimates 1000 protesters today. We have three times as many medievalists (over 3,000) at the International Congress. *We* outnumber *them!*"

Kantorowicz looked at the faces across the auditorium. He was certain he was winning the disputation, so he offered a closing statement.

"That's how you fight racism," he said. "One racist at a time. But with each of us doing our part, in the mix, not on the sidelines." Then, pausing for effect, he repeated himself.

"That's how you fight racism!"

A spark moved through the audience like a crackling of static electricity. Kantorowicz had that effect on his listeners, even when they disagreed with him. Then, as quickly as it came, the spark dissipated.

"But are you the right person to give advice on fighting racism?" Coleman said.

"Yes," said Madeleine Chang. "With all due respect, as far as we can tell, you've actually aided in uniting the Alt-Right. Your work with the symbol from the Voynich manuscript is all over social media and people expect to see it in full use at today's rally. Forgive me, but I find your 'research' to be ignorant, enabling, and appalling. It's racism of the worst kind coming from an academic."

"That symbol ..." Kantorowicz paused. No one but Quint and I could tell that Kantorowicz wanted to blurt out that his research, while fake, had the higher goal of disrupting the neo-Nazis. No one else knew about the FBI contracting Kantorowicz to create the forgery as counter-intelligence. And Kantorowicz couldn't tell them until the big reveal, which was scheduled for high noon.

"Somebody told us you're speaking at the Alt-Right rally!" Leigh Ann shouted out. "Is that true?"

I was amazed that she was standing up to our professor. And what she said was news to me and I assumed to Quint. It couldn't be true. Could it?

"How dare you!" Kantorowicz went on the defensive. "My father ... my mother ... this ... this leg ..."

"Calm down, Dr. Kantorowicz," said Cynthia Wright-Bell. "Everyone in this country is a victim of institutional racism. You can't escape it. You shouldn't take it personally."

"Forgive me," Kantorowicz, said, "but I fundamentally reject the notion of *institutional* racism, which by your own argument creates victims. I reject any argument that denies personal responsibility. The Nazis who sent my grandmother to Auschwitz, who made my father flee his homeland because he was Jewish, these men were not victims of institutional racism.

Neither are the neo-Nazis who are marching today, and neither am I! Yes, I'm a white man who dares to offer ideas, to *argue* ideas, with colleagues of color. But I won't be silenced because you think it's the white man's turn to shut up and listen. I'm here to fight racism. If you don't like my ideas about how to do that, then argue against me, but don't silence me because I'm white."

"Typical white privilege!" someone cried from the back of the auditorium.

"Okay, boomer!" someone else shouted.

Kantorowicz turned and stormed out. When Quint and I went to look for him, he was gone.

# CHAPTER 5 |
## SkyCam3 Traffic & Weather

SkyCam3, WWMT. It's a clear steel-blue day. 75 degrees. Tom Ryder here with traffic and weather at three minutes past the hour.

Freeways running smoothly 'cause, hey, it's Saturday and nobody's headed for work. A reminder: the International Congress of Medieval Studies is happening at Western Michigan U this weekend, so we wanna say, "Welcome back!" to 3000 of our closest friends. Lots of campus gridlock till Sunday from this gathering of scholars, otherwise, expect delays at Bell's Brew Pub, a favorite of medievalists since 1985.

And another reminder: the second Unite the Right march and rally is happening *today*. The march kicks off at 11:30 from Student Parking Lots 34 and 92 at WMU. The Alt-Right agitators will then goose-step down Howard Street until the playing fields between Howard and West Maple at the West Crosstown Parkway. That's within spitting distance of our own News-Channel 3 broadcast tower. So, unless you want to come down and spit on some neo-Nazis, you might want to avoid the parade route and rallying field. The cop shop has projected over 1000 Alt-Right marchers today and just as many counter-protesters, so there's a 50% chance of some hate speech and racially motivated violence and 100% probability of traffic being backed up in those areas.

We're looking at the West Maple playing fields right now and they're clear. A few individuals, whom I assume to be organizers, walking around, but no crowds to speak of. Some of

K'zoo's finest monitoring the perimeter, and what look to be a few state troopers, but so far, no protesters, fa or antifa.

One weird observation: during our fly-over, we noted four white pick-ups parked at the four corners of the playing fields, about a block off the main route. We hardly would have noticed them except all the trucks have writing on their hoods. We hovered over one of them for a closer look and here's what we were able to make out: *Neca eos omnes.*

I thought this was Spanish, but SkyCam3 chopper pilot Jimmy O'Malley, who swears he was an altar boy, says it's Latin, even though he's no idea what it says. So, hey, medievalists, if you're listening, call into NewsChannel 3 and help us out here.

*Neca eos omnes.*

That's all for now. Remember: SkyCam3 Traffic and Weather is brought to you by Bell's Brewery. Bell's: inspired brewing since 1985.

Tom Ryder. WWMT. We'll be back at 33 past the hour.

CHAPTER 52
## Robin Hood at the Archery Contest

Vans from network and cable news outlets lined the eastern perimeter of Western Michigan U as their reporters looked for possible interview subjects among the gathering storm troopers. Nothing was happening yet, but the news producers were ready if and when something did. Conflict made, like, good television. With the possibility of conflict leading to tragedy—how long had it been since Charlottesville?—some of the TV news people believed that the raw material for a News and Documentary Emmy might reveal itself today.

The Alt-Right marchers did not have permission to park in Lots 34 and 92, or anywhere else on campus. Yet this was the rallying point assigned to them by the Kalamazoo Police Department, with the promise to WMU that the marchers would leave the two empty lots and move away from campus as soon as possible, but no later than 11:45am.

How to describe this sad collection of humanity dressed up in their favorite costumes of hate? I expected something more, like, carnivalesque, except where the carnival pitched its tents outside the gates of hell. To be honest, the scene lacked the comic anarchy associated with carnivals. Except for the costumes, the mood was orderly, regimented, even a little boring. I watched as various organizers dressed in coats and ties handed out water bottles and maps of the route with instructions for how to practice non-violence—not kidding!—while at the same time provoking any and all onlookers.

The marchers achieved said provocation through their costumes, tropes of racism and white supremacy rendered in cloth and thread. There were the brownshirts, of course, adorned with black swastikas inside white circles on red armbands. Add a black leather "Sam Browne" belt with cross strap on the bias and you have a militaristic fashion statement for the ages.

For summertime hate mongering, the blousy and sun-reflecting white robes of the Ku Klux Klan couldn't be beat. And they needed no special alterations because of their one-size-fits-all feature! In fact, many of the Klan-identified protestors looked like they really were just wearing big white sheets—the tailoring was so bad it seemed almost non-existent. I'd hesitate to call them "robes."

For the racist on a budget, numerous T-shirt designs could say it all at a nominal cost. From the stars and bars of the Confederate flag to super graphics of "der Führer" to the simple "black on black" preferred by Skinheads, a T-shirt with one of these designs offered an affordable alternative to the fanciness and dressiness of the Nazi officer's uniform, with a bit more shapeliness than the white sheets of the KKK. Yet the real innovators in this runway of hate were the pseudo-medievalists, who purchased their costumes online or created them from scratch, all with an eye toward an imagined past that could mean anything to anyone at any time, hence a medievalism that for them signified racial purity, even though the constituent elements of their garb had never meant any such thing. These were white supremacist costumes for a generation of lonely boys that had, like, grown up reading fantasy novels and playing video games. In their own eyes, at least, they looked cool.

The newest feature in this year's line was the dynamic use of what some circles used to call a "Jewish star," the six-pointed *Magen David* or "David's Shield," rendered in yellow and applied in every possible costume context. Alt-Right members dressed in Nazi uniforms might wear a swastika band on one arm and a Star of David band on the other. The yellow stars didn't offer enough contrast on the Klan's white sheets, so some had black or red borders, or geometric designs like rectangles or ovals, in which the star could float. There were red, white, and black T-shirts that featured the six-pointed yellow stars on the front or back. Once again, the most creative employers of this new symbol of Germanic racial purity were the pseudo-medievalists. The yellow star worked equally well on the front or back of their hauberks and made the perfect device for their shields or helmets.

Every so often, I could hear an incredulous racist ask, "What the hell are you doing wearing a Jewish symbol!?" In response, the star-wearing racists would offer up a quick smartphone viewing of Yale Professor Abraham Kantorowicz, on YouTube, lecturing in Boston about his new discovery in the Voynich manuscript.

"This star is not from the sons of Israel, but from the sons of Germany, chosen by God."

They relished every syllable.

"*Not* from the sons of *Israel*, but from the sons of *Germany*!" The excitement in their voices made them sound like children whose parents had just announced five more days of Christmas.

Idiots, I thought. Yesterday they all hated the Star of David. Today they claim it as their own. It was amazing how little effort it took to move their beliefs in a new direction. Hitler and Goebbels had exploited this very feature of human weakness.

Kantorowicz was nowhere to be seen. We hoped he might be at the playing fields, so we took the Maple Street bus—the last run before the cops diverted the route—and disembarked at the Crosstown Parkway. State troopers were already posted at all the entrances. They didn't stop me as I entered the playing fields. Quint, however, stopped himself and called me back. His skin tone wouldn't be expected on the white supremacist side of the fence line, so he motioned to me with two pantomime fingers that we should walk the perimeter instead. It made more sense anyway; we were more likely to find our professor amid the growing crowd of protesters outside the fences than among the marchers on the inside.

A long speakers' platform had been erected on the west side of the fields. The fence on that side, higher and butted up against school buildings, stopped us passing through. We walked withershins from the southwest corner, executed a quick Magellan around the fields, and arrived at the opposite end of the stage. Standing outside a large gate, we watched the first marchers enter the playing fields. Still no sign of Kantorowicz.

The march went all along Howard Street. Bike cops raced up and down the street, riding alongside the marchers and talking about the weather, asking if they were local or from out of town. They made jokes about missing family barbecues, with the march scheduled for lunch time. They spent an equal amount of time pulling their bikes over to the curb and chatting with counter-protesters. They asked if anyone in the crowd was a professor and acted pleasantly surprised when hands went up. They talked about hating history when they were in school but being really interested now. Or about loving history on account of a favorite teacher.

"The Middle Ages?" a bike cop would say. "That was my favorite part." Then they'd smile and pedal away to another section of the march and engage the white supremacists again. It was fascinating watching them flip back and forth with such ease.

The Medievalists of Color were there in force with signs bearing the usual catchphrases.

"Nazis go home!"

"Love Trumps Hate!"

These slogans were painted in red letters on king-sized white sheets that MoC protestors by the main gate held high above their heads for easier reading.

The one bit of fun with today's group of counter-protesters—peppered as it was with medieval history nerds—was the taunting. Most people are familiar with medieval taunts from *Monty Python and the Holy Grail*, the scene where John Cleese as the French knight calls King Arthur an "empty-headed animal-food-trough wiper." He follows this with "I fart in your general direction. Your mother was a hamster, and your father smelt of elderberries." Such taunts were quite real during the Middle

Ages, and the over-educated *érudites* among the counter-pro-testers spared no trouble in hurling them at their white-su-premacist foes.

"You hedgeborn ronyons!"

"You crooked-nose knaves!"

"Churlish klazomaniacs!"

"Fustilerian muckspouts!"

The insults were lost on the attendees of the Alt-Right march, sadly. It gave new meaning to the phrase "fell on deaf ears."

More and more marchers entered the playing fields. By Quint's count, more than half bore yellow stars of David on T-shirts and shields and signs. Phase one of the counter-intel-ligence scheme—adoption—had worked. But what about Phase Two—disruption—the YouTube video revealing the fraud? Why had that not yet appeared? I scanned my phone but found nothing. It was five minutes past noon. Where was the video? And where was Kantorowicz!?

*

We sat perfectly still as our professor poured hot water into our teacups. This was the usual office ritual, but it was early May. Back in Houston we would already be drinking iced tea. Nonetheless, sipping hot tea with milk and sugar as we sat across from Kantorowicz in his office was a given, like death and Texas.

"So, you're driving together to Kalamazoo?" he asked. We nodded. "Good. Good. Save some expense. Make an advent-ure of it. Takes me back to my own grad school days. Drive safely. Yes?" We nodded again. Quint asked the question on both of our minds.

"How do you plan to reveal our forgery as, well, a forgery?"

"Video on YouTube," Kantorowicz said. "Same way we set up the forgery with the Medieval Academy lecture. I'll be on the video explaining our whole process, leaving out your names of course. Agent Mapp says they can upload it in minutes."

*

Upload it in minutes, I thought.

I looked up at the platform. Speakers were taking their places. Craig Michaels, the campus agitator was there, as was Ted Bilbo, the Nazi leader from 1488. Then, what the—?

Walking up the steps from behind the platform, with his step-stick-step, step-stick-step rhythm, was Abe Kantorowicz.

"What's *he*—," Quint said. "Is he one of the speakers? Why is he sharing the stage with fucking white supremacists!? It's the Holocaust denying Iran conference all over again! It's the interview in *Zuerst* magazine! No, it's worse than any of that." He turned to me, furious and bewildered. "Has he been playing us this whole time?"

I looked at the crowd at the front of the stage, many of them holding up cameras to record the proceedings. Upload it in minutes, I thought again.

"Wait," I said. "We're not finding the video because it hasn't been made yet! Somebody from the FBI must be under-cover recording the talk. *They're* going to upload it within minutes of Kantorowicz's delivery."

"What?"

"That's what'll happen," I said. "It must be that."

It was the only thing that made sense. Kantorowicz was going to reveal the forgery from the stage of the Unite the Right rally. That gave the reveal more legitimacy and power than something recorded in his office or wherever. I scanned the crowd for Agent Mapp. Could one of his ridiculous dis-guises be "neo-Nazi at a rally"? Was Mapp in the front row—an FBI wolf in fascist sheep's clothing—capturing the video selfie of his career?

Then, at the far end of the platform, I spotted the bald Nazi in the neatly-tailored suit, the one we'd last seen offering security to Bilbo and Kantorowicz in the library. His eyes trained on Kantorowicz but he did not hold a camera. In fact, he had one hand under the breast of his jacket, as if he were ready to go all *Grand Theft Auto*. I pointed toward him and nudged Quint, who nodded as he gently lowered my pointing arm.

"Does he have a gun?" I whispered to Quint.

"I'd say, yes," he whispered back.

If the armed, bald Nazi was there to protect our professor, how quickly could that turn to attack, once Kantorowicz revealed our Voynich forgery.

"Where *is* Agent Mapp?" I said. He's the only other person I knew who had a gun.

The emcee for the second Unite the Right Rally was Craig Michaels, the white nationalist who'd spoken at Yale. I looked over to Quint and shrugged, but his attention was fixed on our professor.

"White *people!*" Craig Michaels shouted into the microphone.

"White *power!*" the crowd shouted back. This call and response continued for a few minutes.

"White *people!*"

"White *power!*"

"White *people!*"

"White *power!*"

"Aah, that never gets old," Michaels said with one of his wide, charismatic smiles. "It's great to see you all here and I'm so glad you've come! Welcome to the second of many Unite the Right Rallies!"

Cheers and wild applause.

"I notice that many of you are wearing what they used to call 'Jewish stars.' That's fantastic!"

About half the crowd cheered. Half didn't. Michaels began a new chant, which the participants repeated without irony.

"Jews will not replace us!"

"Jews will not replace us!"

"We at Unite the Right," Michaels said, "want this *German* star to be the new unifying emblem of our movement. I can see that some of you are confused by this, like you didn't get the memo. So, let me introduce Ted Bilbo of 1488 Associates, who can tell you all about this new logo. Ted."

Bilbo took to the platform. To me, he was still the same slimy, Nazi Hobbit who had haunted New Haven for the past academic year, but he earned a decent round of applause from the gathered congregation of haters.

"Many of you have seen the video with Professor Kantorowicz, the one where he discovers the true history of the six-pointed star and how it was stolen from the white races by the Jews. The true history of this symbol confirms the place of the white races, not to mention the treachery of the Jews, who stole this six-pointed star from the early Germanic tribes, our ancestors!"

Cheers and applause for "the place of the white races." Boos and jeers for "the treachery of the Jews." Cheers again for "our ancestors!" Bilbo continued.

"This star is not from the sons of *Israel*," he shouted, "But from the sons of *Germany*! Chosen by God! My Aryan brothers and sisters, if you haven't seen this video yet, you must watch it!"

More cheers.

"And today," Bilbo continued, "we have something very special for you. Abe Kantorowicz, esteemed professor from Yale University, is here to talk briefly about his discovery and why we should all wear the six-pointed star with pride for our white heritage. Professor!"

Bilbo stepped back and took a deep bow, gesturing to Kantorowicz as he approached the microphone.

"Abe Kantorowicz?" said a hauberk wearing neo-Nazi to his chain-mailed buddy standing next to us. "Sounds like some fucking Kike name." His friend leaned in to hear what Kantorowicz had to say.

Our professor stood at the microphone and addressed the audience of neo-Nazis packed around the outdoor stage.

"Let me tell you about our historical method," he said. "The Voynich manuscript has puzzled scholars for centuries …"

"I can't stand it," I said to Quint. "They'll tear him limb from limb when they hear the truth. What's his escape plan? We have to do something! Where the hell is Mapp!?"

Quint ignored me, looked over his shoulder, away from the stage, away from the mob pressing closer to hear Kantorowicz.

"Once we discovered the star of David symbol in the manuscript," Kantorowicz went on, "and found a text that we might translate …"

Quint continued to ignore me, his eyes fixed on the stage and Kantorowicz. He must have known that any attempt he made to plow through the crowd and save our professor would see the mob killing him as well—just for being Black—long before he ever reached the stage. I'm on my own, I thought.

"But it's not real," Kantorowicz shouted above the crowd. "It's not *authentic*. Not historical at all. The whole thing's a fake. Made up by me, for you. No, *against* you."

I was about to take a step toward the stage, when I witnessed Quinton Quick fulfill the destiny of his name. He moved quicker than I'd ever seen any human move. Ever. His Quickness was heroic. He spun around and in three long strides stood before the two MoC protestors holding up king-sized white sheets painted with slogans in red letters.

"Nazis go home!"

"Love Trumps Hate!"

He ripped the linens from the protestors' hands like a magician yanking at a tablecloth but leaving behind all the dishes, then ran back toward me.

"So I'm Black," he said. "What of it!?"

With that, he wrapped his head and body with one of the sheets and tossed me the other.

"Robin Hood at the archery contest!" I shouted, then smiling, disguised myself just as Quint had done. We shoved and elbowed our way toward the stage, two more white-sheeted fools among many.

CHAPTER 53

God will know his own …

"We invented the symbol, made it up to mess with your heads," Kantorowicz shouted into the mic. "Me and the FBI! They set this plan in motion. To mock you. To embarrass you. And here you all are. Half of you wearing the symbol of a people you despise. Believing the symbol belongs to you. But it *doesn't*. It belongs to *my* people. The children of Abraham, Isaac, and Jacob. You've all been duped. Who can you trust?" Kantorowicz yelled into the mic. "*Anyone* who's wearing a star might be an FBI *collaborator!* Anyone who told you that you should wear a *star* might be a collaborator! WHO CAN YOU TRUST!?"

Silence.

Every hater in the rally looked at the haters around them. Disbelieving, disorientated, baffled, they were frozen, struck dumb with shock.

Ted Bilbo bolted from his chair and charged Kantorowicz, pinning him to the floor of the stage with his hands at his throat. He lifted the prof's head and bashed it against the platform. Lifting and bashing. Lifting and bashing. Kantorowicz pounded at Bilbo's back with both fists. He'd dropped his crutch but it was still attached at the forearm, flailing about the air with each blow of his hand.

Fury and violence erupted all over the pitch. With a roar, the crowd shifted and surged forward. Some of the people wearing stars of David ripped their costumes off their own backs. Others ripped at the shirts of those around them. Punches flew. Heads butted. Thumbs gouged out eyes. Hands yanked out tufts of hair. Knees crashed into groins. Teeth hit the ground. Blood spattered every which way.

All of this carnage had a gravitational pull. You got sucked in toward the center of the mass and you couldn't force your way out. It was like one huge corpus of pushing and shoving that battered against the edge of the stage until it shook. But it also overflowed toward the counter-protesters. Some of the MoC members and other academics pulled back and tried to avoid the melee. Others defended themselves and others still took the offense and jumped into the fray.

Into this turbulent mess, Quint and I—two white-sheeted Robin Hoods in improvised KKK robes—squeezed and elbowed and fought our way from the back of the throng toward the north side of the stage.

Quint got there first. In a single motion, he pulled Bilbo off of Kantorowicz and threw him from the platform. For a brief moment, it looked like Bilbo might be crowd surfed over the melee, but instead he sank down into it. Quint helped Kantorowicz to his feet, pulling him toward the steps at the back.

I was still trying to climb up, when across the platform I saw bald neo-Nazi leap onto the stage. He was headed toward Kantorwicz but Craig Michaels—trying to make his own escape?—blocked his path. The two of them bobbed back and forth like a couple of indecisive metronomes, until bald neo-Nazi shoved Michaels off the stage and into the pulsing mob.

I reached Quint and together we got Kantorowicz down the steps behind the platform. As I turned, I recognized the golden curls of a familiar figure standing backstage.

It was Special Agent Nathaniel Mapp of the FBI.

Quint and Kantorowicz moved as quickly as they could along the fence, heading for the main gate and escape. Glad to see Mapp at last, and sure they'd make it, I hung back for a moment.

Mapp was wearing yet another of his disguises, this time a white T-shirt with the logo of the Atomwaffen Division, a black shield with a semi-circle carved out of the upper right corner and a white, trefoil radioactivity symbol in the center.

"Way to, like, blend in," I laughed, gesturing to his T-shirt.

Mapp saw me but carried on, holding a walkie-talkie to his face, waiting to give or receive orders, happy that his counter-intelligence scheme was working I guessed. Before I could ask him what he thought about it all, he spoke into the walkie-talkie in a clear, measured command.

"Hitler to Henry Ford! Hitler to Henry Ford! Go! Go! Go!"

"What's that about?" I asked.

"You'll see soon enough," he smiled.

Then from behind me, I heard a sharp voice shouting a different kind of command.

"FREEZE! FBI!"

I held my hands out from my sides and slowly turned around. What the—?! It made no sense. It was the bald guy in the bespoke suit. I felt Agent Mapp close the distance between us, placing me between himself and the bald neo-Nazi.

"Easy," he said. "I'm FBI, too. Undercover. Put the gun down, brother. I'm Special Agent Nathaniel Mapp."

"Sorry to disappoint you, you tired neo-Nazi fuck, but no. I *am!*"

After that, it all happened too fast for me to register single events. If I'd had the benefit of three camera angles all filming in slo-mo, this is how it would have looked.

The person I'd known for the entire school year as Agent Mapp—Mapp Number One—grabbed me from behind and pulled my body close to his, using me as a shield. He drew a gun and held it to the side of my head.

"Drop your weapon!" yelled the person I'd been calling "bald neo-Nazi," who now claimed that *he* was Agent Mapp, i.e., Mapp Number Two.

"Fuck you!" shouted Mapp Number One.

"Not another step!" shouted Mapp Number Two.

I had to hope that a real FBI agent wouldn't use the body of an innocent grad student as protection from flying bullets. With that in mind, I stomped my heel into the toes of Mapp Number One, then bit down hard on the wrist he held across my neck. He let go just long enough for me to drop to the ground. That same Mapp Number One then fired a shot at the person I now realized was the real FBI Agent, i.e., Mapp Number Two. The bullet missed Mapp Number Two, who didn't hesitate in his response to being fired upon. The time lapse between the two shots was so slight that many people must have mistaken the two shots for one. The real FBI agent returned fire with immediacy and accuracy: a single shot to the impostor's forehead.

The real Mapp rushed over to me.

"You okay?" he asked, as he knelt down to check the fake Mapp's pulse.

"I just had a *fucking gun* to my head!"

"I know," he said to me. Then into his walkie talkie. "Mapp here. Man down. It's Krause. DOA. Behind the platform." Then to me again. "Are you hit? Are you hurt?" His matter-of-fact tone made him sound like a flight attendant asking if I wanted chicken or beef.

"My *ears* are ringing!"

"You'll be fine," he said. Then, into his walkie talkie, "Mapp again. Send someone to watch over Ms. Isaacson."

"I don't need ... You're ... Mapp?"

"Special Agent Mapp," he replied. "No time now. You're safe behind the platform. Don't move. Somebody'll be here in a sec. Debrief later." He turned and headed toward the main gate.

Meanwhile, the two gunshots that almost sounded like one had raised the level of panic in the crowd. The bullet discharged from Mapp Number One's gun had wounded a protestor, though it was unclear which side he was on. The mob expanded, became less dense in the middle. Ideal as a target.

*

"Hitler to Henry Ford! Hitler to Henry Ford! Go! Go! Go!"

At the four corners of the playing fields, roughly a block off site, four drivers in white T-shirts with Atomwaffen Division logos confirmed their orders.

"Kill them all!" the first driver shouted into his walkie-talkie.

"Kill them all!" said the other drivers in unison.

They started their white Ford F150 trucks and revved the motors, more to, like, boost their own adrenalin than for any benefit to the engines. Then, in perfect synchronization, they took off for their prescribed paths. Each truck raced for its respective corner of the playing fields. Some of the counter-protesters on the sidewalks were able to jump out of the way, but many were hit. The trucks crashed easily through the cyclone fencing surrounding the fields. The state troopers were impotent. Once inside the playing fields, the trucks traced out their well-practiced routes.

One truck zigged west, then south, then west again. Another zagged north, then east, then north—each of them running over countless marchers as they went. The remaining two trucks ran these same lethal patterns in reverse. All of them raced toward midfield, their driving so precise that their paths crossed exactly in the center, threading their trucks through the crossing, missing each other with perfect accuracy. Except for its murderous results, the pattern had all the precision and beauty of an aerobatic stunt by an elite flying team.

With a vehicle ramming attack coming from four directions, the panicked crowd was helpless to flee. I hid in relative safety next to the speakers' platform, sickened by the scene, too shocked to look away.

From where I stood, I could see Quint and Kantorowicz outside the gate. They, too, watched in horror, so transfixed by what they saw that they didn't register the second truck retracing the path of the first, heading right for them.

"Get out of there!" I yelled, though I knew they couldn't hear me. I ran towards them.

The grass was dewy, even past noon, and Kantorowicz was still unstable from his fight with Bilbo. Later, Quint told me how he grabbed our professor's arm to get him to safety, but Kantorowicz yanked it back, shaking off his student as the truck bore down on them. Quint snatched at Kantorowicz again but the professor kept pushing him away.

They must have heard the whining of the truck's engine, the cries and screams of the people falling in its path. They turned just seconds before it was upon them. In the very last moment, Quint jumped to safety. Kantorowicz stood petrified as the white truck hit him, crying out as the leviathan mangled his body.

"Turner!"

It was the name of the guy who got killed by the truck back when Kantorowicz was a kid.

Our professor pulled himself up as tall as he could, aiming his crutch like a harpoon and ramming it into the truck's grill. Still attached to his arm, it pinned him to the front of the truck while the F150 and driver sped on toward their escape.

A shot rang out.

Where did that come from? A sniper?

The driver of the F150 slumped forward as Kantorowicz banged the hood of the truck with his free hand. The now driverless truck, with Kantorowicz still trapped against its grill, careened off the playing fields and across Howard Street, plowed into a small house, crashed through its three-season porch and crushed our professor against the front door.

"Bill ... Turner," he rasped.

With that, Abraham Kantorowicz Johansson—son of Amanda, son of Ernst—was dead.

When I relive these events in my mind's eye, I always see Kantorowicz as that little boy on the dirt road in Mississippi, paralyzed with fear, as he watched a silver ornament with a rotary gear and lightning bolt on the hood of an early model F150 racing toward him.

CHAPTER 54
The Debriefing

Quint rushed to the site of the crash. I followed seconds behind him.

The Atomwaffen driver still sat upright in the front seat of the F150. Upon smacking into the house, the airbag had properly deployed. That, and the fact that the driver had remembered to wear his seatbelt, meant that he was in pretty good shape, except for the sniper's bullet that had, like, blown half his brains out.

Our professor's wrenched body was still attached to the truck. Aside from his crutch being jammed into its grill, parts of the bumper had wrapped around Kantorowicz's twisted legs when the truck crashed through the front porch. The top half of his body lay face up across the hood, his arms out-stretched and limp.

Police pronounced him dead at the scene.

The front end of the truck was in the living room of a terrified and distressed homeowner. She yelled at the Kalamazoo Police that she had never wanted "this KKK march" to come down her street, sobbed that "her boy" was due home any minute.

"What am I s'posed to do?" she shouted. "What am I s'posed to do?"

*Jeopardy* blared from a TV in the kitchen—a female contestant was making a run on a category called "Medieval Crusades."

*Its underaged participants were sold into slavery before ever reaching the Holy Land.*

"What is the Children's Crusade?" I said.

"What?!" Quint said.

Tears began to well up in Quint's eyes. He slid down onto the woman's living room floor. I slid down next to him and we held each other close. We stared at the big white truck, at our professor's body draped over it.

"I should have saved him," Quint said through his tears. "I tried to save him but I jumped out of the way instead."

"This isn't your fault," I said. "It's just a stupid, senseless death, done by a white man filled with hate."

"No ... I should have ... I tried ..."

"You're alive," I said. "Abe made his own choices."

The cops finally told us we needed to wait outside. The playing fields looked like a Matthew Brady photo. Numerous ambulances that had been on standby showed up, but there were clearly not enough of them. I saw Reed Coleman across the street, applying a tourniquet to the leg of some guy wearing a star of David T-shirt. Cynthia Wright-Bell stood over him, yelling at Coleman, though I couldn't make out what she was saying. He finished tying the tourniquet, stood up, and began yelling back at her, his arms gesturing angrily. Again, no idea what he was saying but they continued their animated spat as they left the wounded neo-Nazi on the ground and headed back to campus.

Further off, I saw Madeleine Chang holding a cloth to her head, blood caked on her face. Later that night, I remembered Quint telling me about her children and how brave she was.

Quint and I gave statements. At some point we wandered back to the dorm room we'd been using for the last two nights. There was no joy at the International Congress on Medieval Studies. Any papers scheduled for Saturday afternoon were cancelled, as were The Pseudo Society and the late-night dance. In their place, congress attendees held a candlelight vigil at the playing fields, which was still an active crime scene late into the night. The next day, we met with the real Agent Mapp in a classroom on the Western Michigan campus.

"There were 176 injured and 64 dead from the truck-ramming attack," Mapp said. "Ted Bilbo was among the dead. That weasel Craig Michaels got away with minor cuts and bruises. One Kalamazoo citizen died from a stray bullet, the one intended for me. Two perps were put down by law enforcement." We later learned that five of the deceased were medievalists: another professor (in addition to Kantorowicz), and three grad students, all of them white, if that makes any difference.

"A sniper stopped the truck that killed your professor," Mapp said. "One of the trucks got its undercarriage gummed up with bodies, which slowed it down enough for the Staties to intervene. Another truck was pursued by cops, first on bikes, then in cruisers. The driver trapped himself in a blind alley and surrendered without further incident. The last truck got away. We've got a BOLO on the make and model but there must be hundreds of white F150s in Kalamazoo County alone. It's a very popular truck"

The SkyCam3 helicopter later reported that the four F150s were using the dead bodies in their wake to draw a giant swastika across the entire playing field. They took no account that some of their victims were also neo-Nazis.

"In fact," said Mapp, "the other neo-Nazis were the main target, especially the ones wearing yellow stars. We think that's connected to the Latin phrase that was painted on the trucks: *Neca eos omnes.* Kill them all? Can either of you help with that?"

"It comes from the Albigensian Crusade," Quint said, listlessly. "Thirteenth century. A fight between Catholic Christians and Albigensian heretics. They all lived and practiced their faiths in southern France, around a town called Albi. They were all basically from the same stock, so other than their different beliefs, it was impossible to tell them apart. The Catholic knights asked their leader how they could keep from killing the wrong people in battle."

"*Neca eos omnes, deus suos agnoscet,*" I added. "Kill them all. God will know his own."

"Harsh," said Mapp.

Even though he was recording the debrief on his phone, he took a moment to jot down some notes.

"Who was the guy you shot?" I asked. "We've been, like, working for him for the past year, thinking he was you!"

"His real name is Stefan Krause," the real Agent Mapp said. "He was a leader in the Atomwaffen Division, one of the more extreme neo-Nazi groups. Atomwaffen was suspicious of the "unifying star symbol" from the moment we posted it to the web. They're skeptical in general about the Unite the Right movement. We've known for a while that Krause had been surveilling the interactions between Bilbo and Kantorowicz, but we didn't know till yesterday that he'd been impersonating an FBI agent. Much less *this* FBI agent."

"He had us surveilling Kantorowicz, too." I said. "He even had us bug his office."

"We knew about the bugged book," Mapp said in his FBI cadence. "We swept the professor's office every other day for listening devices, but we decided to leave the bugged book as part of the counter-intel op, though we downgraded its capacity to sound as if there was a faulty connection. That way Krause could still believe he was gathering intel, recording the professor's conversations, but the quality would all be low res. Anything else you can tell us?"

Quint took my hand and held it tight. Neither of us spoke.

"Obviously, you can't talk about any of this with anyone," Mapp continued. "Anything that happened in the public eye is in the public eye. Kantorowicz's talk at the Medieval Academy. The YouTube videos. That's all out there and we can't do anything about it. In fact, we don't want to, since it serves our greater purpose."

Mapp looked at Quint and me as if to say, *the location of the Grail must never be revealed.*

"Anything that happened outside the public eye has to stay buried. Work product. Trade craft. Operational details. You can't ever speak to anyone about any of those things. Ever." We both nodded, frightened of what might happen if we disobeyed. Mapp hovered over us for a few seconds, then changed his tone.

"I think, uh … further debriefing can wait. You've both seen … in the last 24 hours. Maybe you … maybe see somebody. My office can recommend … if you like."

He reached into his breast pocket and gave each of us his business card.

"Again … very sorry for your loss."

CHAPTER 55

The Drama's Done

It was Quint's idea to take the train back to New Haven.

We were supposed to leave K'zoo on Sunday, but the conference organizers let us stay in the dorms one more night free of charge. Saturday night I couldn't sleep. Sunday I never left the dorm, sleeping only in fits and starts. Quint kept a vigil with me, leaving only to bring back food. Monday morning, we loaded our stuff from Valley III into the Mini Cooper and started to drive off campus. Headed for I-94, we'd barely made it across town when the panic struck. The Mini was too small. Too exposed. Too vulnerable. Every passing vehicle felt like a threat, even when it wasn't a big white truck. We put the car in long-term parking and headed for the train station. Quint said he could come back for it on his own, if I didn't want to.

"I'll figure it out later," I said.

"I don't mind," he said.

"Just *leave* it!"

Mom learned of the mass slaughter at Kalamazoo and the death of Kantorowicz on the news. She knew I was at the conference and, like, freaked out when she heard that I'd witnessed the whole thing. I didn't dare tell her my part in causing it all.

"Come home," she said.

"I'll be fine."

"Of course, you'll *be* fine, Mol. I just don't think you're fine right now."

"I'm fine, Mom. I *am* and I *will be* fine."

"Your dad said you can stay at his place if you like."

"Mom!"

Quint and I stood on the train platform in Kalamazoo, waiting for the 4:15 to New Haven. Professor Stark came to see us off. She'd stay behind for a couple more days to make arrangements for Kantorowicz's body.

"Where will you, like, send him?" I asked.

"He didn't have family, as far as I know" Stark said. "A mother in memory care ... somewhere. She likely won't be much help. I'll get him to New Haven and let the Administration figure it out. I'm sure Abe will love the irony that Yale University, after harassing him for half of his career, will now be tending to his final resting place. Anyway, they have lawyers who can find out if Abe had lawyers. If there's a will. All of that stuff."

With that, Stark took my hand, then Quint's.

"Look after one another," she said. She stayed on the platform as we boarded the train, waving till we were out of sight like a lone figure in a black and white movie.

Quint and I watched as small towns and farmland passed by the window. It's about twelve hours from K'zoo to New Haven, but long before the moon did its thing and, like, chased away the sun, the rhythm of the train made my eyes heavy and I finally slept. Quint claims I tossed and turned and made weird moaning sounds.

"Nightmares," he said.

Nonetheless, I didn't wake up till NYC, and by then it was morning and only about an hour to New Haven.

The nightmares I had on the train continued, though I got them less as the summer went on. A mashup of white trucks and gunfire and angry Nazis and Kantorowicz, leading the seminar from a classroom, or sometimes lecturing from the hood of a Ford F 150. "What do you see? See? What do *you* see? What do *you*? *What* do you? What *do* you ..." Stars of David morphing into swastikas into a kaleidoscope version of the Sterling Library façade. The swastika on our carrel door transforming into the bloody swastika of human corpses left behind by the Atomwaffen drivers. A rabbit running through New

Haven, or some city, looking for a place to hide. Agent Mapp—the guy we thought was Agent Mapp—in his ridiculous trench coat, pinning my shoulders to the floor and laughing like a mad scientist or a melodrama villain. That's the point in the nightmare when I'd always wake up, which might be at, like, any hour of the night. Sometimes it felt like the dream went on for hours but when I checked my phone I found that I'd only been out for a few minutes. Sometimes these images flashed before my eyes when I was awake.

I shared these dreams with Stark.

"Sounds like PTSD," she said. "Have you seen anyone?"

"A shrink?" I said. "No ... no."

"You might think about it," she said. "Have you told your mom?"

"No way," I said. "She'd, like, come to Yale and drag me home."

Stark laughed, but I could tell she, like, endorsed me telling her anyway.

I didn't want to see a shrink. Didn't *want* someone to cure me of PTSD, if that's what it was. The nightmares linked me to Kantorowicz, to the whole weird academic year. I didn't want to lose that, not yet anyway.

The campus held a memorial for Kantorowicz. In spite of him being such a controversial figure, the service was well attended. Maybe that was the rule. You could be censured and attacked when you were alive, but colleagues still showed up for your final send-off. Stark spoke on behalf of the history faculty.

"Abraham Kantorowicz," she said, "received his PhD from Notre Dame University. He had many prestigious academic appointments during his career, including the Pontifical Institute, UCLA, and Brown before coming to Yale in 2010 as the Rhodes Professor of History. He wrote nine books and countless articles and reviews. He was a pioneer in the field of medievalism, that nexus where past and present collide. His two most important works in this area were *Crips, Bloods, and*

*Crusaders: Medieval Precursors to Modern Gang Signs*, and *The King's Too Bawdy: Urban Graffiti as Medieval Marginalia*."

Stark paused and adjusted her glasses.

"Abe was a tireless defender of the Middle Ages against all stereotypes that proclaimed it a 'dark' age. He also fought against right wing movements who coopted the medieval symbols that he loved so dearly, though his work there has been greatly misunderstood."

There was, like, a slight rumbling through the crowd, as if to affirm the phrase "greatly misunderstood."

"Abe was also my friend. He was witty and stubborn, argumentative and kind, generous, especially to his students. I'll miss him." She stood at the podium as if she were going to say more, then sat down.

Quint stood to speak on behalf of the students. He cleared his throat several times, looked up at the ceiling and began.

"Abe Kantorowicz was my teacher," he said, "my teacher ... in ways that went far beyond the classroom. Professor Stark said that his work fighting rightwing movements was 'greatly misunderstood.' Even now, there are people on this campus who believe he was allied with white supremacists. That he was a fascist or a racist or that he, at least, supported such causes. The truth is just the opposite. The truth is his entire career was one long pilgrimage toward the good ... There are many things I'd like to tell you ..."

Quint paused and looked out at me. For a split second, I felt worried for what he might reveal.

" ... things I'd like to tell you ... that I won't ever be able to tell you. Not that anyone would understand, even if I could. He was my lion. The best lion anyone could ask for."

CHAPTER 56
Final Jeopardy

As the memorial service ended, a lawyer walked up to us.

"I'm Tom Gallitano, with Horwart, Groven, and Gallitano," he said, presenting his business card. "First, I'm very sorry for your loss. There's some good news, I think, in that Professor Kantorowicz has left you something."

Both of us must have looked surprised and happy, but that didn't last.

"Oh, no," Gallitano said. "I didn't mean to get your hopes up. It's just a letter, but ... I know this must sound strange ... you'll have to go pick it up yourselves."

"You don't have it?" I said. "You couldn't just give it to us? Or mail it to us?"

"No, I'm very sorry. Your professor's last request was that the two of you pick up the letter yourselves. I know that's inconvenient, but that's what he wanted. I'm just the messenger and all that."

"Okay. So, where do we get it?" Quint said.

"Here's the address," said Gallitano. "I suggest calling in advance."

Dad came through and had the Mini shipped to New Haven though I hadn't yet driven it except into the parking ramp. Now it seemed that Quint and I were destined for another road trip.

It's 237 miles from New Haven to Cape May, New Jersey, four-and-a-half hours, all of it on the Garden State Parkway. Once you get through NYC, the entire trip is along the coast, so the views are spectacular. Cape May hangs on the southern tip of New Jersey, like a raindrop clinging to the last snippet of peninsula before it falls into the Atlantic. This is the quaint town where Brookdale Senior Living is located, a facility that also offers memory care.

We went to the main desk and asked for Amanda Johansson.

"Are you family?" said a woman with a Caribbean accent.

"Friends of the family," Quint said. "We called yesterday to see about a visit."

The woman behind the desk smiled and called someone to fetch "Miss Amanda," as she called her. She then directed us to the TV room around the corner. *Jeopardy* was on, with the volume set for, like, maximum deafness. Several residents sat facing the TV, but none of them paid any attention to the game, or at least they weren't responding out loud. I nudged Quint, pointed to the TV, and made a face like I was holding back laughter.

"I get it," Quint said. "A game show that depends on memory playing in a memory care unit. Interesting choice."

A tall orderly wheeled in Kantorowicz's mother and tried to make introductions.

"Miss Amanda," he said. "These friends have come for a visit."

Amanda Johansson showed no response. Quint reached out and gently took her hand.

"We're friends of your son, Abe, Ms. Johansson. I'm Quint and this is Molly. Abe is our professor. We're Abe's students."

"We *were* his students," I corrected. Quint gave me that exasperated look that he sometimes gave me when he thought I'd gone too far. Maybe she doesn't, like, know or understand that her son is dead.

"Abe wanted us to visit you," Quint said. No response.

I turned away from her and whispered so she couldn't hear me.

"I don't get it," I said. "We're supposed to, like, get a letter from her. The lawyer was very specific. A letter Kantorowicz left for us."

"If he ever gave her a letter, I can't imagine she'd remember. Or know who to give it to," Quint said.

Ms. Johansson made no eye contact with me or Quint or anyone else in the room.

*He ordered a survey of the English lands in what came to be known as the Domesday Book.*

"Who is William the Conqueror," I said.

"You can't help yourself—," Quint started to say then stopped. He nudged me to be sure I was seeing what he was seeing. Amanda Johansson was smiling.

*… founded by Ferdinand and Isabella in 1478 to fight heresy.*

"What is the Spanish Inquisition?" I said and she smiled even more.

*… the body of electors that chose the Pope.*

"The College of Cardinals."

This time she giggled. And repeated the answer, "College of Cardinals."

The *Jeopardy* champion ran the medieval category and moved on. Quint and I did our best to keep up. She smiled with every right answer. Sometimes she laughed. If our answers were wrong, she made a frowny face.

"Abe was so little when he hurt his leg,' she said out of the blue.

"What was that?" I said. "Was that, like, a breakthrough?"

"Sshhh," Quint said. "Listen."

Kantorowicz's mother stared into space for a good five minutes. We sat dutifully next to her, hoping for some other, like, utterance that would clarify everything. Anything. Nothing came. The orderly reappeared and wheeled her out of the room.

"Okay, Miss Amanda," he said. "You can visit more with your friends next time."

Quint and I sat there, not understanding what had happened. After a while, we got up to leave, stopping by the front desk on our way out.

"Was there anything else?" Quint asked.

"Oh, my goodness," the woman behind the desk said in a hurry. "You're Mister Quint? And you're Miss Molly? Oh, I didn't even realize." She reached into a desk drawer and handed Quint an envelope that had our names on it. "Sorry," she said. "So sorry. Yes, yes. This is for you."

Walking out to the car, I grabbed at the letter, but Quint didn't give it up. He leaned against the door to the Mini and opened the envelope, inviting me to read the letter over his shoulder.

"Dear Quint. Dear Molly."

Kantorowicz never used our first names. It was always Mr. Quick and Ms. Isaacson.

"Please forgive my subterfuge. I wanted you to meet my mother and I couldn't think of a better way to make introductions. I do hope that, from time to time, you'll be able to visit her in the future. She doesn't have much future left, but I know she'd enjoy your company if you came to see her."

So, this was a trick, I thought. A way for him to organize some company for his senile mother.

"By the way," the letter continued. "If you're reading this, I'm most likely dead."

"He knew," Quint said. "He knew and he planned for it."

"I can't possibly tell you how proud I am of both of you. By the time you read this, we'll have faced an evil beyond imagination. I know that you'll both have fought valiantly against that evil, but in the end, very little will have changed. Mapp's counter-intelligence plan will work for a while. It might be harder for the Alt-Right to organize in any significant way, but evil won't go away. Hatred and racism will still exist. Maybe Stark was right. Maybe you shouldn't mix academics and activism. But I have no regrets. And I'm glad you were with me on this journey."

I saw Quint wipe his eye. The letter continued.

"Perhaps each life is its own Voynich manuscript, with secret meanings bound in symbols we can't decipher. We try to decode the mysteries of our existence, of happiness, yet fail miserably, again and again. Is there some undiscovered palimpsest that holds the key? Or is it up to us to create the palimpsest, to forge it from our imaginations in order to construct our own realities, our own bliss? I hope each of you can find a way."

Signed, "With great admiration. —Abe"

That was the end of the letter.

"It's a little contrived," I said. "I mean, he could have just given the letter to the lawyer to give to us. He could have just asked us to visit his mom."

I took the letter from Quint and refolded it to fit back in the envelope. Before I could do so, I noticed writing on the inside.

"Uh-oh," I said and passed it back to Quint.

Quint took the envelope's flap and we pried open the mouth as far as we could without ripping it. Kantorowicz had trained us well. The note was clearly in the same hand as the letter, except, like, strained from having to write inside the confined space. The note was short, but it had a certain "beware the ides of March" feel to it.

"Expect the Spanish Forger," it said.

"This has to be a joke!" Quint said.

"What?" I said. "Like, nobody expects the Spanish Forger? A joke? In his final note to us? A letter that predicts his own death!? No. This is no joke."

"Well, what the hell does it mean?" said Quint, mustering all the outrage he could.

"I don't know," I said. "But I'm a medievalist, and I'm going to find out."

The End

POSTSCRIPT
Why and How

According to Umberto Eco, "The author must not interpret. But he may tell why and how he wrote his book."[1]
Let me try to do that here.

As I write this paragraph, the news on the radio reports that ten Black people were killed in a mass shooting in Buffalo, New York. The white gunman appears to have been racially motivated. First, he traveled for hours to the location of the shooting because it was a predominantly Black neighborhood. He also left behind an internet rant that espoused white supremacist conspiracy theories about the "replacement" of whites by other races.

I started writing this book three years ago. I include the story of the Buffalo shooting only to say that the problem I initially set out to address has not gone away. If anything, it seems to be getting worse.

The issue of white supremacists coopting medieval symbols to promote their racist agenda is real. In Christchurch, New Zealand, the murderer of 50 people in two mosques used weapons inscribed with Crusader slogans. Closer to home, James Alex Fields, Jr, who drove his car into a crowd of protesters in Charlottesville, Virginia, killing Heather Heyer, bore a black shield with medieval insignia. These are just two of many examples.

Medievalists began to take note and address such episodes in 2016, shortly after the election of Donald Trump. Since then, numerous essays and studies have appeared in disciplinary works,[2] as well as the popular press.[3]

At the same time medievalists were starting to address white supremacy outside the academy, accusations began to fly concerning white supremacy within the academy. Papers by scholars of color were not receiving the same consideration as the work of white scholars when it came to conference presentations or publication. There was also unfair treatment of scholars of color in hiring and promotion practices. Such inequity led to the creation of a new collaborative called the Medievalists of Color, which, among other things, critiques the medievalist establishment in an attempt to make it do better.

Most non-academics, if they knew about white supremacists using medieval symbols, would likely find it silly. So they dress up like they're going to a Renaissance fair? So what? And if these same non-academics knew about the disciplinary infighting among medievalists, they would likely consider it petty. As the saying goes: Academic disputes are so bitter because the stakes are so low.

A partial explanation for these attitudes among ordinary people is their lack of understanding of history in general, and the Middle Ages in particular. There is a pervasive sense that medieval studies might be fun, but it's basically irrelevant to everyday life. After all, these medievalists are not solving the unemployment problem. They are not curing cancer.

In spite of such attitudes, confronting white supremacists on their abuse of medieval history could not be more serious. And the stakes could not be higher.

Here's why:

White supremacists seek to create an idealized past, an origin story that conforms to their racist beliefs. Their goal is to help their followers build community around a shared heritage—even a heritage based on a lie. They rewrite and abuse medieval history to construct an all-white Middle Ages that never existed, in order to give their community a stronger sense of identity.

To let them get away with this is dangerous. They must be stopped.

As a medievalist, I wondered how effective the many essays and books correcting false white supremacist history really
were. Did they just "preach to the choir"? As a novelist, I
wanted to create a scenario in which protagonist medievalists
more directly confronted the white supremacist antagonists.

What if medievalists could send a Trojan horse into the
fortress where white supremacists created their false histories?
What if the white supremacists adopted the ideas inside the
Trojan horse, only to find out later that they had been duped?
With that as the premise, what would happen next? Distrust?
Disruption? Derangement?

As for how, the first thing every author must do is build a
"world" in which their characters live and interact. This novel
operates in a world very familiar to me, the world of medievalists. It includes lecture halls and graduate seminars, libraries
and archives, dusty old manuscripts and sleek laptops, study
carrels and meetings and conferences and professional jeal-
ousies and arguments and office hours, not to mention coffee
shops and laundromats and bedrooms with books stacked
floor to ceiling.

Some elements of this novel's world exist in so-called real
life. Some are historical. Some are made up.

To begin, the novel references many books that actually
exist and I recommend them all. The two exceptions to this are
the books "written" by the fictional Abe Kantorowicz: *Crips,
Bloods, and Crusaders: Medieval Precursors to Modern Gang Signs* and
*The King's Too Bawdy: Urban Graffiti as Medieval Marginalia*. The
latter is a play on words with the real title *The King's Two Bodies*,
by the real historian Ernst Kantorowicz. For anyone interested,
the art historian Michael Camille really did study the connections between urban graffiti and medieval marginalia, for example, comparing graffiti "tagging" to name inscriptions in
medieval manuscripts.[4]

There are real institutions in the novel's world: the Medievalists of Color,[5] the Medieval Academy of America,[6] the International Congress on Medieval Studies at Western Michigan

University (Kalamazoo),[7] the Sterling and Beineke Libraries at Yale University, the latter of which houses the very real Voynich manuscript.[8] I've fictionalized the people associated with these institutions, though I've tried to give them the attributes and experiences—good and bad—that I think such people have.

The novel also contains historical events and historical people. Some of these, like Hitler and Himmler and Göring, will be obvious. Others are less well known, like Malskat, who painted the forged murals in the churches at Schleswig and Lübeck. For the historical characters, I did not have them do anything that they did not actually do in history. Malskat really did paint those murals and he really did feel under-appreciated when no one would acknowledge that he had done so.[9]

The one exception to this rule is Ernst Kantorowicz. Kantorowicz the elder (as he's known in the novel) was a real historian, a German Jew much admired by the Nazi elites, until he wasn't. His mother really was killed in a concentration camp and he really did emigrate to the United States, ending his career at Princeton University.[10] To the best of my knowledge, he did not have affairs with much younger female library workers, nor did he father any children. I've made Ernst the father of Abe so that the fictional Kantorowicz would have a back story to work against. I hope that any surviving Kantorowicz relatives will forgive me.

All of the other characters in the book are products of my imagination. My great challenge was to render them as realistically as possible, so that when the audience entered the trance state of reading the book, they would experience real people operating in a real world.

It's easier to create characters whose backgrounds and experiences are closer to one's own. For me, this means white, cis-gendered, heterosexual, able-bodied, neurotypical, male. Some critics argue that authors with my profile should not dare to write about people who fit different profiles. "Those stories are not the white (etc) man's stories to tell," the argument goes. But in a book about people fighting racism, anti-Semitism, and white supremacy, it feels dishonest (and boring and unrealistic) to have a story without a range of diverse characters.

Rendering realistic, diverse characters is difficult, not least because growing up in a racist society has ingrained racist stereotypes in all our minds. I'm no exception. The key is to recognize and work against them.

I've benefitted greatly from a blog entitled Writing With Color, which is moderated by a group of women writers from diverse, intersectional backgrounds. Colette Aburime, one of the blog's founders, says that she wishes "to help writers who aim to write diversely and do it well." [11] Among other things, the blog offers specific advice on how to describe the skin tones of people of color. For example, they recommend using "tawny" or "russet" instead of "cocoa" or "chocolate." The former are specific colors among an array of colors. The latter "food words" are cliché and fetishizing, connected to colonialism and the slave trade. Writing With Color also describes stereotypes and tropes to be avoided, like the "magical Negro," and "the white savior."

In an early draft of this book, a five-year-old Kantorowicz is rescued from an oncoming truck by a Black man, who dies in the process of saving him. Kantorowicz becomes dedicated to fighting racism because of the Black man's sacrifice. Later, the grown-up Kantorowicz saves his Black student from a similar vehicular fate, giving his own life in the process. As a writer, I was very pleased to come up with this plot device. It had a symmetry. It felt familiar.

After spending some time on the Writing With Color site, I came to see the Black man saving the young Kantorowicz as the trope of the "magical Negro," who sacrifices his life for the benefit/enlightenment of the white character. And the symmetry I liked so much when Kantorowicz dies rescuing his Black student was just a variation of the "white savior" trope.

After a good deal of reflection and several drafts later, I changed these sections in order to eliminate the tropes. The black character still dies in the first section, but he's no longer a cypher, put into the plot for that sole purpose. He has a name,

Bill Turner. He has a background story, and a relationship to Kantorowicz and his mother, and a purpose for being on that lonely road where the racist hit-and-run takes place. Young Kantorowicz is now saved by his mother. Bill Turner still dies, though his death is no longer described as selfless and heroic, but rather as senseless and cruel. I made similar adjustments to the later scene to neutralize the "white savior" trope. In both instances, based on advice found at Writing With Color, the fix came from adding complexity to characters who were once two-dimensional. I think these sections read much better now.

I don't intend for this to be a moment of "virtue signaling," where I pat myself on the back for having figured something out that should have been obvious from the start. I'm still not sure it's perfect, if there is such a thing. And I'm sure I've gotten lots of other things wrong. So it goes. As the moderators at Writing With Color say, "Keep trying. Do better next time."

All I can say is that I tried to approach each of the characters in the novel with sensitivity and humility, questioning my own biases as best I could, and doing lots of research, at Writing With Color and elsewhere, with the hope of writing complex, realistic characters.

*The Medievalist* is not a history, though it uses history to tell its story. This may seem ironic since a major theme of the book is how neo-Nazis (mis-)use history to tell *their* story. How the novel treats the neo-Nazis, with humor and derision, may offend some readers. When one of the neo-Nazis confuses melatonin for melanin and wants to use the latter as a sleep aid, the character's ignorance is meant to evoke laughter. But are neo-Nazis really a laughing matter?

The activist Srdja Popovic, who helped overthrow the Milošević regime in Serbia, promotes a comic protest strategy called "dilemma actions." According to this strategy, when white supremacists march through your town, send in the clowns! If the fascists ignore the jokes being made against them, they seem weak. If they respond with violence, they seem mean and stupid. That's their dilemma.

For my part, I choose to stand on the shoulders of giants: Charlie Chaplin and Ernst Lubitsch, Mel Brooks and Taika Waititi, not to mention the Three Stooges and Bugs Bunny! All of them poked fun at Hitler and the Nazis. As with the original Nazis, to poke fun at neo-Nazis is to appropriate back the symbols they appropriated from us and to use those symbols against them. It's a kind of cathartic exorcism that reveals what Hannah Arendt called the "banality of evil."[12]

## NOTES

[1] Umberto Eco, *Postscript to The Name of the Rose*, English translation (1984).

[2] See, for example, *Whose Middle Ages?: Teachable Moments for an Ill-Used Past*, Andrew Albin, Mary C. Erler, Thomas O'Donnell, Nicholas L. Paul, and Nina Rowe, eds. (2019); and Amy S. Kaufman and Paul B. Sturtevant, *The Devil's Historians: How Modern Extremists Abuse the Medieval Past* (2020).

[3] See for example, David Perry, "White Supremacists Love Vikings: But They've Got History All Wrong," *The Washington Post*, May 31, 2017; and Jennifer Schuessler, "Medieval Scholars Joust With White Nationalists. And One Another," *The New York Times*, May 5, 2019.

[4] Michael Camille, "Glossing the flesh: scopophilia and the margins of the medieval book," in D.C. Greetham, ed., *The Margins of the Text* (1997), 263.

[5] For the Medievalists of Color, see https://medievalistsofcolor.com.

[6] For the Medieval Academy of America, see https://www.medievalacademy.org.

[7] For the International Congress on Medieval Studies, see https://wmich.edu/medievalcongress.

[8] For the Voynich manuscript, see https://beinecke.library.yale.edu/collections/highlights/voynich-manuscript.

[9] Jonathon Keats, *Forged: Why Fakes Are the Great Art of Our Age* (2013), 31-49.

[10] Robert E. Lerner, *Ernst Kantorowicz: A Life* (2017); Norman F. Cantor, *Inventing the Middle Ages* (1991), 79–117.

[11] For Writing With Color, see https://writingwithcolor.tumblr.com.

[12] Hannah Arendt, *Eichmann in Jerusalem: A Report on the Banality of Evil* (1963)